WE KNOW
WHAT WE ARE

WE KNOW WHAT WE ARE

Dawn Reeves

sharedpress

First paperback edition published in Great Britain in 2017 by Shared Press

Published by Shared Press
www.sharedpress.co.uk

A catalogue record for this book is available from the British Library.

ISBN 978-0-9574981-8-1

Designed and typeset by Quarto Design
www.quartodesign.com

Edited by Lisa Hughes
www.completefiction.co.uk

Artwork by Ben Kelly
www.benkellyart.co.uk

Shared Press' policy is to use papers that are natural, renewable and recyclable products from well managed forests in accordance with the rules of the Forest Stewardship Council.

To everyone who believes that society
doesn't have to be like this
and everyone having a go,
in whatever way,
at changing it…

CHAPTER 1

December 2008

Saturday afternoon

Against the flow of shoppers being sucked into the main pedestrian drag, Anita is light-footed, trying to pick out the dawdlers, the kind faces, the people unattached to either gadgets or children. It's easier to spot the preoccupied souls, the crawling and the craving; those who are a million miles away and those who want to be anywhere but the present.

"Excuse me." She makes eye contact, smiles. "Hi. We're..."

There's no we. She's drifted away from the portable pasting table that has become their base and left the three campaigners battling a gust of wind for their petitions and leaflets.

"No thanks."

She pulls up the zip on her fishtail parka, glad of the padding, the fake-fur collar and her black patent Doc Marten boots. The coat hides a turquoise sari, which wasn't the best idea, but it's become a canvassing uniform of sorts.

"Could I stop you a moment? I'm..."

"Sorry love..."

A barrage of indistinct football chants blows the short distance from the stadium into the city centre. As the wind picks up Anita competes with blasts of grievousness and injury, derision and partisan cheer. From here it sounds gladiatorial, someone is facing death. It won't be long before the match is over and the hordes head their way.

"Put people first." The blustery squall whisks her voice up and away. "Put children first," she shouts, her pitch rising. "Jobs, justice, climate! The financial crash is costing us taxpayers millions. No bail out for the bankers."

"Errr… No thanks." A young man, who could be a student, answers as if she is begging.

Actual conversations are few and far between this afternoon. With a smidge of sarcasm she jokes to herself: no to jobs, definitely no to justice and no to saving the planet. Except for *Planet Earth*, the TV series, everyone loves that.

As the sky darkens and the shoppers thin, Anita circles back to find the others.

"Five minutes 'til the final whistle." One of her friends taps his watch. Normally she'd hang around, see if she can get one last signature before calling it quits, but the thought of getting caught in the football crowd causes her to shudder.

The drizzle thickens to rain. Her heart thuds dull and heavy in her chest. She is used to being a short Asian woman wrestling her way through a large group of mainly white men, but the problem is that last week she'd been kettled for hours on a demo; a memory that makes her bladder contract and causes her to reach in her bag for a bottle of water at the same time.

Looking down at her clipboard Anita counts the signatures. The total of her afternoon's endeavours is eight names. That's it? The blue biro was running out by the end, meaning that two of those names are barely legible. One man had written his phone number down – "Steve – call me" – as if the point of it all was to cop off.

Anita is determined that her voice is heard, but, yes, that is it, she thinks. I am never doing this again.

Early evening

The windscreen wiper is on full, clicking and scraping angrily as Conor drives his grandad back to the nursing home after the match.

"Nil-nil draw seemed about right…"

Conor wonders if Grandad was watching the same game. The Welders' performance had been woeful and the drubbing was deserved.

"…the rain dampened their spirits and the wind blew that last shot onto the woodwork. The luck was with us today."

Speculation and stoicism would see the fans through to the end of another insipid season. He wasn't sure about the team. Whether they survived or not, Conor would be quids in. He often bet against his own team, thinking about it as compensation for the emotional distress he suffered. If the team did happen to win, then he was supporting the cause.

Leaving Grandad to sweat it out in the suffocating heat of the care home, Conor chugs through the irritable traffic back to his office in the redbrick 1970s civic centre. Working at weekends has become routine, but tonight he wants to check on the money markets.

The caretaker is a man in his thirties who looks like he's off to do a shift on a fairground waltzer. It wouldn't be a bad move. Council shirt sleeves rolled up, a small hoop earring with a golden cross dangling down – it's David Essex reincarnated. They'll all need to boost their income.

"Alright boss?"

"Nothing a win won't mend," Conor replies.

This isn't true, of course. While Conor has been working through the probable impacts of the global financial crisis on the public purse, there's already been a local spike in unemployment. He's the council's chief executive, but as its former finance director he can't fill the car with petrol without noticing the hike in fuel prices and totting up the extra money they'll need to keep the refuse fleet on the road. The hair stiffens at the nape of his neck. Another source of discomfort is the increase in food prices. Their traditional Mr Sizzle burger on the way to the match has gone up, suggesting the cost of meals on wheels and school lunches will follow.

Cuts are coming. Cuts are coming. It had started like a new football chant, emerging from small clusters. There'd been a few early adopters, but most officers hadn't been ready to believe, wouldn't commit to the new tune. Now they were throwing their hands up like a Mexican wave flowing around the civic corridors.

Conor switches on his computer and pulls up the spreadsheets he's been working on. Put your concerns in a numerical cell, apply a formula, quantify the variables and $x + y = $ calm. In some places, the city treasurer or finance director still has an office full of imposing oak furniture, leather-bound statutory instruments and financial reporting standards filed in glass cabinets. That was never for Conor. Even now he's the chief exec the functional birch desk and standard gun-metal grey cabinets still suit him. Don't attract attention, hide your light well; the politicians like that. They rely on him to manage the uncertainties, to say yes to their schemes when election time creeps closer. Which it is doing.

The rain knocks insistently at the windows. That a storm is approaching is a truism. Conor is strengthening his reserves, planning for all eventualities. Rainy day funds are required. Supplementary contingency management, SCM – he likes the made-up name – it's all part of his job. Detectives have whiteboards, webs of photos and arrows to join the dots. Accountants have layers of Excel spreadsheets, columns and rows to tally.

Conor adds in a fallback here, a contract get-out there. It's prudent, but his heart rate is up. He has confidence in his system, in his abilities, but the city is taking a battering, the economy has been trashed. Out of his cracked office window he sees a tree bent over double, an advertising hoarding dead in the road. The flood lights at the football stadium are off. The distinctive shape of the Cemetery End Stand seems to blur, moving almost. Whatever happens, Conor is staying put.

Late evening

Ash takes refuge in the Crypt. It's underneath the Cemetery End Stand, down a short flight of stairs at the end of the service corridor. At least down here no-one can see him. He kicks at the rusted metal "Keep out" sign lying on the floor. The rotting door drags on a sodden pile of match-day programmes. The light bulb fizzles, then dies. He leaves the door ajar. The room is half-lit by a fading yellow strip in the corridor. Unsold cup merchandise spews from a mouldy cardboard box. A soiled teddy bear in a red and black football shirt, like one he'd had as a kid, lies face down in a puddle.

They say the Crypt is rat-infested, but he's only ever seen crushed beer cans, an old burger box crawling with maggots. Like the laundry basket at home when his mum refuses to wash his football strip, the place festers. It could be a room in the swamp crawl game he's got on his Xbox. The Crypt is for losers.

Exhausted, Ash stretches out on the bench. Tall and solid, his feet and arms hang over the edge. He uses his damp kit bag as a pillow, vaguely noticing the water streaming down the walls. He rues his slow legs, his stupid decision, buries his head in the bag and sobs. The club will chuck him out and he'll have to go back to school.

The coach had called him a jessie. It wasn't deliberate; he slid and hadn't been able to lift his foot quickly enough before breaking their star player Dez's ankle. When his friend had been taken to hospital he'd felt like a cockroach, wished someone would stand on him. He can't shake the chorus of abuse from his head, led by the captain yelling, "You're dead man."

There was no way he could go out with the rest of the players to celebrate the scabby draw. He wants to wait until everyone has left the ground, all night if needs be. Above, the ceiling bulges, the slow creak of the frame sounds wrong. A tile crashes down beside him. A wet wedge of plaster skim lands on his foot. Eyes wide open, he sees a pool table-sized section of ceiling plaster, lath and joist fall rapidly. But he's not quick enough to move. The beam lands, splintered ends straight down into his chest.

The hurt is like a white-hot blade, as if he's been shanked. Black spots swarm in front of his eyes. The arm dangling off the side of the bench is trapped, it won't move; the other arm can't reach his mobile. The weight of the joist is flattening his lungs. It feels as if he's drowning. There are steps in the corridor. The sound isn't football boots or trainers. The pain is too much. The Crypt must be flooding. He wants to cry out, but his mouth won't open. As numbness spreads through his limbs he realises this must be it. I'm dying, he thinks. If only I could ring Mum, she'd come. Someone would come...

The thought stops.

Midnight

From the turret of his penthouse flat, Croft sips at his favourite cocktail – the Obituary. It starts like a dry martini, then there's a splash of absinthe, the distinctive liquorice highlighting the aromatics in the gin. It's a complex drink, unusual, yet the end tastes bitter, hasn't been strained properly.

The penthouse flat isn't the investment he'd been promised. Twelve storeys down, he can see the remnants of the outdoor market. The developer keeps saying the council will move it and close the homeless shelter opposite. Idiots. He'd have been better off doing it himself.

That said, Croft likes the square, double-height room. His turret has windows on all sides and a small look-out balcony. In daylight, he can see beyond the city to a more relaxing view of the rolling hills. Tonight, the empty darkness helps him think. Or it would if he wasn't interrupted by the constant, muted buzz of his phone. People only ring at this time of night if there's a problem. He lets it ring, testing the level of need.

"Dead or dying. I can't look…," the football club chairman's tremulous voice on the other end of the line irritates Croft more than the old man's inability to give the body the once over. The uninhabited eyes are always hard to forget. The caller's shaky tone gives it away; he won't let himself beg for help, but he's desperate. You lost your dignity Cornflower the moment you dialled my number, Croft thinks.

"Where is he?"

"In the Crypt…"

That place is for the nefarious activities of players, apprentices and staff – the smokers, closet alcoholics, pill-poppers, bullies, cry-babies and the paedos. It's Croft's business to know those sorts of places. The Crypt is part of the secret history of the Welders, of every football club, probably.

"Sounds like you should be calling 999."

"I can't. No. The boy can't stay here. You've got to help me move him."

"Who do you think you're talking to? I play golf with the chief of police. That isn't something my company does."

"Come on, Croft, we all know what you are, where you've come from."

Croft controls himself. "This call is over…"

"No, no, I need you…"

The more desperate Cornflower is, the higher the price.

"But I don't need you or this."

Does the risk outweigh the opportunity? It's a question Croft wouldn't have bothered to ask himself in the past, but building this operation has taken years.

"I don't know what to do… He…" Cornflower's voice whines. It's a lie. The fat, orange-faced old man does know what to do. He just won't take responsibility for his own shit.

"The death of a kid, no-one forgets that."

Croft knows he's turning the screw, but equally he's serious. It's not that he's gone soft; he's in a different market these days. Dead children. No.

Cornflower's silence gives him a moment to think.

"Here are your choices. You pay me to get rid of your problem. This is a business transaction and, IF I agree to do it, we do it my way. Or you call 999, do the explaining, there's an investigation and your mates in the council don't cough up their millions. You might get away with corporate manslaughter, might not do jail time if you get a decent barrister – they can be pricey. Then there's the family of the dead kid. There'll be compensation, grieving relatives to deal with…"

The contract to provide security for the stadium had proved a decent little earner. Now it's a big fucking diamond. No, hold on. Hold on. The leverage he could get on this one call would give him the whole bloody diamond mine.

"…And there's the shame…" Croft continues. "…No more FA dinners, no more freeman of the city, you won't be able to step foot in your local. Wouldn't fancy explaining it all to the grandkids myself…"

"Fuck's sake. I get it. Name your price." Cornflower caves.

That confirms it. The boy is already dead.

Croft tastes a rich opportunity, Italian white truffle, Wagyu rib eye steak, he can move into a new league here. The logistical challenges will take some creative thinking. Cornflower will be tricky. He's an amateur, vain, talks too much, emotion where his balls should be.

It occurs to Croft that Cornflower might have taken a sledge hammer to a retaining wall or two, speeded up the collapse of the rancid stadium. That would've shown some initiative. But no. Cornflower isn't after the insurance. He's already made some kind of arrangement with the council, has been waiting for this moment.

"Assuming you didn't jerry-build the office block, you stay there. Have a drink if you need it. I'll send my security guy. He'll drive you home."

As a kid he'd been to watch the Welders. The football was crap, but the violent chaos drew him in initially. He ran with a nasty little bunch of oiks for a while, causing mayhem with the visiting fans. The coppers didn't have a clue what was going on. That was what Croft liked about it, outsmarting the pigs. Now he sees the football as a business opportunity. The lame regulators, the misty-eyed punters – their stupidity deserves to be exploited. They bring it on themselves. His eye wanders across to the black block of the civic centre.

Outsourcing the darker fringe activities of the operation had been necessary after his previous run-in with the council. The incident had stung, but setting up a separate entity made sense. His right-hand man became a preferred service provider. What he lost in direct control, he made up for in respectability. He slept well in the penthouse.

The Sweeper, who had been faithful to date, picks up the phone on the first ring.

"Understood, boss." It's a nice touch. A nod to the past.

"I'll get the body out before the rest of the building comes down. Make sure the CCTV is off for the minimum. A minute or two max to get him in the boot of Cornflower's Bentley. Want him wrapped or not?"

"Unwrapped to start with."

The Sweeper is a thug who loves the detail, thinks ahead.

"And the drop-off location?"

Croft's eyes haven't left the council building. "Hmmm. I need to check something, but…"

Out of the darkness comes an idea. Bit of a punt, but let's call it insurance. Plenty of council land available for a shallow grave. The wind smacks the thickened glass hard up here. If this was a proper city, the lights would spread out in all directions. After a mile or so there are only tiny dots on the edge of no-one's radar. Still, an invisible city is an opportunity, he thinks. I might as well own it all.

CHAPTER 2

December 2008

The next day

Conor blinks, stops, shakes his head and moves his gaze on as if mentally taking a set of panoramic photos. From 40 metres back they survey the scene. It's an invisible cordon. There are other men who have stopped there, too; fans quieted by shock. In the centre of the wreckage, they stare at the collapsed stand. Conor knows he's looking at storm damage, but it's as if a bomb has gone off. Sheets of corrugated roofing seem to hover on top of a mountain of wood and mangled metal. The racks of grey plastic seating, like rows of decaying teeth, are eating into the jumbled mess of scrap.

At the fringe of the scene, a commercial bin has nose-dived, polystyrene burger boxes and chip wrappers spew out, beer cans run free across the concrete expanse of match-day parking. A programme seller's booth lies on its side and there's shattered glass underfoot. Fallen trees have brought down the hoardings of C.C. Smith – Audi dealer, W.S Watkins – Bookmakers, Davies and Davies, a local builder Conor knows personally, proud match-day sponsors.

There's a bitter smack of realisation. Conor's season ticket seat, row 50, next to the aisle, is gone, swallowed by the debris. His childhood Saturday afternoons were spent half-watching the match from the Cemetery End, weaving through the forest of adult knees, the reverberation of the warped, bouncing planks a sound fixed in his memory. He'd run up and down the stand to the very top. From there he could see it all: the game, the ground, his street, the road into town, the whole of his world.

Conor feels a downward pressure, a heavy grip that digs through his suit into his shoulder blade. His work-bag is slung carelessly round his neck, pulling his tie out of place. He's 47, but he feels like a dishevelled schoolboy, uniform thrown on five minutes before he leaves the house.

"Mother Nature's inflicted an injury on her sons." Les, the leader of the council, has a tendency to dramatise.

Nearing retirement, Les has the heft of a 1970s union leader, a booming operatic voice, crow's feet spread from his eyes. His normally solid frame is rocking, his eyelashes are spiky, wet with barely concealed tears. As the leader of the council and his boss, Conor has grown to see the value of Les' commitment and bullishness, but at this moment they are equals, fans united in disbelief.

Les rolls his shoulders back and pulls a high-vis vest out of one of his pockets – as if he wasn't a politician, as if he was still a fire fighter. While the younger fans around take poor-quality pictures of the devastation on their phones, Les jots down new details in a pocket notebook. He points at the right-hand wall of the stand.

"Stay back people, level with me." Les assumes the role of fire marshal, over-stepping his jurisdiction, Conor thinks, nothing unusual there. They can all see that what's left of the stand could come down at any moment. Two police officers, arms stretched wide, form an inadequate human barrier. In the face of a rapidly growing mob of concerned fans, Les moves into action, standing shoulder to shoulder with the police. We are all men with the demeanour of small boys, Conor thinks, wanting reassurance.

The structure of the fans' collective history has been shaken to the ground. The Welders' first professional game in their new stand in 1928; 1934 league champions; the abandoned years of the war; the beggar's kit and skinny players of the 1950s; the first cup win in 1968 – stuff he knows about, but doesn't know how he knows it. Second-hand memories, he supposes. Later he'd seen the steady slide down the divisions first-hand. Conor feels his body cave slightly. Not that anyone would notice, they are all experiencing their own personal trauma.

"The lads'll be here soon," Les says. "We'll make the site safe."

Of course, Les will have been on to his old mates in the fire service and the service manager at the council depot, but that's not what Conor is worried about.

"Can't trust the chairman to organise the clean-up. Where is Cornflower? He sent his car for me, but I haven't seen him. He's never put any money into this place," Les spits. "If we don't do something, no-one else will."

He might be right, Conor thinks, but if we do something, that means I'll have to find more cash we haven't got.

Dense cloud cover forms a weighty lid on the scene.

"We'll rebuild it," Les says. It's what the fans want to hear.

"You mean the council...?" Conor says.

"I mean the tax payers."

"We could do the minimum," Conor ventures. "Lock the site down, talk it through with the chairman."

But Conor watches Les look up at the watery sky. What's in the air is a bigger decision, one that will anchor today in history. Conor has seen that look before – Les as war-time leader and evangelist. It means a massive public investment. Which also means that Conor will need to become an alchemist. He'll be required to magic millions out of memories and misplaced belief.

As if a match is about to start, there is a surge of fans towards what's left of the turnstiles. Men of all ages, many wearing club colours, flood the area. The new arrivals are braver, moving towards the rubble. More stupid as well, wanting to pocket a piece of their past. Maybe they are chancers, seeing some value in it, willing to risk the danger.

Conor notices a child, maybe eight years old, trying to push into the crowd. The boy is wearing a red and black woollen hat, and a jacket that's down to his knees with a Welders badge on it. He – or perhaps it's a girl – has lost his dad in the melee maybe? Stupid place to bring a youngster.

"Everyone back," Les booms, as the remaining wall of the stand groans and a metal strut buckles, forcing a crack that releases a brace of breeze blocks. "Over here now!" Les commands.

Conor loses sight of the child. The clanging of metal fencing being thrown from a flatbed truck is like the peal of urban church bells. Grounds maintenance staff in the green livery of the council work with the newly arrived fire crew.

"What about the north stand?"

"Chairman won't cough up for this mess."

"You're right. It was in the paper. Cornflower's waiting 'til a new investor comes and they can do what they want with the place."

"But where will we play?"

Agitated fans punt panic into the crowd.

Already people across the city will have formed an opinion about what has happened and what should happen next. Like it or not, football conversation permeates the life of the city, from news updates to pub chat, whether there is actually something worth talking about or not. Conor can't remember a council meeting that hasn't started without a post-mortem on the previous Saturday's events. The city will be talking about this for years.

As a finance man Conor can't help speculating about the insurance. In his mind, the Cemetery End Stand wasn't just called that because it faced the city graveyard. Fans joked that you could die of boredom in the Cemetery End, but Conor considered it an actual death trap. The amassed junk and detritus of 40 years must have come down with the building. The council's health and safety officers had complained regularly and often been denied access to the ground. Nobody kicked up a fuss, least of all the councillors – to a man and a woman, they were all fans.

Would a storm cause this sort of damage? Conor had been woken in the night by thunder, but still. There would need to be an investigation. The costs, the clean-up, the demolition, would just be the start. A nervous prickle creeps up Conor's spine.

Away from the collapsed wall, towards the car park, he sees the same child. Yes, it's a young girl. Looking under a small pile of debris, she tips over a piece of corrugated iron half her size, jumping back as it slaps down on the concrete.

"Come away from there, young lady," Conor shouts. "It's danger-ous." He starts towards her. The last thing we need is a death here, but then he's torn as he spots a journalist heading towards Les. The girl runs off in the direction of the road, disappearing against the flow of new arrivals – police, grieving fans and grave robbers.

"This will make national news." Les is pumped up by a collision of two of his favourite things: the Welders and press coverage.

Conor bets himself that Les has made a statement and it will be online by the time he gets back to his car. The headline will say, "Council to save the club." He shudders. Les is a big man. The situation requires one.

As if it were already a line in a set of accounts, Les' commit-ment to rebuild the stand will be recorded in black and white. It will be fixed in the minds of the fans and voters. With every word, costs will be racking up, expectations rising. That hand on his shoulder, the pressure, he reassesses it. It wasn't soli-darity, it was an instruction. Raw emotion is being recast as a decision, but it's not that Conor doesn't want it, too. He does. How could he not?

*

The day after Cup Final day, 6 May 1968

Conor had been playing football in the garden since 7am, reliving the victory, the winning goal. He squinted at the brightness, his neck sweating, sticky in his woolly Welders scarf.

"Come on, Grandad." His hand felt hot against the cool skin of the old man. "They're coming, they're coming."

Conor had never seen a victory parade before and was desperate to see the players on top of an open-air bus.

"We've got time," Grandad said. "Let's get you a packet of crisps and a drink."

"Come on. We'll miss it."

They'd stopped at the local shop, but were too late to get a special edition of the paper. The singing began as the fans made their way to the high street. By the time Conor and his grandad reached the pavement, the crowd was four deep.

"Room for a small one?" His grandad asked a couple in front of them, who ushered him through a maze of legs.

Aged seven, Conor pushed his nose out into the street in time to see an open topped sports car herald the cavalcade. Sunlight gleamed on the red bonnet and the huge sunglasses of the driver. Conor's eye was drawn to the two women sat on the folded back roof like Pan's People, dressed in red bikinis with sombreros. Clapping, cheering, horns began to blare. A chorus of "We are the Welders..." went up. Conor felt a football-sized lump in his throat.

One of the Pan's People girls suddenly threw her sun hat in the air and it flew into the crowd. Conor was almost knocked over as the fans jumped to grab it. Everyone spilled into the road, temporarily halting the bus. They were a red and black vein pulsing through the city.

"Special day," his grandad said. "These are the fans you never see at the ground. The ones who read the paper or listen for the Welders' name on Saturday afternoons. And their families, neighbours, workmates."

"Where are we going?" Conor asked.

"Town Hall o' course."

They had gone ahead of the players' bus.

"It'll be a while," Grandad said. "You wait here a minute." Conor wasn't scared amidst the throng in front of the huge, white building. He put his hands over his ears, the noise deafening.

Suddenly he heard his grandad's voice. "That's him." A man in uniform escorted Conor to the front and under the rope barrier. Conor was allowed to sit at the top of the stairs leading to the council chamber with a smart group of children. He hadn't known that his grandad had worked in the highways department. It was the only place in the world Conor wanted to be.

CHAPTER 3

August 2010

Nicole is learning that the distance between how you want things to be, and how they are, depends. That's what her mum always says: "It depends."

Everything depends on something else. But what that something else is, or what the different factors are, seems random, seems to change or remain a mystery. Today Nicole wants to be invisible and it seems like she is. The group of people only a metre ahead don't see her. She can rely on the fact that there's something more interesting to look at.

The new football stadium reaches up to the sky. On top is a steel frame painted brown, a bird's nest made of twiglets. The main entrance is a wall of glass that creates a giant reflection of the statue of Harry Bolt, the legendary number four, Ash's hero. Nicole's shadow fits inside one of his stretched-out legs.

By tagging onto the back of the crowd she's made it inside the two-metre high perimeter fence for the first time. The new ground opens today. Wherever Ash is, he'd want to be here today. Her legs shake, wanting to run; her chest feels light. Ha! She could scream, but doesn't – it's too important.

Every day for the last year Nicole has dodged the security patrols, stuck her nose through the gaps, watching the stadium growing. Searching for information about her brother's disappearance has become a full-time job – or would be if she didn't have to go to school.

How she really wants things to be is like they were before Ash disappeared. She could lean up against him while watching the match on TV. His body was firm, not like their mum's. If you leant on her she'd sink, slump down until the spongy, beige settee swallowed them both. Now there was no-one to steal chips from. No-one to play penalty shoot-outs or invent mad-armed goal celebrations with.

When Ash comes home has depended on:

"When he's ready… When his mate's mum kicks him out… When he runs out of money… When he comes to his senses… When the bloody police get their finger out and find him… When the sodding club do something… When people round here help us… When we find him, because no-one else is going to."

Nicole remembers that the first time her mum said the word "if" she ran to the toilet, her stomach cramping. "If he's alive." Of course, he's alive. But then her mind had jumped to the idea of a traffic accident. They couldn't identify Ash, so he might be in a hospital somewhere and lost his memory. That happens, she'd told herself.

"Proud day," she hears one of the adults in work clothes say.

The group are mainly men, pointing and stamping their feet, talking like they own the place, itching to get inside the stadium. Me, too, she thinks, but it's risky. She doesn't want to get caught or thrown out when she's only just got into the car park.

Unseen, Nicole drifts over to the VIP cars parked in front of the building. She has work to do. Crouching down she pulls a few photocopied leaflets from her jacket pocket. The first windscreen wiper she tries to lift seems glued down. When she tries to tuck a flier under the edge of the bonnet it flies off like a crisp packet in a breeze. Not wanting to waste a single leaflet, she spits on the glass, hoping to fix it; she needs the car's owner to see it and read it.

"Excuse me, young lady."

She bites her lip, should've kept an eye out.

"It's my brother, he's missing."

Nicole uses the photo of Ash in his football kit to draw the man's attention away from her.

"Ashley Brand, played left back, disappeared two years ago. You must remember him?"

The man shakes his head. He's wearing a Welders scarf, what's wrong with him? He ought to know Ash.

"Are you on your own? Not at school today?"

He's blocking the alleyway between the cars. Nicole shoots a look behind her. It's clear. To her left she sees two women she thinks she's seen before. They are dressed up like proper fans on a match day; one is old like her mum, her hair dyed blonde.

"I'm with them." She scoots round the back of the cars and off in their direction.

The man with the car is striding towards them. "Debbie," he calls across. Both women turn round.

Nicole pulls out a handful of leaflets, but is rushing and drops some. She's scrambling to pick them up, scratching her fingers on the concrete, when she realises the man is right by her side.

"Please." Nicole tries to push the paper into the woman's pocket.

"This man is from the council. He might let you have a look inside. You'd like that wouldn't you?"

Nicole freezes. Yes. Yes, but...

"What's your name?" he asks.

She'd so love to see inside. Ash will be amazed when she tells him she's managed to jam her way onto a proper tour.

The man already has his phone in hand. He's from the council, he'll call the social worker and they'll re-assess her. Mum is scared about that.

"They aren't taking you away from me," Mum says. That's why she's never at home, avoiding them.

Nicole sprints to the gate, out and round, down to the cemetery, lungs heaving. Cutting inside she takes the main path between the graves, slowing at the end furthest from the stand. She stops by a large tree, crouches with her back against the trunk. Her breathing slows and she feels better, better to get out of there. The best idea is to go to school, make it seem like everything's normal, she decides, which it will be when Ash returns.

CHAPTER 4

March 2016

If Conor had a pound for every time a council colleague said that the place had changed beyond recognition in the last eight years, he might've been able to avoid another redundancy. The sense of loss in the corridors of the council house endures. His diary has been full of funereal leaving drinks; like a Catholic priest, he keeps his memorial speeches short. That way they can get to the pub quicker and he can bury his own feelings deeper: sadness at losing colleagues and friends, and alarm at the increased risks, lack of capacity and experience.

In reality, the solid 1970s municipal building remains physically the same. Carpet-tile heaven. It's just that the staff are rattling around like lost souls in a giant storage warehouse. Conor climbs the back staircase to the third floor. He's been trying to let the floor to an IT company who are fishing around for council contracts. Good luck with that, he thinks. Those are shark-infested waters.

The only inhabited area on that level is the councillors' suite, as far away from the public as it gets. Conor needs Les to recognise their financial situation is now critical. His finger has been in the dam for years and it's about to break.

Next to the leader's office is the cabinet members' PA, Sandra, who has surrounded herself with a collection of pigs of the world. A farrow of plastic piglets balances on top of the computer screen; a steaming mug sits on a painted tile: "Welcome to the pigsty." Or trough, thinks Conor.

"Go on in." Sandra gives him an anything-for-you smile, almost flirty. He prefers to see it as tactical. They are a breed, these PAs. Three rounds of cuts and they are still here in force. Les is seated at his scuffed, old, presidential, partners-style desk.

Conor and Les have known each other for 20 years; there's no need to ease in.

"The club's finances won't last the summer."

"I know. They say that every year," Les snorts.

Conor sticks to his plan, wanting to get as far as he can without a full eruption. For EIGHT YEARS the club hasn't paid a penny of its contribution to the capital costs nor the rent it owes.

"It represents a catastrophic risk. I have to report it."

For now, though, Conor hasn't informed the council's solicitor. Les rests his head in his hands, deflating as he blows out a long breath. Conor turns his palms down and tightens his fists into a ball.

"You've always been a pessimist, Conor. You'll sort it…"

Conor swallows hard and keeps going. He can't allow Les to revert to the old narrative.

"Don't press them," Les says. "True, they're a bit short of funds. Soak the debt up, we'll be back up next season. A good cup run will see us right."

Pretty quickly the council had slipped into a regular routine of solicitors' letters and debt rescheduling.

"Don't upset the supporters. They are our voters." That's how Les thinks about it. Conor doesn't quite buy that. Because they are councillors, he thinks, they over-stating the connection. Of course, the fans would be defensive of the club, but would that really affect the way they vote?

After the stadium opened the club had outright refused to pay. The Welders had a new chairman, Daniel Croft, who insisted the contract had nothing to do with him. Chase Cornflower was the message; any debt is down to the old man. And the political rub is that Les refuses to take any action.

"No, we can't scare the horses. I'm not going to be the one who pushes the club over the edge."

"Then you might be the one who pushes the council over the edge. Every year the club doesn't pay we have to find another million pounds' worth of savings just to pay the interest on the debt. That's 40 extra redundancies we have to make, purely to subsidise the club. We've been robbing Peter to pay Paul. We took a £4 million revenue hit when the power station closed. We spent all our reserves on the stadium."

Les looks out of the window, like a school kid ignoring a telling-off.

Conor continues, "The level of government cuts is unsustainable. The legal challenge to older people's services means we can't touch that for now and we're paying hand over fist for agency staff in children's services since the decision not to recruit to key positions. It was you who didn't want to get rolled over in the press again. We've hit the tipping point."

Conor watches Les rub a hand over his neatly shaven head, wonders if he's still listening.

"You know all this, but I have a responsibility to spell it out."

Les' first response is predictable if more hesitant than normal. "You'll sort it out, you always do. Save the club, save the council."

"There's nothing I want more," Conor shakes his head, "but we can't go on like this. If we do nothing we could be out of cash by Christmas. We won't be able to pay the bin men's wages, road maintenance, cleaners, social workers, you name it. We'll have to shut up shop." He deliberately forces Les to make eye contact.

"You will be the first leader to... fail, to bankrupt your city."

Sweating now, Les thumps the table and stands abruptly, knocking his chair over. Its legs point up accusingly. Tell the truth to power, they say, and be glad if it thumps the table, not you. Conor knows Les fears a national party clampdown. Central office won't want one of their local councils causing a national outrage. Les would be in the political wilderness.

"Hold your nerve, lad. We've been here before. You officers exaggerate. We all know that…" Les says.

Bankruptcy would be the end for Conor, too, but he'd had to say it.

"Remember the 1980s. If we don't set a legal budget there will be a surcharge on your private bank accounts and prison if you don't pay…" And, he thinks, Les would never be able to drink in the Mechanics again. That had to hurt.

"We'll see, lad. This isn't Liverpool. I'm no Militant."

*

Les' practical response to the situation is a real shock. It's only two weeks after that conversation and, after over 20 years (with only one previous blip when the opposition held power for four years), Les is moving on. This is what happens now, Conor thinks. Politicians mess up and just walk away, dodge the accountability bullet.

"I'm stepping up to the region. That's where all the power and the money are these days. I'll automatically take over the police commissioner role, might even sack the chief constable if he doesn't play ball. I'll have a transport and housing budget we can only dream about."

Les sits in the chair opposite Conor's desk, puts his feet up. Must have cleaned his shoes especially, Conor thinks.

He's been aware of the political manoeuvring behind the scenes. There were a few names put forward to be the party's preferred candidate for the regional role. Les has done well to land it. He can sell it as a promotion rather than skulking off when the storm inevitably breaks in his own backyard. The local councillors will be proud to have their man as the regional mayor – if he wins.

Conor wouldn't put any money on that, though.

"Am I allowed to ask who you want to take over?"

"The group will elect the new leader as normal." Les seems unusually proper, playing the process card. "There will be a competition this time. Councillor Gent will stand against my preferred candidate."

As an officer, Conor is relieved to be well away from that bear fight. But then he thinks again. Why would Gent put himself forward to be leader if Les is backing another candidate? It would be pointless. Unless, Conor looks at Les' smirking face and realises he wants it to look like a competition, but it isn't. It's a set-up.

Les leaves the room smiling curiously. "You'll hear the result soon enough."

Eventually Conor's sources come up with the information. Councillor Gent, the badger-haired deputy, has naturally put his hat in the ring, but Les has backed a late-comer to the contest, a relatively new councillor, Anita Patel, not one of the inner circle.

Really? everyone thinks. What's going on is pure politics. Conor sees Les' game. The cunning old sod. Les won't be able to keep his distance. Not when he drinks in the same pubs, lives down the road and sits next to his colleagues at the football every week; the colleagues he's left in an almighty mess. Then Conor twigs. That's the point. Les isn't going anywhere. Les will keep his hand unofficially pressed on Conor's shoulder and Anita will be lucky to get a look-in. He'll have two bosses and already he knows they will be pulling in different directions.

Save the club, save the council, is the gamble. Or bankrupt both. Conor re-does the odds in his head. The odds on the club bankrupting the council or the other way around are both getting ever shorter, ever more likely.

CHAPTER 5

July 2016

Anita smooths the creases in her racing green shift dress, does up a single button on her jacket, then undoes it again. The cracked red leather seat squeaks loudly. The light bouncing off the gold leaf of the city crest makes her squint. Waiting to be sworn in as the new council leader is hard work. Many a famous backside in this city has sat in this chair. She is being watched, which is to be expected, but more intensely than she'd imagined. Anita taps her shoe on the brass foot-bar. At least sitting here at the centre of the horseshoe of tiered seating she can see it all.

The air in the council chamber is puffed up. Her fellow politicians in their Sunday best trot to their designated seats. The room smells of furniture polish and dry-cleaned suits. Anita watches the nods and handshakes, spots the allegiances, but doesn't join in. It's not that she's above it; glad-handing is part of the job. It's more that she needs people to see her differently today, to see that she's dignified.

The early evening sun pierces a stained-glass window high above. Captured in its rays is her Auntie Pinkie, sitting in a rosy glow of pride. She wishes Uncle Jas were still alive. They both miss him like they would miss tea. It's important to try and make Auntie proud. In private she'd even admit to feeling proud of herself, too. Yet at the same time, Anita is sanguine about the reality of the task ahead. A quiver of doubt vibrates through her.

What if I completely mess this up? She bites down on a nervous smile and locks her hands together to hold still.

The sideshow of the mayor-making begins. The in-coming mayor makes her way down the wide, carpeted aisle, protected by the bearer of the mace, all white gloves and formality, holding the weapon aloft. The mayor's gown is made of the finest scarlet wool, trimmed with full-length facings of fur. It can't be real fur, Anita thinks. The lace neck piece and triangular hat make it look like an expensive fancy dress outfit, a pirate or a Tudor courtier maybe?

These rituals of government are an irritating throwback to the days when politicians thought they were in control. It makes no sense to Anita to look backwards, to think the answers are in the past; a past that never included people like her.

As the procession makes its way towards the courtroom-style benches, those gathered look at the in-coming mayor in admiration, as if the young woman is a bride. Everyone knows the mayor has no power. They are generous and benevolent about it, sentiments that Anita knows not to expect.

In the 1980s, Uncle Jas had his turn with the mayor's chain. A backbench councillor for years, he and Aunty Pinkie, officially his consort, were proud to have been asked and she'd been proud of them. They travelled dutifully from school event to charity function, feet swollen, stomachs allergic to both the triangular white bread sandwiches and the starchy supermarket samosas that had been the only concession to their Indian mayor in the regulation buffet.

"The mayor's role requires sturdy shoes and the utmost courtesy," Aunty Pinkie had said. "It's the effort that seeks us, not we the effort." They weren't looking for the role, the universe needed someone to step up; it asked and they'd responded. When Uncle Jas died, Aunty Pinkie had taken his seat on the council.

In the past Anita had been happy as one of the crowd, holding a campaign banner whenever it was needed and shouting the truth to power whether it was listening or not. But not now. She hadn't planned to become council leader. One first, faltering political step had lead to another. Anita smiles at a memory.

Inspired by the Greenham Common Women's Anti-Nuclear campaign, a naïve but vocal sixth former, she'd joined a CND mass trespass at the local army depot on a Saturday afternoon.

"Stick with me," one of the older and not bad-looking students from college had said. As a small group of protesters surged towards the fence, breathless Anita was swept into the action, gripping the wire until it cut into her hands. A cheer went up as a post toppled. Heart thumping as she scrambled over the wire and into enemy territory, she'd clung to the young man's donkey jacket.

"Run," someone shouted and the group had scattered. The two of them kept running until out of breath, hands on their knees, they looked at each other laughing. They were in the middle of a cul-de-sac of bungalows, army officers' quarters. A curtain twitched.

"Oi!" a pensioner shouted. They ran down a garden path and hid behind a shed. Not wanting to be found or thought an idiot, and totally on impulse, Anita had shut the young man up with her lips. It was the sort of kiss she'd had been imagining for a while; full, clumsy and exhilarating.

On the way to tonight's meeting she'd stopped at her usual petrol station. It was on the same road as that army depot they'd broken into 25 years ago, now long gone. There's a housing estate and a new school, too, on the site now, which is a result really, Anita thinks. The development wasn't directly related to that protest, but how could you tell? As Auntie Pinkie said, it takes time for the water to wear away the rock. Anita flushes, remembering the kiss, but not the boy's name. She'd felt that what they had done had mattered, in a small way; they'd said no. It felt good, in more ways than she'd imagined.

Eight years ago, when Anita first started as a backbench councillor, unsure of her footing, she'd decided to stick with the same
campaigning approach. She saw her job as holding the city to
account on behalf of the people. In addition to her party alle-
giance, she saw herself as part of a loose alliance of the awkward
and unconventional; ambitious for change, but not for a job title.
It was hard to commit to one faction or another. The move into
the spotlight, to the leader's seat, was borne of frustration. In
her job as a youth worker, she had seen the direct effect of the
sinking economy on her young people's life chances and had
quickly tired of residents' complaints about parking and noise.

On a night like this the city looks like it's holding itself together.
The great and the good assembled, serious effort and talk of
progress. But for Anita the response is too slow and too sterile.
She's sick of managing decline. OK, her side manages the city
better than the opposition, they have done some good things,
but it's not enough.

Anita hadn't wanted to stand, but there was duty involved
and she was dammed if yet another middle-aged white man
would get the leadership. Les resigns, shuffles up to the region
and his mate slides into the warm seat. No. It was about time
the city had a woman leader. Anita knows she'll be criticised
and Pinkie has warned her about getting a reputation for being
anti-everything. People already have their scorecards out, judging
her. Losing her integrity is a risk. Sticking to her principals will
be challenging. I might have packed away my old campaigning
boots, she's thinks, and this feels a long way from street politics,
but I'm up for a fight.

The mayor's inauguration is complete. Anita's nerves ratchet
up a notch and she flushes, over-heated. It's her turn. What would
her parents say? They are 5,000 miles away. They always said
she was difficult and had sent her away to the UK at the age of
12. With a struggling food business, her mother would see little

financial incentive to take on a role like this. Her father, a junior lawyer, might view it differently, but there was no point dwelling on it. They were the ones who'd uprooted Anita, expected her to settle and grow in a new world. What right did they have to judge?

Life is complex. Fluid is good, but it's difficult to say anything without placing yourself either side of a deep chasm. Making sure her hair-pins keep her thick, shiny, black hair away from her face, she stretches her neck and re-focuses on the room. She's practised her speech for hours, so that it's in her head. Simple and clear, she knows not to go on.

The idea is to start afresh on day one, have a re-think, get everyone together and set a new direction for the city. The opposition leader leers across. There's a UKIP councillor who curls his lips back to reveal his teeth, like an Alsatian. He's not the only one in the room who won't like what she has to say, but there's nothing she can do about that.

As Anita's name is called and she is duly elected, she looks up at the city crest: "Out of unity is strength." That's something she can believe in. Standing to speak she casts an eye around the room, realising that both unity and strength are in short supply. Our city is in trouble, she thinks, and I must provide hope. If no-one likes me, so what. I'm 42, she thinks. Things have to change.

CHAPTER 6

July 2016

As the inauguration winds up and the council chamber begins to empty, Conor slowly closes the pages of the standing orders book. It's a beautifully bound, well-thumbed, leather tome, little of the gold leaf on the cover remains. From another time, it's a safeguard to fend off any challenges to the way they do business. It keeps them on the straight and narrow – in theory.

"We'll just check what the book says." Conor likes the words in black and white. In public, the politicians like to go by the book; in private, the book of rules goes from "valuable" to a "waste of time" in a blink.

"Just effing do it," is Les' normal response.

"Rules are meant to be broken," Anita has already said.

As he taps his fingers on this manual of sorts, Conor privately acknowledges he operates in an enormous tarpaulin-grey area, re-writing the book every day. Or re-interpreting it, he should say. A nudge here, a stretch there. That's the world they are in now. There's no solid 4-4-2 formation to the organisation, no agile, tiki-taka approach. It's more hoof it and hope. These days you don't know where a policy or initiative might land, let alone who, if anyone, will be on the end of it.

The upside to this is that Conor has more room to manoeuvre. The politicians rely on him to keep the ball in play, to create a bit of magic. The downside is you can't let your concentration drop, never switch off. The treasury is constantly issuing them with trip-wire guidance. Conor is aware that colleagues in other councils have paid dearly for not keeping up.

After 20 years of working together, it's hard to imagine life without Les as his leader. Hard to imagine Les won't be pulling the proverbial political strings. Smiling across at Anita, Conor knows he'll need to work intimately with her and at the same time he wonders how long she will last. At this stage, he wouldn't bet on her lasting until Christmas, although that might be wishful thinking. If she really wants to start with a clean sheet and chooses to unpick his masterpiece of budgeting, Conor's job will become un-doable; his daily grind a numerical hell. Les pulls at his tie as if to breathe more easily. Surely, he's not regretting letting go already?

Conor tries to apply a political shade card to the group surrounding Anita. There are a few clean, bright red stallions, a smaller group of councillors than you might think in a city like this. There are more people in the middle of the spectrum, muted reds and rosy pinks – a comfortable bunch to work with. A group within the group is a mixture of red and yellow, orange but these days without any fizz. Another is red/green, muddy brown thinkers. The reds that are mixed with blue are problematic.

He's wondered before whether Les is so blue he might have joined the wrong party. He skips over the members who are a toxic mix of red, blue, and purple and yellow, they make no sense to him at all. And, of course, it's not that simple; there are geographical alliances to consider and ethnic groupings. The fusion of Asian councillors from the east side of the city are the members Conor knows least well. He could do with an inside track here, an informant who will explain the subtle alliances.

Conor can't imagine Anita being in Les' pocket. Nor who else might form an alternative support base for her. Their side of the chamber has voted for Anita because the numbers are so tight. They want to hold on to control of the council at all costs.

Whether the councillors are persuaded by Anita or they voted for her because Les told them to, it doesn't matter at this point.

On the other side of the house, the opposition took great delight in sitting on their hands when it came to the vote. The opposition leader had actually licked his lips, making Conor shudder. In a city where immigration continues to be a divisive issue, Les must've known a female Asian leader would be more of a provocation than a vote-winner.

"We'll make sure everyone pays their way, pays what they owe," Anita said in her speech. Conor's ears had pricked up at that. He'd caught Les' eye, his face fixed in horror. There were other on-lookers who'd noticed it too. Was it a dog-whistle threat to the Welders, picked up by those receiving on a football frequency? Or was it more of a general reference to corporate tax-avoiders or the council's need to rely on increased business rates in future? Conor isn't sure how much Anita actually knows.

A local journalist had picked up a pencil and, from the look on their faces, the two women dressed in red jackets with neatly sewn Welders badges were not happy either. Matching earrings and a similar swept-back hair style, Conor gives the Debbies, the mother and daughter combo, a wide berth. These extreme fans have somehow managed to head up the Welders Supporters' Club and, worse, they now seem to be the official representatives of the club at public meetings. It's a sign of the times, the chairman delegating his role to the ultras. God help them.

The younger woman had touched the club badge and Conor had groaned under his breath. "Fidelis ad mortem," faith and death – Les might have that on his gravestone.

Rounding up the stragglers and herding them towards the door of the council chamber, Conor finds his mouth is parched. What he'd heard from Anita was the brassy sound of intent, a trumpet of momentum. The new leader stamps across the chamber to the lobby. No fake and shake with the great and good of the city, she heads straight for her activist friends and begins debating the budget. It's 9pm. Conor picks up the weighty standing orders book, holds it like a shield to his chest and heads back up to his office.

CHAPTER 7

December 2008

It's not the collapse of the football stadium Anita remembers, it's the emergency meeting that followed it. Eight years ago and it's on instant recall. When she's tired, stressed or her energy drops, doubts about herself and doubts that she's really understood what's going on at the council creep in. Her brain presses play and she's back in 2008.

The councillors meet in a private bar, the upstairs room at the New Mechanics Institute. The walls are adorned with civic photos; the old town hall in black and white, the new redbrick centre opened in the 1970s. There's a picture of the proud Midlands Miners and a Welders Cup win. The players, like giants, are holding the cup tight, but kissing it gently as if it were a precious new baby. Anita sees that it's important, but there are plenty of other struggles they could be celebrating. What about the great women's lock-making strike? The first gay pride march?

It's two months since she was elected as a councillor and she's still not sure who to sit with. Tucking a handful of hair behind her ear, she throws her bag on the floor and chooses to sit on a stool at the far end of the bar. Les looks freshly shaven, dressed for a night out in light blue pinstripe shirt, clean tan brogues, with a generous navy jacket hiding his bulk. Anita's come straight from a youth work session in a pastel orange t-shirt and jeans. They can take her as they find her.

"Thanks everyone for turning up in a crisis." Councillor Gent, Les' badger-haired ally, calls them to order. He's not the only one in the room who looks stricken. The beer is cheap in here, but the atmosphere is sober.

The word irks Anita. This is not what she calls an emergency. The stadium has just collapsed, so what if one side of the football ground is derelict? As an outsider, it seems a more accurate reflection of the club's situation – all mouth and no dentures. Last night she'd seen her cousin Vikesh, a Welders fan, and he'd seemed perversely proud of the ground's deformities.

Les takes the floor.

"Remember '68? We were cup giant killers, we showed courage against the odds and you could feel it everywhere. The place was buzzing. People were optimistic, happier, proud of the city. They moaned less, they spent more."

Anita sticks her tongue into her cheek. They could be here a while.

"Nottingham Forest, Preston North End, Bristol Rovers, Crewe Alexandra – when the football results were read out at five o'clock on a Saturday, you paid attention. East Fife 5…"

"Forfar 4."

It gets a laugh, but it means nothing to her.

"That's how you knew a place existed and it's still true. A city with a successful football club is on the map. Everyone here wants this club to be in the Premiership, restored to its former glory."

One of the backbenchers raises a glass to that. Anita picks at the edges of a beer mat. Have I walked into a supporters' club meeting by mistake, she wonders?

"A successful football club means a successful city. We need to build confidence, attract investment and jobs. It's about leadership."

Les' pitch is an invitation to dream, an appeal of faith. That is never going to work for her. Anita is just not interested in football, doesn't see why we all have to be, but she can see Les' speech is having the desired effect. She rips the beer mat neatly in half, then quarters. Surely someone else is going to say something? If cuts are on the way, why are we giving taxpayers' money to a football club, a private business?

"And it might be the last good thing we can do before the election, with cuts on the way..."

Anita fidgets on her bar stool.

"I'm a Welders fan," Les reddens, "man and boy. There's 30,000 of us." He pauses. "When we're winning, that is."

The downbeat delivery, the team's blighted history, it's all calculated to have its effect.

"Errr... sorry Les," she can't keep quiet any longer, "but 235,000 people live in this city. We're elected to meet everyone's needs, the whole city."

Heads turn in surprise towards her.

Les' smile drops. "And every one of us wants to feel good about where we live. It's not just the supporters; a win for the club is a win for us all."

"Are we asking the public what they think? This isn't just about us in this room."

Les groans, but it's also a relief to get a "hear, hear" from Councillor Kathleen Berry. At least Anita's not the only one who thinks it's madness to build a new stadium.

"The club needs us, we'll be there for it, but only because there's no-one else. No Russian oligarch, no consortium of local businessmen, we're on our own."

"We haven't got the money, have we?" Anita blurts. She can feel her face flush, the room itself glares at her.

Les snaps, "We wouldn't be here if this wasn't on. I'm advised we can use our reserves. This is our chance to make a statement. A new stadium. It will create 500 jobs. We can use it for conferences, concerts, the club can pay us rent. It's a standard model."

What? That can't be right? We need to slow down, she thinks.

"And if needs be, we can borrow…"

That tests the group discipline, conversations break out.

"…cheaper than the money markets. Friends," he roars, "friends." The sound jars, it's too big in the sweltering room.

"Friends," Anita sees Les is hoarse now, but the group are back with him. "Do we want to be a second-rate team in a second rate-city? Clubs like ours can't survive alone. It's market failure. That's capitalism. Either we let it fail or we step in. And we make it great, a club and a city to be proud of."

She hesitates, thinking, alright, one last try.

"Is this legal?"

Les lowers his chin and turns his body away from her, dismissive.

"We have the power of general competence, a duty of care. Want more? Conor, please tell our new councillor…"

Anita stares at Conor. What's he even doing at a political group meeting?

"Councils all over the country put money and support of different kinds into football," Conor says blankly. "And into all sorts of sports, everything from bowling greens to Formula One. And they build art galleries and theatres. When finances allow."

As Conor is not far from her at the bar, she speaks directly to him. "I'm worried about the long-term commitment…"

"Of course, it's a bloody long-term commitment." The power in Les' voice threatens to knock Anita off her stool.

"I want the club to be for my grandchildren and their grandchildren. That's what you'll never get. You don't know what this means to us. It's our heritage."

Her scalp prickles, hair lifts on the back of her neck. She takes a deep breath. "Our heritage?"

There's a low mumble in the room. Everyone heard that. It feels a long way down from her stool to the swirling carpet.

Les attacks. "You've been on the council five minutes. I'm telling you this is about a new beginning. This will guarantee us victory at the next election. We've got to knock on every door in the city in just under a year's time. What are you going to say...?"

This is Les' killer blow. Making it political puts the group under pressure, seals the deal. He turns his attention to the faithful, who nod, chunter, begin to talk tactics, it's all about winning. Or rather win/lose.

Anita holds on to the bar, desperate not to stumble or fall. Picking up her bag she notices her hands are shaking. They'll shut me out now, she worries, I'll be ostracised. She needs to get out of here at all costs, but her legs feel weak.

Conor is moving towards her. She pulls her bag into her chest, forces herself to look him in the eye.

"What I want to know..." she says, "is what you really think?"

Conor's tongue must tied in a line of knots. Seconds pass. Of course, he must be a fan, but how can there be enough money to build a brand-new stadium?

"I serve at the leader's pleasure," he shrugs.

Right, she tells herself, this is how it is. Don't burn your bridges. Keep your self-respect. Just do this and then you can leave, head up.

Anita looks past Conor and takes a few steps towards the leader. Les is powerful, it's important not to burn bridges so early in her time on the council. Her hand is out, clearly determined to shake his, it'll look bad for him if he doesn't take it.

But instead he leans in close, puts his arm on her shoulder, she can smell a mixture of sweat and tangy aftershave. He looks around, smiling, then whispers in her ear.

"We're a group. Go against this and you're on your own. Fit in or fuck off."

CHAPTER 8

September 2016

The salty butter coating the fat of the bacon in his Saturday morning butty normally lifts Conor's mood. Today he's let it go cold, the congealed grease giving it the texture of a wax candle. Instead of making the usual early start for the football ground, he sits on the bottom stair thinking about work, his hip joint aching. It's going to take all his strength to get up and out. Turning up for another Welders defeat most likely, but what else would he be doing on a Saturday?

In any week Conor would've spent as much time with Les as he does with his partner, Jayne. Over the years that's made him more guarded, he keeps more back. It would just make Jayne angrier. With Anita he's starting again. The characters change, he thinks, but the issues don't. The resource problems become normalised, routine even. Parts of the council have modernised. The Place directorate, what used to be called Regeneration and Planning, has merged with Housing, Communities and a dozen other departments. A many-headed monster in a lean land. It looks like a new country compared to his old fiefdom. The cuts have Balkanised the directorates, driven them apart rather than together. And they all want to leave responsibility for the money to him.

Monday will be his first real encounter with Anita. He's still not clear what her priorities are. She's a strong advocate for children. Whatever she does it'll put pressure on his precarious budget. Stop over-reacting he tells himself. They'll be meeting in the obsolescent city farm, nothing to see there.

"Squash up, love." Jayne wants to sit beside him on the stair. At least she's still speaking to him. Last week her sister, who works in the homelessness team, had received a redundancy letter with his e-signature on it, adding insult to injury.

"You still thinking about Becca?"

She nods.

The stair isn't wide enough for the two of them, but he's glad of the closeness.

"It's a dirty job etcetera…" he tries to jemmy out a smile, "and it's got my name on it."

As a couple, that was how they'd rationalised his work, agreed it was better that someone like him makes the cuts, someone honest, straightforward. He'd felled the budget, feeling the weight of the fallen. There is further to go, but Anita has already said she won't make the sort of cuts he and the other public finance woodsmen know they need.

It's been gruelling to make the cuts. It was always gruelling. Although a member of the public had recently called him the most hated man in the city, what was worse was the sympathetic commiseration from well-meaning colleagues. Poor sod, they think. "You look like you're carrying the weight of the world on your shoulders," they say. No doubt it's intended to make him feel better, but usually it has the opposite effect.

Which is annoying, because, actually, he believes in what he's doing, working to make the city a better place to live. And there are good people working hard here in difficult circumstances.

It's hard to make cuts, but almost worse not to.

Jayne brings him back to their conversation.

"That's still true. But someone's got to *want* to do it."

"At the end of the day I'm an accountant," he says. "I just know how to make the numbers add up," clinging to his professional badge. "I didn't go into this job to make people redundant."

Conor feels like a soldier who signed up to defend his country and finds himself a member of the firing squad. Jayne looks at him like he's the general that just yelled, "Fire!"

Their hips and shoulders are wedged together, stuck.

"I take care of the council's money, I don't make the decisions." She squeezes his knee.

"Stop hiding behind the politicians. You're the one holding it all together. You could let it go, there's a chance now Les has gone, walk away."

"But how would we manage?"

The disappearing grant, the hidden government ring-fencing that ties his hands, the additional responsibilities and staff transferred to them without a home or a budget, they make it impossible and bind him in at the same time. How could he trust that minefield to someone else? His mind flicks to the implications of a low-interest rate environment; he won't be able to use his old investment tricks to generate extra cash.

Jayne says, "It's never been about paying the mortgage. We don't need that much."

Conor realises he's still thinking about the council.

"I'm not sure where your heart is anymore," she says, "or your head for that matter. You've gone. You're somewhere else. You used to be sure of what you were doing and why."

He looks at the carpet, not wanting to make eye contact.

"I do what I've always done. What I do is what I am. My word is my bond," he says, trying for humour, knowing in his stomach that his words are overblown.

She sighs. "You can't hold it altogether, though, can you? You're pretending."

The firing squad image reappears before him, but now he feels like the poor bastard wearing the blindfold. Chest stripped bare. He'll be shot if he doesn't follow Anita's new path or face municipal bankruptcy if he does.

Conor swallows hard, for the final time the firing squad reappears, but this time he's the one digging the graves. Including his own.

"I have no choice. I have to try," he says to Jayne, his stoical fan voice slipping out. However bad you think it is, manage down your expectations.

"It's not all down to you. And you aren't your job. Let's get away for a break, get some perspective…"

His pulls at the Welders scarf hanging limp over the banister, falters, unable to meet her eye. There is so little outside his job these days; snatched words with their son Toby, time-pressured visits to his grandad, the duty of the Welders. Aren't I just like everyone else these days, he wonders? But more so? Or maybe less so – he's back to thinking about the people he's just made redundant.

"This can't go on," she says.

It's Jayne who starts to move, putting her weight on his thigh to lever herself up.

He senses her leaving in a deeper way and instinctively says, "I love you." He says it so quietly she might not have heard. He loves her more than he has ever done. He tries to pull her back down by the pocket of her jeans.

"You need some space to think," she replies. "And I don't mean going to the match."

There are many reasons why he loves going to the match. At the moment, it's because it's the only place he doesn't have to think.

CHAPTER 9

October 2016

When Nicole thinks about Ash, it's usually as a 13-year-old. He's playing football, long, wet fringe stuck to a sweaty forehead. She might be prowling up and down a muddy touchline, the school pitch probably, chatting to one of the dads acting as linesman. Getting your haircut was unlucky, Ash said.

Now and then she remembers him as a 16-year-old. She's sneaked into club training ground, keeping well out of the way of the coaching staff, but she knows he's seen her out of the corner of his eye and it's alright, she won't get chucked out and they can walk home together.

She saves the memories of Ash's Welders debut for when it's hardest; his birthday or hers. If he was alive, Ash would be 24.

Nope. Nicole tries, but she just can't picture him.

Wormy had sent her message at 6.00am. *Crime scene at city farm, check it out.*

It would be better if Wormy, Ash's bezzie mate, could be there, but she'll go anyway. It'll be all over Snapchat by the time she gets to school. The city farm is about a 15-minute run. She'll get there and they will be digging someone up. It'll be an old man, his face will be like concrete, ants crawling all over his neck.

It could be a normal jog except her stomach is rock hard and she's sweating already. She laces her trainers tight, throws on whatever's handy, but never goes out without her black and red beanie.

Slipping out of the home before anyone else is awake and before the key workers on the early shift, Nicole starts her run. Down to the bottom of her road, legs shaky, like the end of a hard training session not the beginning. Breath choppy, no rhythm, she steps straight into the road and is shocked as a car flashes its lights at her.

Pete, the manager of the care home, says she's got a morbid fascination with crime scenes, which she must work on with a therapist. No way. It's research. She's hunting for clues about Ash's disappearance.

The first crime scene she'd been to was at a gas works out of town. Wormy was on security at the gate, drowned in a three-quarter length high-vis. He'd let her watch the police setting up, the victim already had a grey tarp over him. She might've been there only ten minutes before she was chased off. Turned out to be an industrial accident. The second was almost a year later. That was never going to be Ash, but it was useful to watch the scene. An old man had a heart-attack while walking his dog. She'd stayed well back at that point, learnt what to do.

Arriving at the park, she decides against running straight down the long drive to the city farm gates and scoots around the fields. The traffic on the motorway hums away in the background. The farm buildings are shrouded in mist. Ash is alive, he won't be found in a place like this. Scanning, scanning, head twisting so she almost loses her footing. Then she sees. The lake, a park warden, a policeman and a high-vis security guard are staring at the lake. Heartbeat darting, she swallows hard, her saliva thick and bitter.

No. Nicole almost turns back, doesn't want to be here, can't be here. There's a pain in her chest. Please don't let Ash have drowned in there. He hated water. "No", she says aloud.

This is not Ash.

CHAPTER 10

September 2016

As Anita walks into the seminar room above the visitors' centre at the city farm, the outside seems to follow her. It's strange there's no-one around to greet her. A mist saunters in through the Crittall windows, attempting to dampen her upbeat mood. There's a strong smell of manure and damp carpets. It's been raining for days. The place feels abandoned, as if it's given up already. Close us down if you want.

The venue wasn't her choice. The over-sized room upstairs on the first floor swallows the empty table. Their decisions will echo around them. Anita's looking forward to a new camaraderie, maybe even some collective energy. She's expecting some scepticism, but it's her first day, surely she'll be allowed a fair crack?

Placing her coat and papers at the head of the table Anita wanders over to the far window, looking down at a giant pig, fattened on taxpayers' swill. If that pig had longer legs, it could be a hippo.

"I should know this, but do Indians eat pork?"

Anita recognises Councillor Gent's broad Brummie accent as the staircase groans beneath him. Other voices fill the small hallway, they will be here any minute – and then it starts.

"Muslims and Jews don't eat pork, that's right isn't it?" That could be Councillor Ward.

"Not Indian," Les corrects. "Anita's a Hindu."

That throws her, what the hell is Les doing here? He gave up his right to waltz into any council meeting he liked when he resigned. That was his choice. She's the leader now, this isn't a party meeting.

Gent says, "My sons' friend eats sausages when he's at our house, but his mum thinks they're unclean."

"Not those beauties, they're spotless. We aren't getting rid of those pigs. The kids love them."

The three of them appear in the room. Les is wrong on two counts. Three, if he thinks he's still in charge.

"Always best to check when it comes to religion…" Anita says and smiles, her lips pressed firmly together. "I'm an atheist…"

Les stares back, while Gent squirms.

"…and I'm a vegetarian."

It's possible to love animals and still shut the farm. Sentiment won't help them make the difficult decisions that lie ahead. Those pigs could provide bacon sandwiches for half the city. The thought makes her feel more determined and, at the same time, slightly queasy.

"Here's my girl." Les announces her to the group. His voice is cloying, the words inaccurate at best.

"Didn't know you were coming?" Anita definitely hadn't invited him.

"Wanted to make sure the team behaves for the new boss."

Anger almost hooks her. No, she decides; don't get caught, dragged in or down. Still standing by the window, trying to appear relaxed, she says, "We'll give it a couple of minutes…"

She does up an extra button on her purple cashmere cardigan; neck cold, palms sweaty. Watch out for the old guard, she tells herself.

In her inauguration speech Anita had set out her vision of a future where the vulnerable are protected, and the gap between rich and poor closes. Les had warned her; "Keep it practical. Round here, people only care about protecting their own, they don't believe the state can look after them, they don't want us to and they don't want to think that they're the poor."

Determined to start a new type of conversation, she beats down a moment of doubt. There are no good luck wishes, no congratulations on taking up the leadership. Surely some of them voted for her? It feels odd. The energy in the room is low, maybe Les has told them it's just another budget-cutting meeting.

There are two more cabinet members to come. This is the cabinet team: Bardill – they call him Skip, which refers to the size of his stomach; Gent – with the badger hair and small eyes he's not known for his vision; Ward only nods in Les' direction; Kathleen Berry is the other woman, nearing retirement; Morton – old Frank used to teach at her college; and Evans, the so-called hard man of housing. Looking at them en masse, she sees she's missed an opportunity not to re-shuffle some of Les' gang out, deal herself a new hand.

The problem with that, as she'd discussed with Auntie Pinkie while cooking dinner, is that it's not the small 'p' politics Anita wants to be associated with. Mixed in with the smells of turmeric, coriander and coconut were wisdom and love. Cabinet members earn allowances of up to £23,000 a year, a good salary for many families. Pinkie reminds her that the choice can generate fierce and enduring jealousies. Everyone suspected Les of buying loyalty from those he selected, not picking the best candidates for the job. If it isn't working, change it then, was Pinkie's advice.

Les catches Anita's attention. His face says, listen to me.

"Don't worry lads, we're not moving to fortnightly bin collections." Les makes it sound as if he's giving her an instruction. Whatever games Les chooses to play, she decides, take what you can get and use it.

As they start to talk about Saturday's match, she finds her attention drifting. Movement to the right of the pig pen, towards the pond, catches her eye. It's not immediately clear what's going on. Work is underway, or was. Two men, wearing the green polo-shirts of the city farm, are standing well away from the muddy edges. Straining slightly, she sees two police cars. A white van rolls alongside noiselessly. There are three uniformed officers. What takes seconds in a TV drama, unfolds gently. Kit is unloaded, laid out on the ground. Stakes are knocked into the sodden earth with wooden mallets.

Looking back into the room, Les is bent over the table; an arm shields the papers in front of him as if he's hiding his prepared answers. Next to him, Conor, another of Les' men, bends in the opposite direction, a willow sighing towards Councillor Bardill. They are as uninterested in her as they are unaware of the situation outside.

A silver Mondeo parks up and two men in casual jackets get out. Alert, their sweep of the lake draws Anita's eye to a grassy bank at the side of the slow-moving scene where a young girl sits watching intently. From the hoodie and tracksuit trousers she could have been out running, or else it's just regular teenage uniform? As the black and yellow tape is knitted around the pins to form a cordon, a policeman waves the girl away. She moves position slightly, concentrating on a spot at the edge of the pond.

When the crime scene officers emerge in full protective coveralls, Anita's stomach lists. Under the cover of a tree, the girl takes her phone out, quickly filming the scene. She rocks slightly and chews the end of a ponytail. She ought to have grown out of that at her age.

Drawing a line from the girl to the water's edge, Anita makes out a spot, a light stick poking out of the sludge. That must be it. Part of it. Her heart pounds – a bone? She tries to stay calm, but contractions in her throat make her cough. An old memory rises up. A bone in swirling mustard water, a bone sticking out of an arm, attached to a cream kurta pyjama maybe? But not much else. Her first dead body was viewed from a river boat on a family day out when she was about five years old.

It was a human arm, the brown skin shining like a wet branch. There was also a foot, which made her brother, Siddhu, shriek excitedly. Their mother began to cry. The watery grave is imprinted on Anita's memory.

A man wearing a smart jacket and trousers announces himself.

"Excuse me folks, I'm Detective Inspector Jones. Sorry to let you know, we have designated the city farm a crime scene. Don't be alarmed, we've found what looks like human remains. We're going to have to ask you to remain here for a while."

"What?" "Dead?" "What do you mean?" "Is that it?"

DI Jones' body blocks the door. He's also the council's link officer to the police force. The group know him well.

Now people stand, there's the pretence of order as they make their way towards the windows. The muted hubbub gives Anita a moment to compose herself. Her thoughts leap; it's a woman, it's someone's wife, daughter or friend. The start of my leadership is marked by the discovery of human remains, not exactly auspicious. She chides herself for being superstitious, but it's difficult to take her eyes from the muddy resting pool and the girl, now huddled into a ball, limbs like elastic bands wound round her knees.

The others stretch and reach for their phones like passengers on a delayed train, desperate to share scant information they can do nothing about.

"We're all a bit shaken up. Best to leave it for today." Les announces this as if he's still in charge. If his behaviour doesn't change she's going to have to pull rank and tell him to sod off.

"It's incredibly sad." Anita says. "But we should let the police do their work and we'll continue with ours."

"It's going to be a while before we can get the cars out," Gent says.

"Don't want to get stuck all the way out here." Councillor Berry sounds frailer than she is.

"How about walking over to the Highlands?" Anita tries to break the train of thought. "We could use a room at the community centre?"

"Walk?" Gent is incredulous.

Bardill stutters, "Leave the cars here?"

It's a mistake, beyond the pale.

"OK," she says to DI Jones, "we aren't involved, it's an unfortunate coincidence we happen to be here. If we give you our details, can we get out of your hair?"

"Well…"

"OK, good. Here's my mobile," she says. "Please call and brief me later."

Anita lets DI Jones, and Les, know who's in charge now. The sky outside darkens, there's a whispered menace, these things happen here.

"Let's resume in an hour. We can use my office in the civic."

The group like the sound of being back in town. It's secure. As people begin shuffling, Anita suspects half of them might just slope off, finding new ears for the news and new meetings that avoid the difficult subject of the future.

"As I said," Anita continues, "when we set this session up, this isn't about how we avoid bankruptcy…"

That stops them. Les looks back angrily at her. It's an unsayable word in his book.

She takes a deep breath, "…we need to start afresh. It's about how we're going to win the next election."

That's a political trick she's borrowed from Les and it seems to work.

She turns to Conor, finding him difficult to read.

"I'll give you a lift back." It's as near as Anita dares get to an order. There's a flick of an eye movement as he looks towards Les, then accepts.

Outside a policeman guides them over the grass to the car park.

Anita's glad not to be looking directly at the pond. As they pass the young girl, Anita walks towards her, stopping a few metres away, remembering that she'd chewed her own hair as a child.

"Are you OK?" Anita asks.

There's no response, they are almost past her when the girl turns her gaze to Conor, there's a harsh squint, hat pulled down firmly.

Anita walks on. Slamming the car door shut she asks, "Friend of yours?"

"Friend of social services more like," Conor says, "I'm pretty sure she's one of ours."

CHAPTER 11

September 2016

In the car on the way back to the civic centre Conor notices Anita's mascara is slightly smudged. They've never been so close before, only the gear stick between them.

"Can I?" He opens the window. The car smells of coffee cups and gym kit. Anita shivers, so he shuts it again. Council papers cover the back seat. Hung from the rear-view mirror is a Buddha charm, the dashboard has old but still glittery stickers, a goddess with many arms, another he assumes to be the sacred sound symbol Om and the Indian flag. Messier than he expected.

"I remembered the girl because she hangs around the football club."

"Is that all anyone thinks about round here?"

Conor raises his hands in apology. Anita doesn't seem the type to start micro-managing, but it's critical that she trusts him; that she leaves him to get on. He takes the conversation back to work – which isn't exactly safer ground.

"I know you want to re-look at the whole budget, but time is short."

"And you've already got a hit list?"

He shrugs. If he doesn't put something on the table, they'll get nowhere.

"The thing is… the budget is stuffed if we can't bring down the numbers of children in care. And…," Conor hesitates, "our asset valuation suggests we could sell a number of the residential properties to support our medium term financial plan."

"To make a tidy little sum you mean?"

Anita pulls the car up abruptly at an amber light. Conor wishes he were driving.

"And where do we shove the children?" She turns her head towards him. "Up a chimney?"

This is what she meant when she'd said, "We will protect the vulnerable."

To Conor the complexity of children's care is a creaking see-saw. At one end it's sensible and cheaper to try and give children a family home, find adoptive parents or re-house the kids with relatives, however distant. But at the other, the see-saw crashes down, unable to deal with the weight of the children's problems and the heavy costs on the system.

"Children who've lived through the care system can be deeply traumatised. They need a therapeutic environment, love and understanding. While I'm leader," she tells Conor, "we won't be selling those homes. We'll have to come up with something better; for the kids, not for us. And we won't be spending public money on football."

"Could I remind you," he says, tentative, "just how serious the budget problem is?"

"You mean that up to now you haven't been telling us the full picture?"

Is she joking? Or already suspicious, Conor wonders. He aims for a wounded look, pulls his battered satchel from the foot-well.

"We make choices," Anita says. "We find money for the priorities."

"It's just that the figures simply don't stack up."

"The budget is a car crash, I see that. But I'm not going to look away, leave it all to the officers. I need to see clearly how things really are..."

Conor rubs at his forehead. True enough, he supposes. But the budget is a labyrinth and the only map is buried deep in his head. Over the years the accounting twists and turns have become untraceable, un-, well, accountable, he almost laughs.

"Warts and all. Let's go through the numbers together this afternoon, in my office. Nothing is as important as this, right?"

He nods, looks for an excuse. He'd had it all under his control – and the control of a well-meaning group who didn't ask too many questions. This is the second time Anita has asked him to spell it out. He can't. He won't.

His team has spent years weaving a fine tapestry, a safety net of a budget, built on inventive income generation schemes, intricate trade-offs held together by the goodwill of the staff. Anita's blank page approach could take forever, it wouldn't deliver what he needs to keep them safe.

"Back at the farm you mentioned bankruptcy," he says. "If we don't sort out the costs and the quality of care... we're due an inspection, the government could take the decisions out of our hands."

"I'm sure we can come up with something..." Anita grips the steering wheel tightly.

What exactly? Snappy solutions are a delusion, agreements a mirage, temporary at best. Aiming to be conciliatory, but non-committal, he makes a suggestion.

"We have some great social work practice going on," despite the cuts, he means. "Why don't you have a proper look at some of the residential homes, good and bad? We can hold on to any changes to the current proposals for a few weeks..."

"Weeks? This is long-term change. I won't be bounced into sticking with Les' proposals. That's what you're talking about, isn't it?"

The sarcastic voice in his head invites Anita to tell him how on earth they are going to balance the budget. Better still, you do it, Conor wants to say, but, of course, he holds his tongue.

"I'll go to visit a couple of the resi homes," Anita says, "but only because I want to."

They are almost back at the office. He makes sure his work bag is shut properly, trying not to look desperate to get out of the car.

"And I want you to tell me about the football club. I know it's costing us money."

Christ. Conor can feel the colour in his cheeks start to rise. Keep calm – as they say – and give nothing away.

"It's a long story..." he says, "and, well, maybe Les ought to be the one to fill you in. It's political."

"What do you mean?" Anita stabs at the brake, turns her head away from the road and towards him. That was a mistake.

"Only that Les will need to tell you what the group were thinking."

"OK, but I want to know the practical implications."

At the council AGM Conor had been worried about how much Anita knew about the club. It's something of a relief that she seems to be on the first page of the sordid saga.

He tries for another distraction.

"Have you been to a match before?"

Her face says don't be stupid.

"Why not come to the next game? Call it a research visit. It might give you some extra brownie points with the other councillors if you've seen the club in action."

CHAPTER 12

September 2016

The next day Anita is outside Westmeade Residential Children's Home. It has a substantial, neat garden, glossy black railings, two generous bays on either side of a wide door, three stories and an extension – Georgian maybe? It's detached, with a five-foot wall of privet protecting the house from the street or the other way around, Anita isn't sure. Pink geraniums in a terracotta pot on the windowsill catch her eye.

"She holds out her hand as the wide door to the home opens. The manager, Pete Lambton, is mixed race, tall with strong shoulders and his handshake is unhurried. Anita senses the rare possibility of a genuine jargon-free conversation.

"We're on the same side," is what she might've said if she'd met him only a few months ago. From the moment she'd become the council leader people have reacted differently towards her. Words are watched, qualified and hedged. There's fear that a real opinion might slip out and there will be consequences. She knows it's a response to her position, but it's already frustrating. In her mind Anita's still a campaigner, a people's advocate and a leader. Not *the* leader, the voice of the many. Am I behaving differently, she wonders? Of course. I have to.

Inside the wide corridor is like a gallery with quality art work. The pictures are generously framed. One is a powdery charcoal drawing, a thin serious face accentuated by the black glasses of a librarian. It's impressive and vaguely familiar. Another work is a painting, in the style of a 15th century Dutch master, girl without a pearl earring, girl with purple elastic hair band. The one that isn't signed holds her attention. It's printed in a large modern block font, four words in a heavy matt black, "THIS IS NOT ME". The anger compressed under the glass frame makes Anita stand back.

Pete says, "Fantastic, aren't they?" Anita notices Pete's dark chocolate voice. "We put our kids' pictures up like any other home, except ours are better. The kids need more than a roof over their heads."

"Agreed."

He's unusual, arty, cool, she thinks. Attractive, too. Bet the kids here love him.

"In case you were wondering..." Pete says without an edge, "we had an anonymous charitable donation to pay for the art therapy."

Of course. No budget for that.

At the end of the corridor, the gallery illusion ends and a chaotic intimacy begins. Coats and jackets bury what was once a grand banister, rucksacks and shoes hide the chips in the original tiled floor.

Pete clears his throat as if he's making a pitch, performing for a special guest.

"We're all passionate about this place. I mean, what I want to say is," then he smiles, relaxes, "say something happened to me, god forbid mind, and my kids had to go into a home. If it was here, I'd know they'd be properly cared for."

His cheeks flush. "Except I've got two boys and living with seven girls would totally freak them out."

It's the first time Anita has heard anyone say that. She clocks that he has kids, but isn't wearing a ring.

"I mean..." he says, "our approach, our focus is on attachment. We've developed real bonds with the children. It's a different place from when the police visited three times a day. You'll make your own mind up."

Divorced, unattached, she wonders?

"I used to work in young people's mental health a while back," she smiles.

"Funny, I never think of politicians having real jobs. But that's good, you'll get what we're trying to do." The awkwardness melts. Anita wrinkles her nose, feels the excitement of finding an ally. Possibly more.

*

"We'll start the tour at the top, will we?"

On the first floor of the building Anita watches two girls through a door jamb. They are lying on a bed sharing earphones. A framed photo competes for space on a bedside table against hairspray, a water bottle, make-up, half a chocolate bar and a brush, thick with long blond hairs. An open drawer spews t-shirts and knickers; the floor is covered with soft toys, a hairdryer, school books and chargers everywhere. It looks normal, she supposes; happy maybe. No-one ever says that in meetings.

Up a separate staircase there is a converted loft room.

"Do you have time for a chat with one of the children?" Pete asks. "Nicole's pretty distressed at the moment, you'll see why."

He shouts to the heavens.

"Nicole, chick, do you want to join us downstairs for a drink? You can bring your papers."

The lounge is scruffy, but comfortable. Pete is the head of a household, one whose lumpy cushions have seen better days and whose kids leave the place like a bomb site.

"I'm Anita," she holds out her hand and is taken aback. It's the girl who was silently watching over the body at the city farm. Conor was right – one of ours. Does he know she lives here? If so, how? It's hardly an accountant's area of experience.

The girl hugs three fat, pink cardboard wallet folders as if they are precious scrolls.

"I saw you at the farm the other day, didn't I?"

"Maybe," Nicole says. "Who are you?" The question is direct, but the girl's head is down, concentrating on pulling out a single piece of paper from the mass without tipping the whole lot out.

"Councillor Patel is the leader of the council," Pete says.

"Do you know about it? The body they found? Do you know who it is?"

The girl thrusts an old newspaper report at her. It's from 2009, the sub-headline says, *"Hunt for missing teenager called off."*

Anita grips the paper. The image of the bone in the mud flashes in front of her.

"I only know what's been in the press."

In fact, DI Jones' updates have pretty much mirrored the article she'd read. The police have confirmed it's the body of an adult male. They are reviewing old cases and looking at missing persons files. Nothing has emerged as yet, nothing specific, or they might not be making it public.

Nicole snorts.

"Umm... then... excuse me, but what can a leader of a council do?"

The new question is a surprise and a distraction from the clipping.

"I'm testing that out."

The two girls from upstairs come crashing loudly down the corridor, making Nicole roll her eyes, her lips press into a pink brown slash, she wants nothing to do with them. Anita's already sure there's absolutely nothing she can do about the boy in the paper, his chin high, chest filling his football shirt.

"If you tell me what you need, I can be clear what's realistic."

As a youth worker, you learn not to over-promise, that hasn't changed now she's a politician.

"You're just like the others, you say you want to change our lives, but it's all talk…" Nicole erupts. "I need actual help to find Ash. I want to find my brother. He disappeared eight years ago. I was only eight. They said he ran off to London, but I'm worried he's…"

Shifting back in the chair, Anita looks to Pete for help. Her next thought is if the brother was also in care, this could mean a major investigation.

"…Can you do stuff? Like talk to the police? They won't listen to me," Nicole says, running her fingers through her hair, white hands tugging at the ends.

"I'm not sure I…" Anita replies.

The girl's pitch rises. "I need to know now."

OK, Anita thinks, the police didn't find her brother, his body hasn't turned up. The poor kid must be at least considering that the body in the lake is Ash.

Pete's face doesn't give much away. "The not knowing is the hardest bit, isn't it?"

He's good. He's talking to Nicole, but telling Anita that this is a cycle, something they've been through before. He's alive and he's coming home, then he might be dead. It must be Ash, it must be Ash, until it isn't.

This isn't why she's here – spending on vulnerable children is way over budget. Don't get sucked in. Nicole looks intently at the carpet. Anita walks across to the window, preferring not to look at the years of raw pain. It's hard to see the whole girl, because this is all there is – this event. The event, she guesses, Nicole talks about all the time.

"We'd know now," Nicole accuses, "if they'd bothered to search properly. He deserves more respect, he was someone. He played for the football club. Ash's mates said the club lied about his disappearance."

That's a big accusation, Anita thinks. There's really no time to deal with a situation like this now she's the leader. In all likelihood, she'll end up being yet another adult to let Nicole down. There are professionals who can do this better. Yet she finds herself saying, "I could ask some questions. Do you know who the investigating officer was?"

Anita can't say no to a girl who's lost her brother, one to whom she is a corporate parent. Who could? And it's in her interests, the football club connection could be useful, and it will allow her to ask awkward questions, get their attention. Nicole spots a yes, her eyes widen. Anita holds Nicole's gaze and holds a hand up as if to stop a charge on a pedestrian crossing.

"I'll help… if you come canvassing with me tomorrow night."

"Politics?" Nicole turns away disgusted. "Gross."

*

As Pete shows Anita back down the corridor to the front door, she returns to the picture on the wall that had caught her imagination.

"THIS IS NOT ME… That's Nicole's self-portrait, isn't it?"

Pete nods. "She still lives in her other life with her real family. It distances her from the others."

Unexpectedly he asks, "Do you have to rush off? The night manager will be arriving shortly. We could grab a coffee or a drink?"

Anita would love to, but keeps a lid on it. The new reality is that Pete, a good-looking man, not wearing a ring, is also an officer of the authority, an employee, and she's effectively his boss – with a savings target to hit.

CHAPTER 13

October 2016

While Conor thinks Grandad ought to be reclining in a conservatory with new UPVC windows and a Victorian-style roof, Grandad is adamant about living out his life here, never wanted a five-star hotel. Oakhaven is a 1980s three-storey, horse-shoe shaped complex, a municipal care home for the elderly built in solid red brick. At the entrance paint flakes off the metal hand rail, the cracked concrete underfoot suggests the wheelchair ramp needs replacing.

"Times have changed, this place isn't what it was," Conor had said.

"Then it's your job to fix it," Grandad had replied.

Grandad is always ready for an argument about football or politics, but Conor is in the mood for neither.

Earlier today Anita had asked him, "Why cut children's services rather than adults? Don't get me wrong, I don't want to cut either, but I'm interested in your answer?"

He'd dropped his shoulder, done a neat body swerve and managed to avoid the question. Temporarily, though. Anita is dogged.

Inside the building it's bright enough. The number of thank you cards pinned around the reception window just about outweighs the instructions to visitors not to abuse the staff.

"We've moved Mr Walsh downstairs," the duty manager explains.

There are a couple of rooms for residents with increased medical needs. Grandad's new room is dominated by the high-backed medical bed frame, rather than the soft birch wooden headboard he'd had upstairs.

"How do?"

"Can't seem to get rid of this niggly cough."

It's a lung condition on top of a "bout" of cancer, which made it sound like he'd had the flu. Not always ill enough for hospital and fiercely independent, in reality Grandad's not able to look after himself. Wherever he goes Conor sees budgets like leaky buckets, resources and lives draining away. Adult social care is treated like the poor relation to the NHS and he's less and less able to talk about it. Being called miserable or dour is fine for an accountant, but no-one can afford to be seen as negative.

Normally Grandad has a flick through the evening paper, but tonight his hand remains limp on the baby blue polyester blanket.

"I'll give you the highlights." Conor turns to the back page. Grandad will want to know about the Welders. A sub-heading reads *"Welders facing cup melt down."* Aren't we all, he thinks.

The picture is of Daniel Croft, the chairman, on the touchline wearing an expensive coat over a jacket with no tie.

"Want an insight into the man behind the Welders?"

"Not sure I do, son."

A couple of smaller photos interest Conor. He's never seen a picture of the club's old chairman and new chairman together, which is weird. The pictures are separate, but both are in starchy dress suits for a charity dinner. Cornflower looks like he's swallowed a mouthful of woodlice and Croft touches his neck, wanting rid of the bow tie.

"Mr Croft argues that clubs in lower divisions need to have bigger ambitions," Conor reads aloud. Les might've said that.

"The club needs to be free to make the most of all its assets, the stadium, the team and the support. Football's a business that can deliver economic growth. Only private enterprise can generate value."

Grandad scoffs, "After the public purse has paid for the foundations, that is."

"Despite his reputation as a rough diamond, Mr Croft says, 'Everything I've done is to ensure the best future for this club. I'm not proud of some of the things I did when I was younger, who hasn't made a few bob without getting their hands dirty?'"

"Blood-stained more like," a choking sound comes from deep in Grandad's throat. "Your fellow Croft is nothing more than a common criminal."

Conor ignores that. Grandad doesn't understand that these days he's forced to deal with whoever is there. Croft has re-invented himself and no-one cares what's true or not.

"'I want young people to grow up with proper values,'" Conor reads on. "'It's not just about what you can buy these days. Hard work, loyalty and commitment; that's what matters. Someone's got to help kids from the wrong side of the tracks.'"

Social mobility street-style, but it's fair enough, Conor thinks.

"I want this to be a traditional club, local recruitment, we have good talent in this area. We won't be scouting in any African jungles."

That wouldn't have got past the council comms team. Still, Conor and Grandad had hoped Toby would play for the Welders and, if Croft were to come good on his promises it might make another local family's dream real.

"You have to earn your right to say you're a fan," Conor reads. "You can't come here for five minutes and say you're one of us… Our fans put their heart and soul into it."

"Give over now," Grandad says.

"But he's got a point, hasn't he?" Conor replies.

"Careful son, you're thinking like a fan. Half the men that support the Welders aren't stupid either. You hear what you want to hear and you think you can do better…" Grandad continues as if talking to himself. "…People like Croft aren't stupid either.

Sounds humble and authoritarian at the same time, licking the feckless youth into shape. And the dodgy casino licensing scam, the illegal booze operation… No wonder the fans love him. It's collective amnesia."

Accepted business practices these days, Conor thinks.

"You should be on your guard, son. My bet is this isn't going to end well."

Conor turns to the TV page. He can't afford to think like that. People can change, but the figures don't. The article is peddling optimism, a boldness that's the opposite of the club's books – and the opposite of the team's performance. That the club's accounts look woeful is convenient for Croft. It's helped bolster the argument that Croft can't afford to pay his municipal debt.

"You're right, Grandad," He says, even though the old man's bets were often wrong.

*

The ability to calculate the probability had been a gift from his grandad. Conor had virtually grown up in his grandparents' living room, sleeping on the cracked, tan PVC sofa. He can still smell the blanket of crocheted squares that covered him – a mix of his nan's lilac water and slightly singed wool from the electric bars of the fire.

It had been his job to help with the football pools coupon. He remembers straining his eyes and steadying his pen to put the Xs in the tiny boxes, getting the money ready for when the pools man came to collect.

A few years on, Grandad introduced Conor to horse racing and he learned to calculate the odds. When his grandad's legs got bad, they watched the racing together after school. Arithmetic came easily, learning the system came with practice. Wednesdays and at weekends he went to the bookies; Alan Marsden's was on a parade of shops nearby. If they predicted four score draws correctly, Conor would be allowed to stop in the newsagents for a Mars bar. It's only a problem if you lose more than you win, his grandad said. Which he realised was a problem when he'd overheard his nan arguing about gambling with the housekeeping.

His grandad had no strategy, no awareness of the bookies' business, just conviction and hope – which was good – but not good enough. It was never a question of predicting winners, it was about whether it was worth a bet or not; how the bookies had priced it; how to spread your bets; what the form did and didn't tell you.

Conor began changing his grandad's bets to make sure he won more than he lost. He was contributing to the family income, saving them all from the same old rows, making sure there was money for the fish and chips on Fridays. Conor had enjoyed the responsibility, kept the show on the road. That was what mattered. He'd grown up in their eyes. Gambling was respectable for men and women, habitual and harmless. And it provided money to fix things, it was useful. That is what Conor has continued to believe.

Treasury management – he likes the technical name and has his own system. Back in 2006, the team invested everything they could scrape together, including influencing the pension fund trustees, and bunged it in Icelandic stocks. And, according to Conor's system, they spread some bets with Malaysian teak farms and Brazilian oils rigs.

Conor knew what he was doing. There was no way his council would be on the list of councils to be named and shamed in the papers for major losses of taxpayers' money.

"The return *of* our money is more important than the return *on* our money" is one of his stock phrases. It isn't a bad impression of Gordon Brown. "This council's resources are prudently managed."

One of Conor's rules is, if a bet looks too good to be true, it probably is. In the nick of time, he'd got out of the Icelandic freezer, making millions, and giving them a cushion for the shock of the early rounds of cuts.

It wasn't the 1980s, there had been no creative accounting as such, but Conor's virtual financial footprint was all over the globe. To celebrate he'd gone to watch his son, Toby, play in a school match. Amongst a bunch of nervous parents, he'd felt elated, free, he'd been no-one at all.

Leaving Oakhaven in the drizzle, Conor wishes he smoked. Betting tips come in a range of forms. Grandad is right, he needs to look into the Welders' books again. The council has done the due diligence on the club, ticked the boxes, but he knows that's not enough. In the past, there was no point in spending time pursuing a debt that neither he nor the politicians were interested in. Now Anita wants to open the box, dig down to the bottom. It's not hope that's down there.

Conor squeezes his car key into his palm, hoping to override the sense of foreboding, a sense that his luck has turned.

CHAPTER 14

October 2016

Nicole meets the group outside Blakedown flats, a rectangle of Stickle Brick blocks, six storeys high. They are delivering leaflets, ticking addresses off a list. Easy. Nicole did that for years when Ash disappeared. And she knows all about this estate, because she was in foster care here in the early days, while her mum was in hospital. Must've been here two months maybe? It's hard to remember now.

Tonight, Anita isn't in charge. She's just one of the canvassing team. There are seven people and most of them are more like Nicole's age than Anita's, which is OK until she recognises someone from school.

"What're you doing here?" Ed asks. He's in her maths class, looks the same as any other kid, short back and sides, floppy top, not a spectrum spod or a posh boy. I'm here because I want to get in with Anita, so she'll help me find Ash, she thinks. But they won't want to hear that. When in doubt opt for sarcasm.

"Getting fresh air," she says.

"Yeah and the world's gone to shit," Ed replies.

"Who's gonna save us, you and Peter Crouch?" Behind Ed is a gangling six-footer who reminds Nicole of Odds.

Used to the banter, he asks, "D'you want to come with us?"

Anita wades in. "She can stick with me. We'll take North Block."

It's a relief. Groups of people, however welcoming, are tricky and Nicole doesn't want to get into conversation with someone she doesn't know, on something she knows nothing about.

"Watch out," Ed says, "canvassing with Anita can take forever. She'll talk to anyone. You could be there all-night. Bet we finish first!"

"You're on." Anita laughs, "South Block lift isn't working. Even with me slowing you down we should win."

They start at the top floor; Nicole strokes the soft mottled metal interior of the lift. It's the end of the day, the lift smells like the last person's shopping, coriander or parsley.

"We're trying to get people to a meeting about the cuts. But if we get the chance to chat, we ask if they've got any problems we can help with."

Panic shoots through her. "I'm not saying anything."

"Don't worry, just tell them I'm in the building and take a note of the flat number. I'll work my way down to them. Seeing other people's problems might give you a bit of perspective."

Nicole rolls her eyes. "It's not that I don't understand. Left, right, rich, poor, I get it, I just can't see the point. Nothing ever changes. Nobody really has a say."

"Actually, I couldn't disagree with you more." Anita looks narked. "That's the most important thing, the first step."

"Yeah, but who gets heard? I don't." Nicole senses she's won that point, so ploughs on. "You think people are going to change their minds because of you?"

"Not necessarily," Anita replies.

"Then why are we here?"

"Because it matters that we don't just turn up at election time. You don't wait until you need food before getting down the allotment, as my Uncle Jas used to say. We do this so people see who we are. We might not look like them, but we live round here, too."

"You do look like them." Nicole reckons 80% in this block are Asian families.

"Us Asians all look the same?" Anita smirks. "I'm making you suffer for the greater good."

"You just like nosy-ing in people's homes."

Anita gives her that. "Yeah, well, always something different."

Nicole posts the leaflet at number 30; the father opens the door wearing no shirt, his chest shiny with Patchouli oil. The smell wafts towards them. Anita turns away, but Nicole stares at his bulging bare brown stomach.

"Shoulder hurt," he says, walking away to put a shirt on. Anita does a horror film face then whispers, "I've got this, you go on."

Dropping down the echoing staircase to the next floor, Nicole posts the leaflets down to flat 18.

Flat 15. The door is open. "I need new place for baby," a pregnant young mum with a cigarette in her mouth pleads. "Everything too expensive."

Nicole taps an imaginary watch as Anita stops to talk.

"Go on, you finish the block. Anyone else opens the door, say I'm on my way down."

Nicole takes a last bunch of leaflets without having read any.

Flat number 8 keeps the chain on his door. "Why isn't there no youth club no more?" he asks. Nicole knows what Pete would say, but keeps quiet.

"Government cuts innit," Number 8 answers his own question.

Flats 7 to 3 are all sweet. Actually, that was OK, she thinks.

"Don't forget 1 and 2. We only cheat ourselves if we miss them out."

"Yeah, yeah, I get it."

They walk together around the side of the block to Flat 1. A Welders flag covers the strips of glass in the front door. As Nicole tries to deliver the leaflet, the door flies open.

"Oh," a blond woman interrupts Nicole's thoughts. "I know you, don't I?"

Behind the conversation, on the sofa, an older blond woman sits staring at an oversized TV screen. Above it is a framed photo of the old stadium; the two women dressed in full fan regalia are in the centre of the pitch. Nicole does recognise them.

"You run the supporters' club?"

The woman nods, "I'm Debbie and that's Debbie."

"Yes! I'm Ashley Brand's sister, do you remember him?"

The older woman heaves herself off the sofa, pulls down her white cardigan and thumps her way to take control of the front door.

"We do. You've grown up a bit."

Embarrassed, Nicole asks, "Ready for the big match at the weekend?"

"Team hasn't really warmed up yet. Can't expect them to if the fans don't step up."

Having no fans doesn't affect Nicole when she's playing football. There's never anyone watching, but they always play to win.

Anita appears and starts to introduce herself.

"Yeah, we know exactly who you are," the younger woman talking to Nicole interjects. Frosty or what.

"I'm sorry," Anita says. "You were at the council AGM. We didn't get properly introduced. I've met a lot of people in the last couple of weeks."

"Now Councillor Underhill, he was a great leader, part of the community."

And I'm not? Anita thinks.

Nicole takes a step back, adults arguing, leave me out of it.

The older woman looks at Nicole and says, "Sorry chicken, didn't realise you were with her. You want to mind the company you keep. She's not one of us."

"I'm not sure what you mean…?"

"You threatened the club."

"Errr, no."

Nicole wants Anita to hurry up with an answer, but she takes her time to reply.

"I said that because of the pressure on the budget, we'd leave no stone unturned. We'd work with all our stakeholders to save money and our creditors to pay what they're owed. Is that what you mean?"

The old woman scoffs, "If you aren't with us you're against us."

"Well, yes, and everyone else who doesn't pay what they owe. That's my job. I'm duty-bound to get a good deal for local people, which is all of us, including you."

Nicole's pupils widen, she wants Anita to shut up. When there's conflict at Westmeade, which there is, all day every day, Nicole feels torn, or drawn, and so retreats as fast as. It's safer, but you end up on your own a lot, surrounded by people who thought you were on their side.

"Surely you can see if you have a contract, you pay up? Unless you're the President of the United States, that is." The Debbies don't like what Anita's saying. "You can support the club and at the same time be able to see when things aren't right?"

It's sort of right, but also wrong in Nicole's mind; it's not the club that's the problem, it's specific people.

"You don't know what you're doing… have you even been to a game? You know nothing about the club," the older Debbie rasps. "The debt belongs to old Cornflower. If the club runs out of money and can't pay the players' wages, where does that leave us – relegated!"

Nicole stammers, "Relegated?"

"Whoa, that's a bit of a leap, isn't it?" Anita says. "OK, I'm new. I don't know the detail; I'll absolutely hold my hands up if I've got it wrong."

Nicole spots a look between the two Debbies, but can't catch its meaning.

"We'll talk again…" Anita motions to Nicole to leave.

The older Debbie leans across the threshold of the flat and puts a hand on Nicole's shoulder. "We've got loads of old photos of the team through the ages. Maybe we could find a few of your brother."

Nicole looks at Anita, conflicted. Yeah, it might be helpful to have the leader of the council helping you, but right now Nicole is too annoyed with her. She hadn't thought to ask if Anita is a fan. It matters.

"There's a whole room full of Welders stuff," the younger one says.

Debbie gently pulls Nicole into the flat.

"I promised Pete I'd have you back by 8.30pm." Anita lowers her brow.

Who is she to tell me what to do? Nicole wants to stay. The chance to see the old photos, maybe there'll be other things, information?

"I'll call him."

Door shut, it's not what she imagined. The room is too cramped, too hot. The TV screen is so big the faces of the presenters on the early evening show are almost life-size. The volume makes it hard to hear yourself think. The Debbies don't seem in a hurry to find any photos.

"Best to stay away from her. Football and politics don't mix."

Nicole doesn't reply.

"Our chairman pays for the supporters' club. We wouldn't be here without him. He respects women. Daniel Croft is real gent."

Being here is a mistake. Nicole forces her mouth into a smile. At least she knows not to put her foot in it about Croft. Wormy had spelled out how Croft had taken over from Cornflower as chairman of the club when the new stadium opened. Nicole still lurks around the club, drifts there whenever there is nowhere to go, nothing to do, drawn back to the last place Ash was seen. One of the girls says it's like self-harm, but what do they know? Even from the outside she learns things about the new ground. It's interesting, the coming and going of staff, players, suppliers, cars, although she's frustrated at not finding anything specific.

*

The change of chairman hadn't sunk in until she'd had a run-in with Croft a couple of years ago at a charity night thing, when she'd started sneaking into the car park.

Pete had said the new chairman probably wouldn't know anything about Ash. The club is a big organisation, he'd said, but she was braver now, wanted to ask a few questions. As Croft's top-dog Range Rover pulled up, Nicole had hovered, then walked slowly towards him, shakily holding out a leaflet. There was no way Pete would have let her come here alone, but she'd been desperate, sick of emailing and writing letters asking the club for meetings, trying to get information of any sort.

"Mr Croft, excuse me, Mr Croft." The words had come out too quietly.

"Ashley Brand disappeared six years ago. I'm his sister. We're still looking for him."

She'd seen him in photos, he always looked too smart for football, not posh, cocky sort of, like he knew he was on the money, but now Croft's face looked weird, fixed like he'd had Botox. His fringe was too short, it made his forehead look enormous, and he was too close, looking into her eyes, not at Ash.

"Can't help you, love. Sorry."

Wormy said none of the lads trusted him, that she shouldn't try to talk to him. Nicole had also overheard Pete tearing a strip off one of the girls for being in a Croft pub, even though she hadn't been drinking.

"I need to know what happened in 2008. You must know something. You know Cornflower, he would listen to you."

"Try him. Nothing to do with me."

"Cornflower isn't here, but you are…"

"Shall I get this runt out of here?" the man next to Croft had said. Nicole had tried to dodge to the side, but the man had grabbed her arm, squeezing it through to the bone. Another security guard had arrived; she was in for it now.

"Take it easy everyone, the young lady can leave of her own accord," Croft had said. The men had seemed to relax, the thug had let go of her arm. "It takes guts to go up to someone like me. You've got spirit. That's good. When you get a bit older you can come and work with us. We like to help people from our side of the tracks."

"Never!" She'd shouted in his face. "Ash is dead. You must know something. My mum said…"

"Your mum is…" There'd been a flash of anger on Croft's face that had made Nicole stumble backwards. She had assumed her mum had been speaking in general terms, everyone on their estate knew to steer clear of Croft, but did he actually know her mum?

He'd shaken his head to the heavy. "Seems she does need someone to show her the way out."

The man had snatched at her arm again, dragging her away from Croft, who had already turned his back and was walking off across the carpark.

"Listen to this carefully," the man had spat in her ear. "We know who you are. You like to play football, don't you?"

Nicole heart had thudded, her brain had raced. Shit. How did he know her?

"Come anywhere near Mr Croft or this club again and I'll take a hammer and shatter your ankles bones…"

Shit. He must have seen her asking around the club. "Let me go…"

"…Then I'll to go to work on your knee caps, might even crack your pelvis just for fun."

Before the man had released his grip on Nicole's arm he had sneered, "Not a good idea refusing Mr Croft." He had tried to kick out at her, but Nicole had twisted and broken his hold. "Now… FUCK OFF."

Back in her attic bedroom at Westmeade, wrapped in her duvet but still shivering, Nicole had concluded: I will watch Croft like I'm making an undercover documentary. They wanted to scare me off. They must be hiding something.

CHAPTER 15

October 2016

Anita parks in a temporary car park on an old school site. It's doing a brisk trade on match night, despite the potholes and lack of lighting. As she opens the car door she hears the indistinct, miserable mumbling of the football crowd. Chances aren't fancied, mention is made of injuries, talk of defeats snatched from the jaws of victory. What am I doing here, she wonders? A young man bangs on the bonnet of the car, startling her. She catches his eye and is relieved to see entrepreneurial enthusiasm rather than hostility.

"Five pounds, darling."

The fuchsia pink pashmina she's wearing doesn't exactly match the fan's red and black scarf, but he stashes the money in a small black man-bag and sticks a thumb up at her. His assumption is that she's off to the match, why else would anyone be here?

Anita bites at the corner of her lip and smooths down her trench coat. Her neck and shoulders are stiff, exhausted from back-to-back meetings. Two boys, possibly seven or eight years old, tear past her, knocking her bag.

"Sorry, love," a man says, "I promised them pick-n-mix."

She's arranged to meet Conor at a burger stand. It seemed like a good idea at the time, but now she can see a legion of fast food options, a supply corps of vans ready to feed their army. He could be anywhere.

Apparently I'm joining the prawn sandwich brigade.

It was a new thing, messaging Nicole. The girl was serious, already asking for updates.

King Prawn more like, Nicole had replied.

Queen prawn actually.

Wanna borrow a scarf?

Anita isn't about to pretend to be a fan. Conor was right about coming to a game and Les had been only too glad to sort out a VIP ticket.

At the end of the street is the City Stadium, built by the council. It was supposed to herald a new era of success, but for whom exactly? It hadn't produced the return on investment that the city needed. Towards the gloomy stand, fans walk the narrow streets of the St Peters neighbourhood, chests out, chins up.

The glare of the floodlights makes Anita feel exposed. In the bubbling, multi-cultural mass of the city centre no-one pays her any attention. Tonight, she's an interloper, the brown-skinned woman in the middle of the majority-white male crowd.

The terraced streets are buzzing with trade. There's a boisterous queue outside a Chinese-owned chip shop. A group of three young fans are pre-loading on corner shop lager. The Balti House at the end of the block is packed. She wonders how much money these shops would make normally. The football crowd must keep some of them afloat.

Sari shop owners stand outside, staring curiously at the parade of motley fans walking down the middle of the road, more cocksure now, like they own it. Hands punch the air as the more vocal men declare their love for this or that player, their hatred of the opposing team, culminating in an orgasmic communal release for the object of their affections…"WEEELLLLLDDERSSSSSS".

She smiles despite herself and hums, "Maggie, Maggie, Maggie, Out, Out, Out." There's the same "taking over the streets"-type feeling, a similar solidarity to a demo. Anita had been on an anti-war march in the summer, it'd been a cracker. It wasn't the old left crowd, but a younger and more glamorous mob. Arab women with big sunglasses and jewelled headscarves glistening in the sun, badged-up distinguished peaceniks, coach loads from all over the country exercising their right to protest, to demand change. That's the difference. What do this lot want? To best their neighbours in 90 minutes, go home and watch the highlights on TV.

Anita is grudgingly impressed, 20,000 people turning out en masse every Saturday. If only we could mobilise them, get them interested in something other than their right to watch and pontificate about a sport. Would any of them miss a match to try and stop a war? Dream on.

Despite herself, the noisy pre-match atmosphere shifts her mood, the buzz is infectious, trepidation tips into excitement and it feels safe, only home fans would take this route.

"Hey, Aunty, Mrs Council Lead-ah," she looks for the voice in the crowd and is relieved to spot her nephew, Vikesh. It's OK to be Asian if you wear the team colours week in week out. She waves and keeps moving; the dense crowd slows as they near the stadium.

"Tonight's programme." "Get your Welder here." "The Fabricator." The match-day programme and fanzine sellers' chorus starts up as she keeps her eyes open for Conor and the appointed burger van – Mr Sizzle's.

Tonight, she could have been at any number of meetings, supporting campaign groups, or making a public speech, all critically important to the city, but right now, at this moment, this is the only show in town.

The smell hits her. Smoke and meat fat in the air make her taste buds stand to attention. She hates it and feels hungry at the same time. Mr Sizzle's small, white burger van – *Serving the Welders for 40 years* – is part of the street furniture. The world of the football club, the men, the misery, the traditions and their "historic" burgers, too. Football sits alongside her world. Different worlds that choose not to see each other. But Sizzle, she knows; the van, not the man. He exists in many of the parallel lives of the city: the ritualised chaos of the city centre on a Saturday night, the DIY car park on a Sunday morning, at the Mela and chasing pink pounds at Gay Pride. Conor is nowhere to be seen. As she approaches the burger van the scene looks wrong somehow. A thin, sharply dressed customer stands with his back to the van, talking into a mobile, surveying the scene, drawing a semi-circle with his eyes, marking out his own exclusion zone.

Anita notices the expensive ankle boots, stitched leather sole, smart jeans with a neat turn-up, a thin-lapelled suit jacket. His football scarf is tied in the same way as her pashmina. His mouth turns slightly up at the corners, there's a smear of a smile on his face, but it doesn't move, is devoid of warmth.

Two men block the left-hand side of the van, lathering ketchup on their burgers. They are wearing expensive-looking leather jackets and have close-cropped hair. One of them keeps a constant eye on Sizzle's customer as he accepts, but doesn't pay for, his burger.

Anita thinks she's seen his picture in the paper, but can't recall a name. Something to do with the club? An ex-player maybe? He's clearly watching her as she approaches.

"You're not our average fan," he says, as if he knows her.

"Probably not," she says it lightly, unsure of her ground.

"Welders fans are proud to have no class."

"And you're a cut above?"

"Oh yeah. I'm special."

Anita makes eye contact with Sizzle.

"Veggie burger please." She's glad of the big man's generous face and his nod to modernity. Not that she's hungry. It won't taste good, but she's making sure he keeps it on the menu by proving there's demand.

"Might've guessed," the special one sneers.

In India being a vegetarian doesn't need the justification required in this meat-addicted society.

"Sorry, I didn't catch your name," Anita is polite, but unimpressed.

"Mr Chairman to us," Sizzle interjects.

That stops her. The club chairman here? But wasn't the club chairman an older guy with an embarrassing tan?

"And that's £3.50 please, Councillor Patel."

The football boss puts his burger down, wipes his hand neatly on a napkin and holds it out for her to shake.

"Yes, I know who you are, but I didn't expect you to be so..."

Anita's eyebrows lower a warning.

"Good-looking," he says.

Her frown fixes.

"I hear you're not much of a fan."

How would he know that? As Anita tightens her hand into a fist then releases it, she gets a tingle of suspicion in her fingertips.

"I've accepted an invitation to the directors' box..." she says, thoughts scurrying.

She's an idiot, under-prepared. In her book everything is political, yet she's not taken the match seriously. Sizzle hands her the burger.

"If Les Underhill's to be believed, I'm not on your Christmas card list either."

He's right, but why would Les have said anything at all?

"There are some official questions I need to ask."

"Oh no, Ms Patel," he spits out the Ms and the P. "We don't talk business on a match night, spoils the atmosphere. Has Les told you nothing?"

A knot grows in her stomach. She scans the crowds walking past, hoping Conor will arrive and there will be an excuse to call this to a halt, re-group and have the conversation when she's ready to have it.

Maybe the chairman thinks she's not listening, because almost out of the blue he says, "Ask yourself this, shiny new Ms Council Leader: why you?"

"What?" She feels her pulse rate spike.

"You don't get it, do you?" he repeats; "Why you?" he smirks, "And why now?"

He nods to the skinheads and turns his back on her; smarmy bastard. She won't dignify the comment. It's a tactic to get the last word, the upper hand. She clenches her teeth, opens her mouth to say something and then thinks better of it.

"We'll see you in the box, Ms Patel. Lads..." They stomp away.

The "why you?" question isn't destabilising as such. Auntie Pinkie had gone through the possible scenarios with her when she'd decided to stand. It had been her own decision, but if it was convenient that she was a woman and looked good to a grow-ing voter base in the Asian community, she'd take that. What catches her is why Croft is talking about it. If he's involved is there more to it? She puts the veggie burger down on the counter, folding her arms.

If Les was setting her up to fail, why and how aren't clear. In the election for leader, she had beaten Gent convincingly, maybe too convincingly? And the "why now" question disturbs her. What else is she missing?

Catching Mr Sizzle's eye, she says, "I see the boss doesn't pay for his burgers then?"

"The accumulation of marginal gain, I think they call it these days."

Sizzle can see she's not following.

"Yes, he's an expert at exploiting a situation is Mr Croft..."

"Not THE Daniel Croft?" Her face flushes red hot.

Croft had a murky reputation on an estate adjacent to her ward. It was a name everyone knew. There had been an incident involving Croft and the council. She digs in her hard drive. The details are buried beneath the flood of new information she's had to take on board recently. A young girl was murdered and her body was dumped in a commercial bin. The murderer had worked for Croft, and there had been a hornet's nest of fake alcohol and a Croft planning application for a super-casino.

"The very same. Which version of reality have you been inhabiting?"

Ouch. Anita picks up Sizzle's jibe. This is worse than their party leader getting caught out not knowing the popular TV stars. The players, the coach, you can't help knowing their names; they're in the paper all the time. The stand is called the Cornflower stand; she'd assumed the old man was still the chairman. She's lucky only Sizzle heard that.

Anita has taken an instant dislike to Croft, but, as Auntie Pinkie says, "fairness is the eye of the beholder," you don't have to like everyone. I've wasted time, she thinks. If I'd known it was Croft, I'd have started questioning our relationship with the club sooner.

CHAPTER 16

Nicole had been wondering all day if she'd meet Councillor Anita and magically there'd be an extra ticket, a chance for her to see the match. Like, durr. As soon as she'd seen Anita at Mr Sizzle's talking to Croft, Nicole had pulled down her red and black beanie hat and taken off. Sprinting through the underpass she'd finally slowed up in the narrow, terraced streets of St Peters. If Croft had seen her she'd be dead.

Trashing his car wasn't one of my better moves, she thinks. The bastard's got a restraining order out against her. As she turns to stare at the stadium, the Cemetery End appears to be resting its elbows on top of the terraces. The cosy two-storey houses, that's where Nicole would choose to live if she could. Close to town. Friendly. People for her mum to chat to.

She sits on the pavement. The street is calm now, the party's moved on. Nicole hadn't stayed long enough to see what Anita's face was like when she'd been talking to Croft. Would she be able to trust Anita? They are supposed to be going to the police station together tomorrow. Like scoring a goal from a perfect free kick, you can't just want it to happen and like FA Cup magic it will. It's a test and it's up to Anita to pass. Nicole has to let Anita turn up and see what she can do. If she doesn't trust Anita at least this once, nothing will change and something has to. Or Ash will stay lost to her.

Ash would have approved of her performance at this afternoon's game. She'd kept her shorts clean, stayed on her feet, no lunging tackles, pushed up when she could.

"On the overlap Nic, go, go, go."

Pete calls her an attack-minded defender. She's definitely not the tallest, nor the fastest, rarely scores the winner. And so what if I've got square shoulders and I'm flat-chested, she thinks. Better not to get noticed. When she'd complained to Pete that her feet were too small, he'd bought her some bright red football boots.

"The opposition won't be thinking about your small feet, all they'll see is a flash of red coming at them."

Nicole loves the number 3 shirt. It was 1-1 at half-time. The school they are playing are under-16 county champions last year and they've never beaten them.

"You're holding it all together at the back, keep it up," Pete had said.

She'd flushed, glad some of the others had heard that. There are decent players in their team, friendly enough but not friends. Nicole has never told any of them where she lives. On their touchline, choosing not to sit in the run of garden chairs that made up the bench, were the coach – not a shouter – three fairly quiet parents, the centre forward's boyfriend and Pete. He didn't make it to every game, but she played better when he did.

With 10 minutes to go, lungs working, thighs stinging with the cold and sweat, Nicole had intercepted a pass just into their half, made a run down the left wing, saw the captain's blond ponytail in the corner of her eye, focused totally on the ball and put in the cross. Just like she'd practised with Ash, it floated into the box. The captain got a head to it, but it crashed against the woodwork.

"Argghhhh bollocks!" the captain shouted to the sky, dropping to her knees. That had been the chance, the last action of the game.

"Language," the coach had said half-heartedly. "That was the best we've played all season."

"Victory lap, victory lap, come on."

Nicole had flung out her arms like a plane and followed the captain, gliding and swooping. They had made it to the goal mouth and had fallen over each other laughing, a pile of muddy aching legs.

CHAPTER 17

There's a flash of hi-vis, a neon guardian of the club's universe, directs Anita to the VIP entrance.

"Expecting a good win tonight," he says, his words positive, his tone cautious: both hopeful and resigned in advance of disappointment. Dare to believe, but not too much because you'll probably lose and it will feel worse. Anita wrinkles her nose. Some people feel the same about politics. She steers well clear of that type. They are the ones who'll be on their way home before the trouble starts.

The realisation that she's dealing with Croft has taken the edge off her unexpected excitement. The encounter was a blessing, though; the stakes are raised; forewarned must be forearmed.

The stadium's VIP foyer has the look of a mid-range hotel. A low desk with a large vase of lilies, their heads already bowed. A young blonde woman dressed in a black suit with a gold name badge mouths a welcome and points her up the stairs.

Many of the doors to the hospitality suites are already shut, a waitress piles ketchup stained plates on a trolley. There's an odd combination of smells, the stale sweat and beer of a student union mixed with the lavender of an air freshener, as if someone's hastily run up and down the corridor before the guests arrive.

A brass plate indicates the directors' suite. The walls are covered with photos in cheap frames. There are pictures of teams, middle-aged men in suits shaking hands, old men in suits with young players, men in sports kit and not a women's team in sight.

"Come on through." Conor is waiting for her. "Sorry to miss you earlier."

Was he? Presumably Les has put him on duty. His skin looks three shades brighter than when she'd seen him earlier, younger somehow, with his thick hiking jacket and striped scarf. By the glass sliding doors out onto the stand itself, she notices the red and black carpet is worn. The men are wiping their feet as they come in and out of what might be their own front door.

In the open air now, the atmosphere wraps her up, tucks her in. The brightness makes a stage of the pitch.

"Not quite the theatre of dreams," Conor says, "but we call it home."

There are no empty seats in the house, the fans' faces are sprinkled with anticipation. There's a burst of song. Well, song might be pushing it.

It's not immediately obvious where the chants start; they are individual whispers that transform in seconds to a choir: "We're by far the greatest team, the world has ever seen."

Are they being ironic? She looks at Conor's' expression. Right now, he believes the chant. They all believe it.

She looks up to the tier of seating above.

"It's a capacity crowd – 28, 000," Conor says.

If they are all paying full price for their tickets, week in week out, Anita wonders, how can the club be in financial trouble?

As she focuses on the rows of seats around them, she's bewildered by the crowd. Her eyes flick from one man to the next. Her fellow councillors are here in force.

Councillor Bardill, mouth full of steakwich, garbles at her, "Didn't expect to see you here Councillor! Good on you!"

"We're the ones in red. Shooting towards the Cemetery End," Councillor Blake explains, patronising but gentle. To the left, in the neighbouring block of seats are more of her colleagues, Councillors Allen and Ford – all of the cabinet and most of the resources committee. Councillor Evans shakes her hand, holding it longer than usual. Kendrick pats her back as he takes his seat. They are seeing her not as part of the family, but a welcome visitor.

Conor shows her to a seat next to his; in the centre of the row, directly in front of Les. Scrunching the printed ticket in her pocket she reminds herself to pay for her ticket, doesn't want to get tripped up with accusations of favours. There's no sign of Croft, which is a relief and a concern; better to have him in her sights than not.

Les' hand presses down on her shoulder. "Need a win," he says, insistent. "We can count on your support."

Her smile, like her support, is temporary and conditional. She focuses distractedly on the advertising hoardings directly in view. Les stepped aside to lead the region, yet she can't shake him off. A Volvo dealer has a freshly printed sign whilst an estate agent is using last year's faded one. Uninspiring, but it must be generating income for the club. A local solicitor has an advert sandwiched between Mr Egg – whoever that might be – and a money lender. A signboard bearing the name of a local builder is hung beneath a banner: "Thanks to our match-day sponsor." This is about small-businessmen, their chests puffed up like robins, being seen to put their hands in their pockets for their club. The lack of slick professionalism works better for Anita. She makes a mental note of the builder's name in case she needs some work done.

A tinny, old reggae instrumental she remembers from uni days is cranked out of the Tannoy as the players run onto the pitch. The crowd stand to attention. She's five feet tall and they tower above her.

"Here we go," Conor says. "I always get prickles on the back of my neck at this point."

The 1970s electric organ is cheerful, the fans begin to sing "Der, der, der der... der da da der," and the song winds up to a chorus, where there is a roar of "Fuck-off-West-wich."

It's the first mass chant she hears, loud and powerful. It contains humour and a provocation, an audible local hatred. She understands the way the fans enjoy the repeated curse as if they are still kids in a playground, or as she'd been as a younger woman on a demo, a sweary rebellion.

The announcer welcomes the opposing team. It's a fairground voice reading a list of players' names, each one greeted by a ritualised response, "Who?"

When the Welders' first names are read out, the men around her exercise their throat muscles, shouting out the surnames. Knowing all the players' names binds them in. All eyes, hers included, face forward as the whistle blows. Up close she sees the players as athletes; their physiques are toned and taut. The number four looks more like a rugby player, possibly carrying excess weight, but muscular, fearless. The number ten is lithe, tall and angular, the teenage spots on his face and neck still angry. He's not much older than Nicole. The speed of the game impresses.

There's a player close to the touchline dancing a tango with the ball at his feet. His head, high and haughty, not looking at his opponent, he turns his neck and shoulder, appears to move in the opposite direction, the ball is miraculously still beside his foot and he's free. Anita finds herself clapping, watching the ball, acknowledging the precision of the arc as it floats 40 metres from one side of the pitch to the other.

"Started well," she says. It's innocuous and the team appear to be attacking the correct goal.

Les says, "They're half asleep more like. Bloody wake up you morons."

She twists her head. Les is frowning, it's apparent that she's not supposed to pass judgement. Whatever she says will be wrong.

The opposition attacks.

"He's got the touch of a gruffalo," someone shouts. They laugh to disperse the tension.

Conor's hands dig into his thighs. It's a surge – short passes her eyes are not used to keeping up with. What appears like six or seven men in blue advance towards the Welders' goal. The wave of anxiety around her makes her gasp.

"What...?"

The ball has disappeared into the stand.

"You don't know what you're doing." A derisory chant begins.

"Corner, poor decision," Conor interprets, bending in so close she can feel the warm air from his mouth on her neck.

"We love you Welders we do, we love you Welders we do ooooooh..."

When Anita turns around, she's startled to see that it's Les leading the singing. Her head is level with his thigh; if she looks up she's staring directly into his groin. He holds the note, a people's Pavarotti, standing up, he leans back, opens his chest and booms. As the last of the air leaves his lungs, he raises his arm expectantly at a group of fans in the adjacent stand who take up his chant.

"Ooooooh... Welders we love you."

He is their leader, as he was in the council; he's followed wherever he goes.

As the corner is taken, she imagines Nicole practising her corners with Ash. A player jumps into the air, his head rising impossibly above the rest, suspended like a ballet dancer. I'd be better off with Nicole next time, she thinks, then realises she's contemplating coming to another match. She's enjoying it.

CHAPTER 18

As sharp as the tone of the referee's whistle, Anita senses the atmosphere switch. An opposition player rolls on the ground in agony. Suddenly the men around her begin swearing. It's fascinating and intimidating.

"You're playing like a fucking girl."

"Get up you ponce."

"He dived. Book the filthy cunt." The words come from a fan in the stand above.

If she'd still been wearing her Sari and DM boots, her fiery student self, she'd have challenged that kind of language, but that isn't the battle she's here to fight. She supposes there are other stadiums where things have moved on; where women aren't collateral damage.

Conor reddens slightly, "It's a free kick. Lucky it's not a penalty," he says. The men are tense, expectation tips towards fear.

A few rows below the box, two blond women in full fan regalia whistle and jeer – about the incident not the comment. She recognises them from the AGM. The older woman pumps her fist, "Defend this." Her head turns, nodding at Les.

Anita's eye is taken by the referee's shaving foam spray can, drawing a line over which the Welders' defenders must not tread.

"Get back," Councillor Gent shakes.

There's a moment of silence before a barrage of sound from the away fans at the other end of the ground hits them. The opposition have scored. The rival gang is giving their team a beating.

"For fuck's sake," Les yells.

Conor looks at his shoes. There's an awkward void before the game resumes. The faces of the fans are cartoons of anger, disgust and humiliation. After the re-start, even Anita can see mistakes are being made, tension bouncing between the players and the fans. A pass fails to connect. From their seats she can clearly see the goalie shout at the defender. The fancy footwork fails. From the home fans' end, a crowd behind the goal begins a call and response chant. The call is hard to hear, the response sounds like a shopping list.

Buy a corner shop now – Buy a corner shop now
Sell a cheaper lager – Sell a cheaper lager
Banks' mild – Banks' mild
44p a can – 44p a can

Conor isn't making eye contact, already embarrassed, she assumes. She turns to councillor Gent. "What are they saying?"

Gent shakes his head, but it's clear he knows what's coming. "It's a few mindless morons, take no notice."

Buy a take away shop – Buy a take away shop
Sell a cheaper poppadom – Sell a cheaper poppadom
Chicken Rangoon – Chicken Rangoon
£1-40 – £1.40
Curry Sauce – Curry Sauce
32p a tub – 32p a tub

Smuggle in Ranjit – Smuggle in Ranjit
On a forged passport – On a forged passport
Ranjit's got Aids now – Ranjit's got Aids now
Buy a terraced house now – Buy a terraced house now

Send for all your relatives – Send for all your relatives
20 in the bathroom – 20 in the bathroom
40 in the bedroom – 40 in the bedroom
30 in the kitchen – 30 in the kitchen

Her hand goes to her ear as if she could block out the noise. She'd like to leave now this minute, but is frozen solid. The abuse isn't sung by everyone, but it's as loud as any other chant. The opposition's goal seemed to be the trigger for it. Anger steams off the fans, while the cold of the plastic seat begins to seep into her spine. She doesn't trust herself to speak. To those fans, it's nothing, it's a joke. Because their team are losing they feel powerful belittling others.

"I'll be making my views about this clear to Mr Croft." Councillor Bardill rubs his huge stomach as if the abuse has given him indigestion.

Anita's heart races, she squeezes her eyes shut. Rationally she reads the papers, knows football violence is on the rise again. but she'd been completely unprepared for the visceral reality of it. The friendly welcome has evaporated. In its place, the atmosphere is acrid, spiteful. It's not about her, she doesn't believe the fans will do anything to her, the directors' box will keep her safe, but she scans the crowd hopelessly, trying to see where her nephew, or any other Black or Asian faces, might be, hoping they will be alright.

She stares at the other councillors in the box, appalled. Les doesn't meet her eye. Hands fumbling in her bag, Anita gets her phone out and records what she can. She's been in nasty situations before where it's important that there's evidence of what's going on. As the chant weakens and fades, the fans return to the game until she actually hears:

"Get your tits out for the lads," an adolescent man yells at a young woman carrying two coffees.

"Bit busy at the moment," the woman chirps back.

The attempt at humour is spirited, but Anita is completely deflated. When the whistle goes for half-time she staggers quickly out of the directors' box. The executive ladies toilet is out of order, so she's forced to go down the stairs to join the mass of fans. The carpet disappears, the walls are un-plastered breeze-block, and the small heels on her Oxford brogues click down the concrete steps. The bogs are on the ground floor, under the stand, where seething fans queue for soothing tea and hotdogs.

"My hamster can run faster than Redman, he should be back on the bench."

"They'll be happy with 1-0, watch 'em park the bus."

"We'll be playing in the bloody Conference if we're not careful."

The overpowering smell of the toilets, not ten metres away, races up her nose. She decides not to queue, then sees the older Debbie is three places in front of her. The layers she's wearing are constricting her voice, white polo neck jumper under a sweatshirt and a hoodie all under an over-sized football shirt.

"Call ourselves fans," she says to everyone in the queue. "It's our fault if we don't win. We're supposed to be the 12th man."

Wheezing makes her stop momentarily.

"Pathetic. And some people haven't been supporting us at all," she turns her shoulder, staring directly at Anita.

Tonight was supposed to be about networking, seeing it for herself, just that. Her lips flatten, blood pumping. As she stamps back up the stairs, a violent memory surfaces.

She'd been linking arms with anti-racist campaigners, tightly packed in the second row, three metres away from far-right protesters spitting at her. Hatred louder than the police banging their riot shields. Wanting to put her hands up to wipe her face, but being too scared to break the chain. She will not be intimidated.

Although she'd been shorter than most, she'd made eye contact with two of the BNP mob. One in a sweatshirt like a school uniform with a badge sewn on by his mum, the other man-child she recognised from one of the youth groups she's supported. The men linking arms in front of her, members of the Anti-Nazi-League, could taste a fight, were even hungrier for it. Now she's here, the historic connection between football violence and racism seems like a crackling fuse wire.

Conor had suggested she call today's attendance research. As far as Anita is concerned, the evidence is conclusive. The outcome resonates far deeper than football team affiliations or even political allegiances. In contrast to the ringing chant is the unspoken intention. It's "us" and "them" – and you can never be "us."

CHAPTER 19

A chilly air charges in from the stand. Conor rubs the back of his neck, turns his gaze to the red and black carpet.

"I'm really sorry," Conor says. "Sorry you had to witness that. Neanderthal man still grunts in these parts. The club hasn't got a grip on it. It's totally unacceptable."

Anita throws off energy like an electricity substation, no-one else will go near her.

"How can the council be associated with this?"

Conor respects Anita's anger, although he suspects she'd get a better reception from most of the councillors if she'd run off in tears. It's easier for them to deal with. Easier for him.

"We can report them to the FA," he offers.

"Yes. And what about us? What would it take for any of our councillors to challenge that kind of abuse? They just don't think it's their job. I'm the Asian, so it's down to me to complain?"

Conor knows she could throw the same accusation at him. What would he have to say? I'm not a racist, but I've heard that stuff before and said nothing. In the moment, amongst all those men, it's hard to make a stand. Five minutes until the second half. Conor can't wait. The Welders are losing. Unvoiced fears are shared in tuts and mutters, their team's failings are personalised. It's "we" who are inadequate, inferior, not up to the job. Down go the pints of bitter to drown their bitterness.

Conor's always thought that the difference between sport and theatre performance is that you can't predict the ending, it's unwritten, unpredictable. But a familiar emotion, like a virus, spreads through the crowd. He's not immune to the despair, all is lost.

Conor spots Les deep in conversation with Croft and feels Anita bristle. Les' face says "come and have a go if you think you're hard enough."

Anita's eyes narrow like she might.

"We'll have to adopt a more attacking formation," he says by way of a distraction. "Bit of a risk, but could work. I mean, could be more exciting for the neutral."

Anita couldn't care less, nodding at a small red sign on the wall, "Show racism the red card." Conor sees it, too.

"We'll come back to the racism issue, it's the chairman I'm after."

Conor flinches. That can't happen. Anita in a rage, Croft and Les in a cabal, the team losing, it's bound to kick off.

"What about a snack?"

He grabs at a plate of burnt chicken wings on a nearby trolley and thrusts it towards her.

"I'll pass, thanks."

Flustered Conor tries again, "Vegetable samosa?"

"No!" she replies. Conor makes himself big, puts his body between Anita and Croft.

"This club owes the city money and he's got some explaining to do."

"Not now," he half whispers, "don't talk to Croft." Conor feels a flush of adrenalin. "Not now..."

"Why not? What I have to say should be public record."

Conor feels his scalp prickle. It was a mistake to bring Anita here. The noise of the crowd rises a notch.

"Either you tell me exactly what the situation is, Conor, or I'm going to have a very public chat with Mr Croft. And I'll invite those reporters to listen in..."

"Of course," he says, thinking that he will tell her what she needs to know when he's ready and that at all costs this matter must be kept away from those local hacks. There's enough poison and conspiracy on a normal Saturday to fill the stadium.

The councillors in the directors' box begin to shuffle outside back to their seats. There's chanting outside.

"We hate Westwich and we hate Westwich, we are the Westwich haters."

Conor hears the chant through Anita's ears.

"It's a 90-minute hatred," he says. "It's not real…"

Anita looks at him, incredulous.

"Sup up lads," Les' voice rises above the troops. It's a call to arms, time to get serious.

"Conor!"

"Definitely, no problem," he says, forcing a smile. "Let's go for a coffee, maybe a drink. Ask me anything."

"No, now."

"Sorry, but the game… it's a six-pointer. Means a lot. A draw will do."

"Now!" She begins to walk towards one of the reporters.

"OK, OK," Conor says hurriedly. "Let's go into the reception area, it'll be quiet there." In the abandoned reception, they sit side by side on a small, purple-striped sofa. Conor perches on the edge, scanning the area for a screen.

"Right, what's going on?"

"Ermmm…" If he says it quickly, keeps to the numbers, need to know only, it'll be less painful.

"It's a 35-year agreement. The club's total debts are in the region of £55 million, about £23 million to the council. We borrowed the money cheaper than the club could. They haven't paid it back, so we service the debt, pay the interest and add it to the overall bill. It costs us around £1 million every year. It's all documented, we are water tight. We've taken legal advice."

"I've read the legal advice. It doesn't say what the real problem is."

His teeth are clenched.

"Under Les' leadership, we were instructed to extend the credit, reschedule the debt regularly. Up until now it's been manageable."

"Hang on, you mean we have to make an extra £1 million of cuts just to re-finance the football club debt?"

"Well… errr." He can't deny it.

"You're suggesting we shut the children's homes, sell the buildings and carry on financing the football debt. Is that it? Is that what's in your budget proposals?"

This time there's a deafening roar, a goal for the Welders. Conor grinds his foot into the floor and bounces off the seat like a small boy who's been grounded and can hear his friends playing outside his window.

"Why haven't we dealt with this in the chamber?"

Conor looks at his watch. Thirty minutes go, he thinks, we could get another one.

"It's a standing item on the finance committee agenda. We've debated the club and the debt every year for the last nine years. It's in the accounts, it's in the annual audit report, the independent auditor's letter, it's been to scrutiny committee every year and it's in our risk register."

"Hidden in plain sight."

"Not at all…" He feels his back stiffen.

"You've used red tape to obscure the situation."

"No. I don't accept that, we've followed all the procedures I think you'll find…"

"Bullshit."

"Many councils manage worse debts than this."

"And that's supposed to make it OK?"

"Remember, your councillors are fully behind this."

Anita tries again; "There is a contract. The club was supposed to pay us rent. Why didn't that happen?"

"What do you want me to say?"

All Conor can think about is getting back to the match. She leans in so he can smell her musky perfume.

"The truth! Was Croft deliberately defaulting? Was that the real agreement? Les gave Croft the nod, told him he didn't actually expect the club to cough up? Tell me or I'm going straight back in to Croft, match or no match. If he thinks his cosy arrangement is going to continue, he's got another thing coming."

There's a roar from the crowd. Conor taps his foot, desperate to see.

He takes a breath, can't keep this up.

"I suppose you could say it was accepted that there was no political will for further action."

"Why?"

"It's complicated." Too quickly Conor's left the safety of the numbers.

"Tell me…"

"There are real problems and fictional problems. Everyone wants the fiction that the club is getting back on its feet and we can't jeopardise it now, there's a foreign investor coming. It will be different this year, that's what the club says… It's not denial…"

"It looks exactly like denial to me. And what about you, Conor, tell me you don't buy all that. Where was your professional advice?"

Conor winces internally, but moves on seamlessly, as if Anita hadn't said that last sentence.

"…It's a point of view. And we manage the implications, as with any contract."

"That's it? Blind optimism coupled with our desperation to avoid the blame for putting financial pressure on the club? That's official council policy?" Anita is shaking her head.

"You'll have to ask Les about the politics…," he shrugs.

"Hiding behind the elected members all of a sudden?"

Ouch. What can he say? Les has made sure the personal controls the political and that maintains the status quo. Already the two-boss scenario is harder to negotiate than he imagined.

"…Everyone contests what the real problems are. The public thinks we're the problem. We're incompetent. Croft will say we inflated the costs, we're exaggerating the debt to compensate for the cuts. Croft lawyers have already tried to say it was an illegal deal in the first place, so they shouldn't have to pay it back."

"That's unbelievable." Anita looks for lies in his eyes.

"It's true." Conor holds her gaze. "The fans believe we'll be the reason the club fails and, of course, we're all corrupt. That'll be the accusation."

"It's completely perverse. We're so worried about being called corrupt, we don't challenge something that's fundamentally wrong."

"I'm just saying, people believe the story they want to," Conor says.

"There's never just one story is there and stories change," Anita replies.

"Yes and no," he says. "The club has to be here and the city has to support it, that story is pretty fixed."

There has been one council that let their club go the wall and that hasn't been forgiven.

"I'm no expert, but I can see what's in front of my eyes. The stadium is full. There are sponsors. The team, to be frank, can't cost that much. Where are the numbers that show they can't pay?"

Anita pulls an A4 sheet of paper from her pocket. Conor recognises it as a print out of her complimentary ticket.

"Do all the councillors have regular freebies?" she asks. "Croft buys their silence about the club debts and it's cheap at half the price? Un-bloody believable."

Conor sighs. "Les believes in the club, but not in the numbers. Belief trumps reason for the fans."

"But Les, and the others, they aren't ordinary fans. They are fans with civic responsibilities. They are sworn in legally, with elected responsibilities, just like I am. We have a duty to serve all our communities."

"The risk that we will destroy the club is too great. The Welders are forever."

Fear trumps belief. He stands up agitated, sensing something. "Conor, what is it? There's more?"

He doesn't answer.

"What do you want Conor?"

He wants this conversation to be over. He wants to see the game and he wants the club debt off the books. He's wanted that since the start. But there's another problem. Les sees things completely differently. The old leader doesn't even consider it a debt, he considers it as an on-going investment.

Les has said, "If Croft owes us money, we've got a hold over him. Over the club. It gives us influence. It's tantamount to ownership."

It's not true of course, but how does Conor explain that to Anita? The answer is he doesn't even try.

"I want us to win," he says, full of anguish as the crowd sounds another attack.

Conor stands up. He's drawn by an ungovernable force, up the stairs towards the boxes or a screen. The Welders have scored. There's a wave of euphoria, cheering, clapping, stamping and singing. "We love you Welders we do."

He stops and turns towards Anita, "We've done it! Unheard of!"

There's a sudden lightness in his muscles. Conor had confessed and instead of ten Hail Marys, he'd been blessed with a win.

"Go back to your boys," she says. "I didn't choose this fight, but it's on. And you, Conor, you need to decide which team you're supporting."

Taking the stairs two at a time, he wants to drink in the exaltation. His skin prickles as he hears the crowd sing...

We know what we are
We know what we are
Pride of the Midlands
We know what we are...

CHAPTER 20

In the police station reception, Nicole puffs her cheeks out. More waiting, another plastic chair, sweaty smell, three people in a queue moaning about losing their phones. Like all they want is a number for their insurance claim.

"Where's the council woman?"

"Anita isn't late," Pete says, "we're early. Remember she got you this meeting."

The robot doors zip open, Nicole jumps up. Right, Anita is here. Let's go, she thinks. Yet it's another ten minutes before DI Jones comes down to meet them. Nicole glues her lips together to show her disgust. Pete says taking offence is a default strategy for teenagers. Yeah well, when there's cause.

"It's your meeting, so stay as long as you want. If it's not useful you can leave anytime," Pete reminds her.

We've only just got here, Nicole thinks. And they always say that: "This is *your* meeting." Even though there's always more of them than you. The systemers she calls them, social workers, key workers, police, teachers, health visitors, whatever. They aren't all bad, but most of them don't feel alive to Nicole. Like their juice is being drained and they can't recharge. And if you don't play the good kid, they switch off.

Pete isn't like that, but then he's someone else's dad.

*

"Jonesy..." Pete shakes the detective's hand.

They are definitely mates, but Nicole is unsure if that makes the policeman OK or not.

"I'll leave you to it then."

She swallows hard. It would be better if Pete stayed, but he's already told her he needs to go to another meeting.

"See you later?"

Nicole smiles then realises Pete is talking to Anita. There's too much Anita. At the match with Croft? With Pete?

"Good to see you again, Nicole," Jones says.

Picking up her rucksack, Nicole holds the folders close to her chest. They are led into a part of the police station she hasn't seen before. The sign says meeting room, not interview suite. There's a stupid countryside picture on the wall, a man-sized tissue box, soft green covered chairs. This must be the bad news room. Her heartbeat sounds loud in her ears. Maybe I came here with mum? It's hard to remember all the details.

"Thanks for seeing us," Anita smiles, cosy-cosy.

The policeman asks Anita, "How's everyone doing after the city farm?"

"It was a shock," Anita replies. "Thanks for asking."

Nicole blurts, "Why aren't you asking me how I'm doing? It's my brother we're here to talk about. I want to know if he's the body in the lake."

Jones invites them to sit down, but Nicole prefers to stand, leans against the flimsy wall.

"I'm sorry Nicole, it's public knowledge that we haven't been able to identify the body."

The room closes in, her mouth is dry.

"Why not?"

"We need specialist equipment to dredge the lake or we can't get a complete picture. It's a question of resources."

"Surely this is a priority?" Anita asks.

There's no need for Anita to butt in, I can speak for myself, Nicole thinks. She's unsure if she can trust Anita after seeing her with Croft yesterday. Somehow it seems unlikely that she would be working with him. If anything it sort of feels better. Anita is on her side right now. Two against one. And there's a sort of relief. The body isn't Ash, or at least, not for now.

Jones stalls. "Let me fetch your brother's file, see if anything new has come in on your brother's disappearance."

Nicole groans, bangs her head against the partition.

"Told you! This is what it's like. Waiting for nothing." Nicole can't stop her voice from rising.

"You could've checked before we arrived," Anita says.

"If you find the skull, you can get the dental records. Dr Andrews was our dentist. Ambler Road dentists."

"Yes…" he pauses, "you've given us Mrs Andrews' details before."

Jones seems to be looking at Anita a lot. Does he fancy her or is it because of her job? She might be more useful than Nicole had thought.

Nicole pulls out a piece of paper with her questions written and numbered.

"Can I see Ash's file? Did you find his phone? What about the witnesses?"

"I'm sorry I can't show you the file and, no, we didn't find the phone."

"Argggghhhh," she bangs the table. "Why can't I see the file?"

"You could put in a freedom of information request," Anita suggests.

Yeah, she's heard of that, doesn't know what it is exactly, but it clearly gets up Jones' nose.

"The coach lied about the last time he saw Ash. Said he'd been at the hospital with Dez, but I showed people at the hospital Ash's photo. They hadn't seen him. And the chairman said he'd seen Ash two weeks after he'd disappeared. Why would he say that?"

"We're going over old ground here," Jones says.

"Yeah, well, I'll just keep asking until I get an answer, won't I."

Nicole is rooted to the chair.

"I'm not going 'til I've asked all my questions..."

"Let me get you a drink and I'll have a word with the Chief," he says and leaves the room.

It's capital A awkward, alone with Anita. What are you supposed to say to a person like her? Nicole picks up her phone and flicks through her photos to find a picture of Ash.

"Show me," Anita leans over.

"Ash isn't smiling in this picture, but I like this snap."

In the shot his hair is coppery brown, not ginger. Nicole's is straight, jet black. When one of the temporary girls in Westmeade said that there was no way they could be brother and sister, Nicole had flown at her. So what if we had different dads? She'd almost been transferred, but Pete saw the girl was deliberately provoking Nicole, he knew how hurtful the words "half-brother" were.

"Ash was the best."

"Tell me about him."

Nicole judges Anita. She is concentrating, she sounds for real and, anyway, it's always easy to talk about Ash.

"None of my mates' brothers would give a toss about their little sisters, but Ash wasn't like them."

Anita gives her the adult go-on-type nod.

"He cared, y'know, properly. He was always there."

"I tried to be there for my brother, Siddhu, before I came to the UK. Ash sounds lovely..."

Nicole is unsure whether that means she's supposed to ask about Anita's brother or not, so she continues...

"We played footie every night..."

"You play?"

Anita has been alright, she supposes. "The school started a team, but mostly it was kicking around in the garages. I mean, it's nothing but... We had number 3 as the goal. Some of the other garages were used by smackheads or, like, garage 16 was too close to the houses. And I wasn't always in goal, Ash didn't treat me like a girl..." Nicole knows she is smiling to herself, losing sight of who's in the room.

"Ash had a mean left foot. When he wacked it against the door it sounded like thunder, the reverb was... immense. It was our pitch. We made a bench from breeze blocks, scuffed out the weeds so it was nice, we practised for hours. Ash could make the ball stick to his heel. He taught me to take corners, float it in."

Flicking through the photos on her phone, Nicole holds up a picture of Ash in front of an abandoned garage, a buddleia growing out of the roof like a tattered flag, marking their territory, a white door with a number three, like an angry W on its side scratched into the paintwork.

"Ash was a proper coach, made me tackle him hard, made me take like a million penalties. Said we had to practice coz that's the worst thing about the England team. Only the Dutch are worse than us."

*

DI Jones returns his hands full with two white plastic cups of water.

He addresses Anita. "I've had a word with the chief inspector and he's asked me to pull together a full report and email it across to you. The chief's taking a personal interest in the case."

That's a wind-up.

"Why are you sending it to her, it'll just sit on a desk forever. You can't fob us off like this. You say this meeting is for me, but that's crap..."

"I need you to stay calm, young lady," Jones says.

The muscles in her legs shake under the table. They are just saying they are looking at the case. They've said that before. Nicole feels her breathing quicken. There's no way she wants to burst into tears in-front of them so she has to get out of there. They haven't got a clue, not a clue.

"Can you send the report within 24 hours? I'll share it with you and Pete," Anita says.

Nicole stands, quickly packs up her rucksack.

"Bloody jobsworth." Air, she needs air, has to get outside, right now. Away from this poxy room.

CHAPTER 21

"That went well…" Anita isn't impressed.

Jones looks at his watch. "Nearly 15 minutes, I'm getting better at this."

Anita takes this to mean that Nicole has stormed out of meetings in a shorter time than that. He'd played the meeting with Nicole straight enough, not overly polite just because she was there. But no wonder he's wary. Nicole just accused the chairman of the football club of a cover-up, possibly involvement in Ash's disappearance or even murder if you took Nicole's line of thinking to its conclusion. Get that wrong and Jones could get seriously burned.

Which prompts the question – how should she take this suspicion? Anita needs to know more before she decides, but her gut says if Croft is involved, however marginally, there is something in it.

"I should go after her…"

"Just one thing… Do you know the family?" Jones asks.

He's checking the territory; asking if's a personal interest. Anita had come to the police station, because she'd promised to help Nicole and wanted to prove that she keeps her word, that she hasn't sold out, that she's still got time for real people. And she'd wanted to see Pete again.

The link to the football club is a bonus. After the horror of the match, Anita is weighing up her next move. For want of a better start to the battle plan, here she is.

Although she's taken Nicole's side on principle (that you support the weak against the strong) things are different now – as leader of the council, she has to be sure of her ground.

"It's a duty of care issue." Anita resorts to organisational speak. Any duty evokes the possibility of a legal challenge. Jones nods, taking her interest seriously.

"Nicole's brother disappeared around the same time the stadium collapsed, but we couldn't make a connection. Believe me we tried. We heard different stories from different people. It was a messy, confused time and, despite that, the players' statements either said nothing or were in line with the club. Word perfect…" He sighs, then continues, "Nicole wouldn't let it lie, kept turning up with a banner and it escalated from there. We've cautioned her for wasting police time and violent behaviour on two occasions," Jones pauses. Pete hadn't mentioned that.

Despite having the whole city and its extended family to worry about, Anita's gut is still telling her to stand by Nicole. If Anita had been in Nicole's scruffy trainers, she'd have been equally frustrated and angry. The girl is a Catherine wheel, fiery sparks fizzing around a central lightning rod.

"It's a bit unhinged, attention-seeking hormonal girl gets obsessed, but, you know; I feel sorry for the kid."

Anita stares at him. Did he really say that? It's not the use of the word that bothers her, although in her experience no-one describes a man as unhinged. The problem is that's what he actually thinks about Nicole. And he thinks he's talking to one of his own. Anita takes a deep breath. Normally she'd pick him up on that, but on this occasion decides to pump him for information.

"What have the club said about all this?"

"Official statements mainly, but Croft's lawyers demanded a restraining order with an exclusion zone to keep Nicole away from the club," Jones says. "I hear you're interested in the club?"

How would he know that? Anita's instincts tell her to tread carefully. Policemen have sources and maybe there's been some kind of black and red brotherly nod from Les.

"Due diligence," she says opting again for legalese.

"Hmm," Jones says. "On the debt or the bankruptcy rumours?"

The skin on her fingertips tingles. Anita has little reason to distrust the police these days. They've made progress locally on hate crimes, tackling homophobia and community liaison. Yet old habits die hard and she's sceptical about his motivations. She's careful not to give him an opinion that can be repeated.

"Are the police investigating the club?"

He shuts the door; they appear to be weighing each other up.

"Nothing formal at this stage, but in the spirit of working together," Jones says, "we'd be grateful if you'd share your plans about the club with us."

It occurs to her that he might be a fan. She keeps her face open.

"Like the council, we've got previous with Croft: loan-sharking, counterfeit goods, tax avoidance, criminal damage. Remember there was a murder in the city centre – Laura Awsworth ended up in one of your bins?"

"Yes," she shudders.

"The murderer, a serial rapist, you remember surely..."

Jones is testing her, annoying habit.

"...it was one of Croft's men. Croft was behind that super-casino fiasco. But there was nothing the CPS could make stand up."

What Anita is waiting to hear is the connection between Cornflower and Croft, but Jones trails off.

"Right," she looks at her watch, "I have to go. Promised I'd get Nicole back safely..."

Anita has deliberately ignored football of all kinds. It takes effort not to breathe it in, not to know even the basics through osmosis. The debt and threat of bankruptcy at the club, that's the same as the council. And every other public agency she knows. And a fair percentage of the households in the city. We're all in a leaky boat, 300 metres from shore and three missed mortgage payments away from being totally sunk.

*

In Anita's car on the way back to Westmeade, Nicole slumps like an empty airbag, fingers picking at one of the faded stickers on the passenger side window.

"Well done in there," Anita says.

No response.

"Have you ever been arrested?" Nicole stares out at the darkening sky.

"I've been cautioned," Anita responds economically, playing down the number of times she's disturbed the peace. She was also arrested for non-payment of the poll tax, but doesn't want to get into that now.

"Got anything to eat?" Nicole asks.

"There's chicken tikka crisps in the glove compartment, but we'll have to share."

Nicole helps herself.

"What are you thinking of doing after? With your life?" Anita asks.

It's Nicole's final school year, after all.

"I'm asking because I'm interested and it's my job."

She gets nothing back. Not dissimilar from chairing the education committee for the last two years. It's clear Nicole's mind stretches only as far as her next thought, which is always about her brother.

"What about your mum?"

Immediately Nicole sits up straight.

"What about her?"

"You said she wasn't well?"

Nothing.

"How did you end up at Westmeade?"

"Why d'you think?"

It's 4.30pm, the ring road is getting busier and a longer journey might be useful if she's ever to squeeze out any information, but Nicole changes the subject.

"I could live in this car. I bet it cost more than our old house…"

It's a large Skoda Octavia, left by a cousin who'd gone back to India.

"…Bit messy though. You got kids?"

Nicole's looking at the gold rings on Anita's fingers, a child might not realise that none of them are wedding rings. In India jewellery is worn differently. A toe ring would be a marital give-away.

"I'm not married. No children."

"Weird."

"Uncomplicated," Anita replies.

It's better when young people say what they think. It's less tiring than talking to her colleagues. Sometimes Anita drops a hint or two about Mangalore and the arranged marriage "that didn't work out," and the consequences. It leaves a space to let people make up their own story about Anita's life. When she overheard someone saying she was divorced, she didn't correct it.

As a kid Anita had spent hours listening at the closed door to her father's study, her head on the cold, tiled floor, trying to push her ear closer to the gap, hoping that once said, the heated words might cool and float downwards where her ear could catch them.

The conversation usually started with her mother asking, "What are we going to do with her? Always problems."

There was a stream of minor infractions: arguing with her father, her teacher, a police officer who falsely accused her of stealing in the market, repeatedly being caught exploring the adjoining neighbourhood, running around with boys and climbing trees. It hadn't been deliberate; curiosity got the better of her. The world was out there and she wanted to see it.

They couldn't have been surprised when she refused to dress up and sit silently as the talk turned to future husbands. She hadn't intended to bring shame on the family.

Behind the study door there were negotiations and re-negotiations. When she couldn't hear the voices, she'd bang at the door. "I won't do it!"

Her fear of being sent to live with a strange family generated an angry resistance. Why did she have to marry anyone? Why couldn't she stay with her parents? Anita adored her smart, beautiful mother and was in awe of her dad's ability to tell stories that helped explain the world. She would argue forever to stay close by.

"Enough." Her mother emerged, arm raised, her father in the background, whisky in hand. A decision had been made.

"We'll speak when you're calm."

Anita kicked at the heavy, locked mahogany until the wood was splintered, the door frame cracked. What they saw as their daughter's rebellion was love. Anita tried to tell them, but they wouldn't see it. The reward for love was exile.

Her parent's decision was that she would be sent to the UK to "finish her education." Anita felt the shock in her bones. Sent to a new continent, to family she'd seen only once in her life.

On the endless plane journey to England, as she chewed at the plastic wallet hung from her neck that labelled her an "unaccompanied child", she vowed to be in the room when it mattered and to become the person who said yes or no, go or stay.

On her first night in this city, as she cried and shivered in the small box room at Auntie Pinkie's place, she thought that love didn't count; if they loved me how could they send me away?

＊

Bumper to bumper in traffic now, Anita looks closely at Nicole. Their situations aren't remotely similar, but Anita understands the drive.

Nicole breaks her thought pattern, "But you're rich?"

Youth worker, teenage counsellor, local politician, it's not the stuff football players' mansions are built on, but it might seem like a fortune to a child in care.

"What about other family options? Were you fostered?"

"Nope," Nicole rubs her eyes hard. "Why're you asking? Is this about shutting Westmeade?"

That's a bit of a leap, but she's cleverly turned the attention away.

"We are looking at options. I told you that."

A choking noise comes from Nicole's throat. Anita hears it as a stifled panic.

"You're supposed to be helping me and now you want to shut us?"

"I didn't say that."

"Do the police actively think Ash is alive...," Anita goes for a diversion. "Or is it just that they think his disappearance wasn't connected to the stadium collapse?"

"Some crap."

"A bit more specific, please?"

"They made up a reason for him to run off to London."

"They don't make up reasons, they try to discover them."

"They tried to make out he was gay and he was ashamed about what happened at the club to Dez. Like there was something going on."

"Was he gay?"

"Does that matter?" Nicole says it like a challenge. "Ash wouldn't have run off, he wouldn't have left me like that. They didn't investigate properly... they didn't talk to his real friends."

Anita doubts that can be true. Surely they interviewed the other players? Ash doesn't sound like a loner.

"Some players I don't know said Ash'd been sleeping in the changing rooms, hanging around the hospital."

"Sorry?" she asks. "Ash wasn't living with you then?"

"He stayed over with his mates a lot. Mum got a text saying he needed space. We looked at that message a million times. Ash wouldn't have said that. Mum could be like, hard work, but the coach and the chairman lied. The police said they saw texts sent two weeks after we last saw him. Two weeks! No freaking way. They told everyone that Ash said he was sorry about Dez, but they could all stuff it. And that he was going to find a club down south. As if! And why wouldn't he send a message to me? It was all wrong, everything was wrong. It's lies…"

Nicole stutters.

"Why hasn't anyone else said anything about this?" Anita asks.

"Because I was ten! No-one believed me. Not then, not now. I mean, until I got to Westmeade. Pete believes me. Or at least he says he does…"

Anita slows the car; she wants to believe Nicole, too, and is glad of the respite of the traffic lights to steady herself on the steering wheel.

They pass most of the journey in their own thoughts. Anita finds herself thinking more about Pete, hoping in the late afternoon gloom that Nicole can't see her lick her lips. As they are approaching Westmeade, Nicole is crystal clear.

"I'll prove it to you," she says. "You have to talk to Wormy, Odds, maybe even Dez. They knew what was going on."

Nicole gathers the precious rucksack into her lap.

"OK," she says, "get yourself inside."

I have a city to run, Anita thinks. It's early days, but she needs to make an impact and maybe if she can get something on the club she can get the council out of this ridiculous debt situation and save some money. And Nicole needs her, which makes Anita relieved, of sorts. Wrinkling her nose, she acknowledges the good feeling of being able to respond. It's something immediate, something practical she can do.

CHAPTER 22

8.20am. In the council's basement is the print room. Conor finds the soft, rhythmic clicking of the new copier machines calming. He focuses on the discount he's just negotiated on the lease agreement and the income the team have generated by delivering services for their neighbouring authorities. It's small beer, but every swig counts when it's always your round.

"Welders 0 – Syndicate 1!" The diminutive print room manager, Ivan, limps across to greet him.

"Shall we leave our winnings in?" Conor says.

The staff football syndicate runs itself, it's all done online and there's a policy about winnings – they are accumulated to pay for the Christmas party. But he asks anyway. The World Cup sweepstake, the Grand National and the Christmas Savings Club, they also get administered in the finance department. Not officially and not in works time, of course. His team are honourable, trusted.

"We could buy the Welders a new striker?" Ivan has a sardonic laugh.

It'd been harder than he'd thought to get a real picture of what's going on behind the scenes at the club. More tightly knit than an Italian defence. The office staff were either too loyal or scared, but eventually Ivan's niece, an admin assistant at the club, had given him what he needed. She's been going out with a bookkeeper at Langhams, who look after the club's accountants. It's the brotherhood and sisterhood of fans, those who will do a favour for a fellow fan without question. They all have the club's interests at heart.

Screengrabs of the club's books, spreadsheets and the notes to the management accounts are now in Conor's possession. He rubs his eyes hard, as if to clear the acrid smoke that's stopped him seeing this before.

There are reasons he's not been on the case until now. When the previous chief executive retired, Les had asked Conor to step up and to save money he'd taken on some of the finance director's remit himself, downgrading his previous role to a head of finance. One of his talented managers had been given the job, but was too in awe, too grateful perhaps, to ask questions. Excuses not reasons.

Anita is the one who's causing the pain. She's the one who's made him see that the numbers in front of him are not the whole story. And he has to stay ahead of her.

"They couldn't even pay the window cleaner this month," Ivan scoffs.

Or wouldn't, Conor thinks. And he can't remember the last time the council house windows were cleaned either.

"They could try turning off the floodlights," Conor says. "Saves money and playing in the dark might add something to our defence." He takes his leave with an appreciative nod.

"The odds on staying up must've improved after the win?"

"We live in hope…" Conor replies, smiling with his eyes, his mouth can't quite make it.

Back at his desk, Conor rolls his sleeves high and tight above his elbow. Trying to put Anita out of his mind, he gets to work on the file. It's clear he's been looking at the club in the wrong way – caught ball-watching, not seeing the bigger play.

Old Cornflower had run up debts and regularly announced losses, his declared ambition for the club overshadowed by his conspicuous spending, the villa in the Caribbean, the helicopter taxis to and from Heathrow to the stadium. Given the scale of the city and the club, the behaviour was delusional.

When Croft had first turned up at the club a small group of fans had argued he couldn't pass the fit and proper test, but the protest had gone nowhere. Most observers, fans and local press, were relieved that the embarrassments of Cornflower were over. Croft got the nod from the FA, he was part of the establishment, had references from the previous council opposition leader and played golf with the former police commander. In truth, they all wanted to believe in Croft and as long as the due diligence boxes were ticked and the numbers stacked up, any other doubts weren't Conor's concern.

Papers pile up. Conor spreads documents across the floor. He steps cautiously around the sheets, a tango of sorts, moving back and forth, a tight interplay between the club's accounts, the file on Croft and the insider information he'd got from Ivan's niece. Conor tries to listen to the numbers. Normally they tell him a story, but these numbers are mute or, he suspects, gagged; with good reason.

As he works his way through the club's accounts for the last 15 years, he spots an evolutionary leap from Cornflower to Croft. Although Langhams' accountants still sign off the books, it's clear there's someone new involved in the Croft era. An accountant who's worked in the city maybe? Conor had never been tempted to work in the city. If he adds up what he's in control of and what he influences – the pension fund and other public bodies, the fire authority, the police and parts of the health sector – it's much larger sums than a typical number cruncher in the city. He is fortified by the responsibility and relishes the chance to do his duty to serve his city. And although the greater good often feels out of reach these days, he'd still rather be here.

The new city accountant giveaways include a set of too-clean accounts, too-convoluted notes and too many letters scattered like a half-completed crossword puzzle.

It's unclear if the words refer to individuals, companies or countries. There are new suppliers listed that aren't registered at Companies House. A sister company named WMK77 selling management services registered in the Netherlands? He thinks of Cornflower's home in the Caribbean and gets the whiff of a Dutch Sandwich tax evasion scheme. Then there's a group called PEAG and another DC77 in Dublin? Alarm bells ring, the "double Irish" tax scam has been widely reported, too, and Conor is alert, but it takes some detective work. And sophisticated tax arrangements would only be worthwhile if the club had lots of profit?

Pushing his chair back, he stands, literally scratching his head. It's wrong. Definitely wrong. There are too many transactions. Especially in the first year, transfer fee-type sums of money, when every fan knows they didn't buy any players. The office feels too small. The air in the room moves as if the ghosts of city treasurers past are shaking their heads. Conor has to get out of here. Professionally it's his name that's on the stadium deal.

I love this club, he thinks. Its weaknesses only make it more loveable. We've got a dodgy chairman – aren't they all? It gives us something else to moan about. He thinks of the outrage he's happily chuntered away in the pub, the times with Grandad when they've put the club (and the world) to rights from their comfy armchairs.

Croft's accountants have created an impressive illusion and Conor has enthusiastically helped maintain the illusion. It's in the job description of a fan. Love requires the illusion to endure. From the council perspective, he's used his considerable financing and political skills to keep things looking exactly as they were. That's what everyone wants. So that he and the thousands of supporters in the city can ignore the reality.

✳

His phone pings.

Anita's message says: *I've got info on Welders, be with you in five.*

There'd been no sight of the leader yesterday. Social media confirmed they had been in the same building at the same time, but Conor had deliberately kept his head down, spent time with his team on a zero-based budget review, stripping the spend back to its base. They have to set a legal budget and with Anita refusing to make cuts that feels impossible.

He swallows hard as the attached photo fills the screen. It's a snap of a crumpled leaflet, Anita's purple nail varnish visible in the corner. *Missing teenager.* He knows he's seen this before, but even if he hadn't recognised the boy, the football shirt glares at him. Christ! The girl, the body at the farm and now this? He checks Anita's latest media posts. There's more. *Have you seen Ashley Brand?*

Five minutes? I'm not ready for another round with Anita, he thinks, trying to stack the club's accounts into order. She's still angry from the match, she's stockpiling ammunition. He needs to know everything there is to know and be prepared for her next move. There's nothing to hide, but there's no time so he scratches for the keys at the bottom of his bag, locks his office door and heads down the back staircase.

He stops to send his reply at the first-floor landing,

Off to meeting, catch you later.

Looking down he catches a glint of the zingy lime green glasses of his audit manager, Mrs Massey, talking to Anita. External audit, audit committee, audit investigations sub-committee, they have a job to do, but they walk through life facing backwards, always looking at the past. If they turned round they'd realise the council is at the edge of the precipice and Anita's irritating idealism just might tip them over.

Doubling back through the planning department, Conor heads for the quiet of the committee suite. This time of the morning there's never anyone around. The doors to the council chamber are open, the rows of empty seats, wood panels and stained glass are like a church, providing him with sanctuary.

The city shield glares at him: "Out of unity is strength."

Conor thinks that unity is only ever temporary and strength comes from predictability, yet with Anita around every day predictability seems to be slipping further from his grasp.

CHAPTER 23

The dense black shadow of the warehouse forces Nicole to slow down. "He said to wait round the back."

The side of the building is a murky alley. Darkness doesn't always equal danger, she thinks, but finds her breath quickening.

"You sure we're not going to get mugged?" Anita follows behind, heels click-clacking. Nicole scrabbles for her phone, uses the torch to flash at the young man lumbering towards them.

"Pay per snap," he says with a crooked smile.

"Wormy!" Nicole punches his arm in greeting.

"You nearly gave me a heart attack." Anita over-reacts.

The smokers have wheeled three bins together, prioritising protection from the wind above the smell of dank cardboard and rotting cabbage leaves, one of which has wrapped itself around Nicole's trainer.

"Sorry Piglet," he says lightly.

Nicole puts her tongue out at him, smiling through the gloom. Piglet was what her brother's friend had called Nicole in her previous life, when she was still Ash's kid sister.

"Don't let the man on the spybox see us." Wormy motions towards the security door at the back of the building.

"This is Anita, from the council." Nicole worries Anita might spook him. "She's gonna help me find out what happened to Ash. She's alright, it's just for us."

A nearby generator kicks in, covering Wormy's unease.

"What d'ya need to hear?"

"We've got to show the police Ash didn't run off."

Wormy considers the request like he's been asked a difficult question in class and wants to get it right. He's wearing a grubby work sweatshirt, frayed round the cuffs, with a logo in place of a school badge. Nicole hopes Anita can see he's true, got no reason to lie.

Ash might have looked like this now, Nicole thinks. He'd be 24, wide-framed and substantial, except Wormy moves slowly, deflated somehow, and his coffee-coloured skin looks grey in this light. Wormy puts his arms heavily around her shoulder, conspiratorial, as if they are discussing team tactics.

"No way he ran off. It wasn't his fault, but Ash proper messed up Dezzie's ankle. The club had big money on Dez being sold to a Prem club. It was a done deal, he'd been up there, had the medical. Coach was screaming murder at Ash. Suspended him straight off. I never saw Ash again. He never replied to my messages. When I asked the coach, he said Ash fucked up and he ain't wanted here. Good riddance he said. We all heard him."

Nicole is wrapped in the story even though she's heard it many times before.

"And you told the police this?" Anita asks.

"No comment."

Nicole says what Wormy doesn't want to. "No-one speaks to the police..." Although privately she wishes they would, she understands and hasn't given up hope that Wormy will change his mind. "...And no-one speaks out against the club if they want to play football, not here, not anywhere."

"You got it." The tension in Wormy's body makes Nicole's skin prickle.

Anita asks, "You didn't see Ash, but you spoke to him?"

"Nope. No word."

Wormy swallows thickly. Hurt, he's still hurting.

"That bullshit about Ash texting the coach to say he'd legged it. No way. And even Cornflower said he'd talked to Ash about leaving the club a week after any of us had seen him. Why would Ash talk to Cornflower about leaving the club? Cornflower barely knew us. We weren't valuable…"

"But together you were."

"They were only bothered about the stadium. S'all about the money for them upstairs."

Nicole looks at her feet, knowing what's coming.

"We were nothing to them." She already knows Wormy thinks they killed Ash. "For real Piglet, Ash ain't coming back."

"Didn't the police track the phone?"

Nicole's glad Anita keeps it practical.

"Those back-in-the-day phones, no way."

Wormy's arm is still round her, holding her steady.

"Were you both on contract to the club then?"

"I was a member of the academy, but my mum paid for that. We pays them, they don't pay us, unless you're Dez."

Nicole sees Anita look surprised.

"Yep, they do that," she confirms.

"So I was on the books an' I wasn't. I sat on the bench enough, so's they can keep taking the dues." Wormy hangs his head.

Nicole tries to kick the offending cabbage off her shoe. Wormy continues.

"And your mum paid for Ash?"

For the first time Nicole hesitates. "Someone at the club, mum said."

"Ash was proper good," Wormy says. "Not priced up like Dez, but valuable. He wouldn't go to London. Not without a deal, no way no how… and he wouldn't go without me." He shakes his head slowly. "We had plans; we were going to move clubs together; we knew everything 'bout each other's game, solid at the back, could've earned us some notes in the Conference.

"Another thing, Dez lied. He said to the police that Ash came to the hospital, like days after the accident, to say sorry."

"Why don't you believe him?" Anita asks.

"He was backsliding all the way. When I pushed, Dez said he saw Ash, but didn't speak to him. Like Ash was supposed to be in the corridor, but was too shamed to step to his bed. Then he said to me, he wasn't sure it was Ash because he'd done so many painkillers. Coulda been. Dez was off the scale, his deal coulda gone down, career over. He'd say anything the club wanted him to… And Dez is slow, a genius on the park, but you know…"

"Not academic," Nicole says.

"Next week I was dropped, sent back to school, but I was 16, wasn't I, and I'd missed so much I couldn't take no exams or find another club. Too late. I didn't have the legs. Man…"

"Come on Worms, you're so fit, you've gotta play again," Nicole tugs at a handful of his sweatshirt.

"I ended up in this wacky warehouse. An' that's all she wrote." The cheek of the smile has gone. Wormy moves his arms away from Nicole's shoulder, taps her softly on the back.

"I'll chase up some ghosts, then walk round the front with you."

He runs energetically out into the yard, picking up some bubble wrap blowing wild, no longer chasing his football dream. He's a man, 20 is a man. Nicole doesn't get it, what keeps him here?

"Don't be a stranger little piggy. Take Miss Marple to see Odds. Maybe even Dezzie. Gotta slide."

Glad to be out in the street again, the street light is a pallid white, but the wind drops hopelessly.

"Do you need a lift?" Anita asks.

*

The car door clunks shut reassuringly.

"You didn't say anything about the match. Come on, it was a great win."

Anita ignores her.

Nicole opens the glove compartment and, finding nothing to eat, twists her body around to see what's in the mess on the back seat. Leaflets and council papers are in both foot-wells, there are two bags of shopping, vegetables, fruit and crisps on show.

"Can I?" She's already half-opened a packet of Bombay mix.

"Where're you going?" Nicole asks. "Dress, lipstick. Extra shiny hair. You look… expensive."

Underneath her coat, she's spotted Anita is wearing a silky, pearl violet shirt.

"Do you always talk about the cost of everything?"

Nicole sighs. "If you don't have any food you talk about it all the time."

She can see Anita turn up her nose, but, like the systemers, Anita carries on with her questions.

"What allowances do you get?"

"Don't you know already?"

Anita shakes her head.

"We get a grant. We get one lot for clothes, books etc. I save what I can, in case."

"In case?"

"You take it away."

"Me?"

"Yeah you, and them."

A message from Wormy arrives.

"Right. Odds is in Winson Green. When can you go? He knows stuff."

"I'll talk to DI Jones," Anita replies, holding back. "That's down to the police."

"It's not. One of the girls in the home books prison visits to her dad online. I can do it for you. What about tomorrow?"

"Hold on," Anita says, "prison visits weren't part of the deal."

CHAPTER 24

From the car, Anita watches Nicole disappear through the door of Westmeade and her thoughts turn to Wormy. What reason would he have to lie? She's learned over the years to trust the people without power, the ones with nothing to lose.

She knows that Nicole won't deviate from her path until Ash's disappearance is solved, but she fears it won't be solved and Nicole's fighting spirit will be exhausted, that she'll become a hollow zombie teen. It's an all too familiar narrative for a kid in council care – alive but dead to life. Anita trusts her gut, and there's something compelling about Nicole herself and her version of the truth.

She thinks about the fathers buying their sons a place in the club's academy, buying hope that they will be the one in a thousand who makes it, buying bragging rights in the pub. The reality today is that whatever ticket you buy, college, university, internships, apprenticeships, it's a lottery. But somehow it's worse for Wormy and young men like him. They are sold a line; that "You have the legs or you don't." He's internalised that early failure and thinks he deserves to spend the rest of his life lifting boxes onto a conveyor belt in a darkened warehouse. Young people need experience and skills, not fake dream tickets in a fake market.

That's what politics is supposed to do, sort that out, yet so far the council hasn't exactly made progress on this issue. They'd talked about alternative provision on the education committee and approved the football club as an educational supplier on the basis that it was somewhere disenfranchised boys would actively want to go and learn. The club had been given money to pay for a teacher on the premises. They'd had help to put standards in place. Remembering the debate, the way Les and the others councillors behaved, fires her up.

How much time did the councillors spend talking about education in comparison to football? Even when it was education at the club? And it wasn't just how much they talked about football, it was the way they talked about it, too. Like the young players, they never challenged or questioned what was happening. Didn't act like adults. It was all about the game, never about the boys as boys, about their lives. Did the club keep any of their promises? Weren't they just ticking boxes, yet again pocketing the taxpayers' money? The bloody Welders.

The intervention in Nicole's situation is high risk with little likelihood of a good outcome for the young woman, but now the risk is growing legs and walking into Anita's life, right into the town hall. Ribs crunching a millimetre tighter into her lungs, Anita decides she has to get on the front foot, start dealing with the club or it will affect her own politics, her story.

Anita switches gear, turns the engine on and makes her way to her date with Pete. She'd been reluctant to talk to Nicole about it. Pete can handle that. And in any case, it isn't going to be a relationship – just sex with a decent, attractive man without baggage. The inappropriateness of it hasn't put Anita off, not a bit. Yes, it's wrong, she's technically his boss and she's supporting an emotionally vulnerable child in his care, but it's the fact that it can't develop into anything that makes it a useful proposition – a good release from the tension of the new job, a good lift from the general political gloom. There's no time for anything else.

Can't have it all, don't want it all, she thinks.

*

As Pete closes his front door and takes her coat, static electricity makes the silk shirt cling to her skin. Knowing his boys are at their mum's, Anita invited herself back to Pete's place. It was fast even for her, but? So? She stops on the first step, then takes each stair deliberately, pausing, letting him enjoy the view from the landing. Her neck is hot. At the top of the stairs she holds her hair up, not bothering to undo the rest of the buttons and peels the purple shirt over her head. Pete holds the door to his room open. Men's bedrooms are always cold she thinks, rubbing the goose bumps on the top of her arms.

"Here, let me," Pete says. His firm hands rub up and down her body, heat steams off his bare chest. She enjoys the expertise with which he undoes her bra strap and his admiration of her free, full breasts. Anita parts her lips, craving his mouth; fingers tingling, she unbuckles his belt.

She should probably say something like, "This has to be a secret" or… "Don't think this is… something," but in the moment she loses the ability to speak. Turning Anita around gently, Pete unzips her skirt, one hand is inside her knickers, caressing the cheek of her bum; the other finds its way to her stomach and up to lightly brush her nipple. She tenses her leg muscles, not wanting to fall forward, enjoying the rippling sensation through her body. Knowing exactly what she wants, Anita lies back on the bed.

It's almost midnight. In the car on the way back to her place, there's an essence of him still inside her. Concentrate on the road, she tells herself. The sex had been unusually tender and urgent. By the time she gets to her part of town, though, Anita has decided that as a one-off it couldn't have been better, so best to leave it like that – a golden burst, an expansive release. They are consenting adults, but technically she, or rather they, could be in trouble. If they were to have a relationship there could be a clear conflict of interest when it comes to cuts and it could give ammunition to the opposition, press or the watchers, the self-appointed scrutineers she fears.

Satisfying flings are her thing. Affairs are exciting and containable, and it's always better to avoid the inevitable crash when they won't leave their partners and kids or some cause or other takes her in another direction.

Arriving home, she slows the car before parking. Her mood dips abruptly, cardboard packaging blows across the drive. There's a crunch of crumpled plastic under the wheel, which is odd. Immediately Anita's shocked by the look of the front door. Rubbish is stuck around the sides of the letter box, like it hasn't wiped its mouth properly.

As she opens the car door, she sees that there's a two-litre milk carton stuck under the wheel. The recycling bin is completely upside down to the left of the door and the main bin is on its side under the apple tree. What's going on? Her heartbeat races, she fumbles getting her keys out of her bag. As she walks towards the door it's clear that whoever has done this has spent time here. Someone has pushed the contents of her food recycling box through the brushes of the letterbox into the hall. She can smell the coffee dregs; there are teabags, carrot peelings and an egg shell that can't have been easy to push through.

There's an empty bottle of wine smashed angrily on the door step. Pushing the door open grinds the debris into the carpet. She checks the lounge. There's no break-in, but this is an attack. Whoever did this must have known when the bins are collected, that her bin would be out ready? It must be a neighbour. Her left hand shoots up involuntarily to protect her face as if she's facing another blow, but no, no-one's here.

Then her eye is caught by small movements in the waste. Maggots, hundreds of them, are eating their way through the mess and into the carpet. Someone has emptied a box of live fishing bait through the door. Swallowing her saliva uncomfortably, her eye is caught by a dead mouse and, scurrying along the corridor, a live one.

Horrified she wants to call Pete, but dismisses the urge. It's too personal and she doesn't want to be seen as needy. Steady, she tells herself. Do the right thing, call the police.

When the police have established there was no physical threat, they inform her that it isn't a priority, they'll send a scene of crime officer round in the morning and that she can take photos and clean up what's on the floor.

In the empty kitchen Anita takes an age to stretch a pair of rubber gloves over her shaking hands. She begins brushing up what she can and runs the Hoover over the biscuit carpet, letting it suck up the hatred. The afterglow of her time with Pete is sullied. All she can think about is who has done this?

The far-right mates of the teeth-baring UKIP councillor were riled when she became leader. There'd been a report to the council's community safety committee on white nationalist group activity in the city. Most of the councillors thought they'd disappeared, but after the Brexit vote these groups had started emerging again. The report mentioned Britain First, Combat 18, Blood and Honour, BNP, NF, English Defence League, white power skinheads. There is an Eastern Europe fascist group, not in her ward, but there had been an incident a few months back. That this is a targeted attack sends a bitter spike of adrenalin down her spine.

Pictures from Anita's past swipe across her line of sight. The pages of her favourite book, *To Kill a Mockingbird*, being ripped up by two racist girls at school. Her black patent shoe on the gravel next to the live train tracks after she'd had been shoved by a youth off a station platform; the youth laughing and hiding in a big group of men. Then a boy on her first day at college calling her "pretty for a Paki". That hasn't happened for years, but since the referendum she's been expecting it. When she'd asked a white taxi driver recently, "How's life," he'd replied, "It'll be better when your lot have gone home."

She's pissed off plenty of people herself over the years, but nothing this personal. Her mind drifts back to the racism at the match. The smell of the coffee and rotting vegetable peel turn her stomach. Anita switches the Hoover off. I can't stay here she thinks.

Reversing back out of the drive, she anticipates the relief that refuge at Auntie Pinkie's place will provide.

CHAPTER 25

Anita takes a moment to breathe out, to remind herself that she is safe here. On the mantelpiece there's a gold-framed photo of her cousin's wedding, filled with the extended family. The carved soapstone lions are en garde next to the fireplace. A warm pink, block-printed throw from Jaipur covers the sofa. Aunty Pinkie mutes the TV, hypnotic news tickertapes across the screen. Raising the intricate net curtain she checks the terraced street. A blanket of stillness silences the night.

"Let me make tea," Pinkie says.

Heat flushes down Anita's neck. She snatches at her pashmina like a bandage too tight at her throat. This attack, she thinks, why her, why now? The question reminds her of Croft.

"I have to do something."

"Slowly, slowly," Aunty presses the air down with her hand like a brake pedal. "Come through to the kitchen."

"Not the attack. I need to focus on the substance, the debt, the football club."

"You're in shock." Sitting at the table, Pinkie holds her hand, encouraging Anita to repeat the details of the violation, share the pictures. Looking through the photos on her phone, the mess seems small in comparison to the size of the hallway, the solidity of the house. Anita blinks it away, forces herself to move on.

"The football club owes us £23 million, they've refused to pay back any of it and we've let them. Les is out of the firing line and I'm in it."

This is like a nightmare where she's pinned to the podium in the council chamber, naked. Her skin crawls.

"I am also shocked," Pinkie says. "Deeply appalled."

"I feel…" Anita's mind reels back. She could scream at her own stupidity. All those conversations back in the summer when she'd argued that a different leader, a different perspective, could bring change. She'd naively gone round asking her colleagues for support, without realising they were voting for her because somehow she had become Les' preferred candidate; the vanity of letting herself believe that somehow she was winning hearts and minds, that she'd won the leadership on merit.

"They…" she swallows hard, counting up how many of the councillors were at the match, were in on it. "…this is not a fair fight. Les must have realised the budget was coming to a crunch point… the football club debt wasn't tenable."

Les had refused to act against his own tribe and admit he'd got the council in a serious, high-risk situation.

"It all happened way before my time, but I'm going to be the one that falls on my sword. He put me in as a stooge to take the blame. They are vipers and cowards… Les knew this was going to happen. They've played me." Heat burns inside her cheeks. "They set me up to fail."

Shaking her head Anita's protector pours the tea from a bright blue ceramic pot into mustard yellow mugs.

"There are good people there…" Pinkie talks as if she's still on the council sometimes, "…but fear of failure, of being found out, is a powerful motivation."

Anita had to push so hard to get the information from Conor. Only a handful of the old guard could know, trusted allies of Les. There's no other explanation.

"What I can do," she thinks aloud, "is start legal action to recover the debt."

Anita pulls off her silver earrings and flicks her bangles over her wrist onto the tea tray. The timing of all this is critical.

"If we don't act now, nothing changes, the budget has to be set and we bail the club out for another year..."

Scenarios swirl. There's no money and the worst happens. The river Tibble floods and they can't afford sand bags. She is forced to close Westmeade and Nicole is homeless. Or an old person like Pinkie, she had a fall last year, what if she gets sent home from hospital too soon and there's no money for a care package. She could have another fall, could die alone.

"...And I'll have to sign off an indefensible budget. If I don't sign, we don't set the budget – I'm legally responsible." Anita knows this means she can be held personally liable, that councillors, unlike government ministers, can be sent to prison for overspending. "...Les isn't liable, it all happens on my watch. It's all down to me."

"I'm not sure about this." Pinkie stirs the teapot slowly.

Shaking herself, Anita stops short of a bark. "Surely any right-thinking person can see that reclaiming the money from the club is the right thing to do."

"Daughter..." Pinkie sits opposite now, holding eye contact, "we all see things differently. Do you know what they see or what they need?"

Anita pinches her lips together, sucking the air in and out through her nose. When she'd arrived in the UK, she'd been polite, helping with the cooking and cleaning when Pinkie asked. It was a new experience and they'd shared the kitchen space comfortably. It had taken years before she allowed Pinkie to hug her. Anita had watched Pinkie try to connect with her, try to make up for her absent parents. Aged 18, when Anita had struggled to decide what to do with her life, Pinkie had listened, supported her to make her own mind up. A deeper bond had formed.

She sees the value of Pinkie's advice, but it usually means taking more time, listening hard, consensus-building and compromising. Anita tries not to roll her eyes. In the past that's sort of worked, but this issue is so clear-cut and there's no time for considered reflection.

"I'm not naïve. I've just seen half the cabinet at the match. They won't want anything that makes their precious club look bad, but their heads are in the sand."

"No doubt, no doubt, but legal action isn't the only way."

Anita jumps to thinking about direct action. That's what she knows, what she's good at. But in this financial tangle, it's hard to see what she could do. A sit-in at the club? Dig out her old Doc Martens and paint some placards? She'd be laughed out of the party, sent back to the nutters' corner, totally ignored. Her job sets her apart from this now. She's supposed to be the establishment, she thinks, and Les has pushed her into this dirty corner.

"Legal is what the organisation does, what it should have done years ago."

Anita gulps the hot tea.

"Think about who will get hurt by this. The club will be hurt by your actions. I'm not saying they behave well, they do not. You know how much damage I think competition can do in our world. But the club enjoys the support of many people in the city. We know that much." Pinkie worries, "You are picking a big fight."

"They hate me whatever I do. The club has brought this on itself. I don't have a choice."

"Take your time. You are new, allegiances are built over time. You need friends you can rely on."

That's true, she thinks, and it's her own stupid fault for not prioritising that.

"I would prefer my taxes go to a children's home rather than a football club. I would imagine many others would, too."

But where does the power lie? The voices of the fans are loud and time is not on her side.

"I'll manage it." She says this more confidently than she feels. "There's a meeting tomorrow. I'll put it to them, set out my case. There are plenty of people who aren't interested in football, who will want to see services protected."

Pinkie sips her tea. "It might seem like a choice between football and services but it's not that clear-cut, is it? What is actually possible? There are regulations…" she cautions.

The mention of bureaucracy flattens Anita's battery.

"Conor says you can't do this or that, because that's not how the system works. This account can't be used for those purposes. The accounting conventions don't allow for that. So what? If the system doesn't work, I say fix it!"

People in bureaucracies, officers like Conor, give up too easily. When a system needs changing they act like it's impossible. They pretend they have no choice, when that's exactly what they are doing, Anita thinks, choosing not to change.

"It could damage your leadership. They won't want to hear it from you…"

The wordless look that follows says something they already know. Pinkie means that they won't take it from a woman and they will resist even more, because she's an Asian woman. And that's it; that's why Les chose her, because his followers won't be led by an Asian woman.

It's not all 60 councillors in the city. Some have gone along with her so far, not because of her politics or her ability, but because she smiles and doesn't make them feel stupid. Some tolerate her because of Uncle Jas and because she has grassroots support – not that the Burnswood Stop the War Coalition will hold much sway when it comes to it.

Les' gang were openly cutting and digging. Councillor Gent had questioned her understanding of public finance, suggested she needed "support" – underlining the word with a long drawl. Anita could've bitten straight through her tongue. Did any of them totally get it? Wasn't it constructed like that to keep out anyone but accountants?

The other woman in her cabinet, Councillor Berry, had poked Anita with an old stick, she was "too passionate" and "over emotional". How was that for gender solidarity? The rest are holding back until Les tells them it's open season.

"And it could be risky for us…" Pinkie says.

That means risky for a conflated group of Asian communities. Wherever "we" come from, "we" will get blamed if this goes wrong. This time it's a memory of her Uncle Jas' voice that rings in her ears as if she's a teenager again. Jas is telling her to be good – don't rock the boat. Pinkie is suggesting take the slow route around the problem. Her concerns are legitimate, but neither strategy works. Anita doesn't want an argument. She just wants to get on with it.

"You're right. I'll need a few allies, but my leadership's a sham unless I take this on."

Anita puts her hand on top of Pinkie's. It feels warm, solid, if a little stiff these days.

"Thanks for letting me stay."

"It's your home," Pinkie replies. "If you do this, do it with love in your heart, not through anger."

Don't tell me that now. It's not fair. The club stands for everything that's wrong with this city. It's the opposite of everything I believe in. The club can go to hell.

CHAPTER 26

The light from Anita's mobile guides her across the hall landing. Careful not to wake up Auntie Pinkie, she shuts the door to the small guest room before putting the light on. When she lived here there was a cheap, self-assembled desk, piles of books, politics and music magazines and dirty washing. The clutter removed, a tealight flickers and a small brass statue of the Hindu god, Vishnu, the protector and the preserver, smiles at her from the neat bedside table.

A pair of cotton pyjama bottoms and an old purple sweatshirt are folded on the pillow of the single bed. The fabrics smell of essential oils. Pinkie has been burning joss sticks.

The latest phone message reads: *Have u booked to c Odds?*" There's a link for Winson Green Prison.

Anita knows you can book online, but it still makes her smile, the rigmarole that was required in the old days when she'd visited poll tax protesters. Realistically, it's hard to see when she'll find the time to indulge Nicole now she's made her mind up about the debt. The teenager will have to wait. Anita starts work.

The first message is to Conor: *Can u forward all legal docs re: debt agreement? How much have we paid in solicitors' fees so far?*

The next request is to an old lover, Namjeet Kaur. A principled legal aid solicitor wearing braces and novelty socks – those were the days – he now works as a barrister in a London chambers. Perfect. He'll be independent and enjoy rubbing up any provincial judge who stalls the process.

Sounds ominous & most intriguing. Call now if alone.

Not to disturb Pinkie, Anita pulls on a jumper, creeps downstairs and sits on the sofa. Her eyes adjust to the slither of light between the curtains.

"And is there the political will for this?" Namjeet pauses as if to make sure the jury is listening.

"Come on Nam, this is me. I'm committed to it."

"Darling, you've been committed to more just causes than we've had curries. I'm not talking about you. I take it the council hasn't considered this instruction formally?"

The small notepad in her lap is covered with biro, swirling spiral doodles turning in on themselves.

"There's been a report every year recording non-payment and approving the re-scheduling of the debt."

"But this… how should we call it… is a dramatic escalation of hostilities?"

"It's that obvious?"

Anita is glad she's talking to a friend. As she fills Nam in on the details, he questions her hard.

"And the audit letter hasn't picked it up? You've received no other legal advice recommending a new approach?"

"Do we need that? The size of the debt, shouldn't that justify it?"

"Where's the hook? Be under no illusion, this will be fraught with difficulty. Whoever set this up knew what they were doing."

Dropping the pen Anita concludes that means Conor, not Les. She chews her lip feeling let down. Les gave the instructions, but Conor made it happen. It's easy to see Conor as the fall guy. In some ways he's in the same boat as she is, with severe seasickness, but still… his considerable brain power was used on this and, at best, it was hardly transparent.

Her resolve strengthens.

"Of course," Nam says, "in the light of the current unprecedented financial constraints etc etc. You would be acting prudently, if for example you had information that the club were at risk of administration."

Conor didn't exactly say that, but is he still holding out on her, she wonders.

"And you would be the first authority in 20 years to cut its football club adrift," Nam pauses for effect, "but it is a tough road to take, unless there's any evidence of impropriety. It sounds like the club pushed the council through an open door."

Sinking down into the sofa Anita is again taken back to that first meeting after the stadium collapsed. She'd been on her own, none of the other councillors needed pushing into the deal.

"It's worse than that. They walked through arm in arm."

"I must warn you, you should expect a significant backlash. The council has been the cash cow for the club. They won't give that up easily."

Anita imagines Les' contorted face when he hears the news, the spittle flying.

"I think the backlash started as soon as I was sworn in," she admits. His message is understood.

"Indeed," Nam says, the clipped voice holding back his own irritation.

There's still an acrid taste in her mouth from the incident on her front door step, a powerlessness she's desperate to spit out.

Nam moves on to business. "Look, here's how we'll set the cat among the pigeons. We keep it contractual. On behalf of the council, we'll give legal notice to the club to repay its debts within three weeks. If not, a statutory demand will follow to commence wind-up proceedings. We will freeze the chairman's assets."

That's her game plan. Whilst it's a relief to have one, at the same time the flow of blood to her fingers speeds up, she smiles involuntarily, but feels her stomach lurch. Sleep is impossible now. Wind-up proceedings? If she was serious, of course, it could come to that. It is serious. And huge. It would leave a crater in the life of the city. Namjeet agrees to speak to the council's legal officer in the morning. Anita prepares some scenarios showing how the club's money could help turn things around, keep the children's homes open. It's simplistic, but could be useful.

She fetches her laptop, the backlight is strong. There's research to do. She and the Internet have a long night ahead. The list of councils in conflict with their local football clubs is longer than she'd expected. Like dysfunctional couples, blame and bitterness infuse rows over planning applications. There are spats over health and safety regulations. There's manipulation over money-making opportunities for the club, permission to use the stadium for concerts for example versus constant complaints of broken promises to the community.

That hits home to Anita. Croft hasn't delivered on any of it. He's done nothing to develop football for girls. Like too many clubs, it's a box they say they tick, a condition of getting an FA license. Croft doesn't bother with lip-service, there's not a hint of equality. If the club is a partner of the council, it should actively reflect the council's values. It can't remain a boys' club, there's the wider community to think about.

Is the relationship between the council and the club corrupt? It's morally dubious for sure. But if there's personal financial benefit for Les or anyone else, Anita will root it out. They can't rely on the FA. How could they have any credibility – giving a license to someone like Croft in the first place? More money, less leadership, less scrutiny. That's how it seems to Anita. It's an embarrassment – and the public thinks that local government is corrupt? For god's sake. She makes a note of a few stats to back that up, just in case. Her list of actions gets longer.

Anita knows her plan will be unpopular, with her colleagues and with the public. There was a survey, though, recently, she reminds herself, that said public trust in local councils is increasing. We aren't some fly-by-night organisation. We're not rogue traders, she thinks. The more transparent we are the better. If I've got it wrong and suddenly the club pays up, it'll be embarrassing but so what. That's what I want. I'm not proud.

It starts tomorrow and she must be prepared to go to all the way. Before crawling into bed Anita remembers Nicole's message. The world is always letting teenagers like Nicole down. Now isn't the time to back-pedal on her commitment to the girl.

Prison visit is on.

She wrinkles her nose, falling into a troubled sleep.

CHAPTER 27

Tonight Conor steers clear of the files, switches his computer off and opens the metal clasp on the window fully. Then shuts it again, imagining that Anita's got binoculars trained on him right this minute. He scrapes a hand through his hair, rubs his neck in an attempt to stay calm. Making sense of the Croft accounts is the priority. Different thought processes are required. Can he see through the numbers to the wider story?

There are not too many scenarios here. Croft is clean, that's the official line, what the accounts say on the face of it. Or Croft is dirty, but it's a smudge here and there, his face wiped with a spit on a handkerchief. Or Croft is toxic, polluted, contaminating the city like the dirty manufacturers of old.

He pulls a proverbial envelope from the re-cycling box and sets out a theory. Screws up the manila paper and starts again. Another proposition emerges, one that relies on the dirty Croft scenario being true; one that could explain what's been happening. The idea needs testing. Ideally, he'd talk it all through with his grandad but the old man is in bad shape.

Could he trust a colleague in another authority? It's too risky. He'd have to explain how he's got himself in this position. The respect he's accrued would be wiped away. It's hard enough to let Jayne see his vulnerability and she'd never understand this.

His stomach starts to rumble. It's 9.30pm. Kill two birds he thinks, making his way into the city centre.

The burger van has been recently upgraded with a new red sign. Conor appreciates the black-painted modern typography, "A touch of class," it says. The counter looks spotless, sauces and napkins arranged in perfect order. It's parked in its usual night-time pitch. Conor has been a match-day regular for 20 years and normally enjoys the philosophical banter as much as the food. The city centre is already busy. By 10.30pm Sizzle's van will be a magnet for the pissed and the pitiable, lining their stomachs to avoid being sick and, at the same time, increasing the chances of that.

"Alright son. How's your grandad?"

Mr Sizzle has both elephantine hands and memory.

"His health's not so good these days."

"Thought we hadn't seen him for a while."

Conor feels a flash of guilt; he hasn't visited Grandad this week.

"Make me one with everything." Conor stares at the menu board behind Sizzle's head.

"Ah... the old Buddhist special..."

Conor is not really in the mood for jokes. "Got a lot on at work," he shrugs.

"I met your new leader. Quite the looker, but not what I call a fan."

"Some of us are trying to keep the faith."

"Faith is an enigma... Burgers on the other hand..."

Conor watches the melting cheese turn the meaty patty into a gold medal. "...are a fiver."

The economic exchange over, Conor hovers. There's no easy way to start a conversation like this. "As an expert on many aspects of the club and the city... I'd like to test out a theory on you... off the record so to speak...." Sizzle, armed with a hygienic spray gun, blasts an empty griddle pan. Times have changed from the days when burger-men poured hot mugs of fat down the city's drains. Conor ploughs on.

"Let's say, for example, a local businessman, Mr X, shall we call him, buys his local football club…"

Sizzle taps his nose, "…some call him a rough diamond made good, but some know better."

"Correct. Mr X buys his local football club at a knock-down price with money made, shall we say, somewhat dubiously on past performance… and takes advantage of a generous loan from the public purse." The big man snorts, immediately catching the drift. "Mr X brings in new food concessions and two new bars in the ground, courtesy of an uncharacteristically liberal licensing committee I might add; to the detriment of existing traders… and what have your lot done about it…?"

That immediately takes his thoughts away from Croft and to Les; he chaired the licensing committee for years. A streetlight flickers madly behind him and dies.

"I'll check that, but yes… all the new facilities and services are provided to the club at exorbitant rates by a management company…"

"Let me guess, it's run by X." Sizzle thrusts his spatula under a burning burger.

"Over a period of five years, Mr X vests his shares in a management company, in a holding company, takes it offshore and continues to channel cash from his criminal dealings through the football club bar." Conor pauses, doesn't want to patronize Sizzle, but needs to know he's with it so far. When the big man nods he continues. "X recovers his original investment but the club finances still look poor and they refuse to pay a penny back to the taxpayers."

Both men chew on it.

"So there's your answer, son, you go after the offshore company. We've all seen that on TV."

"Have we? Some bits of the jigsaw are missing." Conor finishes his burger and screws up the paper napkin.

"Two hot-dogs mate," a 20-something man in a thick jacket interrupts.

"Croft is re-inventing himself as the new Abramovic, if you'll pardon a distasteful analogy." Sizzle replies to the customer, "Two dogs coming your way," but his attention stays with Conor. "Abramovich was a mechanic turned stock trader turned oligarch, imprisoned in the nineties, came out a megalomaniac with added greed."

Conor feels bad about underestimating Sizzle, who is turning out to be more erudite than expected.

"...Bought his luck." The big man taps his nose. "You can learn everything from a Channel 5 documentary. Not a patch on *Panorama* mind.... Post-truth era or not I still take the BBC every time."

"It has to be more than greed, doesn't it?"

"Remember our Mr Croft had a run-in with the law a few years back, gets off with a rap over the knuckles and he's out for revenge."

"Against who?"

"Anyone who stands in his way. Or even anyone who argues back. That cost me my marriage," Sizzle shakes his head, muttering.

Christ, he is in the way of this man. Conor rocks on his heels, his mind jumps to Jayne, to his son, Toby. He'd assumed that Croft wanted respectability and that respectability is a smoky old members' club with jackets and ties, a behaviour code, sanctions and the possibility of exclusion. If Sizzle is right and that respectability has had its day, this could put his family in danger. And suddenly he doubts Sizzle. What's his relationship with Croft now? Cowed, but angry, or in his pocket? Is Sizzle likely to tell anyone that I've been asking questions?

"Shares, stock trading..." Conor tries to bury his fear by returning to the earlier more detailed part of the conversation.

"Many a "venerable" England manager has tried to set up a hedge fund in the Caribbean." Sizzle looks pleased with his own joke.

That's something Conor knows about. His online investment habit has been personally profitable over the last few years, and there's Selka, a tipster, if you could call him or her that. It's got to be worth looking into. With Les in power he hadn't needed to look so closely at Croft; the situation was pretty unpalatable, but not unstable. The politicians provided him with an element of cover, so to speak. Now Anita is asking to see the records, he sees how flimsy his shield actually is.

Which is that Croft has been deliberately hiding the truth and could even have been perpetrating a serious fraud. But even that doesn't justify his own lack of rigour. It's bad enough having someone like Croft in his own orbit; now it seems they are on a collision course.

He can beat himself up when gets home, but for now he presses on. Understanding what's been happening, if not the how or the whole reason why, helps stabilise him.

"One more thing," Conor asks. "Any idea why Cornflower would want the club off his hands?"

"That I can't answer. If he'd sold the club before you lot re-built the stadium that would've made sense. The place was a death trap, ought to have been condemned. Your lot did him a big favour."

"We invested in the city and the club."

"That's not what Comrade Patel says, although I dare say, you're both right."

"And if my theory is true…?"

"Plenty of conspiracy theories in football, son – 20,000 fans, 21,000 conspiracies, you work that one out."

The new customer spurts a runny version of English mustard onto the hot dogs and the counter. Sizzle tuts, picks up a dishcloth without comment.

"If it was a Channel 5 documentary I'd watch it."

"Would it change things?" Conor's voice is monotone; he squares his shoulders without any strength.

"Ask yourself this," Sizzle says, "you're a fan, your grandad's a fan, does it change things for you?"

CHAPTER 28

New day, new resolve. Like a tonic of old, a take-away cardamom lassi energises and refreshes her. Until she gets inside the council building. Anita makes her way to the stately committee room 3. She hates this room. Large framed photographs of her predecessors sneer down at her. Even though Les is not here, an Underhill – possibly Les' father – patronises her from his elevated showroom portrait. Neither Uncle Jas or Auntie Pinkie ever made it up there.

"It's time to get serious."

As soon as Anita begins to set out the legal action she's discussed with Namjeet, Councillor Gent interrupts.

"Ridiculous! You were at the match. We won! This season will be different. The passion is back."

Fans always demand loyalty and passion. On the terraces she'd heard them shout, "Show some desire!" They beat their chests, threw their arms about, gurned in desperation. To Anita the fans' behaviour has more to do with a general permission to show basic emotions – joy, fear, disgust and blind faith. There's nothing wrong with that, the football ground is their safe space, but surely what the club needs isn't passion – it's skill and ability, and it might sound naïve, but some tactics would help?

"Let's think rationally about it," she argues. "We've got an organisation to consider."

Councillor Gent's response takes it to the extreme. "You'll bankrupt the club. The whole city will be against us."

He makes the whole thing seem unarguable. In the space of extremity, there's no possibility for change.

Bracing his huge stomach against the table, Councillor Bardill stretches out his arms, imagining the force of public opinion like a gale blasting at him. "I'll lose my seat if this goes ahead."

Anita wishes there was more diversity in the group. At least they wouldn't be speaking with the same voice – against her.

The eyes of the councillors' portraits hung around the committee room glare at her. She tries to be as clear as possible. "Not everyone has football as their first priority."

There's a ripple reaction, the jaws of the boys' club drop one by one.

Anita has no choice but to press on. "If we carry on propping up the club, we are turning our backs on vulnerable children and adults."

Councillor Berry takes offence where none was intended. "The government is doing that, not us. We've been working hard for years on poverty and inequality."

Anita had been counting on Kathleen Berry's support. Although in retrospect Berry had only ever supported Anita's commitment to engaging the community. Not to making change.

Then she'd looked to councillor Frank Morton. He was with her before, she could rely on him.

"I'm not saying you're wrong." He shakes his head in discomfort, meaning why didn't you come to me first? He continues, "This will affect the party. They'll never give their blessing to this."

"You're seriously worried about that?" So what if they get a telling off? That was something she was sure she could handle.

"We'll all get pressure from HQ. Lose a few seats next year and we lose the council. It might jeopardise the constituency seat too. The numbers are too tight, it's too risky."

Dazed, Anita tries again.

"We could mount a serious campaign around the issue. Get out there, talk to people. You'll be surprised how many will support it. Everyone has to pay what they owe?"

Ward smirks. "That's that then." He looks under the table at his phone. They all have their phones out. What's he up to, Anita wonders.

The others seem to relax. Frank's assertion that this isn't their decision to make, his appeal to the party hierarchy, takes the pressure off.

"Wait," Anita says. "I know this is difficult, but let's make up our own minds. If the party wants to give us advice, we'll listen. But this is a democratic organisation. And we're elected to make local decisions."

Idiot, she tells herself. Ward is Les' ally. Again she curses herself for not re-shuffling the cabinet, not dealing herself a better hand. And she's been spending too much time with Nicole. Missing the basics.

Walking across the room to switch on the lights gives her a moment to breathe.

"I've already taken informal legal advice on the matter. Council's solicitor is talking to the barrister as we speak."

"We're spending more money on legal fees?" Gent says. "This is ridiculous."

"Isn't anyone willing to take Croft on? He's a key part of the problem. We need to stop thinking that the club can't pay. It's Croft, he's refusing to pay."

Anita looks around the table. Mentioning Croft's name was a mistake. They are scared. Ward gets to his feet.

She tries again. "If we don't stand up for ourselves we are lost. This is standard legal procedure to recover an outstanding debt…"

Phones begin to buzz in the room, the sound grows to a swarm. Anita peels off her jacket, feeling over-heated, and then looks in her bag to see if her own phone is ringing.

"Errr…" Is it an emergency? What's happening?

"This legal action, I want no part it." Blake makes for the door.

The rest of the cabinet gather their papers, disappearing as quickly as they can. She's barely had time to finish speaking. They are hardly out of the door when the chaos starts.

Her phone is screaming at her. Twitter alerts flood the screen. The number of updates and emails climbs so rapidly it becomes a blur.

Her intention has been leaked.

Council leader threatens Welders with bankruptcy

It's from an *Evening Post* reporter. Hell. Was it Ward? One of them must've messaged Les? In the minutes that follow the messages get more offensive. A stream of troll comments emerges from the swamp. Every councillor is used to abuse, it goes with the territory. She's had malicious comments before, but nothing like this scale.

Fucking bitch wants to have a go at us…

Fucking get your hands off our club

You don't know what the fuck you're doing

We're going to fuck you over…

Fuck you Paki slag

We will gang rape you Delhi style

Anita's eyes bulge, oh god it could happen. She starts to hyperventilate, desperate for air she sucks in short, rasping breaths. These vile men want to reach through the screen and kill her. Fumbling, she turns the phone off, throws it on the table, fearing she might vomit.

Frank says, "I'm sorry Anita. You've said the unsayable. This is nuclear. I'll talk to HQ, see if I can dial it down… try and… well…"

Then he's gone, too. Her shoulders freeze. Anita finds she can't speak. There's a knock on the door. It sounds like someone is trying to break into the committee room. Oh god, are they here already?

It's Hayley, the council's communications manager.

"Thought I better come and find you? Are you alright?"

Amongst the roaring demands of the press, TV enquiries, Anita tries to focus on the issues, not the intimidation.

"Let me get you a coffee. You're safe here. We can call the police. Then we can make a start." The young woman is kind and efficient, her voice says positive, her face says Christ what've you done?

There's no way Anita will duck any of this, but she's been thrown in front of a juggernaut. In her first interview with the *Evening Post* conducted from a council landline in the press office, she hears herself say, "The level of cuts the government is forcing us to make is unsustainable. We need to balance our priorities…"

It's not her voice, she sounds like an answer phone message. The scenarios she'd worked on last night are lost from her mind.

"We'll be forced to make more redundancies if the football club doesn't pay up."

What she says isn't wrong, but she's unschooled.

"If the football club doesn't pay up, we'll have to close our children's homes."

That's the quote that gets repeated. It's over-simplistic. It irritates everyone, including the people who care about the children's homes. I'm a campaigner, not a politician, she thinks. Emotion can win an argument in a campaign, but Les, the politician, knows not to have the argument in public. Never mind the football club; her own skills and abilities are failing her.

Two hours later she stumbles her way down to the civic car park in the bowels of the building. The blackened concrete makes the air bone-cold. Inside the car the sound of the engine calms her, but when she lets the handbrake off and puts the car into reverse, immediately there's a slight sink in the chassis, a quiet crumple, like a drink can being crushed. Has she forgotten how to drive, she thinks? It wouldn't be a surprise.

Letting the car roll a few metres, the wheel rims screech in pain. She presses the pedals down hard, yanks on the brake and gets out. Her legs wobble, heart's racing. How could she have missed it? All four tyres slashed. Steadying herself on the bonnet, she sees the side panels have been keyed, the scratch a gunmetal grey scar. The car is sticking out into the exit lane.

What if whoever did this is still here? She scans the parking bays through glassy eyes. It could be someone at the council. Trying to push it, her hands cool on the metallic paintwork, but make no impact. There will be security here somewhere, but the thought of looking for them in this miserable labyrinth makes her put her back into it.

Finally, the car crunches forward 30 centimetres, enough that other vehicles can pass, but across another bay. Breathing heavily, she gets herself into the lift and up to reception. Relief at the bright lights makes her mouth dry. The caretaker is sympathetic when he finally understands the jumble of words that spill out.

Anita heads for her office, shuts the door, slumps into her chair and calls DI Jones. Instant retribution for daring to suggest they challenge the club? By someone who knows her car. She cares about the car, not the metal box exactly, but the private space it gives her, where her off-guard, messy self lives. Still, what really unsettles her is Nicole's message.

WTF?

CHAPTER 29

She wakes in her old room at Auntie's place again. Pinkie is providing an impenetrable shield for Anita should any local hack pick up her scent. A woman in her forties shouldn't keep running home whenever there's a problem, she thinks. But she's safe. The smell of cinnamon and all spice from the kitchen is restorative. Even with the window open to listen for disturbances on the street, she'd sweated through dreams of being locked in her car boot, her hand bleeding as she smashed the rear brake light to let the air in.

There is so much to do that Anita fails to concentrate on anything. Pinkie has gone shopping early. The mundane can be soothing; it's the usual routine. After the adrenalin of last night, sitting still isn't an option. She sends a message to Conor to chase the legal advice. Not in a hurry to return to the civic centre, she decides the solicitor can come to her if necessary. Auntie's kitchen table becomes a temporary desk.

DI Jones' number comes up on her screen.

"How are you doing this morning?"

"Fidgety, I suppose." It's an understatement worthy of Conor. In her mind the written words have become a mob of real people out searching for her.

"We've got someone working on the social media threats. We classify it as malicious communications. You're lucky it used to be a brick through the window..."

"Lucky?"

"Sorry, no, that's absolutely not what I meant... There's already one or two of the tweeters we could charge with inciting hatred."

Anita hasn't thought about where this might escalate to. Jones tells her that fans are mobilising outside the council offices. There's talk of a pre-match demonstration – oh the irony! Anita had wanted to harness the energy of the fans for the greater good. And there's a Facebook page; Welders Against Politicians has 3,600 likes. Keep sport and politics separate, they say, but nothing is separate any more. What about keeping business out of sport?

Anita trawls the web, hungry for alternative views. There are anti-Croft fans, but they aren't aligning themselves with her. The viral diatribes about the future of football are more interesting than she'd imagined. Will the European players have to leave the UK with Brexit? Yeah, right.

At the Premiership level, football is a sophisticated content business, selling talent in a de-regulated market. It's like modern day slavery. In the lower divisions Anita finds talk of a growing movement of fan-owned clubs and anger at the lack of funding for the growing women's game. It's all political. She texts her nephew, Vikesh, the Welders' fan. At least he might talk to her.

"The CCTV from the car park looks like a young woman, too dark for identification, wearing a football hat though..." he leaves this hanging.

Does he think it's Nicole? The caution for criminal damage, hints of violence, the Croft restraining order. It would be hard to stomach if it was.

Anita hadn't answered Nicole's last message; an angry teenager she could do without.

"If it's football fans, it's not the same lot that put rubbish through my front door." A dark presentiment grows in her stomach. That threat had returned to her in the early hours. If

Pinkie is right and the other attack is race related, two separate groups of people are seriously angry with her. Anita paces around the living room as they talk.

"We can't say unfortunately, no prints. You've rubbed a fair few people up the wrong way."

True, but how is she supposed to respond to that? The police have leapt to the assumption it's fans. The trolling and calls have continued, Anita understands, although she's stopped herself from looking.

"When we met at the station I asked if you the council had any plans in regard of the club." DI Jones is cautious. "I take it the leak had some substance? I mean, it might benefit us both to share what we know."

"It might," she says, not feeling very trusting this morning.

The threats don't change the facts. However badly she's handled it, however culpable the council has been in not taking action against the club sooner, it doesn't excuse this behaviour.

The council has looked up to the club like a star-struck kid hooked on the glamour of an abusive, older gangster. The council, Les particularly, wants to please the people, but however much it gives, it can't. And the fans, also in awe, have joined in the latest kicking. Most right-thinking fans should be able to support the club and admit that, in this case, they are wrong. Being a fan doesn't mean accepting everything.

"I'm not sure what's illegal at this stage and what's a breach of contract. The club are hiding something and it's possible the council are, too. And there are definitely inconsistencies in what the club told you and what Ash's friends say."

"All conjecture, I wouldn't trust that lot..."

"You mean the club or the kids?"

The thought gives her an idea.

"I'm planning to visit the prison today in connection with the Ashley Brand case. Paul Oddsman, do you know him?"

"I know his reputation – unreliable, basically an average kid who messed up, got in with the bad lads."

Aren't they all like that, she thinks.

"Nicole suggested he had evidence about Ash's disappearance."

It's a long shot, but she's got nothing better to do and it'll give her something positive to report to Nicole.

"One more thing…" she asks, "the body in the lake?"

"I'm saying this just to you, but I've seen enough to know that there's a strong probability… the timing and the circumstances… it might well be Ash."

The details are hazy. Eight or nine years ago, Anita had just joined the council.

"So what's the hold up on the identification?"

"Budget cuts. The resources for dredging the lake have run out."

Keep politics out of services, she smiles bitterly to herself.

"Bloody politicians, eh?"

CHAPTER 30

Nicole likes kicking the bright red football against the soot-stained brick wall – target practice. In a restricted parking area meant for emergency vehicles, she fires the ball from her boot like an automatic weapon. Masonry dust from the dried-out cement trickles to the ground every time the ball pounds the wall. Anita is walking tentatively towards her. Too right; be scared council leader.

"Are you alright?" Anita asks. "Pete said you might be here."

"Pleased with yourself?" Nicole shouts above the morning traffic, keeping her focus on the ball, not needing to see if it hits the target.

Last night she'd dumped her football kit on the lounge floor and sprawled on the sofa listening to the local news. That was a first. Her eye had been caught by the sight of the Debbies being interviewed outside the stadium. The younger one was wearing a black and red, Russian-style fur hat, seriously over-done make-up and carried a banner saying "Save our club."

"We're fighting to keep this club alive," the older one had said. "Councillor Patel will bankrupt the club."

Gobsmacked, Nicole had shouted for Pete.

"It's true then. Anita is trying to destroy the club?"

Pete had looked at the TV and done the twirling fingers by his ear sign to suggest the Debbies were mad.

"The supporters' club want to take legal action of our own against the council. It's their fault for lending the club the money in the first place. They didn't have the power to do it. We understand the club were in negotiations with an overseas investor, but that might not happen now the council have stuck their oar in. The chairman would be well within his rights to demand compensation." The older Debbie had looked deadly serious and, Pete had a point, she did look a bit bonkers.

"Don't listen to that crap," he'd said. "It's pure speculation. There's been no official statement has there?"

The younger Debbie's voice had ended the news item: "Patel's got a vendetta against the club. We're calling on all real fans to show their solidarity, protest at the civic centre tomorrow night."

Pete had said, "That's sensationalist. Why don't you phone Anita yourself. Maybe something else is going on?"

Nicole's own experience of the press in the reporting of Ash's disappearance made her alert to bullshit, but why would the Debbies lie? She had spent the next couple of hours reading social media comments, searching her way through the news to make sense of it. The balance of comments seemed to agree with the Debbies. There was a video interview with a football finance expert and he'd said, yes, bankruptcy was a possibility.

Firing the ball against the wall again, she barely hears Anita say, "It's not like that. The club is acting illegally."

"You are fucking unbelievable..." Nicole tightens her jaw. Puffed up with scorn, she enjoys swearing. Just try and tell me to watch my language and this ball is coming straight at you.

"Me and Ash, we loved the club. You must hate it or you wouldn't bankrupt it."

The ball smacks the wall sweetly. Not looking up, she's aware Anita is moving around to her left-hand side.

"Don't believe everything you read. The club won't be bankrupt. But it is dirty and the situation has to be put right."

Nicole scuffs the ball along the ground. This time it rolls away towards the stand. Sprinting, flicking it up with her right foot and volleying it with her left, the wall seems to flex as if it were the back of the net.

"You don't get it, do you?" she tells Anita "The old chairman, Cornflower, he wasn't that bad. What I want to say is... that doesn't matter. Those people, the suits, the managers, even the coaches, they aren't the club. They don't stick around. Only the fans are always there. No-one's bigger than the club."

"That's just words. The club is a business like any other."

Nicole's hears her own pitch rise, Anita isn't listening.

"We make the club. The club is nothing without the fans. You hurt the club..." – the angry ball cracks against an imaginary cross bar on the wall – "you hurt us..."

That's the truth. Nicole's black sweaty fringe sticks to her forehead, her cheeks rage red.

Anita says, "I wouldn't have done it if there was another way. The club has to pay what it owes. The council has to care for everyone, including you. Every year our resources are cut. We can't do everything."

"Why not? Everyone owes money. Pay it back another time."

Nicole watches Anita's arms flap in frustration. "It's not that simple..."

"That's bollocks." Nicole is breathing hard now, running back and forth, aiming the ball nearer to Anita.

"Can't we find somewhere to sit down and I'll explain." Anita looks impatient.

Yeah, right, that's not happening.

"Explain what? You know nothing."

Anita tries to stop the ball with her foot, but fails, as if that would work. "What would you do in my shoes?"

"Don't ask me. You wanted to be the leader. You love being in charge."

"I'm trying to help, trying to do what's right."

Nicole thrusts out her chest. "Yeah, well you're crap. And the girls in Westmeade say you're going to close us down."

"Nicole, would you please calm down, I can't talk to you like this."

"You don't care about us, but you won't sack your new boyfriend will you?"

That shuts Anita up. Nicole has already guessed something has happened between Pete and Anita, but when Pete mentioned it she blanked him. *Whatever.*

"The council wouldn't need the money if the councillors weren't on the take."

One of the cleaners had said that in the kitchen the other day. Pete had defended the council. Nicole knows it will get up Anita's nose.

"No Nicole, that's rubbish." Nicole sees Anita's trying to hold it together and smirks. "Use your brain. You've seen my house, my car. The club owes us £23 million. Do I look I've got that sort of cash?"

Standing still, one foot on top of the battered ball, Nicole puts her right.

"You've got more than I'll ever have."

"Look, there's no need to get emotional. It's complicated, but if you just listen for a minute. I know you're attached to the club and to Westmeade…"

"Attached! Shut the fuck up!" she interrupts. "You haven't got to a clue! Me and Ash, my mates, my hood, what I talk about, what I watch, what I want. The club's the only place where I know who I am."

"I'm trying to explain."

"Why can't you listen? You're taking away my roof. I'll be on the streets, is that *right*?"

"Nicole, it's not like that... You just need to understand..."

"No. You need to understand!" It's screams that come out now, but Nicole can't stop.

"Come on..." Anita snaps. "You're being stupid..."

That's it then. Game over.

Throwing her rucksack over one shoulder and picking up the ball, Nicole darts round the corner, wanting to put some distance between them. Starting the walk back into town, she yells, "That's so shit. So wrong."

No-one is listening. She gasps at the air, hoovering it in as if she hasn't eaten in days, then throwing it back up like she's swallowed too much. Two days ago she'd allowed herself to get a bit hopeful. Not exactly optimistic, but ready to believe that things were going in the right direction. Stop it. Her throat is so dry she could gag. Just stop it. They'll think you're weak, they'll treat you like a child. She hugs the ball.

As she trudges back into town, the last place she wants to go is back to the home. The last couple of years have been OK, she's managed to keep playing football, although that's about it. Her room is alright, but the other girls, none of them like her. Even Pete, he's changed.

CHAPTER 31

Anita is left feeling punctured, her head aches. It's not fair of Nicole to run off like that. She knows it's never a good idea to say the word stupid to a teenager. I suppose I'd probably have run off, too, Anita thinks, throwing her hands in the air in an "I give up" gesture. I couldn't hold it together and I should've done. I'm the adult, whatever hell is going on in my world.

On the other hand, Anita doesn't want to be part of that old story – the child throws a tantrum because it can't get what it wants (no matter how impossible) and the grown-up picks up the pieces. That's what Les does. He treats the fans like spoilt kids, lets them think they can have it all. And expects they'll love him for it. Does that work for you, Les? They might love you for a while, they might vote for you once, but then what? They lash out at you? Or they don't if, like Les, you walk away, put someone else in the firing line.

It's hard not to be cynical and being right is no consolation. That's exactly where modern politics is, Anita thinks.

The concourse feels abandoned, desolate. Anita calls a taxi. As if Nicole were still here, she says out loud, "If the club I loved, the club I thought I was part of, was corrupt or criminal. I'd do whatever I could to fix it. That's why I went into politics. If the system doesn't work, get in there, at least try and sort it out."

No-one is listening.

*

"The prison please." Anita opens the message from Nicole with Paul Oddsman's official prisoner number.

The cab driver is a young Pakistani man. Anita is slumped down in the far too soft seats of the Cavalier. It makes her feel small, as if she fits entirely into the driver's rear-view mirror. And he looks back far too often for her liking, but she holds her tongue, focusing instead on the endless grey-black Victorian stone wall around the perimeter. Before they reach the drop-off point, she shakes her head at a hoarding advertising *Grand Theft Auto 5*. Ironic or clever placement? It doesn't help.

There's a small, almost invisible, door in the huge original arched gates to the prison.

"Visitors' reception 200 metres to the right," a guard directs her.

Anita walks alongside a young mum, who might be Nicole's age, pushing an expensive, chunky-wheeled buggy. The young woman looks her up and down and turns away. It could be her imagination, but Anita's photo is everywhere at the moment, she hopes that Odds hasn't seen it and doesn't react similarly.

It's a long time since she's visited anyone in prison. The airport security-style scan is to be expected, but having her mouth swabbed makes her want to gag with guilt when logically she knows she's done nothing wrong. A guard lifts Anita's hair up for the back of her neck to be scrutinised, which makes her face redden. When the drug dog doesn't stop to sniff her legs, she composes herself and resolves to be here as long as it takes.

It's the intensity of the noise in the visitors' room that's overwhelming. Forty prisoners and their visitors, harvesting words and emotions, condensed in time and space. An officer checks her visiting order and shows her to a low table.

Odds stares down at the floor, his shaved head revealing an oval shaped scar, more like the imprint of a coin or a sovereign ring. It reminds Anita of something that Croft or one of his minders might wear.

"I'm Anita Patel. I'm helping Nicole Brand. She's trying to find out what happened to her brother."

"Yeah, Nic sent me a message. But who are you?" His head still down, but his eyes looking up, taking her in.

"I'm a councillor."

"I had a counsellor when I first got in here. He was good like, helped me cope. Man that first year was bad."

Normally Anita would've corrected him, but she isn't keen to give up her lucky break.

"How are you feeling now?" she asks, playing up the counsellor role.

He speaks slowly, but without hesitation.

"You're Nic's counsellor, not mine."

"Sorry, it's a habit."

Odds starts off defensive, but warms up, "I'm doing alright, studying for a GCSE, wanna get my head sorted."

"Good for you," she nods. "Nicole needs closure and she thinks Ash's disappearance is to do with the football club."

"Why didn't she come?"

"She's at school. Were you close to Ash?"

"Yeah, course, back four, y'know."

Odds still defines himself as a football player, which is better than becoming an inmate.

"When the stand came down, everyone forgot about Ash. Dez was out for the foreseeable, the team was dying in the relegation zone. It was like he was long gone. Ash got bad luck on him. Pissed off to London, the coach said."

Odds pulls down on his grey sweatshirt, turns his body away from her, ashamed, "Except I was the one that should've pissed off. Got out while I could. Ash wasn't bad. Wrong place, wrong time. He couldn't stand being at home sometimes so, like, he hid out at the club sometimes. We never told Nicole that."

"Sounds like a difficult time." Anita empathises, but tries not to over-egg the concern. Essentially, I'm lying to a not very bright kid, she thinks. She's not particularly happy about it, but he's unlikely to open up otherwise and she needs to come out of here with something useful, although what that might be is anyone's guess.

"The first few weeks were mad. Didn't know where we would be training or playing. Weeks they didn't pay us, so I needed the cash and ended up doing the bag run. It was all wrong after that."

She wants information about Ash, but senses there's something here.

"I'm sorry, I don't really understand. What was going on?"

"Proper grief like, insurance problems, security, health and safety. The chairman needed someone to go with the Sweeper to fetch the bags. You never say no to the chairman. He said I could handle myself. And I s'pose I thought I could. I could be the muscle. Got paid for the assists, better than my wages, so I said nothing and carried on."

"The Sweeper?" A football position, she wonders.

"Cleans up for Croft." Odds is not joking, his voice is hesitant, eyes are fixed with intent.

"What bags?" she asks.

"Cash bags. There was a round. Pubs, nightclub, the garages."

"And you weren't taking it to the bank?"

Odds leans towards her, "You sure this is confidential?"

"Absolutely." Anita says. She doesn't want Les, Croft or any of the fans, for that matter, knowing she's been here, she thinks, but already she is sure this is Jones' territory.

"That kinda money doesn't belong in a bank."

Does he mean it's counterfeit? A baby being bounced on her mother's knee next to them wails high above the adult voices.

Anita moves on as quickly as she can. "Did you tell the police?"

"Nah. Not then. I was scared." Odds points his two forefingers at her like a gun, then points at his head. "Croft pubs, weren't they. And Croft garages, where drugs were dished out."

Playing the supportive professional for all it's worth, Anita draws out the story.

"Croft was using vulnerable young players to launder money?"

"Yeah. You gotta realise Croft was always bad, way before he took over the club. Bad men don't change, but they do get respectable. That's the way it goes."

She nods. "And you were involved in a stabbing, related to the money?"

Odds wraps his arms around him like a straitjacket, his cheeks burn. There's a flash of anger, but it seems directed at himself. Faltering slightly, he admits, "I started carrying a knife, like, for protection. Next time I got in a fight, I used it. Not on purpose. Lost my balance and chipped another kid in the thigh. Bloody stupid right, knife could've gone anywhere. He could've died and I ended up here."

Odds' body crumples back into the chair, deflated.

"Croft can go fuck himself."

"Would you tell the police now? About the money, the delivery bags?" He drops his head again.

"No-one crosses Daniel Croft. He's done the worst thing he could do to me. Took me away from the team. I... I lost it all."

"Would you do it for Wormy, for Nicole?"

Odds sits up straight, scans the visitors' room.

"Could be worse for them if I do."

Nothing feels particularly safe to Anita right now. The last thing she wants is Nicole or Wormy to be in harm's way, but there's definitely more and she doesn't want to leave. The digital clock sounds a techno alarm. Time's up. None of the visitors move quickly. She smiles at the baby, distracted by the movement around them. As she puts her coat on she hopes to drag out what extra she can.

"Do you think the club had something to do with Ash's disappearance?"

"He was collateral damage."

This time his head drops so far forward that the back of his neck is fully extended, his skin blotchy and reddening. It's almost a bow.

"Sorry?"

"Watch out for the Sweeper, find the old Bentley. Wormy can help."

He is talking in riddles now, but Anita knows the thing that's said in passing, at the end, is always critical. She bashes her calf awkwardly against the low table. One of the wardens, not much older than Odds, points to the door.

"Just tell me – what do you mean?"

"Time up. The door's that way."

"Collateral damage – Ash was caught in cross-fire?"

Anita puts her hand on Odds' shoulder, the young man's skin has a caustic, clinical smell to it.

"That's enough." The warden tries to stand between them.

"One minute, that's all."

"Look after Nicole, she's a good kid." Odds says, "Good footballer, too."

"Quickly – was there a shooting at the club?"

"Now Madam! Security!" The officer grabs her arm.

Odds shakes his head, she's got something wrong, he's already turning away. A reinforcement security guard arrives, towering above her.

"Wait!" No, no, no. "This is important. Wait."

Odds has said what he wants to say, doesn't want more trouble, doesn't look back.

Fortunately it's quicker to get out of the prison than in. Vexed she finds her phone, taps in notes: Cash/bags, Bentley, Sweeper. There was something else. Insurance? I can't leave it like that, she thinks. It's all too vague. Anita had promised Odds that was confidential, but... Shit. He told her what he told her for a reason and it was criminal. There isn't a choice, she's already justifying what she knows she has to do. Again, she's going to let a young person down.

Odds is trying to make something of himself. A few qualifications are a flimsy platform from which to launch a post-prison career. There's little hope for the football rejects in the labour market, let alone young men with a record for violence. Poor kid. They are all poor kids. Adrift. Not without resources, but without a plan B.

At 3am, in bed in her own room, Anita drifts in and out of sleep. She sees a block of charcoal grey, the slab of the stadium under a thunderous matt sky. Was Ash involved in the money laundering? Maybe he knew too much – or not enough? Her thoughts spin inwards. I care about that girl, I care too much, but she can't see that. As far as Nicole is concerned, I'm no different to any other adult. I'm nothing to her. Anita's heartbeat slows to a mournful thud. I'm an outsider, one of them. Not one of us.

At 7am the insistent buzz of the phone wakes her up, but exhaustion means her movements are too slow to answer. Pete leaves a message: *Call me as soon as you can. Nicole didn't come home last night. She's taken a bag of clothes. Gone.*

CHAPTER 32

It's 8am. Conor feels his quad muscles groan as he reaches the top of the stairs. His raised heartbeat jumps a beat at the sight of Anita waiting outside his office.

"Morning." Conor smiles his normal, resigned smile, a we're-in-the-trenches-but-we're-here-together-type face. His downbeat tone aims for empathy. Most of the staff recognise and return the intent. Not Anita.

"I suspect the club has been laundering money. I've spoken to DI Jones," she says quietly.

He motions towards the door, fishing in his pocket for the office keys. The bunch is too big, his car key tears at the silk lining. He hates being watched. Slow down for god's sake. The corridor magnifies the sound of the key as the catch opens. He keeps his tone even,

"Come on in... are you OK after yesterday?"

He's not deliberately trying to change the subject and he's sympathetic. Yesterday's political bloodbath has shaken him, too. The walls of the corridors seem too narrow, there is no room to wriggle.

"Not really... Anyway, I went to Winson Green, spoke to a possible witness. Can you look again at the finances, find something that might help?"

"Not sure what I can find, but I'll happily look into it," he says. To his own ear, Conor's voice sounds too loud, falsely confident.

Anita's eyes scan him up and down like an MRI, and again, down and up, as if the imaging unit in her head had somehow failed to capture him. "You'll know where to look."

"Are you trying to imply something?" Conor bristles. "I knew absolutely nothing about this," he says. "How would I?"

"Sorry," she throws a large leaf-green leather bag on his desk. "Didn't get much sleep."

Christ, what next?

"...An ex-player, Paul Oddsman, told me they regularly picked up bags of cash from pubs owned by Croft. There's a garage where drugs are dished out to small-time dealers... It wasn't exactly clear, but it sounded genuine."

Conor remembers Odds. Going back a while now, the Welders had a promising defence, kept a dozen clean sheets. Of course, the strikers at the time forgot how to score. Another year, another relegation battle. Yes, Conor thinks: Odds, Wormsworth, Brand and Deadly Dez – who almost made the big time, but was now back on loan. Brand was the one that disappeared, the one in the leaflet Anita had sent him. The brother of the sister, the girl he recognised as a child in their care. Worse than their fire alarm, there's a deafening blast in his ears. The child Anita is "helping".

He makes a mental note to see the children's services director as soon as he can, cover all bases.

"What did DI Jones say?"

"The same as you, he'll look into it."

Anita tails off looking worried, digging angrily in her bag for her phone, flicking menacingly at it for messages. No-one has mentioned drugs in relation to the club before, but it sounds credible and the money laundering accusations support his own theory. He runs through the consequences if Anita is right.

It's just possible that the political balance could tip in her favour. Les is too close to the club and to Croft, by association at least. It'll cost the old man support – and it will affect confidence in me, Conor thinks. What it will do to public opinion is unclear; like a football match, the mood of the people can change in a moment, a misplaced pass here, a two-footed challenge there and the hero and villain switch places.

If the club is acting criminally and there's proof, it won't just be the council taking action to recover debt. Conor will be sucked into a quicksand of multiple investigations. The council will never get its money back and the club will go under.

Conor searches his crowded memory files for information about Les and Croft's relationship. He remembers asking Les' PA, Sandra with the pigs, to check the diary to see when Les and Croft had met. There'd been nothing at all, which seemed odd. He was always making arrangements on his private phone, Sandra had grumbled, it drove her mad. Conor's focus comes back into the room.

"God knows what pressure Croft put the players under to get involved in his criminal activities."

It wouldn't be so difficult to get eager young lads to do your bidding, Conor thinks. As a Welders apprentice, his son, Toby, was asked to clean the boots of the senior players, hose down the showers, run errands; whatever was wanted, you did it. It was normal and you knew to keep silent. When Toby had hinted that was much worse than that – bullying, victimization, pranks that turned into vendettas on the pitch – Conor, the eager dad/ fan, hadn't paid it too much attention.

"Do as you're told son," Conor had said, "or you won't make the bench."

It had all seemed OK until the day Jayne had arrived early to pick him up from training, had seen the club culture first hand and had raised hell. The next week the club had banned the mums from the training ground. The dads were still allowed in.

"Pure sexism. This is not the 1970s, for god's sake. You knew what was going on? Why didn't you say something?"

Jayne ripped up Toby's contract, metaphorically speaking of course, the club was paperless. There had been no difficulty in finding a new club for their son, one where nobody was bullied. For Toby, it was a good result. He'd made good friends, his game improved.

If he could wind the clock back he would, would have said something, done something himself. He'd got stuck on the dream he shared with his grandad, that one day he might see Toby leading the team out in black and red, had been unwilling to see the problem. The idea that Toby, if he'd stayed at the Welders, could have been one of the players coerced by the club into criminal activity casts a weighty shadow of culpability.

Conor is shaken out of his memory by Anita's bhangra ringtone. She mouths "later" and leaves like a student dumping her dirty laundry at her parents. Expecting someone – him – to sort it.

"Wait – the budget! Anita..." She's gone.

The day starts again. Eight meetings later the muscles at the top of his neck, the ones that tuck in under his skull, are strung tight from the tiny movement of nodding. The team has gathered outside his office; the strained voice of his number two, the head of finance, is amplified in the corridor. No-one is talking about the football club debt. They've moved on to the implications for the budget. They want reassurance about their jobs. Not that his colleagues would believe him if he tried to give it to them. They manage the accounts for a living.

It's 4.45pm. One of the PAs puts her head around the door.

"It's the bank on the phone."

Conor nods. Christ. He hasn't actually spoken to anyone in the bank for years. It's first of December, a number of significant contractual payments are scheduled. Hands sweating, he knows what's coming.

"Mr Walsh? I'm sure you're aware of the situation. The council budget has gone into the red. We need to set up a meeting as a matter of urgency."

"Of course," he says, digging his pen as far into the desk as it will go. Blood-like ink starts to flow. "We were planning to call you, too."

There's a temptation to call it an IT failure, buy himself some time, but excuses don't inspire confidence. Which is what's missing. In the past, if they needed to extend their overdraft it would be done electronically without question. The mumbling outside the door grows. Conor can usually trust his team to keep their heads, but they can see what the bank can see. While she has been so decisive about the club, Anita hasn't made the cuts, decisions have been left hanging and so has he. Her leadership is both resolute and irresolute, principals strong, practice weak. The inconsistency infuriates him.

"I'm tied up in the morning," he says, "but later on tomorrow is fine." Even a few extra hours will help.

He opens the door to talk to the team.

"We all know it's both a temporary blip and a long-term problem. Let's do what we can. Scrape together everything we've got. See what's down the back of the sofa. Every penny."

That's it. It feels so domestic. So personal. We've all gone over our overdraft limit, haven't we? Stoicism is all he's got. He tells them to endure.

Energy on zero, Conor calls home.

"I've got to work late, sorry love."

"You were supposed to drop in on your grandad," Jayne says.

Conor hesitates, the care home have called him again, his grandad has developed pneumonia, hospitalization is on the cards.

"It's your choice."

Conor would prefer it if Jayne didn't throw everything back at him. He hears Jayne thinking, then she says; "Anita's right isn't she... about the club?"

No, he thinks. Anita is wrong about the club, but right about Croft. If Conor wasn't in such a maelstrom about the damage she's causing and where this might end, would he think differently? He might admire Anita's courage. He might even have helped her, given her a real chance after Les stepped aside?

"It's not that simple."

Conor tries to keep his voice light, but his mind has moved on. Selka, the share-trading? He needs to make his theory about the club's corrupt financial practices concrete, back it up, work harder at it. What's missing? The question he hasn't been able to answer is this: Where's the money? If Croft is laundering money through the club, where the bloody hell is it?

CHAPTER 33

It's midnight. The TV is on mute, the radiators cool in the living room as Conor, on his laptop, tries to trace the dirty money down the virtual back alleys of the international finance system. What we've got here, Conor thinks, is a new breed of parasite; a toxic bleeding canker slowly poisoning our grand old horse chestnut tree. We can't prop up the tree with wooden struts; either the council will have to fell it for health and safety reasons or it will just die. Neither possibility appeals, but both are already highly probable.

But it's not just one tree. The wood, the forest, the eco-system – the league, the FA, FIFA – they're all infected. It's too big for anyone to fix. In a separate window in the corner of his laptop is a trail to the lucrative lands – offshore. If Croft is sucking the money through the membrane of the club and out again, it has to get into the club somehow.

Selka, the market analyst, a tipster who Conor likes to imagine as an athletic 35-year-old blond woman living in Oslo.

Selka: I'm on the move. How about you?

Paddy Roach: Anywhere interesting?

Roach is Conor's trading name; a fake ID set up to amuse himself alone. Paddy Roach was an old goalie, nearly signed for the Welders once. Grandad called him the one that thankfully got away. Paddy Roach was crap.

S: BVI

British Virgin Islands – that's interesting. Of course, Selka would know all about navigating the clear, blue, murky waters of tax havens.

PR: Going sailing?

S: Fishing around. The water's warm.

This is not idle chat. It's a game played in code. Conor acts as if he knows the keywords, as if he has the type of money that would make him interesting. Sad really, what accountants do for fun. Conor decides it might be better if he thinks of "her" as just an algorithm. Or more likely a 25-year-old garage trader in the American Mid-West, high on numbers and Red Bull.

That said, he's watched Selka for a while, traded well on her recommendations with his own money. Just to keep his hand in. The investment tips were solid, the information speedy, "her" manner light.

PR: No sharks?

Always on the move, Selka finds safe harbours, and here I am, thinks Conor, rolling in the deep. Selka passes on a link to a blog with attractive numbers: 52 Wk low. 56%. $71.8 +7.95 – +12.45% Erngs/Shr: 4.22. Yield: 9.09%. It's a small group of people that speak this strange, hybrid language, who see the money to be made. Another time maybe? He feels the pull of a punt. It's a good bet and it could provide Conor and Jayne with a safe exit route. If his worst fears about Croft are realised, he'll be done for one way or another. What catches his eye is the offer of consultancy services; he's not noticed this before.

PR: Do you provide search facilities? Can you find companies operating offshore?

Bullish is good in this world.

PR: I'm interested in a particular investor.

S: That's a specialist search service, but it's possible.

It's a lucky break.

PR: And a specialist fee?

S: Message me privately.

Conor hears Jayne padding to the bathroom and waits in case she comes downstairs. How would he justify this next dive into the deep water? Though the council pays for *consultancy* all the time, this is stretching it, even by Les' standards. Still, extraordinary times demand unprecedented action. The only risk these days is not taking a risk – he read that in his *Public Finance* magazine only last week.

The supplementary contingency management – putting what was left from a number of dormant accounts into the Welders' Welfare Fund – that was a rational strategy, wasn't it? His fund is tucked neatly away, all traceable for auditing purposes, but nothing that a councillor looking to fund a pet project would spot. It means he has a fighting fund.

He rocks backward and forward on the edge of the sofa; his neck feels corded. Not everyone would see the logic. It could be seen as illegitimate expenditure and if Mrs Massey, the auditor, spots it there will be an investigation. His reputation would be damaged, although he'd survive that, and, if his favoured position with Les was jeopardised, so what? He's starting to think he needs more distance from the old man anyway.

At the top of the risk register is that he'd never know what Croft is really up to, the council would lose even more money, he would be able to fix the budget and would get sacked anyway.

Rubbing at his stiff neck, he hesitates. This money could help take the council back into the black. Eyes watering, he logs in to the council system and makes the $20,000 transfer from the Welders' Welfare Fund. It's necessary for the bigger picture.

He snatches some sleep in lieu of news. The central heating murmurs and in the early morning light there is a new message.

Selka: Daniel Croft has registered an interest in a new private equity fund based in Anguilla. Looks like he's the cornerstone investor, got major skin in the game – big balls and back up.

Respected fund managers issued a prospectus last week, there was a road show in London and they're touting for deals. We can track any fish they catch, but it'll cost you... proper money this time.

Croft can't have done this without advice. Not the Croft from the Highlands estate. Not even the accountants who had reworked the club's books and stitched up the council so exquisitely could operate at this level. Croft's going global. Conor can see why the private equity market would suit an investor like Croft, seeking to maximize returns offshore, nothing publicly listed, buying directly into private businesses – their nature unspecified – one businessman to another. Hedge funds are better regulated these days and that would put someone like Croft off.

PR: What if Croft's contribution to the fund came from questionable sources?

The laptop is hot on Conor's thigh.

S: Impossible. It's got to be clean before this kind of operation kicks off. The returns are excellent and totally legitimate. You interested?

Selka sounds like an agent now, probably gets commission on any lead.

PR: Sounds promising.

He smiles bitterly. The way things are going at the council now, he might pass the tip onto his investment manager, Jason. They could earn a few precious pennies. Investing in this type of fund is like giving your money to a hot-shot professional to gamble with, someone who convinces you they can win big. And probably they would win more, because of the size of the fund. You're buying a seat at the big table with stakes to match.

As he's about to shut down the computer a final message comes through.

S: If there had been a problem with Mr Croft's contribution, it would be earlier in the money trail. Someone's taken this money to the launderette.

PR: Thanks for now. Got some dirty washing of my own to put through the ringer.

Conor slaps the lid of the laptop shut and shoves it away from him. Croft owes the city, the council is likely to be bankrupt, people are losing their jobs, he's risking his job. And Croft is making millions.

Does it change anything, Sizzle asked? Not if it's all legal. All Conor's got is proof that the money is neatly packaged in an offshore investment fund.

Under the hottest shower his scalp can bear, Conor thinks again. He only knows where the money goes. Where it comes from and how it gets there is just supposition. What can he do? No proof, no allies, no prospect of this getting any better? Drying himself off, Conor thinks again.

The only other option is to go back to the start of the chain. Where does the money come from and how does he clean it? It's not his job to investigate drug dealing, but, he tells himself, you can't sit back now. Scrolling down to find DI Jones' number, his finger hovers over the button. He should ring now. Just call him he thinks. But tell him what? I've just had a hypothetical conversation, paid for with unapproved council funding, that proves Daniel Croft is doing nothing illegal. Shit, he's truly on his own here.

But then again, Conor knows the police won't have the resources to investigate this sort of fraud. We're all in the same leaky, listing, sinking public finance boat, he thinks. Professionally I'm taking responsibility. It's financial forensics, unconventional, yes, but as Grandad might say; "Do what only you can do." He finds he needs no justification to pursue his line of enquiry – Croft.

No-one else knows as much as him. The risk is that not only is Croft defrauding the council by not paying the debt, he's using the council's money to kill the club. He puts the phone down and creeps back upstairs. Jayne is sleeping, oblivious, the beautiful curve of her neck and shoulder just visible. God, he loves her.

CHAPTER 34

"High-risk behaviour," Nicole grunts to herself. That's what Pete would call it. They give me grief, she thinks, but it's Anita who's made the club "unsafe", and put Westmeade "at risk". And Pete's on Anita's side now. Why would he go out with her? That's "inappropriate".

Leaving Westmeade at night feels good. After the row with Anita, she'd skirted back to the home. There'd been a police car out front. It wasn't exactly unusual, but this time she'd felt the police were looking for her. It could be something to do with the restraining order or she's been reported truant – that's happened before. The place is dead anyway, Nicole thinks. If she went back it would be padlocked and wrapped in giant cobwebs, like a condemned mansion in a cartoon.

There are two obvious places to go, places that remind her of Ash. Their appropriated football pitch at the garages, she could always find him there. That was where the grainy picture of her brother in his old football shirt was taken. They'd been kicking the ball about next to the garage with the number three scratched into the metal door. She would be alright there.

The club is the other place. It's not 100% safe because of Croft and she doesn't know the new stadium as well as the old one. But still. It was like a second home to Ash.

Her rucksack cuts into her shoulder. Nicole's packed a bottle of water, packet of cheese and onion crisps and three flapjacks, probably mashed at the bottom of the bag already. It was a risk bringing one of the files on Ash's case with her, but if she'd left it at the home she might never see it again. The file with her precious photos in, that was hidden in Pete's office with a note. He's a traitor now, but he wouldn't bin that. More than his job's worth.

Nicole's first choice is the garages. The last time she had been there it was summer, she'd felt her brain was fried. It was a spur of the moment thing. Pete had gone mad, just because she'd slept out one night in a scuzzy garage. The other girls stayed out with disgusting men all the time, how was that fair? It was nothing. She'd left the metal door open a few inches at the bottom, giving her a slice of light. It was cold, but calm. Lying down she watched the clouds make potato-print smudges on the moon.

Arriving at the garages Nicole automatically gets the football out of her rucksack, but decides against playing. It's late and she doesn't want to give the neighbours a reason to ring the police. If the police ask her name, she'll make one up.

Steph Houghton, captain of England. Ha! They wouldn't have a clue about women's football. And if someone asks what she's doing here, she'll say, "I'm waiting for my brother."

Like always.

*

Nicole shivers. There's no moon tonight. Take control. Play your own game. Right this minute, she doesn't know what any of that means, but at least feels better for the pep talk.

Without the street lights, smashed or switched off to save money, she stumbles. There are potholes in their hallowed ground. Their old football pitch is pocked with puddles of stinking brackish water.

"Urggghh…"

Her eyes adjust to the dark. The layers, as many as she could get under her jacket, are helping, but water has seeped through her thin pumps into her socks.

"Yeah, right," she thinks, a torch would've been good. The one on her phone isn't throwing off anything like enough light. She's got her charger, but is unsure if these garages have plugs. Never cared before.

She tries the door of the third garage, but it's locked. One night, it's just one night. Doubt shadows her steps. She tries garage number five, then seven. The even numbers are locked until she finds number eight open. Rolling up the garage door is easy enough, but the smell of petrol, mixed with fox excrement, makes her push it straight back down. Can't stay in that one.

"Why do I get the crap?"

There's no light bulb inside, but she stays put. In the gloom she finds a sleeping bag on top of a pile of flattened cardboard boxes.

"Euww manky. Only if I'm going to die," she says to no-one in particular. As it begins to rain, she shelters inside, sitting on her rucksack as close as she can to the door.

As she begins to nod off, suddenly a powerful torch light sweeps the garages, stops on her open door. Nicole dives for cover, throwing the sleeping bag over her head. The smell of sweat and urine makes her want to heave. Whoever it is bends down briefly, flashing his torch inside. The mound of her body wobbles like jelly.

The footsteps seem to back away from the door. She wants to call Pete, but instinct says don't move, don't show yourself. Would she phone Anita? Anita would come – duty of care – she'd have to. Nicole cracks her knuckles. Only when I'm actually dead, she thinks.

Trailing the light from her phone along the workings of the door, she tries the handle. It catches a lump of skin on her thumb, blood pours and she loses her balance, rattling the metal door. It echoes loudly. The footsteps return.

"Fuck this rain, man."

If the man opens the door maybe she can rush past him. Make it to the road.

Three minutes have passed since she last looked at the time. There's rough ha bloody ha laughter, but she knows they are not joking. Junkies can be violent, strong; one of the girls in Westmeade went to hospital after her boyfriend slammed her head against the wall. "Didn't have a clue what we was doing," she'd said to Nicole. "I don't think he was trying to kill me but…"

The young man boasts, "See that security guard run. He saw me, he ran far, far."

"Faster than you, wasn't he? He Bolt-ed!" they laugh. "And you, fat boy, you nowhere near. Lucky man, we didn't tell you to go back and do him."

"I heard something."

Under the appalling sleeping bag the air tastes of puke. If they get her, they'll rape her for sure. She shivers. Forcing herself up onto one knee, but staying low, her hand and fingers shake as she sends a silent text to Wormy.

Garages help. Now.

It's not much, but it's all she dares send and Wormy is the only person who knows where she means.

"Stop pissing about and get inside. We need to be out delivering."

Number eight never used to be a drug garage. Maybe they're all abandoned now and the dealers just use whatever one they want?

Pulling on her rucksack, she gets ready to run. They are coming from the left. She bends down by the wall on the right, hoping the fat one is nearest to her.

"Fuck. You left it open." There's a roar as the door rolls up, faster than she's ever seen. She has the element of surprise, but the dazzle of the torch disorientates her and her legs buckle before she can launch herself beyond the men.

"What the fuck…" One of the men lunges at her, grabs the strap of her rucksack. She pulls it with all her might. For a second she thinks she's clear, so runs a few metres then finds herself yanked back by the strap. A third man grabs her jacket with one hand. Her red and black Welders hat is pulled off and her pony tail whips round her face in the dark. The man catches it with his free hand, twists it until she screams in pain and anger.

"Let me go, you fuck…" she rages.

A hand comes from nowhere and slaps her across the face. These men don't care about hitting young girls.

Legs crumbling, her neck screwed round over her shoulder, Nicole is forced onto her knees on the gravel, the man still holding her hair like a dog chain.

"I just tried the door. I wasn't doing anything, please let me go. I should've been home ages ago. Honestly, I'm… I'm… I just needed to get some space."

The three men are wearing denim of different sorts. The leader wears a posh-looking coat. He barks orders at the slow one.

"Throw me the bag." Unzipping it, he pulls out a stripy red jumper and the folder of information on Ash.

"Homework!" He spits sarcastically, throwing it in a puddle.

Tears of fury prick her eyes, a growl rises from her throat, skin tingles, nose bleeds, the bastard. Photocopies, hand-written notes of her own home-made witness statements, precious team sheets, the matchday programme from Ash's first game and fliers splay out into the dark water. A newspaper clipping is taken by a gust she can't feel and blows off towards the garage. Years of work, everything she's learnt about Ash's case is in danger of disappearing. She's memorised it all, but who will believe her?

She mouths into her chin, "Fuck you, I hate you."

The man doesn't hear, but something distracts him. It's the photo of Ash, the one she loves. It's landed on the floor a few feet away. In the picture Ash isn't smiling, but his eyes are bright, chest proud in his old Welders shirt.

Temporarily paralysed, the energy in her body plummets. The leader drops her hair and puts a boot on her back, crunching the knobbly bones of her spine. She has no resistance.

"Who are you?"

"I'm Nicole; I used to live here when I was a kid, over there."

Stupid idiot to just blurt that out, she thinks.

"If you lived round here you'd know the garages are off limits."

She keeps her head down, looking at the ground, catching a glimpse of an expensive black shoe, a loose lace dangling in the wet. Maybe I could knock him off balance?

"I used to play football here with my brother."

"Where's big brother now then?" he snarls.

And then she gets it. Shit. Fuck. She's heard this man before, been threatened by him before. He was with Croft that time at the stadium. Wormy thought it had to be a guy they call the Sweeper. Does he remember her?

"Ashley Brand – he played for the Welders."

The mention of the team distracts the others.

"Welders are losers," the fat one says.

"Villa are the money."

The joker says, "Yeah, some kids did used to play here. Yeah, yeah, I remember Ash. He was OK. Your mum was a total wacko." He mimes a straitjacket. Nicole's heart pounds. If she was strong like Ash she'd have broken his neck.

"I was only in the garage five minutes. Let me go."

The leader grunts, lifts the pressure on her back. She won't be able to knock him over, but without waiting for a reply, she scrambles to her feet, grabs the bag and scoops up what she can of the sodden file. Run. Grit gets caught under her nails, gravel tears at the tips of her fingers. The photo is left behind. Run.

Clearing the underpass, she finally slows to a jog in the middle of the road in a narrow, terraced street on the edge of St Peters. Breathing hard, she finds a small space between two parked cars and sits out of sight on the pavement. There's not enough phlegm in her mouth to spit onto the road, her mouth is too dry. Blood from her nose has dried on the file. Digging in the rucksack she pulls out a flapjack, but the water is gone. Adrenalin makes her feel drunk. Where now?

The street is dead. She could cry, but what's the point.

*

In the near distance the stadium looms; a magnetic hum draws Nicole towards it. Mindful of the CCTV, she pulls the hood over her head. If she breeches the restraining order again she'll be arrested this time, sent to prison. But where else does she have to go? The row with Anita seems like years ago. Tracking back to where she was playing football, her heart sinks as she realises she left her ball at the garages.

Next to the emergency vehicles parking bay is a substantial wire fence. Pushing her fingers through the hexagonal wire, she yanks it back and forward. It bends but doesn't move. Then she notices a loose section at the bottom. Bending down she pulls it off the ground, to give her enough room to slide under. The rucksack goes under first. Then, like a worm, on her belly, she crawls. The wire catches her hood, leaving her hair exposed and tangled like ribbons through the metal. As she scrambles under she stifles a yell as the hairs are wrenched from her skull. Then she's free and onto her knees. She's done it, through. Ash, she thinks, I'm here. I'm in the stadium.

Getting to her feet she picks up her bag. Maybe she can…

As she takes her first step toward the stadium the movement triggers a security light. She drops to the floor until it goes off then spots a possibility.

*

The smaller the space, the safer she feels. The programme seller's booth is about the size of a telephone box. Not enough room to stretch out her legs, unless she stands up, which would give her hiding place away. There's a grey, plastic-moulded stool and a battered cardboard box with one ripped programme left from the last match. That derby game feels like forever ago. It's too dark to read the small print. She digs around in the rucksack to find her phone, then empties the contents on her lap, turns the bag inside out and runs her fingers along the seams like a drug cop looking for a hidden compartment. The mobile's not there.

After slapping hard at the empty pockets of her jacket, Nicole accepts it's gone. She sucks in all the air she can to avoid bursting, braces her feet against one side of the booth and smacks the other wall with her fist. Completely stupid. Her connection to the world must be back at the garages. I'm dead without it, she thinks.

Curling her body around the stool, she buries her head in her bag and lets herself cry. Salty tears make the split in her lip smart. Spitting on the edge of her hoodie, like her mum with a hankie might've done, she dabs gently at the grit in her chin.

She's not asleep, but when the security light comes on again, Nicole's eyes struggle to focus on the beam that sits squarely on the ledge of the hatch above. Cramp attacks her leg muscles. She quietly re-packs the bag, desperately wants to stand up, to walk, run, get out of here.

Across the tarmac, the security guard is checking the doors to the stadium are locked. Nicole watches intently as he stops at the VIP entrance, barely ten metres away. He presses in a code, opens it and disappears inside. It's a chance, but if he's doing a check inside the building and hasn't locked the door behind him she might follow him in and not be seen. She copies the pattern his fingers made on the pad. Click. She's in.

There's a glass double door, then a kind of lobby area. The reception counter is in darkness. As the guard's footsteps head up the staircase, she runs like a cat, squeezes behind the counter and under the desk.

Don't breathe, don't move. Safe, but not safe. The sky outside is still dark. She's hung around here before in the early morning and there's always activity, cleaners and ground-staff coming in, later office workers. Think straight. There's no game tomorrow so the executive boxes will provide respite. No-one will be here until Saturday morning, two days away

Nicole's relieved as loud door slam tells her the guard has left the building. She makes her way upwards. Her neck is sweaty where her hair has been trapped inside her hood. At the end of the corridor she finds a storeroom door open. This time she can stretch her legs out, there's a stack of multipack water bottles and her pillow is a pile of cotton table cloths that smell like a hospital bed. Safe enough. For now.

CHAPTER 35

Conor had switched on the small kitchen TV on the black marble-effect worktop. There'd been a feature on the local news last night. Conor had been twisting spaghetti around his fork when Anita had said clearly: "We are serving notice on the club. If they don't re-pay the debt in three weeks, the courts will issue a notice of wind-up proceedings. We've been asking politely for years, we've been left with no choice. The impact on the city if the club doesn't pay what it owes is that we will have to make more cuts. Children's services will be decimated."

Uneaten, his spaghetti had slid back onto the plate, the empty metal fork had clinked on the enamel of his teeth. The TV item had cut to a talking head. The older Debbie had read a reaction statement on behalf of the Welders Supporters' Club.

"We will save our club. The Welders are the heart of this city, the club gives us pride; it generates jobs and investment. We need to take back control from people who have no business interfering with how we do things round here."

It was enough to put him off eating, full stop. Conor wondered who'd written that for her. It was uncharacteristically coherent and typically irritating with its Brexit-like high notes. The news anchor highlighted the online backlash and death threats Anita had received. The last shot of Anita was of her storming through the protestors outside the council reception, her arm protecting her face.

Then the news cut to Les, casting himself as the peacemaker.

"I propose a negotiated way forward. Let's sit round the table and sort this out. We should be thinking ahead, it's a critical time for the economy of the city. Stability is everything. The council should write the debt off, wipe the slate clean. Fresh thinking is what we need."

Conor had dropped his fork. Simplify and exaggerate, that was Les' way. And it was clever. Les' voters would approve. Who cares that it was Les who'd made the grand decision to re-build the stadium in the first place or that it was him who'd refused to tackle the debt. Was anyone interested that it was Les who'd chosen Anita to take the reins?

Conor picked up the plate and threw the rest of the food in the recycling. He'd already increased the bad debt provision. It was too much. The auditors wouldn't stomach it. The government might step in. The bank could withdraw their support. He couldn't grovel again, there would be no more overdraft facility. They'd extended their temporary borrowing with some major suppliers just to keep afloat.

Anita is right to make a connection between the debt and services, but it's too literal, the financial connection too indirect for an accountant's liking. Real people's jobs have gone: people like Jayne's sister, Becky, Jason, his social worker mate, Gary, a classroom assistant at his son's school, Geoff, the park warden. In fact, there was no longer a parks' department. It was all hidden.

Conor feels alone; stuck in the middle of the incendiary mix of Anita and Les –Anita the fire-starter, Les the bellows; different approach, similar result, he muses. The rest of the staff and the city are seeing the flames crackle. He can't afford it to catch, for a blaze to engulf them. He has to put it out.

*

Something new is required. Normally Conor's lexicon of shrugs, nods and intimations are more effective than words in giving the politicians the reassurance they crave. He doesn't tell them too much, looks concerned and confident, let's them add their own interpretation. Keep control, that's the point.

The staff need more. They like the mix of solidity and gentle cynicism, the grey mantle of the anti-hero that Conor dons, but – there's always a but – they are exhausted by the constant flux, the pressure of the council living at the edge of its means and on high alert for the latest in-coming storm. They need to know someone has their back, that he will fight their corner.

"I'll be in committee room 2," he tells Mrs Massey. "Debt review meeting."

His audit manager has swapped her zingy lime-edged glasses for an older, more austerity-style pair – she's watching his every move. The investment manager, Jason, has removed his ear buds. Loyal supporters though they are, they must be wondering how he copes with the unstoppable force that is Anita. Funny how the latest management theories speak so positively of disruptive thinking, he thinks. They don't have a clue about the crippling reality.

As if he still occupies the hot seat, into committee room 2 walks Les. He has no right to be here and, Conor thinks, it could anger the rest of the region, if it gets out that Les is still trying to run the show here.

"You need to retract the debt order, halt legal proceedings now," he says.

Conor stands quickly, walks towards the door, firmly pulls him aside. "The leader, the cabinet and the management team will be here in five minutes. I'm sorry Les, but you have to leave now. It's not appropriate."

Les snatches his jacket off as if he's staying. "Appropriate," he scoffs. "I've told Councillor Patel to stop. She's gone too far."

Conor is glad he wasn't party to that conversation.

"I'm serious. This is a business meeting. Anita will be here any moment. If you've come here for a fight, please do it somewhere else." Conor is surprised how strong his voice sounds. Les is out of line being here. And, actually, as he thinks back to the TV report, Les' so called "fresh thinking" really only benefited Croft and could make it worse for the council. "Anita was supposed to agree our budget, take the flack, not dish it out," he says under his breath.

Conor widens his stance, feeling a tightening in his chest. Les hasn't said this explicitly before. It confirms Conor's worst suspicions about Les and his reasons for choosing Anita. Political expediency is distasteful, but he supposes you don't run a city without sacrificing a few of your own along the way.

"Remember, Les, I warned you we would soon hit a tipping point. Anita has pushed us to the edge. We'll be struggling to pay the bin men's wages if we're not careful." Conor lowers his voice, leans in, getting a smack of Tabac after-shave. "I can hold off from issuing a section 114 notice for another month or two."

No finance director in his right mind would choose that option. It would be professional suicide. It's a technical way of saying the game's up, telling the city, the government and the country, we cannot pay our bills. And then there would be the personal shame, the failure, his inability to sort the problem would stay with him.

"The government will be all over us. Never mind the club debt, we'll be out of business, bankrupt."

"Don't cry wolf to me," Les snorts. "We're not having services taken out of our hands by this bloody government. I won't have it. The party won't have it."

And neither will I, thinks Conor. He can well imagine that Croft would lean on Les to put a stop to Anita; whatever works to avoid paying what he owes. But Les is playing politics with the budget. Having a go at him as if he hasn't been supporting him all these years, been part of his team. And what is Les? Suddenly a pawn in Croft's game? This rankles deeply.

"I manage the business, you manage the politics. Can't help you there."

Les purples. "We're supposed to be saving the club. Croft is livid. Mark my words, Anita won't be around much longer, but neither might you, son. You know who controls the group here."

"Subtle." Conor ladles on the sarcasm.

Speaking truth to power is something public servants talk about a lot, but if he's honest Conor hasn't done much of it. And there's the reason Les has threatened to sack him. Is it weakness? You can't have Scandinavian-style services and US levels of taxation is a maxim Conor repeats regularly – and they all nod and ignore it. But the truth-teller has never had any power. It's resign or be sacked.

"You have to leave now."

Les sees Councillor Ward arrive and turns to greet his friend, all smiles.

Sweating now, Conor checks his phone. There are two messages.

Director of children's services: Nicole Brand, child in our care, reported missing, leader and police involved.

Anita: Can't make meeting. Continue with legal action. Absolutely no cuts to children's services. Will call tonight.

It's the leader's job to turn up to critical meetings. How else does she show leadership? He tugs at his tie. This is completely crazy. She drops a bombshell on the city and the council, and then goes AWOL. He can't work like this.

Alone in the committee room he looks up at the light, hoping for clarity. Maybe threatening the section 114 wasn't such a good tactic? It's akin to being a whistleblower, which was bound to wind Les up and it also goes against Conor's own team ethos.

He believes they should be able to sort out their own problems. But where does that leave him?

Conor still wants to save the club, although now, if he can only do one thing, he wants to save the Welders from Croft. He's the one with the bottle of lighter fuel. Get rid of Croft and that would quash the flames. If if if. If Conor could prove Croft was acting illegally and if the police charged him with money laundering, fraud or intent to defraud, he'd be out of the picture.

A bankrupt club doesn't seem so bad at this point. If the club can't pay, it would have to appoint administrators. That would be good. They are often accountants, Conor can deal with them, a cool rationality would return.

At the same time, if he can't come up with any evidence against Croft, he's got to find a way of playing for time, turn down the heat, reduce the emotional and physical stakes.

It occurs to him that the first question the administrators will ask is: what measures have you taken to resolve the situation before court action? In reality, the closer he's looked at Croft the further away from him Conor has wanted to be. If Conor's right, Croft wouldn't want a public investigation now and neither does Conor. That could be useful. There's nothing for it. He has to see Croft in person. Today.

CHAPTER 36

Croft's office is more stylish than Conor imagined. The white-walled room has an empty, frosted-glass desk and low-level birch cabinets. On a pale grey, Scandinavian-style modern sofa there is an open copy of the *Financial Times*. It looks like a fashionable estate agents. Judging by the expensive-looking speaker, Croft is a man who likes his music. Irritated and, if he's honest, nervous, Conor wonders if all this is a front? On credit or paid for by the council?

He stands at a wide, chest-height window, angling his body half at the pitch, half at the door. Croft is bound to be making him wait deliberately. As he hums the fans' anthem, *We Know What We Are*, he realises that whilst he's spent many matches in the directors' box with Croft, they have barely spoken and only about the Welders. Conor takes a deep breath as the door opens.

"Should've known he'd be in the bar. Follow me." One of the office staff leads him away from the VIP area towards the club bar in the West Stand.

"I know my way from here, thanks." Conor feels better without the small talk.

The familiar double doors are open, but it's clear the bar is closed to the public. The lights aren't on, but the screens of the gambling machines flash intermittently. Conor looks round the bar at the signed photos, the red and black flags hanging limply from the ceiling. This is more like he'd imagined. His confidence grows.

Croft is on his own at a table, his head bent over a laptop. Wearing a short-sleeved, slim-fitting, checked shirt, his graying hair cropped close, Croft looks smarter than Conor remembers. A colleague or, Conor corrects himself, probably a henchman, is also there. He's in his forties, heavily built, wearing a red-trimmed, single stripe Fred Perry top and black braces. A stylish skinhead – maybe the boss insists on a dress code.

"Mr Croft." Conor doesn't smile, keeps his voice low and steady.

"I told you to talk to my solicitor." Croft barely lifts his head.

Arrogant sod, Conor thinks, determined not to react.

"I'm here at Councillor Underhill's request." It ought to at least get him a hearing.

"Begging in person?"

Conor hasn't physically hit anyone since he was ten years old, but he feels the temptation. "I came to see if we could help you," he says.

It's partly true. He has to be seen to be making contact with his debtor and he has a proposal of sorts, but it's a risk, and neither Les nor Anita knows he's here. An old northern soul tune that Conor recognises is pumping out of the speakers, "Better use your head" by Little Anthony and the Imperials. I'd better, he thinks.

Croft's eyes remain on the screen, he grunts throatily, "…I don't think so."

Conor has plenty to say about the £23 million that the club owes the public, but he swallows it temporarily, forcing himself to smile. "Councillor Patel thinks…"

"She's not a problem for me, Mr Walsh." Croft looks up at him.

Conor continues through gritted teeth. "The legal action is something we can both cope with, but an independent investigation will tie our hands. We'll both have to open our books to the police."

This also fails to get Croft's attention. The next song up is "Nothing But A Heartache."

"It's a headache you don't want... When you're trying to convince investors to buy into in a private equity fund."

Conor had wanted to hold that back, but he needs Croft to take him seriously. It works.

Croft bats down the lid of the laptop. "What is it you think you know?" The chairman's voice is mocking, his flinty eyes narrow in anger.

"Bringing investors in, it's all a matter of confidence."

And confidence is a game. Conor stands his ground, still and calm.

"What would you know about that? The council is a joke."

"The public purse is worth £1.9 billion in total, about £9,000 per head of population, not all ours, of course..."

Croft feigns disinterest, adopting a loose body posture, but Conor knows the number has caught the attention.

"...and I'm interested in investments that generate income. What do you think we do with our pension fund?"

It's possible that Croft might just be cocky enough to think the pension trustees would put money into a fund he fronts.

Croft points to the chair as an instruction to sit. "My question's the same. What do you want?"

Conor continues to stand, lifting himself up in his shoes, focusing on his own irritation rather than Croft's hard-man reputation.

"The simplest way for the negative press to go away is for you to pay something towards the debt. Take the wind out of the new leader's sails. Tell everyone Anita's got it wrong, you're already paying it back like any responsible lender."

Croft laughs, "You think I'm stupid?"

It isn't a bad plan, Conor thinks. If Croft pays off some, it would confirm that the debt is his and might establish a precedent. Croft is getting good advice and listening to it. Never mind, maybe there's something else here. He thinks fast, toes twitching.

"And/or you could pay the council something towards the other debts you owe; your contribution towards the health and safety officer; the building control fees; planning gain that was part of the original stadium deal. Demonstrating reasonable behaviour can have a value legally. It builds trust."

Croft calls round to his colleague, "Sweep mate, turn the music down a moment..." In the sudden silence, he asks the man, "Have we done the collection this week?"

There is the briefest of nods from Croft's man.

"I'll make a goodwill payment, one-off, ex gratia..." Croft voice sounds dismissive, with an edge of boredom. It doesn't fool Conor. Giving any money away will hurt.

"...Bring Mr Walsh three bricks. No, let's say four. We're supporting our city..."

Wait, he's giving me cash? He's giving us a bung? Conor tries not to react to the insult. He thinks I'm the stupid one. There are protocols for logging the money formally so as to be above suspicion, but there's nothing to be gained from throwing it back in Croft's callous face and taking the moral high-ground. Principles equal weakness to Croft and his ilk. And if he accepts the cash everyone – him, Les and Croft – are happy. Is being in hock to Croft any worse than being Les' personal financial advisor?

"...Make sure it goes on something useful, like paying the bin men's wages," Croft smirks.

Christ. That tells Conor that Les has phoned Croft since this morning's meeting. Thank god he didn't share his theory about Croft's operation with Les. Conor tries to understand the situation. Why did Les go blabbing straight to Croft? It's a betrayal, but why? It doesn't make sense.

"We'll send you a receipt," Conor says, ladling on the sarcasm.

Croft goes behind the bar to turn the music up. "Soul Time" by Shirley Ellis cranks up. Conor wanders over to the photos. An action shot of a player catches his eye, a number eleven heads the ball whilst three feet off the ground. The player's concentration is evident, the muscles in his neck are bulging, certain of a goal. Whatever Croft thinks, this is a noble sport.

In minutes Croft's man comes back with a supermarket carrier bag.

Thick elastic bands barely restrain the wads. If opened there is no chance of getting them back under control. Conor decides to drive straight home. The bricks are too big to be a £1,000. More like £5,000. Croft has just given him £25,000 and he acted like it was nothing. Most people in the city don't earn that much in a year.

The smell of the cash, red wine stains, old books and mould fills the car, forcing Conor to open the window. The notes are dirt magnets for grease, dust and the odd hair. It's as if Croft has given a homeless person a fiver. Croft has dismissed the whole city.

At his kitchen table he rips open one of the packets. Counting it out, it's clear the crumpled currency has lived many lives. Notes in this condition, folded and passed through grubby hands, should have been taken out of circulation by now. The last time he'd seen notes like this was in his early twenties when he worked as a cash-teller in Marsden's bookies.

Slowing his thoughts down, Conor realises that Croft could have just given him a big clue. This money hasn't come from the bank, it's come from the street. What is a football club doing with such large amounts of cash? The fact that there is so much cash on the premises doesn't prove money laundering, but evidently this cash is not clean. It isn't getting on a plane and going to a private beach in Anguilla in this state.

Spotless, that's what Selka said. Then he smiles, his teeth gleam under the kitchen lights, he enjoys the feel of the bite. He's had an idea, a good one. Times have changed, of course, but it has to be true that one place lots of cash turns up in is betting shops. And anywhere there's lots of cash, people can be tempted to do wrong. It's not the only way Croft could be washing the money, but it's a good place to start. And if it works, he gets the proof he needs to free the club from the parasite's grip. He finds an envelope and stashes two thousand pounds in his pocket. The rest he leaves wrapped in the carrier bag and puts it in an old sports bag amongst the junk in the cupboard under the stairs.

He picks up the phone to call Anita, then puts it down again.

CHAPTER 37

If Conor had a dog, he wouldn't be driving around town trying to find space to think. It would have to be an active dog – a silky retriever perhaps, bred for a purpose and a good companion. Yes, regular dog walks along a quiet tow-path would give him the time he needs to make sense of the aberrant world of Daniel Croft.

The traffic is slow enough along the Weston Road that he spots a pattern. A payday loan shop next to a take-away next to a charity shop next to a bookie's – and repeat. Sat at the lights it's possible to see a group of school kids in a chicken shack, eating nuggets from a carton and throwing chips at each other. Two of the teenagers pile noisily onto the street; one chases the other at speed across the road as the lights are changing.

Conor slams the brakes on and the trailing teenager misses the bonnet by inches. Shaking, he immediately pulls the car over and gets out.

"Are you alright?" he shouts.

"Paedo," the teenager shouts, disappearing down a side road.

He used to know this area. The first job he'd had at Marsden's bookies was around here and there's a familiar-looking newsagent a few doors up. Buying a bottle of water, Conor notes Marsden's is long gone, the shop front now sports the familiar purple branding of a bookmaker's chain. The clean bright lights draw him closer. There's still an hour to kill before Conor is due to meet Jayne at his grandad's nursing home. Here might be as good a place as any to take stock. I could even put a bet on for the old man while I'm here, he thinks, the morbid knowledge that it could be his grandad's last hitting him with momentary debilitating fear.

Do we become more or less like ourselves as we get older, Conor wonders? Pushing open the heavy door of the betting shop he could be 14 again, listening to the results being announced from Catterick or the Curragh, avoiding the regular who'd be digging the small blue biros into the shelf or stamping the leaky pens into the carpet. The bitterness of a losing streak barely contained.

Conor would hunch over the corner of a large table, his arm hiding the betting slip, filling it in like an exam. A teenager in a poor pensioner's world, Conor had studied hard to maintain the regular modest wins that he would present to his nan.

*

Inside the bookies the tables have gone and there are life-size cut outs of the top European football players, not one in a red and black shirt. Conor keeps his coat on to hide his suit. Not that anyone would say anything. No-one looks at anyone else here. All the attention is focused on the casino machines, not a traditional fruit machine in sight.

"Fixed odds betting terminals are the crack cocaine of the betting industry." That's what Anita had said at the licensing committee meeting. AKA B2s, the license allows you to bet up to £100 per spin every 20 seconds.

Anita had made a name for herself as a councillor early on with a campaign to restrict the clustering of betting shops at the city centre end of Weston Street. "All bet's off" had been spirited, but it had been over-ridden by Les in what had seemed at the time a defence of working class men's right to enjoy frittering their money away and central government's laissez-faire approach to licensing and planning policy.

"People need protecting from these blood suckers," she'd said.

We can look after ourselves, Conor had thought, although looking round at the pale, drawn faces Conor concedes Anita had a point. He isn't like most people here.

Older and wiser, he knows he's too clever for this crude game to catch him. Stepping up to the B2, Conor confidently opts for roulette. It's been a while, but he knows how fixed odds work. He's just reminding himself, that's all.

The clean bills from his wallet slide into the mouth of the machine almost magnetically. First he places three bets – £10 on red, £10 on black and £1 on zero. At worse he's going to lose £1. He wins £36. Click, in a second the computer asks him to bet again. He goes for £20, red and black, again minimising his losses. He wins £14 this time, click, plays again, but loses small then wins again. In less than two minutes Conor is wiped out of the cash in his wallet. He's still up – but only just.

A flash of adrenalin makes his eyes blur, he takes a few steps back and looks around. Take a deep breath and just walk out now, he tells himself. Then he feels in his jacket pocket, retrieves his bankcard. The B2 has him.

"Excuse me." A young woman in her purple polyester corporate shirt puts a hand across to wipe the machine with a sterile cloth.

"Can I get you a cup of tea?"

"No, no thanks." Conor wonders if she's seen his bank card.

"Do you want to set up an account? We can transfer your winnings directly to your bank."

The machine tells him he can get a printout of his earnings at the cashier's desk. There are legitimate receipts, minimal losses, almost no regulation and the machines bring in massive profits. If you know what you're doing, big if, you can minimise losses, probably no worse than the cost of doing any business.

Not everyone is happy. An older Asian man thumps the machine next to him and an alarm goes off. A wheezing security man appears and the man is told to cool off. Not barred though.

"I'll take the tea, if that's OK?" Conor perches on a stool watching the activity.

There are four hungry machines, two being patiently fed by young men wearing a non-descript jeans, jacket and trainers uniform. Unhurried and clearly regulars, they know what they are doing. The clever prosper and the weak become addicted, he thinks – or at least that's how he used to think.

As Conor watches them, the picture in front of him comes into focus. The young man nearest to him has a wad of dirty cash, just like Croft's money under the stairs at home. Hyper-alert now, he imagines the money like petrol passing through the machines. The process transforms the cash into fumes and then it's released into the atmosphere, like a cloud of cash, it's value travelling across the city, blown in a particular direction.

Could that be it? The terminals are how Croft launders his money? In the football club bar, where he'd met Croft not two hours earlier, were two of these monsters. Was that what Croft's skinhead was doing – feeding the machine? Now he thinks about it he's sure there was another machine in the Legends Bar at the Cemetery End? And one in the club lounge.

How would Croft get a license for so many? Who would know or care? Les immediately springs to mind. The staff in the bookies should file suspicious activity reports on peculiar transactions; he remembers that from years ago. It's possible they could be bending over backwards to support the club, but they certainly wouldn't be reporting anything if they worked for Croft, of course. No-one hears anything, no-one says – let alone does – anything.

That's how organisations work. It happens in the council, although the fear is not as acute or obvious as it must be in Croft's organisation. Conor's colleagues rarely question him. Or they might, but they don't do anything about it. Talking about what's wrong feels like action, but it's not. And the more people that see the problem, the fewer people think it's their job to take action. Well, except Anita that is.

Conor's been swimming head up through the city's polluted canals, avoiding the dead bodies and shopping trolleys. Anita has pushed him under, made him swallow the contaminated water, and he can't get rid of the putrid taste of Croft's sewer.

CHAPTER 38

On her way to Westmeade Anita takes a sharp left, deciding to check the city farm, just in case. It's a short detour, the park is deserted, the farm centre shut. The discovery of the body might initially have made the place a magnet for zombie-obsessed teens, but now, at 8am, even the early dog walkers are giving it a wide berth. A private security guard in a hi-vis jacket kicks his heels against a nearby tree, yellow police cordon tape still blows in the wind, now well and truly breached.

Remembering that first morning, Nicole staring at the lake being dredged, Anita stops. Teenagers are skilful at creating an invisible wall around them, one that at first looks impenetrable, but is vulnerable to bursts of emotion. Yet Nicole had contained herself in front of that watery grave. It must have crossed her mind that it could've been Ash. If the club had something to do with Ash's disappearance, it's possible that they were involved in bringing him here? Whilst the sight of the bone sticking out of the mud has stayed with Anita, how must it have been for Nicole; thinking that might be all that was left of her brother?

In Anita's bag is an inch-thick wodge of old council reports that should make an adequate mat. As she slumps down, her backside grinds the impossible choices contained in the pages into the sodden grass. Damp seeps through the reports. Seriously, they are good for nothing.

Tear ducts itch, her nose starts to run, thoughts spin inwards. She cares about Nicole too much, seeing in the girl a similar anger and determination to her own at that age. And although Anita knows that, just like every other adult, she has disappointed Nicole, she won't, can't, let it end like that.

Anita lets her head roll back onto the morning dew, looking up at a blurred palette of greys. She hasn't slept properly in days. Her decision-making has been poor. Has she helped the situation at all? Tears halt in the corner of her eye. She'd needed a moment to gather her thoughts, but she's not helping Nicole here.

Taking her time, legs wobbling as she gets to her feet, she refocuses. A young man was murdered and dumped in this lake. Holding on to the shock is important, the sadness, too, but now getting angry is vital. We have to be able to feel something, to demand answers, to do something or otherwise what is there, she thinks? Only debilitating helplessness, a resigned acceptance that the people responsible for this can't be stopped.

The security guard propping up the tree must have been watching her. "It's a tragedy," she says, looking towards the water.

He nods to the ghostly neighbours.

"Yes, they are sending the boy on his way now. All done here."

Anita shudders. They've identified the body. Oh god, she thinks. The police will make an announcement. Nicole won't hear it. Or she will and she'll be alone.

*

"80% of missing young people aged 15 to 19 come home or make their whereabouts known within 24 hours," DI Jones tells Anita. She's on the phone, sitting in the car outside Westmeade.

"So 20% don't. We have to look now."

"We've already been trying to make contact with Nicole."

"Because?"

"That's a matter we need to talk to Nicole about. We've had the preliminary autopsy back."

That's it then. They've confirmed its Ash's body and they have to tell Nicole first. There are many reasons Nicole might've run off, but the strongest might be that she thought the police wanted to question her. The girl is about to find out that the body is her brother. Anita wants to reach out to her, but they parted badly. Their argument is on a loud loop in Anita's head, yet for Nicole it would be well down the list.

"The missing persons team know what they're doing."

Yeah right. An echo of Nicole's voice rings loud in her ear.

"There's an officer on their way down to Westmeade and I've spoken to Nicole's social worker."

"Well I'm here already and she's not."

"You sound upset," he says on the other end of the line.

"I am. And I'm beyond pretending that everything's alright. I want her found."

She fails to muster the voice control to sound authoritative and struggles to lock the car; the bunch of keys is an unsolvable Rubik's cube.

"That's our job," DI Jones says.

"No, it's all of our jobs."

The corporate language means something real.

"Understood." He slows his speech, conciliatory, "but we'll do the leg work."

Jones is a good officer, but the situation has been escalated and he's resorting to the "leave it in our capable hands" approach.

"No," she says calmly and confidently, "now's the time to take collective responsibility. We need to trust in a joint approach. In a crisis, everyone needs to play their part."

Individual thinking won't work. Anita needs to show leadership and influence others to navigate a safe passage home for Nicole.

"And we'll mobilise a community search." Anita stands her ground.

Four of the Westmeade residents, girls in night club-length skirts and ankle boots, click down the tiled path on their way to school. There's a "For sale" sign lashed to the Georgian railings. The bloody estates department! Is that Conor trying to force her hand, she wonders, or just an over-zealous property officer with an income generation target. Anita yanks the T-board sign until the wooden post snaps in two.

"Nutter." One of the girls looks across half impressed.

"Sorry about the "For sale" sign," she says. "I didn't approve that."

Pete looks as though he's about to say something caustic, then changes his mind. Anita hasn't seen this before, his eyes narrow searching her face for a lie.

"Look, I'm not behind it. It isn't policy. The council officer who put the sign up is probably a Welders fan," she continues sarcastically.

His voice is cold. "This is traumatising for all of us, especially the girls."

Lovely Pete is nowhere to be seen. They are his surrogate daughters and he has two children of his own to support, so of course he's worried.

"That's why I said what I did about the club," Anita says. "That's why I had to force the issue. It's an impossible situation. You know that."

He does know. He just doesn't like it. Professionally there's nothing in it for him to play nice when his service is being cut, his home sold off. He didn't choose it, didn't vote for it.

"When I agreed to stand as leader, I had no idea how bad it was. But I'm not hiding from it. I'm here and I'm not going to carry on talking to myself. I came to help find Nicole; I'm desperate to find her, to know she's safe. If you don't want me here just say."

"I don't really." His sneer cuts into Anita. They had slept together, for Christ's sake, doesn't that count for anything? She stands swaying, unsure whether to make for the door.

"Nicole's never been missing this long before. She thinks you led her on. You didn't just reject the club, you rejected her."

Anita crumples inside, but holds her body steady.

"Look, I know a lot of people in this city. I've been organising communities all my adult life and I'm the leader. That's got to be useful for something."

He nods, stretching out a stiff neck.

✻

The first call Anita makes is to Carol, an overstretched school administrator at Nicole's school. They'd met on a campaign to save maternity services at the local hospital. "And by the way, I'm right behind you on the football club," she says. "Don't keep bailing them out. It's immoral."

Next is Toni, one of her old muckers, a sports development officer. "Actually, I remember Nicole, pretty talented player," she says. "Text me her photo and I'll check with the ladies' football league. Teams know other teams; lots of women will have played against Nicole. And…" Toni wants her say on the Welders, "… the fans could run that club better than Croft."

"You or I could." Anita hangs up. That's a thought, but there's no time to let it percolate.

The tenants' association is a resilient, well-organised group, happy to put the word out. Zoe from the surprisingly well-networked LGBT group is a Welders fan: "I'm not saying you've got it completely wrong about the club, but don't destroy it, fix it."

It's the sort of thing Anita would normally say herself. Colin, who runs the disability alliance, ran as an opposition councillor in her ward, but they sort of get on: "Men's football is the richest sport going, it gets all the attention. What about wheelchair sports or women's football even? How much money have you put into that?"

It's a good question. Vic from the Ward Partnership says, "We could bring loads of young people into that stadium, do something different, creative."

Suresh from the taxi drivers' association asks, "Why doesn't our hockey club get that kind of support?" The police have already asked them to keep a lookout.

Auntie Pinkie will see if she can bring the different Asian community leaders together. That's a significant task given the diversity, but they will give Pinkie a level of respect that Anita won't enjoy. And with the Muslim community reps, it will save Anita from going over old ground about planning permission for a new mosque.

The phone burns her ear; some of it is good to hear, like balm on the sore of hate and vitriol. These aren't people who make it into the news, but they are ordinary working people who see helping as a natural impulse. She sweeps her hair behind her ear.

"I hate this waiting…" Pete gives nothing away.

"We need to find Wormy."

Anita doesn't know his real name but Pete nods. Of course, he would know anyone who's important to Nicole.

"And the women from the supporters' club, the Debbies. Have you come across them? Nicole talked to them a few weeks back when we were canvassing."

Her throat dries, Anita stops and looks at Pete. Resting his forehead in his hand, shielding his eyes, he blows out a long breath.

"It's my fault." Pete says. "I was in a meeting, had my door shut. Didn't see her leave."

"No, it's mine." Her eyes are glued to the floor. Anita's fear is that although Nicole clearly left of her own accord, now she can't come back.

"Could someone have taken her?" She hadn't meant to say that out loud.

Pete looks up, staring intently at Anita. "No, I mean, it's unlikely. She's fit and fairly strong, knows not to get herself in stupid situations."

"She was angry with me and she's angry with the club. With Croft."

"That was the first place I told Jonesy to look for her."

CHAPTER 39

Conor leaves the betting shop and heads directly to Oakhaven Care Home. The grass has been cut and the leaves of the evergreen shrubs are softened by the drizzle. Conor is pleased to see that the metal handrail has been freshly re-painted, like a watercolour wash; the puddles beneath it have a muddy green hue. The wheelchair ramp still needs replacing though.

Best not explain what's been happening at the club, Conor thinks. If he was this ill, he wouldn't want to hear it. Reading the papers is bad enough. Grandad endures the daily disappointments of a world he struggles to recognise, but the indignities of illness – needing to be lifted from the bed to his chair, not being able to keep his dinner down – those are a different order of suffering.

It's part truth, part excuse. Conor fishes a hankie from his pocket, gives his nose a fierce blow. His sombre mood is broken by the sight of Jayne waiting in the reception area with a bunch of roses.

"For me?"

"You're late," she smiles.

The duty manager catches them at the top of the corridor. They will need to discuss an end of life care plan.

Conor tucks in his top lip. "Let's see how much life there is left in the old dog first."

"Excuse him," Jayne says playfully. "He thinks that passes for having a sense of humour."

He makes his way down the corridor, leaving Jayne to gather the detail. At the end of the corridor, his grandad's new room is next to an emergency exit door where the ambulances pull up to take residents on their final journey. Jayne asks one of the care workers for a vase. Grandad always planted roses in the small garden at the back of their council house. Nan loved the fruity fragrance of the pink-orange tea rose.

The deterioration in the old man's face is painful to see.

Grandad pre-empts the usual pleasantries. "As well as can be expected under the circumstances."

It's a masterclass in self-restraint. It's only 6.30pm, but Grandad is already in his cotton tartan pyjamas, ready for bed, dinner finished an hour ago.

"Want us to see if we can get you a better room? I hear they have Sky Sports and a minibar in the east wing."

Grandad's old room on the first floor had been compact, but it had a nice view of the trees, a comfy chair with soft wooden arms and an old gent next door to talk to. This room is sparse, the bed more like hospital than home.

"This'll do fine. Nothing a lick of paint won't sort out."

Conor shrugs. "It's an outsourced maintenance contract. We haven't got the resources anymore for one-off works…"

For years they'd had a running disagreement on the best way to run public services. Grandad preferred in-house, Conor taking a pragmatic approach, whoever could provide it cheaper. What they had agreed on was what's important in public life: transparent local democracy, a fair day's work for a fair day's pay, affordable housing for those who needed it. All this was still true, but as Conor had tried to explain before, "…it's austerity."

Grandad looks at the muted TV.

"No, son," he says wearily, "it's a choice. Privatising services, making cuts, it's shameful."

Best not to talk about politics, Conor decides.

"Good result in the derby match. Prentice holding it together at the back. That young lad, Obi-Jones, has really found his feet. Six goals in eight games, looking like a good buy."

Jayne places the flowers on the low window ledge.

"First politics, now football, I think he's trying to kill me off. Thanks love."

His grandad's hands make a shaky steeple, resting on a fragile frame. His refusal to talk is unusual.

"Come on, Grandad, you're a Welder 'til you die."

"I am dying, son."

There's no edge of humour to catch hold of.

"Course you're not…" Conor tries to make light.

"Didn't we talk about scattering your ashes on the pitch?"

"No, son. I've been thinking. I want to be with Mary. I lived for that club while your nan was alive, but you don't expect your wife to go first, do you? If I had my time again, I'd spend more of it with Mary."

Conor puts a hand on the quilt, lightly patting the thin leg underneath. For the last few years the crowds and the physical effort of going to a match have been too much. Grandad looks at the photo of his wife on the bedside table. Mary is the same ruddy, Dorset woman Conor loved, too.

"All those matches, all those years, all that time I could've spent with my darling girl. The club's an idea, it's not real."

The old man turns his head to the window.

"I'm sorry…" Conor stops. Did he really hear him say that? All his life, all their lives, it's always been the club.

It's too hot in here. The heating bill must be sky high.

He doesn't know how to respond to Grandad.

"It's nothing, son. It's two hours on a Saturday afternoon."

"Don't say that…" Conor whispers, afraid his voice will break.

"No, son, I've been a widower too many years. I see things differently. I see them for what they are. Son, you've got a lovely wife and a good job. You're a public servant."

"I got that from you…," Conor says, hoping to distract his grandad with reminders of his days at the highways department – filling potholes, maintaining the verges, taking care of the drainage – but he struggles to say the words. They sound too small, not nearly enough.

"…It's important work." Conor shuffles his chair forward until it touches the bed.

Grandad's breathing is so shallow it's hard to believe that the air will reach his lungs.

"Get your priorities right, Conor. All that matters is what you leave behind."

Conor struggles to speak.

"Life's not a gamble lad, it's a choice."

Grandad's eyes shut. Tears prick.

Jayne puts the cups of tea down and hugs Conor tight. "He's asleep, he's not…" Her face is wet, drenched in sadness.

At the end of life there is relief – the relief from suffering, but also the comfort of simplicity, the mess of competing priorities falls away. The focus is on what's important, what's real. Conor sucks in a sharp breath, recognising the clarity with which his grandad now sees the world. His old man is released from doubt.

"Shall I drive," Jayne says.

"No," Conor snaps, snatching the key fob out of his jacket.

In the empty car park his Canyon Grey VW Touareg is an oversized box, an expensive slab of nothing. Body taut, he crunches the gear stick into reverse. The car lurches backwards too fast. Shit. He sits there, unable to move. Grandad can't have really meant it. The club was just an idea? All those years? All those matches? They went to the games together. Him and grandad. That was real. That was where he'd seen his grandad laugh and joke and be serious, he was a respected man. That was where…

Conor's throat contracts... that was where he'd seen his grandad cry. That Cup Final day. Not even at Mary's funeral would Grandad let himself show his real feelings.

Forgetting that the car is still in reverse, he stamps his foot on the accelerator not the brake. The car flies rearwards, smacking into a low concrete bollard. Fuck. Conor thrusts open the door, but doesn't get out.

"Love..." Jayne puts a hand on his shaking leg.

His reply is barely a whisper.

"How can he say it was nothing?"

CHAPTER 40

The fuzzy heat of Pete's office gives Anita a headache.

"I'm going to have a drive around. Call me if..."

Pete nods. They are united in the search for Nicole, but that's all. From Westmeade it's an easy switchback through her ward to St Peters, not far from the stadium. The lights of the sari shops shine eerily on the white mannequins. The fragrant smell of the Shahi Spice takeaway, run by Auntie Pinkie's second cousin, would normally lift her mood and remind her she is among friends, but she has no appetite.

The physical darkness of the stadium and its neighbour, the cemetery, make a random sighting impossible. The wall and the barbed wire remind her of the prison and Odds. In the terraced street nearest to the far stand, there are plenty of lights on, but mostly the curtains are closed. It's a long shot. Anita pulls over, gets out and approaches a front door. If Nicole had made for the stadium last night, someone might have seen her walking this route. The police haven't done a door-to-door yet, so she makes an impromptu start. Anita adopts her canvassing persona: smile, stay calm, try not to look like a Jehovah's Witness.

"Sorry to disturb you..." Families are watching telly, getting kids ready for bed.

"Have you seen this teenager?"

The photo of Nicole on her phone is almost of another girl, toothy, eyebrows raised, hair out of her face. An old school photo, picked to show her features.

"Sorry no."

"If you see anything, the local police number is on the back."

"Sorry to disturb..."

"No thanks."

At the next house a curtain twitches. She is observed and the doors aren't open.

"This teenager's gone missing. Her name's Nicole Brand. She was last seen in the area... We're helping the police with their enquiries..."

She's too stilted, needs answers too badly.

"Have you got proof of identity?"

Proof of who I am? Anita looks for her driving licence obediently, but he's closing the door already.

"Sorry love, no, not seen anything."

At the next door the woman asks, "Are you alright? What's wrong?"

Anita recognises she's sounding more desperate and blurts, "I have to find her. I have to find my daughter."

She shocks herself with this, feels sick, unconfidently maternal. No-one bats an eye that an Asian woman is looking for a white daughter, all they see is raw emotion. And the response is, that people sound sorrier, look scared for her, imagining themselves in the same situation. Anita doesn't know how to roll it back. If she feels like this now, where does she go next?

*

Back in the car she's about to turn left at the roundabout, thinking about the other kids that go missing. Does the council get involved? Then slam, an almighty thud shunts the car. She's thrown forward, jolted up and, as the air bag inflates, is pummelled back against the seat. Behind she hears a vehicle reversing. The weight of her head on top of her neck is like a concrete block balancing on top of pipe cleaners. Anita rolls her eyes up to see the rear mirror.

There are two men in a van, they could almost be laughing. Trying to focus on their faces, she realises at the last minute that they are coming at her again. Thwack. This time the airbag protects her against the impact, but her neck is half-strangled by the safety belt. In the wing mirror she sees one of the men get out and start walking towards her car. Christ, they are going to kill me. She gasps for air, trying to make her hand move to press down on the central locking button.

"What you doing, man?"

Anita can't see who is speaking.

"Fuck off back where you came from."

There's a mess of shouting. Horns blow. She sees cars backed up behind them; two taxi drivers get out and walk towards the van. The van driver yells something, his mate jumps back in, bumps up across the grass reservation and screeches off. Hit and run. Two private hire drivers, young Pakistani men, have saved her. With her relief, blood starts to flow to her brain, to her fingers. One taxi driver puts his head in view of the windscreen.

"Aunty, aunty, you alright? I saw them. Bad people. The police are coming."

His concern makes her cry.

*

Life slows down while she waits for an X-ray in the corridor. Lying prone on a trolley is preferable to the bumpy ambulance ride here.

Anita gags on the bile in her throat, but she forces it back down, not wanting the pain that the retching movement will cause. She keeps her eyes shut, looking up at the glaring strip light hurts. Her nephew, Vikesh, arrives with another cousin, Bali, and Auntie Pinkie, looking ashen.

"Daughter, daughter," Pinkie pats her hand.

"I'm OK, don't worry."

"The police should be giving you protection, this is the third incident." Pinkie says this pointedly at the PC standing a few metres away from the trolley.

Vik shuffles a plastic chair next to the bed.

Anita asks, "Can you call Pete at Westmeade for me? I said I'd go back."

Vik nods taking the phone down the corridor. Maybe Pete'll come?

As the pain killers take effect, thoughts form and dissolve, scenarios swirl. The men who could've killed her float away. She's weightless. Nicole is in the ether, maybe she doesn't want to come back, but she has to want to. Nicole would come back for her mother. Could I be her mother, Anita wonders? It's a ridiculous thought. Just a thought that she lets go, unable to focus on anything in her drowsy state. Could Nicole fight for something other than Ash? For her own future?

Hours pass. She wakes wanting to go home. There is soft tissue damage, ringing in her ears, moving her head is difficult and the muscle spasm in her neck is excruciating. Cousin Bali negotiates a police escort to his place. DI Jones organises security. Pete sends a message to say he'll come to see her in the morning. And if she's up to it, the police will come in the morning to take a statement. There's no news about Nicole.

What Anita wants more than anything is to keep this attack on her quiet. It cannot become news, more news about her. It won't be cast as a story about a politician attacked for standing up for what she believes is right. it'll be something for the fans to cheer: uppity immigrant woman gets what she deserves.

It's hard to know what to think right now. She used to believe that the economic, social and environmental situation in their city and the country in general... well, in the world really...

might have to get worse before it gets better; before people care enough to make lasting, meaningful change. She knows that change hurts and, although up until now it hasn't been her that is hurting, she also knew that it would be her turn soon enough. And here it is, physical and emotional pain. Her body cramped, her heart assaulted by the trauma.

She ought to be able to stand it, she thinks. Seeing her own self-pity as an ugly sore, she shamefully tries to pull her cardigan over it. She looks at Auntie Pinkie's front door; the bright, white net curtains are a sign of safety. I'm 42. She squeezes the packet of painkillers in her pocket. Things are changing. This is the cost – to date.

CHAPTER 41

It's 10pm. Conor packs the club accounts and files that cover the office floor into a white plastic tub. It won't be easy, but the Welders cannot be left in Croft's hands. If the club is taken down in the process, so be it.

He finds a rubber thimble at the back of his desk draw. Old technology. No waxy, new plastic notes here. The dirty notes are an artefact of a parallel cash world. Their dog ears are weary, the metallic stitches frayed, easily split at the seams. The raised print of the "Bank of England" lettering, which should feel like Braille, is smooth and the bills have been creased so often they are as fragile as ancient parchment. In the legitimate world, these notes would've been withdrawn.

The act of marking the notes and recording the serial numbers is therapeutic. It reminds him of more simple times, counting the cash at the end of a long Saturday afternoon working in the bookies. His thoughts have been veering from the deep pointlessness of doing anything at all to a crazy stream of consciousness action list. To-do notes cover every inch of the inside in his brain.

The simple act of writing the numbers one after another, marking the notes, forces him to slow down. The system Conor has settled on is an overelaborate mix of colour-coded neon highlighter pens and the first three letters of the names of his favourite football players. He will be able to identify them anywhere. JA66 915043 SMI lime green. Archie Smith right back 1998 – 2004.

He knows his plan might be considered ridiculous, that it could be dangerous even, but he believes it's the only possible way to gather the evidence required for Croft to be arrested for money laundering. Follow the money, that's all there is to it. The Queen's face on the notes taunts him.

The first few steps are easy enough. He photographs Croft's money on his desk, writes out an official finance department receipt for the money from Croft and puts it in the post tray for delivery to the club. Then he makes a written declaration of intent, a statement of what he's going to do.

It would have been good if he'd got someone to witness his signature on the document. Another accountant maybe? Someone from his professional body? No. He's missed that window. It's too late. He's lost count of the times he could have asked for help and chose not to. It wasn't pride that stopped him from asking, it was the shame of admitting he'd got himself in this mess in the first place. You have to make yourself vulnerable to be a good leader, they say. Which is ridiculous. That wouldn't work with Les, never mind Croft.

Motivated by the thought of Croft in the dock, but also by the image of his grandad, eyes closing, life and love for the Welders ebbing away from him, Conor ploughs on. The pile of marked notes grows painfully slowly.

He imagines the plan will play out like this. An undercover cop, late twenties, dressed in trainers and a hoodie, uses the marked money to buy some drugs, a load of weed to smoke with friends. The cop records the deal and keeps the dope seller under surveillance. The takings are dutifully delivered to the garages, much as Paul Oddsman had described to Anita.

The money is transported to the club. Conor isn't worried about whether or not the apprentices are involved, the important thing is that the marked notes are fed into the B2 betting terminals in the club bar. DI Jones arranges to raid the club, they open the machines and there it is, neatly numbered. H37 145569 DAV pink. Kevin Davies – prolific striker in the 1980s.

The police pull Croft's financials, they've followed the money and exposed the scam. The quicker they can put a significant number of notes into the local economy, Conor thinks, the quicker they'll show up at the football ground. Any drugs purchased will be disposed of, taken out of the system.

Of course, the main issue with the scheme is that there isn't an undercover cop. The police aren't involved. Could Conor buy the drugs himself? Would that be so crazy? It's completely out of character, but he can tolerate greater levels of risk than most people; he's trained for it. Like a nervy high jumper going for a personal best, the bar is well above his head. His stomach contracts, the ends of his fingers twitch.

"Do what you can son," Grandad used to say. What Conor can do is take action, take matters into his own hands, take his dying grandad's words and make something happen. Good people have to make things happen. Conor clings to that. The police haven't got the cash, he has. And he doesn't want to risk Croft getting off on a technicality if the lawyers accuse the police of entrapment.

Conor desperately wants the police to have everything under control, wishes that they were on their way to arrest Croft this very moment. Then he could stand down. He calls DI Jones.

"Is this urgent?" Jones isn't happy at being disturbed so late.

"Yes! How's the investigation into Croft's money laundering going?"

"That's not critical right this minute. When there's something significant that I can share, I'll definitely call you."

"But you are formally investigating it?" Conor drops the highlighter pen, taps his fingers incessantly on the desk.

"I can't tell you..." Jones says flatly.

Conor interprets the response as a no. "Why not?" he asks.

Is someone in the police protecting Croft? Way back, when Croft made an application for a super-casino, there had been a suggestion that Croft played golf with the chief constable. A former leader of the council, Davina Clarke had supported the application. He's always trusted Jones in the past, but Croft has bought influence before.

"I can't tell you."

"What if I could provide you with evidence?" Conor says.

The financial future of the city rests on it. They must prove that the council has been the subject of serious fraud.

"What evidence?" Jones' irritated tone now has a hard edge.

"I need to know what standards of proof you're working to. What will definitely nail Croft? Would physical, traceable notes that have been used in criminal activity do it?"

"Tell me what's going on, Conor. Evidence is our job."

Conor wants to yell down the phone, but you aren't doing anything, are you?

"Police regularly rely on council officers for information to support their cases," he says.

"That's true, but how come I get the feeling you are about to do something stupid..."

The plain magnolia walls of the office start to spin. Stupid? Jones has already decided that he's being stupid? He's thought this through. What does Jones know about private equity or the impact of a collapse in public finances? Conor decides not to share the details of the plan.

"I'm only doing what's absolutely necessary..." he says, wishing he'd talked it through with Jayne. But she'd have picked the wax out of his ears, made him listen properly to his own words. She'd have told him to stop, would say it was arrogance, thinking he could do it all alone.

DI Jones re-iterates, "You stick to your job, Conor, let us do ours."

The risks make him so uncomfortable his feet have run a marathon under the table. Drug-buying is illegal and the business of drugs is dangerous. Croft's people are known to be violent. There's a risk that the money won't end up at the club; that Odds' information is out of date and when DI Jones turns up they'll find nothing. Conor decides he could live with the potential embarrassment.

Waiting isn't an option. If he chooses to do nothing, it all continues. Croft screws the city.

"You're not listening to a word I'm saying, are you." Jones sounds exasperated.

Conor doesn't care, he's well past that.

"I'll be in touch shortly." Conor hangs up.

As the clock in St Peter's church sounds midnight, he stands at his office window staring into the darkness. All the buildings have blurred into one sombre mass. His reflection is a blank avatar, he feels hollow, an empty soul. Will another solution come? Something that will save him from himself? Slowly he returns to his desk. Nothing comes, it's this or nothing. Conor marks his last £20 note. WM18 756091 ASH Black. Ashley Brand. In Anita's book that would be another reason to take action against Croft. He takes it as a sign.

Life's not a gamble, his grandad had said, it's a choice. He knows what he has to do, but he's on his own with this one.

CHAPTER 42

Where do you buy drugs these days, Conor wonders? It was never his thing, even at college. In those days he was more interested in finding somewhere you could drink after 10.30pm. But you always knew someone who knew someone. That is probably still the same, but his network these days is too small and he's too old, too straight. What will he say? He realises that people in the city inhabit completely different parallel worlds and speak different languages. What are drugs even called these days? If you believe everything you see on TV you just walk out of the front door and some hoodie or other comes along and virtually forces it on you.

He wishes time would speed up. That it would be over. Shaking numbness from his hand, Conor notices the dark dent in his forefinger. The last time he'd held a pen for so long must've been his final accountancy exam. The essay in strategic financial management won him the Arthur Collins Memorial Medal. Jesus, the past isn't a different land, it's a burnt-out star, shedding no light on new solar systems.

It's almost 2am. Resisting the urge to turn his work computer on, Conor searches the Internet on his phone: "How to buy drugs." Amongst the hits for prescription drugs and the dark web, there's a Twitter trail to a Neighbourhood Watch blog where residents report suspected drug dealing. Conor finds a link to a small area, no more than three streets on the Highlands estate, Croft territory, and only ten minutes' drive away.

Worrying that he hasn't marked enough notes and that he might be driving around for hours, Conor heads down the narrow stairs and out of the back exit to the silent building. The situation requires bold action, he tells himself. He feels as prepared as he'll ever be and yet completely unprepared.

In the car, he firmly grips the steering wheel. His fingers smell of the dying bank notes. Time seems to slow. He talks to himself under his breath.

"Ought to have brought a coffee for a stakeout."

The terraced streets are hushed, parked cars line the roads. After doing a slow circuit of the area, he finds the spot from the Neighbourhood Watch video, in view of the junction and the two roads named on the website. The cold keeps him awake. Running the engine would attract attention.

Twenty minutes pass, nothing. Then an old black Mercedes crawls up and stops, two young men occupy the front seats. It could be an unmarked taxi? Out of the shadows comes a short, barrel-shaped man. Under his puffer coat he wears a hood up hiding his face. Conor spots what could be a potential buyer approach the front passenger side of the car. The electric windows whir slowly down. It looks like he's holding out a cigarette; possibly asking for a light, but he rests his free hand on the window frame. There's the merest sense that cash is being exchanged. Like a sprung trap, a fist closes around a packet that disappears instantly. Deal done. That's it.

The old Mercedes pulls away. Conor jumps out of the car, following the buyer around the corner and half-way up the next street.

"Excuse me mate. Errr... Can you help me?"

The young man runs off. Fifteen minutes later, the same hand-off happens with a middle-aged woman.

"Back off," she shouts as he approaches her. "I'll spray yer."

The next young man he follows struggles to get his keys out of his pocket and into his front door, desperate to partake of the completed deal...

"Piss off."

Conor hopes he looks rough enough after the last few days to pass.

"Help me son, I've got cash," Conor says, pulling a wad out of his coat, enough to get his attention.

"Look… I haven't done this for a while. My supplier's got a drought on. I'm in a bad way."

"Yeah, you look it. You itching?" The man is still suspicious, his eyes furtive, checking the scene.

A round face with black, pinpoint irises looks out from the hood at the cash in Conor's hand.

"Can't help you, mate."

"I'm not police, I swear…"

"You can't be Five-0 dressed like that."

It takes a moment for Conor to get the reference, *Hawaii Five-O*. The young man's eyes return to Conor's cash, now in full view.

"You need a number; you need to be trusted…"

"Can you give me a number?"

"It'll cost you."

Of course, you buy trust in this game. Conor pulls out a wedge of cash and offers £100. He can see from the hoodie's face that he thinks Conor is acting weird.

"You wanna be careful showing big cash money round here. Get yourself done for less than that."

Conor tries to stay calm. He's right, but the cash will all be recycled into the system. The buyer brings the dealer's contact up on his mobile.

"How much is it nowadays?"

Nowadays? That makes Conor sound like a pensioner.

"I thought you said you had a dealer?"

When in doubt, say nothing. It doesn't take long for the guy to move on.

"Brown or white?"

Conor hides his ignorance with what he hopes looks like absolute desperation.

"White." Must be cocaine.

"£10 a point, £240 a third."

Conor realises how cheap the drugs are. He'll never shift the cash at this rate.

"Will they sell more?"

The young man looks at Conor, detached somehow, as if the whole conversation is insane. Toby does that sometimes, it's infuriating. Conor takes a risk, pulls out more money in the hope that he'll get access to someone higher up the chain.

"You know it's all crack round here. Not planning to off yourself?"

This time Conor sticks with a shake of the head. The less he says the better.

"Alright. Another £100. Say Toenail sent you." Numbers exchanged, the man takes a snapshot of Conor, snatches the money from his hand and slams the door in his face. Who would willingly call themselves Toenail? It's unnerving. Conor's urge is to retreat, drive home, give himself the space to think, but that's exactly what he can't afford to do – let the doubt in.

His mind gets hooked on the idea of sending a message to the dealers. Better than ringing, far too easy to mess that up.

Got number from Toenail. 18 Keeley Street. Need gramme of white.

Is that right? There's no time to mess about with small quantities, but he can see that the dealers wouldn't want punters setting themselves up on corners. It would be harder to manage the supply.

Using his own mobile was stupid. Conor's throat is contracting, pencil thin. He waits for what seems a lifetime. The radio is tuned to a local phone-in show. A fan is moaning about Anita: "What does she know about football? Nothing! She hasn't grown up with football, has she? It isn't her culture, it's ours. The council should piss off."

It's all passion and no pragmatism. Virtue shines out of the club's arse.

"These people can't see the reality in front of them, can't see the bigger picture."

Irony pricks at Conor's eyeballs as he realises he could be describing himself. Well… him in relation to the club. The argument about whether or not they should've done a deal with the club in the first place, that's fair enough, but it was legitimate, Public/private partnerships were all the rage under the previous government. Les loved them. Conor could see PFI blowing up long-term and had limited their exposure, yet he hadn't foreseen the lethal smog at the club.

Once you're in, you're in. They can't walk away now. Anita is right.

"I mean…" he breathes in acknowledgement, "yes, Anita is right."

The phone buzzes.

£1k – Addison Street corner.

CHAPTER 43

Swinging the car around, Conor puts his foot down to get back to the Highlands estate. There's no meet-up time. Is he expected just to wait? Only 30 minutes have passed since he clocked the first deal. Is that brisk business or a slow night? One of Conor's investment rules is that if a deal looks too good to be true, it probably is. The trouble is he doesn't know if this is an investment or whether it's good, bad or a trap. Steer clear, he'd normally tell himself. A spike of adrenalin rushes through him. He pictures Jayne asleep in bed, Toby home for a visit, what if they were somehow dragged into this? Maybe it feels too easy precisely because it is too easy.

Is this happening all over town, 20 minutes' drive from his own house, all over the country? Trying to calm his nerves, Conor tells himself that if he doesn't like the look of it he'll sit tight, wait until they've gone, try something else. But what exactly? The car parking spot he had is now taken and Conor finds he has to park closer to the main road. That's OK, but he's on foot and it's beginning to rain. Thanks to the council's alley-gating scheme there are few shadowy spots to shelter in. The best he manages is to lurk behind a rancid-smelling wheelie bin in the doorway to a vacant shop unit. Rain seeps into his toes. They are taking too long. He stares at his phone, trying to hide the light from view, and checks his emails to avoid doubt taking hold.

There's a message from Selka. He logs on to the forum. Could he be further from a private equity deal in the Caribbean?

S: Plenty of froth around Croft's private equity fund.

C: Who?

S: US$5k gets you detail.

The price is an exploitation that Croft himself would be proud of. The club commonly adds surcharges for cup games and, like the rest of the fans, he groans and stumps up. A Mercedes pulls onto the street. Conor assumes it's the same car. He'll reply later, now's not the time to move.

An hour passes, he starts to dwell, the message taunts him. Who is investing alongside Croft? The private equity fund is legal, but if it's like-minded companies, it could be someone who has made their money in the arms trade, sub-prime mortgages or debt packages. That helps politically, increasing the pressure, the moral repugnance if Croft is in toxic company. It'll force the FA to review Croft's suitability to own a football club, avoiding tax at the top end of the business and criminally evading it at the bottom. For speed he pays Selka by phone from his and Jayne's own savings account.

Conor stuffs the phone back in his pocket and walks out onto the pavement, waiting under a streetlamp. Inside the car the passenger is on the phone. Conor realises Toenail from Keeley Street could have sent the dealers the snapshot. It might not be a problem, but he doesn't like the idea of having his photo being in the possession of the dealers.

The car doesn't stop until it's in darkness 50 metres ahead. There can be no hesitation, Conor thinks. Walk slowly, slowly, just do it. The car window disappears; inside Conor sees taxi cards on the dash board, empty cans of red bull, the driver looks like a student – square glasses, hipster beard.

"The cash?"

Conor counts out £1,000, but let's the lads see that there's more in his inside jacket pocket.

"Nice motor," Conor says sarcastically. It's a battered, old Mercedes.

"Attracts less attention."

The passenger keeps his head down, thick curly locks fall into his eyes as he checks the notes. He passes Conor a thin blue carrier bag, the drugs are in a weight-lifting protein tub not much bigger than a can of beans.

"Is there more?" Conor tries to keep his voice steady, but he feels the adrenalin racing.

"This our limit ol'man. You want more; you have to agree terms with Dev."

The driver smirks vacantly without taking his eyes from the road ahead. The passenger pulls out another packet.

"Think you can shift this?"

Fumbling to count out a new batch of notes, Conor senses that the two small fish partners disagree. They are breaking their own terms.

£2,000 – two grammes, deal done.

"Yeah, so we got your picture, we got face recognition software, your address is easy, give us a few days and we'll have your wife's credit card details."

Christ, Conor hadn't thought about that. It's agony, but he forces himself to walk slowly. When the Mercedes is out of sight, Conor picks up speed running back to his car. In the silence of the night, his heels clip articulately on the pavement. Getting rid of the drugs is his next priority. Jayne will be asleep. That much should be straightforward enough. She won't wake if he flushes them in the downstairs toilet. Then again, he thinks, don't put them into the city's water system. They'll be recycled faster than the cash.

It's 3.30am. The skin on his scalp prickles. There can't have been CCTV. Dealers would never operate in a place where there are cameras, would they? Driving home he senses something is wrong. It's not immediately obvious, there are so few cars on the road, but when the black cab behind him turns off, there is the Mercedes. It might be a coincidence, stay calm. At the ring road Conor crunches the gears, his hand slipping on the stick. He decides to do a full circuit of the traffic island, sweat helping him grip the patterned leather on the steering wheel. The Mercedes driver gives him a nod and peels off to the right, taking the dealers in the opposite direction to Conor's home.

He ought to feel relieved, it could all be fine, but it's not. They have his picture, his mobile and his number plate. And, shit, it was him that was supposed to be documenting this whole event. He's got to talk to DI Jones as early as he can.

In the middle of the night, every traffic light seems against him. Home is a generous, modern, detached house built in the 1980s on the edge of town. It's at the end of a row of bungalows. His arms hang heavy, barely guiding the Audi in. Not until he gets in sight of the bungalows does Conor realise there's another car following him. No point in trying to turn around and drive away, he'd have to cross one of the gardens. Heart pounding, he pulls up sharply. Don't let them see which house he lives in. Keep them away from Jayne. Slowly he opens the door. If they want more money they can have it, if they want the drugs back, they can take them.

The car, possibly a Vauxhall Corsa, parks behind him. Two men dressed in dark colours get out; with relief he sees one of them is in uniform. Oh shit. Time seems to slow down as the police constable talks into his handset. The more senior plain clothes officer holds his badge out. Then he twigs, shit, they are going to search the car. He picks up his phone and scans the message. What he sees makes the blood pulsing in his ears so loud he barely hears the officer's words.

"OK, I'm Detective Paul Winters, that's Sergeant Anthony Stevens, Police West Midlands. Can we have your hands on top of the car please, sir?"

"Errr... What? Yes, I mean, were you following the Mercedes?"

Conor is babbling. It doesn't make sense. Why would they stay with him and not the dealers?

"We need to search the car, sir. "Stand still if you don't mind."

Conor hits his head on the roof of his car.

The constable takes one look on the passenger seat and sees the packages.

"It's not what…"

Patting Conor's jacket, he immediately feels the brick of cash.

"OK," he says brightly, "that was easy. Name?"

"Conor Walsh."

"OK, Conor Walsh, I'm arresting you on suspicion of possession and intent to supply a class A drug…"

As his rights are read, Conor shouts, "Get DI Jones. I'm a council official. He knows me, he knows about this."

Except Conor hasn't told him yet.

"Which is your house?" the detective asks. "I'm assuming you don't have any objection to us having a look round?"

What can he say? There's no way this can end well. He stamps his foot to stop his leg shaking.

"My wife's asleep…"

"Not for too much longer, mate."

The detective takes a firm hold of Conor's upper arm, moving him away from the car. He tries to focus his thoughts to stop fear taking over.

There's £20,000 unmarked drug money in the cupboard under the stairs. It comes from Croft, a man who owes the council £23 million. There's a contract with his name on it – Conor struggles to swallow, tries to cover it with a cough – a contract that he's not enforcing. What it will look like is a bribe.

CHAPTER 44

Nicole's exhausted body had finally let her sleep in the safety of the cupboard and then she'd struggled to wake up. Dreaming, I've been dreaming about mum and Ash, she thinks, that's all.

She remembers her mum. Fragments: a vegetable stall on the market; cauliflower brains, carrot nose, potato head; ice cold hands. She recalls an expensive camera, not to be touched; a blue shoebox full of postcards, white chocolate and crosswords. She'd looked for her mum, like they'd looked for Ash: in shops, parks, the pubs in the city centre.

And there were friends' houses, fewer of them. One of her mum's mates had said she could stay there, but that had seemed wrong. Then there was a row about the police with another friend. She'd bolted then, too. Here at the stadium there's a memory of being outside, not let in. Ha! Now she's inside, but too scared to go out.

Nicole's stomach tells her it's lunchtime, but she can't be sure. There will be people at work. She lies down again, sleeping fitfully. Her chin is sore, fingers grazed, throat dry, stomach hard, but thankfully not rumbling. Basically, I'm OK, she tells herself.

More dreams: the garages, the slit of light under door, gasping, the air tasting of petrol, the disgusting sleeping bag suddenly coming alive and crawling towards her. The papers in her file are lost leaves in the book of Ash's life.

When she wakes, cramp and aching joints force her to creep out. The starchy smell makes her nose itch. It's boring and her head aches, but it's almost dark so it might be 5 or 6pm. Now what? Run for it? Run where? She tries a few doors before finding a hospitality room with a door that leads out into the stand.

Sitting down Nicole can see onto the pitch unobserved. The lines are being painted. Old men are taking their time. She understands they want to get it right. "Mum never left me anywhere," she remembers telling the social worker. "We were just looking for Ash in different places, trying to check as many places as we could." They weren't impressed. Adults would talk to her if she lost her way and bring her home. No biggie.

"If I find Ash, mum will recover, we could go back to our old place," she'd told Pete. He'd shrugged a maybe.

She'd wanted him to say, "Yes pet, you're right."

But in care, they don't let you dream. Her mum had been in and out of hospital. Now she was older, Pete had helped Nicole understand her mum's her mental illness, her long-term drug and alcohol abuse, her grief. She lived with an old aunt in Leeds now. And anyway, there was a new family living in their old house.

Nicole watches the old men pack up their things. There's a crackle and a hum as the floodlights are switched on, but at half-power. It's a ghostly stage, with the audience of one in the stand, almost in darkness. I'll be considered an adult soon, she tells herself. I'll be fending for myself, will have to register as homeless. Bloody Anita, although if she had her phone she'd send Anita a text. Anita would know what to do next, she grudgingly admits.

When the building falls silent, Nicole roams the corridors looking for food. Of course, there is food, there's hospitality. On the first round of security checks she'd been downstairs checking out the offices, had to sit on the toilet with her feet up for half an hour. Wormy would've loved that.

Scouring the team photos on the walls of the staircase, she comes across an old picture. Dez is there, Wormy, Odds and there, finally, is her brother's beaming smile. She wishes she could talk to Wormy now. It's hard to believe she's actually here, inside the VIP lounge where the suits watch the games. VIPs? Would there be CCTV? She sees a spycam in the corner of the room and shuts the door quickly. There don't seem to be cameras in the corridor and if there is someone watching they would've been after by now.

Most of rooms are locked. Did Ash ever come into these offices to get his wages? Nicole remembers that this place wasn't built back then. She makes a mental note to find the photos upstairs of what it looked like before. What takes her down the stairs below the reception is instinct. Part investigator, part fan, she knows this is her one chance to see it all.

The air temperature drops as she descends. Did they build this new stand directly on top of the old one? Another fragment: she remembers the shocking sight of the stadium collapsed. Wanting to walk near to it, but feeling afraid. Men shouting, but wind whipping the words away. A mountain of rubble, debris scattered like an obstacle course. She wishes she hadn't left her jacket upstairs.

Beneath ground level, the bare concrete walls smell damp. The corridors are narrow and without light. Her eyes refuse to adjust. Ash wasn't afraid of the dark. Come on, there's nothing here, she tells herself, nothing to be afraid of. Ash wasn't afraid of anything. Moving her hand along the wall, she takes a step forward, stops, then another. Her heartbeat thrashes in her ears and her legs won't let her continue. Freaked out, she bottles it. Taking two steps at a time, she charges up the stairwell until she's above ground again.

Back in the safety of the generous linen cupboard, her file of papers on Ash's disappearance seems thin now. Nicole lays them out, re-reading the details of old stuff and learning by rote the recent report the police sent to Anita. It was more than she'd been able to get.

There's a profile of the old chairman, Cornflower. It's a newspaper report from when he left the club. It had him coming out with some stupid comment about leaving the club in safe hands, talking about him flying to the game in a helicopter. He looks like an under-cooked turkey, rolls of pink fat under his chin with a red, raw, bare chest, standing outside a villa in the Caribbean. Wormy called him the plantation man, but he wasn't *bad* like Croft. Just fat and greedy, Pete said. What was important to Nicole was that it was Cornflower who'd first agreed to sign Ash; he said Ash had promise.

Nicole doesn't bother to read about Croft. For the last two years she's studied everything there is on him; that's one GCSE she could pass without revising. Employer, entrepreneur, service provider and then business angel, one with dirty wings who puts a chain round your leg. Like you'd ever take money off him; let him own you. It's supposed to be young people who can't retain information, but it's adults who've forgotten that Croft is also a loan-sharker, drug-dealer and alcohol-faker. There were the girls who got raped and the one who died. Nicole shudders, thinking she could've been raped in the garages.

It was Pete who'd said, "If you want answers you need to go to the top." He was talking about something else, but the idea had stuck and after that time Croft had told her to FUCK OFF, she'd been convinced he was hiding something. It had been easy to trace where Croft would be, at football matches, at meetings or that charity dinner. Croft also had trolls. Proper Welders fans who would slag him on social media and write in forums where he would be. OK, she had stalked him, watched him in his expensive clothes, flash car. Yes, she'd shouted abuse, got in his face, but she couldn't let him forget Ash.

After the restraining order, Nicole's social worker had written to Croft requesting a reconciliation meeting, but he hadn't replied. Sweating, she looks back now, relieved. It's too hard to sit still. Agitated she creeps along the VIP corridor, past the executive boxes to the small hospitality kitchen. Stuffing a packet of crisps in her pocket, Nicole freezes. There are voices. Opposite the kitchen is the directors' box. Someone is watching TV. The sound is faint, but it's clearly the news. That would make it 10pm. It could be security guards, but if it's the same as last night, they don't make their rounds until midnight.

As she inches towards the door, she hears the local news music and recognises the female newsreader's voice. Then there are words, a fragment, just seconds. A jagged sound wave that's imprinted on her memory her forever.

"...DNA evidence has confirmed the deceased as Ashley Brand, a local teenager, reported missing, thought to have been living in the London area."

CHAPTER 45

A wave of shock almost bowls Nicole over. For the last two years she's been turning up at crime scenes in the city, checking Twitter feeds, police reports, even the council newsfeed on "staying safe". Places and situations to avoid have been a magnetic force, drawing Nicole in.

Wormy had sent her that text about the city farm. Security had told her the remains were of a young man and he could've been wearing a football shirt, but there hadn't been a sense of Ash at the farm, not like there was at the garages. The foreboding, though, was real, an electric pull that had kept her by the muddy water's edge. Bringing a shaky hand to her forehead, she realises that secretly she's always known that Ash was dead. Denying it so many times, over and over, she'd tried to convince herself he was alive. Deep down, she knows she'd been saying it because she didn't think she could cope with the crushing reality. And now he's actually dead, she's actually crushed, actually wants to vomit, to scream her head off. Nicole's belief that she'd find Ash had given her a reason to go on and a protective shield from the downwards spiral that her mum experienced.

It's hard to hear what the newsreader is saying about the cause of death because her heartbeat is pounding so loud. Through the door jamb she sees the silhouette of a man facing the screen, taking a step forward then rocking back. It's almost a dance. As he drops his shoulder slightly she sees something in his hand. It's

Croft and it could be a gun. Fuck, maybe she should just run, but she has to hear the news.

In the cutlery draw is a steak knife, the blade designed to cut meat. This will have to do, she tells herself. Outside the door to the box she hears a phone ring. Nicole presses down the door handle as slowly as she can, opening the door a fraction and keeping the edge of her toe in it. She can't afford to make a sound.

The TV goes silent; there's a clatter as a remote is chucked onto a nearby table. Not a gun then.

Croft blows a short, hard breath, "Yes, it's on the news... Calm down, calm down for fuck's sake. Listen to me..."

He seems to move the phone slightly away from his ear, waits, then says very deliberately, "Cornflower, if you don't shut the fuck up, I'm putting the phone down."

Nicole remembers the icy tone from the first time Croft threatened her.

"...When the police call, you tell them what I told you."

She knows she should carry on listening, but her legs are shaking, she wants to kick the door down. Cornflower? He liked Ash? What had he done to Ash?

Croft's voice is cold.

"The police have nothing. I have the evidence. I've got the car... You requested my help, remember. You told me he was alive. That's not how my man found him. That costs extra..."

Clenching the knife hard, fury makes her feels strong, she fights back tears. Cornflower is shouting, mangled sounds on the other end of the phone.

"...You got what you wanted. The stadium. The deal. I took this shitty business off your hands. Eight years later you want to re-write history?"

It was them – Cornflower and Croft. Ash died because they had some shitty business deal? *"That's not how my man found him."* Nicole repeats Croft's words silently.

An image flashes before her, she's sinking the knife into Croft's back.

"Like I said..." Croft continues. "...You say nothing. Not one word. I'll deal with Underhill. Get a lawyer and sit tight. I'll talk to..."

Who? Who's that? Other people knew? Is Croft talking about the police? Do they have someone corrupt in the police force? And are they going to get away with it? The thought sends a shock of electricity down into her hand. That's it. Nicole thrusts the door open.

Croft is standing with his back to a wide, black pane of glass, framed by the darkness of the pitch. The room is broad but shallow, smaller than she thought. He's only maybe four metres away, his deep-lined face staring straight at her.

"My brother's dead," she spits, full of rage.

Without thinking she runs towards him, the knife in her outstretched hand. Croft instantly picks up a chair as a shield, dropping his phone in the process.

"Put the knife down."

Nicole launches herself at him. He jabs the chair at her arm, it doesn't make contact and she jumps to the side. Raising the knife above her head, she swipes it diagonally downwards, like a sword. He's too quick, the chair comes crashing down on her arm. Still gripping the knife, Nicole staggers back. Croft follows up, swinging the chair like a baseball bat.

Crashing down onto all fours, Nicole looks up as Croft kicks the hand that is holding the knife. She yells in pain as her wrist cracks and the knife flies across the room.

"I heard you. Cornflower killed Ash and you moved him."

As Nicole tries to stand, Croft drops down on top of her, a knee digs into her chest, pain sears through every nerve-ending. He's sitting on top of her now, she can't move, can't breathe.

"Just shut up and calm down."

"You can't kill me," she screams. Images flash through her mind. He's going to beat me until I'm unconscious, shove me in the boot of a car and dump my body just like Ash.

"I don't want to kill you. I didn't kill Ash. Whatever you think you heard, you've got it wrong."

"I know Anita Patel. She's the council leader. She's coming. She'll bring the police."

Croft pulls a phone out of his pocket. "Recognise this?"

Out of the corner of her eye, Nicole sees it looks like her phone. Shit. Croft's man, the dealer from the garages, must have picked it up.

"No-one's coming, Nicole."

"Yeah, but they know I'm here." It's bravado. He's right. "Anita's my friend. You can't touch me. I've got a file. We... we know. We know about you. Everyone on the estate knows what you are, drug-dealing, pimp, loan shark..."

"You're upset, Nicole. I understand. More than you realise..."

Nicole tries to twist her body, kicks out her legs, trying to dislodge him. The deep frown lines are like scars on Croft's face. He grunts, lets her roll away, guards the door to the box.

"...It was an accident," Croft says. "If I could change what happened that night, believe me I would."

"Liar!" she screams.

Nostrils flaring, Croft reaches to pick up his mobile. "I'm upstairs," he commands. "Get here now."

Nicole rolls onto her hands and knees, trying to catch her breath. I need to get out, right now before anyone else gets here, she thinks.

"Let me help you, Nicole. Once you leave that home you're on your own. I'm a rich man. I like to help kids from our side of the tracks. Come and work for me. I'll get you extra football coaching."

"Never. You bastard. You dumped my brother in that lake."

The chair she's sitting on has a gold metal frame; it was strong enough to send her flying, so maybe...? Mustering all the force she can, Nicole picks it up and runs at the glass doors that lead to the stand. The glass cracks, but doesn't smash. Bastard. He took my family away.

This time she jabs the legs into the glass until it shatters. Icy, cold air blasts through the hole, filling her lungs, making her double up with the effort.

Pulling her hoodie over her head to protect herself from the glass, Nicole tries to climb through. Behind her she hears the door to the suite fly open, the Sweeper, the drug dealer from the garages, launches himself at her, bringing her down to the carpet on top of the broken glass. Pain rushes up her arm as a shard of glass stabs into her hand.

Cowering on the floor, Nicole is forced to look at the triangle shape, sticking out of a pool of blood like a shark's fin.

"Don't hurt her," Croft says. "I need time to think."

"The police will be here soon, I'll tell them everything." It's a last attempt at defiance, but her chin tremors, head spins.

"Use your brain. Who are they going to believe?"

Nicole can't respond.

"Yes," Croft hesitates, "the kid's in shock, needs to cool off. I'll ring the police. Tell them she broke in here, hysterical. She attacked me and ran off. She'll be on CCTV somewhere in the building."

"We can't have the police anywhere near here." The Sweeper sounds angry with Croft. "I can't afford that and neither can you. Timing is critical."

"Trust me, better that I invite them here, they find nothing and we're clear."

"What shall I do with her?"

Dizzy, shaking, blind through tears, Nicole flinches as she smells the Sweeper's sweat.

"Take her downstairs."
She shuts her eyes.
"Take her to the Crypt."

CHAPTER 46

Croft locks the door to the directors' box behind the Sweeper and Nicole. What the fuck is he going to do with her? He walks to the smashed window. The thick soles of his smart leather boots softly crunch the glass into the carpet. The girl is strong, quick and inventive. In her place he'd have done the same. Worse probably.

Rubbing his hand hard over his chin, he is stumped. What can he do with her? His fingers knead his cheeks, the skin feels dry, paper thin; the bones of his skull barely beneath it. He's about to make the biggest deal of his life and this resurfaces.

The darkness of the pitch often helps him to think, but now as he looks down he sees the outline of a young player; a substitute is warming up on the touchline, kicking his heels to his backside, making shuttle runs, knees pumping high in the air. The ghost of Ash is back.

Croft turns the chair Nicole used so effectively the right way up and slumps down.

"Believe me Ash…" He chokes his words out, on the one hand wishing that the boy and his half-sister could hear him, on the other feeling safe in the knowledge that they can't. This is his bloody cross to bear alone.

"…When I agreed to help Cornflower," he says to the spectre, "I didn't know it was you. Didn't want details. There's not a day goes by that I don't think about that mistake."

There's a relief to saying the words out loud, like a scream when you're in pain, Croft expels agony into the night. It's not forgiveness he wants, it's a release.

"Son, I swear I did all I could for you. All your life. I paid for your club fees, transport, maintenance, the rent on the house you grew up in. I'd have done more if your mum'd let me. After she fell pregnant, your mum didn't want anything to do with me. It was over before it started. I…"

Hearing Cornflower's voice after all these years, seeing the picture of Ash on the news, Croft's body had begun shaking. The adrenalin of the fight with Nicole had overtaken, but as the rush subsides, he feels his left leg start to bounce.

"I'd have killed Cornflower for hurting you, but it was expedient to keep him alive, an insurance of sorts. Believe me, I've made him pay."

He grinds the glass diamond chips into the carpet, forcing himself to think. What could he usefully do with Nicole? When the girl had started watching him, he'd begun watching her. Tried to help her, too. Made a charitable donation to the residential home she lived in, made sure she wasn't bullied, but money couldn't buy her what she wanted. Ash was never coming back, life was tough.

The Sweeper is right. The timing of this is critical, couldn't be worse. His eight-year plan is coming to fruition, it has to happen, and when it does Croft will be part of the 1%, the richest men in the country. The import of the fund isn't the money, though; what it will buy him is more precious.

Legitimacy is the new respectability. You can be respectable and still be dirty as hell, after all. Legitimacy will make him untouchable.

What stands in the way of that is Anita Patel. Local government to Croft has always been a joke, but in global money markets the standing of any part of the state is prized. Blue chip. It adds value, infrastructure, assets, democratic accountability and it comes with a seal, the rule of law. He needs Patel to support him. Where direct intimidation has failed, now he can get to her via Nicole. It's, shall we say, fortuitous, if not bloody lucky. He'll keep Nicole as an incentive to Anita to fall in. And he'll threaten her life.

Fuck. Standing again and looking out at the pitch, the ghost of Ash seems to stare directly at the box for a moment. Croft turns away, unable to face him.

Sometimes irony has a bitter, but not unpleasant, aftertaste. This time the irony is like a dose of chemo. There has been an integrity to his career to date – if Daniel Croft threatens you, you rightly live in fear of your life. He's never made a threat he won't deliver on. Until now.

CHAPTER 47

Custody Sergeant Maggie McGee talks Conor through the process as if he's had a long time off work and has forgotten the drill. There's a new sheet to sign.

"Automated at last," she sighs; her voice and skin are jaundiced – too many night shifts under the monochromatic yellow light. There's a computer file on Conor already. The grounds for arrest are clearly stated, evidence outlined. The chipped, birch wood counter provides some stability; he slumps, presses his forearms down and knits his fingers together in a hopeless prayer.

"So, Mr Walsh, you have the right to ask us to let someone know you're here."

He nods, concentrating on keeping his neck vertical, not trusting his voice.

"Your wife is listed as Jayne Walsh. She knows already, doesn't she?"

Jayne's steady determination was given away by a tiny line of anguish between her eyebrows. At 4.30am, standing barefoot on the front door step in silk pyjamas and a sweat shirt, she'd looked terrified, confused, angry and beautiful.

"What were you thinking?" She'd rubbed the heel of a palm across her chest as if to help her breathe. Her face said, surely now we can stop this ridiculous pretence?

Conor was being escorted firmly by the elbow towards the car. He'd looked back longingly. Hopelessly. Jayne had closed the door quietly, not waiting for the police car to drive off.

Sergeant McGee is on auto-pilot.

"And you've refused a duty solicitor?"

Panicking, he'd thought he could come up with some sort of story. The truth had seemed ridiculous. He wasn't thinking straight, there was no way he could look a serious professional in the eye.

"Errr... I might."

"You can make a request at any point in the process."

The process is all there is. More efficient than he imagined, but suitably de-personalised, distant. No-one is interested in the actual content of his story. He needs more than a solicitor doing their duty.

"Did you say you had a day job?"

That throws him. Conor is the chief executive of the council, yet according to the police paperwork what he does is supply drugs. That's how the system now sees him. The opposite of how he's seen himself – negative not positive, immoral not moral, dark not light. Thousands of staff see Conor as the face of the system, integral to it, boss of it, it's in his DNA. He is Mr Municipal.

"You'd be surprised who we've had through here." The sergeant's interest picks up.

From her point of view it looks like a real crime, he supposes. It certainly doesn't look good and, although his story is straight and well thought through in his own mind, they probably hear all sorts of justifications.

"And you still work at the council?" she asks, without irony.

Do I? There's an ache at the back of his throat, it's hard to swallow. The system will treat him fairly, but his activities will be judged as gross misconduct. Instant dismissal. Who will get the budget sorted? Find the cash for the wages? Jane and I, we'll have to move, he thinks. If she stays with me.

"We'll do your bloods..." Sergeant McGee says.

They think he's a user, that underneath his easy-iron shirt and polyester tie will be the welts and sores of a junkie.

"...then you can relax in the cell."

Relax? Is that a joke.

Keeping his composure he asks, "Could I to talk to DI Jones. We've worked together before."

"Original, I'll give you that," she sneers. "The arresting officer will decide what the charges will be. We'll let you know in a couple of hours."

Conor nods. The toilet is a tiny cubical to the left of the reception counter. A custody officer waits outside while he soaps his hands two, three, four times. The realisation that he won't just lose his job forces Conor to straighten up. He could be sent to prison. Bloody hell. His grandad can't know. Grandad might not make it to the weekend. This'll be the news that finishes him off.

The monastic cell is exactly as he'd imagined. The only feature is a single, empty shelf that hovers effortlessly two feet from the floor. Shoeless, his socks wet at the toe from the rain, Conor lies down.

He has assumed he'd be a Welder 'til he died. He'd thought that by removing Croft he'd be able to – what? Keep propping up the club until a new owner could be found? It was sincere enough, but in the plain light of the cell it looked naïve. Conor had convinced himself that the club and Croft were separate, that the childish illusion that he *belonged* to the club was unchanged.

To Croft, a lifetime's loyalty was just an asset to be stripped. What could be exploited would be exploited. Conor had known for years that he was a mug. It wasn't so bad; the fans were all mugs together. Handing over their cash, being ripped off by Croft and probably Cornflower before him, it was a perverse badge of pride - a choice, a collective delusion.

They all knew what Croft was and yet they'd taken off their Welders scarves, shown Croft their proud jugular veins and invited him to bite. Conor's criminally stupid act wasn't trying to catch Croft with laundered money. It was *not* doing something years ago.

Just before he'd been lifted, Conor had been looking at his phone like a teenager, as if it had the answer to everything in life, as if "slide to unlock" was a secret key to get him out of this crazy situation. In black and white on the screen had been Selka's reply, the information he'd paid for, the answer to who was in bed with Croft.

Conor jerks back in his seat.

S: No-one.

What?

S: Croft's fund is light. Word is they were putting back the launch because there were no deals. No investors biting. Croft had to bundle in collateral, a juicy slice of public debt and an asset…

No, he thinks, please no.

S: It's a UK soccer stadium, recently built. Do you want in?

Croft had no intention of paying back the council, but somewhere along the line he'd also seen the potential to use the stadium as leverage.

Conor had thrown the mobile onto the passenger seat without much force, despairing. It had bounced up, hitting the glove compartment and disappeared into the footwell, all lights out. No answers.

Croft is gambling it all, thinks Conor. Our history, our memories, our identity, the backbone of what it means to be who we are round here. All that is being packaged up and used as ballast for a fund no-one wants.

On the bed, Conor curls his knees in tighter. A heavy arm shades his eyes from the strip light. A Welders chant emerges from his subconscious. He's known it forever. He sang it on the terraces with his grandad, their lungs like bellows expanding to bursting point. Years later, he and Toby had belted out the words, growing inches taller, the chorus binding them in a force field that obliterated doubt and fear. The fans are connected in the vibrations of their souls, not as individuals but as one.

Conor starts to hum, but the tune is dead in his throat. He mouths the words.

"We know what we are…"

There's no sound.

"We know what we are…"

It's empty. The meaning gone. He can't continue.

I don't know anymore, he thinks. I don't know who I am.

CHAPTER 48

In the cold, cramped police interview room, Anita relives the moment the van drove her off the road. The pain has sharpened her memory, crystallised the facts, helped her to speak minimally and with precision. The pre-meditated nature of the attack is what scares her most. Violence on demand, at a click, there could be a re-order. Completing the written statement police record Anita digs the biro into the paper. Still, couldn't the police have taken the statement at her house? She needs to conserve her energy.

Wherever Nicole is, Anita hopes she hasn't heard the news about Ash. Hearing news like that in the wrong way is another injury. It's an injustice.

"We informed Nicole's mother and the press jumped on it. Impossible to control a message these days," DI Jones says. "None of us are happy about that."

She blows out a shallow breath, the neck collar brace she's wearing itches. Keeping still is the best way to manage the pain in her neck.

"So…" Jones says, partly resigned, partly empathising, "there's another reason we wanted you to come into the station this morning. One of your lot taking the law into their own hands."

Baffled and intrigued, Anita takes her time to stand. Not that long ago "her lot" could have been any number of activists, protesters or politicos. The council covers anyone and everyone, even Nicole. But here and now, she isn't really sure who her lot are, or if she even has a "lot" anymore.

Moving to the next room feels like a waste of effort. The blank box is a replica of the one she's just given her statement in. A man has his head down, a finger taps on the empty table as if it's a calculator.

"Conor! What on earth?"

Gradually lowering herself into a chair, holding her shoulders steady, Anita rests her head in her hands, eyes shut, neck muscles screeching at each turn.

It's 9.30am – he should be at the budget meeting; they both should be.

"The club..." he murmurs blankly, "we have to eliminate the club. Get rid of it completely."

"No, we have to save the club." Anita replies before Conor's words have registered. "What did you just say?"

"I said sod the bloody club, it's toxic..."

"What?" Anita hasn't heard him swear before. It's as shocking as if Auntie Pinkie has cursed. "You've changed your tune."

"So have you." Conor sounds deflated. "The club is a mirage, it was a toy for Cornflower, it's pure business for Croft. They give the fans false hope and the fans, like me, just suck it up, wilfully blind dreamers."

"Yes, the club is a petty-minded brotherhood, insular tribalism is rife. I hate the aggression and the competition, it's an anachronism..."

Conor manages to smirk. "Yes, but what have you really got against it?"

"What I'm saying is, we have to look at it differently. Reclaim it for the whole city. The club generates commitment, passion, loyalty, all things we can build on... We need to use it, make it ours."

Conor mumbles, "I don't believe what I'm hearing. That's one hell of a U-turn."

Last night, in the fleeting gap between the painkillers and the return to pain, a new possibility had emerged. This is a battle that's harming all of us, she'd thought. I could've been killed, who knows what danger Nicole is in. The council and the city are threatened. We can't let it become a war. Unable to sleep again, she had come to a realisation; it doesn't have to be like this, we can turn this around.

When the pain returned, she'd reminded herself that Nicole loved the club, there had to be a club for her to come back to.

"I could say the same…"

Anita notices a plastic police tag on Conor's wrist, as if he's been in hospital. She turns around to Jonesy.

"What have I missed? What's going on?"

Conor turns his chair slightly to stand and steps towards the wall, spreading a palm out to hold himself up. The sweat rings on his shirt could be arms bands, but they don't do the job and she sees he is about to sink.

"You look like I feel. Just sit down will you."

DI Jones steps in. "Mr Walsh has been caught in possession of a wholesale quantity of class A drugs. We are considering a range of charges."

If it didn't hurt she might've laughed. Unbelievable.

"You?"

"It seems his concerns are more about the activities of our friend, Daniel Croft."

As clear as Anita's statement about the car attack had been, Conor's tale is murky. There are confused timeframes, an odd code for marking twenty pound notes. Details of international private equity and the price of cocaine make her flinch. Slumping into the chair opposite, Conor won't meet her eye.

The bit about the fixed odds machines she could've told him years ago. It was part of a local campaign she'd led – and one that Les had ignored. Connections fizz, thoughts speed ahead.

Anita has to check what role Les played in this. Was he chair of the committee at the time? Had he interfered?

"We've been watching this outfit for months. There's no point arresting them for £10 deals. We've been looking for the management, unusual incidents like Conor here. We've got clear links to Croft, but no evidence. We suspect the drugs operation is sub-regional, much wider than Conor could've imagined. He's only succeeded in proving his scheme to himself. There are too many variables, it would never have made a difference in court."

It was so obviously a ridiculous plan. Drug dealing cash could've ended up anywhere. Conor's face is flushed, his throat contracts.

"You idiot." She says it as kindly as she can.

He's done the wrong thing for the right reason, she assumes.

"...You still think you can fix things. You're secretive and individualistic. Drop the 'quiet man, just doing what you can' act. It's fake. Underneath it you're an arrogant man..."

Anita stops, remembering the tweets that accused her of the same behaviour. "You think you always know best." Nicole had thrown that one at her a few times.

"I'm glad you've changed your tune," she says, "but why now? You knew Croft was a criminal."

"I didn't know about the money laundering."

"I told you weeks ago. You didn't believe me."

Anita's head throbs, thinking back to her first football match, remembering the effort she had to go to to wrench the information from Conor. She can't spend the energy she's got left on him and she can see it's more complex.

"My head told me you were right, but we'd done the due diligence, ticked the boxes... I suppose I didn't want to know." His voice breaks as if losing a signal. "I didn't know it for myself. In myself... And then..."

Conor's eyes are dry but vacant. In different circumstances Anita might've held out a hand to him.

"Any chance of a cup of tea?" she asks Jones. "You aren't a drug dealer, everyone can see that, Conor, you're a public figure, a good public servant, I know that. We don't need you to be a hero; we need you to do your job."

His throat bobs wildly, "I'm not going to be sacked?"

Anita tries to appease Conor; she's sympathetic to a point.

"I'll do what I can," but she knows she won't try that hard. Gross-misconduct is pretty clear. Short-term he will be useful. Conor is tainted now. She can't afford to have him on her team.

CHAPTER 49

Conor sees steel in Anita's eyes. Has he noticed that before? Her head is up. He can't help thinking it's a pity she didn't apply that kind of determination to the budget. DI Jones comes back into the room, tea in hand.

"I'll co-operate fully," Conor says sincerely to both of them. "Just tell me what I can do."

"I can give you a few more minutes," Jones looks at Conor, "and then we'll need to escort you back to your cell."

"Right," Anita says, "if this city, if we, are going to have a football club, it's got to be a club for everyone: families, girls, boys, community groups and people who want to play other sports – hockey, rugby, dance classes in the bar – training, sports science links with the university. Look what they've done at Loughborough. Let's get some expertise in there. And while we're at it, a micro-library?"

Conor keeps his head down, cringing inside. Not this.

"I need you to think. Find us a community-owned solution. Find a way we can transfer the asset. And I don't mean dump it on people who can't afford it, integrate the club into the local economy. Find a way to include people who can't afford a ticket. We need proper apprenticeships. Make it like you want it to be. Proper rules and behaviours. A club that unites us, not divides us. I mean it. No racism, no violence, no hatred, no sexism or homophobia. We've got to create something new."

Conor sees Jones holding his face firm, giving nothing away. Normally Conor would do the same, he can't afford to alienate Anita any further, but there's not a bone in his body that wants this.

She continues: "There's a different history to the game of football and we can be a part of that. I want to be a part of it. I've done my homework, this isn't new. Some of the biggest clubs in the world are fan-owned. St Pauli in Germany, Barcelona, there are some interesting approaches in the UK, too. Actually, more interesting than the football itself, well to me that is. We can adopt a model that works for us. It's the intention that's important. Fans from other clubs have achieved amazing things…"

Conor doesn't know what to say.

"You know more about this than I do. Work with us on it."

Conor wonders who *us* is?

"We need you." Anita's phone bleeps. "Pete's found Wormy and is coming to pick me up. I'll be at Auntie Pinkie's place."

As she turns to leave Anita challenges him. "There will be no club at all if we don't change it. Is that what you really want?"

No words come. Ten minutes ago Conor wanted to destroy the club. He tries not to squirm, but the chair gives him away.

"I get it," she says. "You'd rather have no club than a community club? Croft bringing the club down keeps you safe. Yeah, I've seen that. Failing is safe, you're used to it."

"I'm just trying to think practically."

Anita scoffs. I walked into that, Conor thinks.

"You hate Croft, but you don't like this either. You say you want to help, but I'm hearing nothing. Are you going to sit back and undermine it? There's always someone else to blame, but, d'you know what, after all this, I can't believe you don't even want to try?"

Conor is paralysed.

"It's the chance of a lifetime for a group of fans, isn't it? Run your own club. Even better, *own* your own club. I mean properly, as a collective group of fans working together."

His mind jumps to the financial logistics. "You mean transferring the asset, giving the fans the stadium?"

"Taxpayers paid for it, didn't we?"

If we did this, Conor thinks, technically we'd be mitigating a loss of amenity the community have incurred. But he needs to think carefully. Conor looks at Jones as if pleading to be taken back to the cell.

"I'm asking you to go with your heart, to do the right thing this time."

Time melts away, stretched seconds, a long minute, maybe more.

"There's a lot you don't know about football," Conor mumbles, seeing even more ridicule surrounding them.

"So what? I've got more guts than you. You're just like the rest of the fans, moaning away in the stands that your daddy chairman won't buy you a nice new striker to make everything better."

"Break it up, you two," Jones says.

"You're prepared to take huge risks, even breaking the law, but commit yourself in public, get stuck in when you've got no control over the outcome... No. That's the difference between politicians and officers." As quickly as her injuries allow, Anita stands. "Conor, you're a coward."

*

The custody suite is dead at 10am on a Friday morning, the opposite of how it must be at 10pm. Conor walks ahead of the PC, familiar now with the form.

"We pay enough for our season tickets already. I won't be coughing up more for a *community club*." The PC must've been listening whilst guarding the door. He sounds enlivened, talking insistently into the back of Conor's head. Conor's toes curl up in his socks. Only ten seconds in and people are agin it. He doesn't turn around, wants to be left alone, to escape the smell of his own stale sweat.

"I went to AFC Wimbledon once, got a cousin down there. Piss-poor quality. Three balls were hoofed out of the park in the first 20 minutes. Where's your seat then?"

"Cemetery end. Row 50, where Horn Man is," Conor replies automatically.

The PC picks out a pen, checks his watch and logs the time on a card outside Conor's cell. He wants to get home to talk to Jayne.

"It's not worth the risk," the PC says. "Better to stick with the Welders – at least we might win something worth having."

Les or any number of the councillors might have said the same thing. And so might I, Conor admits.

He hadn't noticed last night, the key to the cell is the same as a plastic hotel card. They will soon be charging for a night in here.

"It'll look pathetic," the PC says, "a community team in that huge stadium. Mind you, have to say the old one had more character and history."

Even if he wanted to argue Conor would have to agree. The fans had never really moved in, made it their own.

"It'll never happen," the PC concludes, slamming the cell door. "We're not like that round here."

CHAPTER 50

Nicole drifts off to sleep again, then wakes up, tear ducts prickling. Cautiously she peels one eye open as if expecting to see the Sweeper ready to boot her in the stomach. It's a black cell, only a sliver of muted, red light under the door. The air tastes of dying trainers or is that her breath? What would she give for clean teeth? Whatever. It doesn't matter. Croft called this place the Crypt. She's heard Wormy and Ash mention the Crypt, but that was in the old stadium, where they went to have a drink or a fag, to escape the mental world of football. It's just a name, she tells herself, but it sounds like a place where people die.

The police have probably told her mum that Ash's body has been identified and she'll lose it, get sectioned again. It's not the closure Nicole had hoped would ease her mum's pain. And worse, when she finds out Croft was involved, well, there'll be no coming back from that.

Each new consequence forces her further into a dark place, but what if they don't find her down here? What if the police never hear her evidence and Croft walks?

Cold dribble from the corner of her mouth has dried on the tatty gym-crash-mat that's become her bed. Her arms in front, as she turns to move, a thin plastic binder cuts into the skin at her wrist. In one palm her fingertips feel a cotton wool pad held in place by plasters, the glass shard has gone. No memory of its removal exists. Head fuzzy, she wonders if she passed out or was drugged.

Ordering her thoughts distracts from the pain. If she's alive now, it's because Croft needs her to be, but she has no idea why or for how long. There's no way out. The news item about Ash's death replays in her mind, making her cry at the horror of the situation.

"Oi," a woman's voice barks. "Stop snivelling."

Her heart jumps, she pushes herself to a sitting position, back against the wall, knees in tight. As the door is unlocked, there's a second or two of grey before a blinding bulb is switched on. There are two of them: bleached blonde hair, matching Welders scarves.

Fuck. No. Her head jerks back hitting the wall. No, that's impossible. She tries to shade her eyes with her tied hands. Gulping hard, words fail her. Them?

"You're as deranged as your psycho mum," the older Debbie says.

No more, she wants to scream. Her brain's over-loaded, circuits shorting.

"We tried to help you." The younger one makes it sound as if Nicole has rejected them. "No-one can say we didn't."

What? They did nothing.

"Complete waste of time." The mother is dismissive.

The daughter sets about untying her and putting a tray of food and drink on the floor. The older one keeps licking her lips, her fat tongue like a garden slug. Up close Nicole sees the younger one's eyes looking everywhere, wild eyes, too excited.

"There's a can of Coke in that carrier bag. The chairman is too good to you. Wants you looked after until he can find out whether you talked to the police and your social worker. He could've pressed charges against you."

"Charges? Anita will tell them…"

The name has become a shield of sorts. It slips out on instinct. The old Debbie, jaw jutting out, interrupts Nicole. "No kid.

Patel's going nowhere. Mr Croft will sort her out. Doesn't take a hint. We made a mess of her place..."

"...trashed her car..." the younger one finishes the sentence, "...and now we hear she's in the hospital. With a bit of luck her neck'll be broken. She deserved that."

Nicole's stomach lurches. "I don't understand."

"You hurt the club, you hurt us. Simple as that."

Nicole had said the same thing to Anita in their argument. More or less. What's wrong with these women? Everyone says things they don't mean. They don't act on it. Adrenalin shoots through her body.

"I love the club, you know that," Nicole protests. Except right now she would bomb the place to bits if she could.

"So you say, but you attacked the chairman with a knife. You're going down for that." The older Debbie's tone is unfeeling, heartless.

Had Croft said he was going to use that line? She can't think straight. No-one would believe that?

"Look, it wasn't like that. He's responsible for what happened to my brother. Haven't you seen the news?"

"We have. Mr Croft told us. He wasn't surprised. He's got a restraining order on you already, hasn't he? After they identified the body, you had a fit, broke in, hid out upstairs, got a knife from the kitchen and attacked him. He tried to calm you down, offered to take you back to that kids' home but you went mental and smashed a window with a chair."

"You lost your brother a long-time ago, Nicole." The younger woman's voice sounds kinder. "Stop this vendetta against Mr Croft. It's got you into a right mess."

"They drugged me, my stomach's kicking off." Nicole senses the younger woman's listening. "I need to go to the toilet."

"There's a bucket there."

Nicole sees a yellow plastic bin in one corner.

"No freakin' way."

The smell of stale sweat creeps out of the neck of her hoodie.

Young looks at old. "Surely we could let her use the ladies…"

Old glares back. "No. We're doing Croft a favour. He could've asked the Sweeper to do this, but he asked us. So we're taking no risks. This wild cat would stab us as well if she got the chance."

"I wouldn't, I just…"

Mother says to daughter, unguarded. "Use your head, girl. Croft's got the kid in the Crypt for a reason. We do as we're told and he looks after us. People in this club respect us these days. All those years we had to put up with Cornflower taking the piss. Treating us like shit. I've worked hard for this. I'm not risking anything on her."

"But…" Daughter is unnerved.

The old woman drops her voice to a whisper, puts a hand over her mouth. In the empty room Nicole still catches an echo off the wall.

"Besides, we do this right and Croft owes us. It's protection."

Nicole groans. "Please undo my hands," she says. "My stomach, I won't be able to get my jeans down quick enough."

Old Debs says, "You'll be surprised what you can do when you're desperate. I'll be back tomorrow." There's the falsest of smiles. "If you're still here then."

CHAPTER 51

Anita's eyes follow the rivulets of rain on the passenger window of Pete's car. The tiny streams of water merge and split, some fat drops splat and fall. The pestering tone of her mobile draws her attention away from the blur of the ring-road.

"Councillor Patel," the voice is a bullet, "you know who this is."

Anita's eyebrows jump, she darts a gaze at Pete, mouthing the word "CROFT".

"I have nothing to say to you."

Pete pulls the car over. Anita slumps down in the front passenger car seat as if Croft is somehow there, watching the car from the top of a building, sniper at the ready.

"We have a mutual friend, who I hear you are interested in locating." His tone is matter-of-fact.

"Where's Nicole, tell me now."

"The girl's safe, staying with a friend of mine. Obviously she's had some shocking news, needed a bit of time out, I'd say," Croft snorts.

"What are you talking about? Where is she? I need to talk to her."

A nerve in Anita's neck jangles down her arm to her hand, little finger buzzing.

"We'll get to that. You and I need a talk. You didn't get the message I take it…"

She looks at her phone, swallows hard, "Errr, no, there was no message."

"Next time you might need more than a neck brace and some pain-killers."

Croft had paid the white van thugs to run her car off the road. Of course it had crossed her mind, but it made no sense. Pete puts his hand back on Anita's leg to stop it shaking. He's mouthing, "PUT IT ON SPEAKER," but she can't move the phone from her ear.

"Just tell me what you want."

"It's straightforward…" Croft pauses, "Like I said, you and I have a quiet chat. No police. No social workers. Until that happens, the girl stays where she is. I'll send you details."

In panic, Anita tries a bluff, "I've been to the police already…" It might be the wrong thing to say, but it's sort of true. They were at the police station earlier.

"Yeah, well, I'll await their call."

"I want Nicole."

"We know that. We're doing you a favour looking after her. That kid is running wild, likely as not she'll take herself off… That would have consequences…"

They could do without a child-in-care scandal of course, but that's not what he means. That's what criminals do. They exploit weaknesses, in systems and in individuals. They threaten the family. Her mind flashes to Pinkie. Croft must know where she lives. Anita holds her breath. I'm already being forced into playing his game. I'll have to do what he wants. And if I do it once, it'll only continue. I won't be acting in the interests of the community or the city, he'll own me. And…

Croft interrupts her thoughts; "Nicole might never be seen again. I'm sure you understand me…"

This is Croft; he makes people disappear. A menacing ear worm chomps its way into her brain. Nicole was right; Croft was somehow involved in Ash's death. Jaws clenched, Anita holds it together.

"You want a ransom? What is it? Tell me what you want?"

Croft ignores her.

"This isn't my phone. We never had this conversation, so don't get any ideas about running to your mate DI Jones. You're dealing with the big boys here, councillor."

He hangs up.

"Do you want me to call Jones?" Pete asks.

Anita shakes her head, forgetting the consequences of moving her neck, but this time she feels no pain. Smacking her fist on the dashboard, she lets out a growl.

"I'll kill him. With my bare hands if necessary."

There's a sense of release as her own violent intent is expressed.

Anita throws the phone into the footwell, not wanting the poison to be near her head.

"Not yet I mean... Let's get to Pinkie's place."

Use your brain, she tells herself. We have to get Nicole back, get Pinkie and maybe even Vikesh out of harm's way, break any hold Croft might think he has over me. They are ten minutes away, but Pete's foot covers the brake as if they are descending a mountain pass and it's taking twice as long.

Remember, she thinks, you have something Croft needs.

CHAPTER 52

As they turn the corner Anita sees two men confronting Pinkie. Her hands are held up, palms flat towards them as if there's a gun.

"Jesus," Pete swerves into the kerb.

Before the car has stopped, Anita flings the door open, leaps onto the pavement.

"Back off…" she yells.

As the taller man turns in slow motion towards her, she recognises his bulk, the jutting chest. The big man is Les.

"You?" Anita staggers to the neighbour's wall. Propped up by the brickwork, the quickening in her blood seeps away. Les is the last person she wants to talk to.

Pinkie rushes towards her.

"I'm sorry," rasps Anita, "I thought they were threatening you."

"No, my dear," Pinkie strokes Anita's arm. "I'm ashamed to say, it is you they came to threaten."

"I don't care who you are," Pete says, "sod off."

Croft's call blares inside her head.

"You'd better hear them out." Pinkie grimaces.

To compose herself, Anita links her arm through her auntie's. A winter wind whips through them.

"Can we go inside?" Les asks. "Talk like adults."

How can anything he has to say be more important than Nicole?

"Say what you have to and then, please, just go."

Anita is sure she's met the man with Les before. As he holds out his hand, she sees the red party rose pinned to his tie and accepts the handshake.

"Gerry Anthony," he says, failing to add that he's the regional organiser, the party's enforcer. Now she remembers him, smiling obsequiously at the council AGM. Les has called in re-enforcements.

"They've organised a meeting at the Mechanics tomorrow night." Pinkie's tone is gruff, furious on Anita's behalf. "A vote of no confidence. They say you have to resign or be expelled."

"What? You encouraged me to run for leader and now you want to ban me?"

"Your actions are bringing the party into disrepute." Les sounds as if he's quoting from the rulebook. He looks odd, as if his spine is pinned to a rod. He's almost moving mechanically. This is the sort of bullying behaviour he is famous for and she wouldn't be surprised if he was enjoying himself, playing the big man again, re-taking power.

Anita's neck begins throbbing again.

"I consider this an outrage." Beside her Pinkie's voice is unusually tight, full of emotion. "They say you have lost them traditional votes, too much negative publicity."

Anita has rarely seen Pinkie so angry. "Traditional votes? You mean white votes."

Pinkie wags her finger at the party officer. "Don't we count? Thirty years ago my late husband and I campaigned for you, introduced you to Asian families in the area as a friend. How dare you say Anita's face no longer fits? I will speak to the elders. We must not risk divisions between our communities."

Maybe Gerry Anthony hasn't understood her auntie's strength. She's always been an unofficial spokesman for a significant minority group in the city – and their elected representatives. Pinkie also commands respect amongst some of the other ethnic groups. Anita is proud of her. She was proud of Jas, too. Jas and Pinkie were a force for unity.

"If the council doesn't set a legal budget, there'll be no need for an investigation." Les is unmoved. "It'll be front page news. We'll be a laughing stock. The first council in 30-odd years that failed to agree a budget. We'll be judged as incompetent."

The party official says, "The party is weak; we can't afford any more gaffes."

As much as she wants to get inside the house, Anita is swept into the debate. She can't let that go.

"You're unbelievable. This government has forced us into an impossible situation. What services are left will be absolutely decimated. And you've given them a get-out-of-jail card. Your deal with the bloody club and Croft makes the situation worse. That's what you don't like. I've made it public. In the meantime, people in need are feeling extra pain because of you and you're worried about political embarrassment?"

Gerry blocks the path to the house, her route to safety.

"Look Anita, plenty of councils are self-sustaining. They don't need grants from the government. They raise income from business rates. We've lost the argument that the government should fund services."

"Don't patronise me. That might work for a few councils in the south with high land values and low service demands, but don't kid yourself that works round here. We should be fighting this all the way."

"You need to grow up, Anita." Les snaps.

The fact that Anita doesn't smack Les in the face right now is a mark of how much she's grown up. In fact, Anita can barely remember her young self in her Doc boots, collecting signatures. She takes a deep breath.

WE KNOW WHAT WE ARE

"It's better than giving up."

"You've no idea how this game is played. I made a mistake in recommending you to the members."

"Yeah, you made a mistake alright," she replies. "And this, Les, is not a game."

Anita's ears are ringing. Unless I come up with something right now, this is my choice, she thinks. Either I sign the budget and let Croft and Les' gang continue the spiral of decline, force the city into a living hell, or I don't sign the budget, get chucked out of the party, possibly sent to jail, the government send in a task force and the city is still a living hell.

"Have your vote of no confidence," she says. "Let your gang decide what they need to decide. We've got more important things to do."

*

Pinkie runs a bright blue flannel under the hot tap, squeezes it out and passes it to Anita as she joins them at the table. The sensation of the warm flannel on Anita's hands and neck brings only minor relief. Seeing Pinkie so distraught, struggling to find a way to turn this around in her head, makes Anita want to cry. They have talked for hours about their place in this city; their commitment to the community, their civic duty, about integration and assimilation, about generations, economic migrants, asylum and refugees, about young people, small steps and acceptance. About learning to live together. About their love for the place. About what makes a home.

Anita's thoughts return to Nicole, an image of Vishnu the protector flashes into her head, his four arms are out wide to gather her up, to keep her safe. There is knocking at the front door.

It's Pete. "They've gone. Let me call Jones," he says. "You're ready to drop."

The satin make-up bag that contains the painkillers is where Anita left it earlier that morning. The sweet tea helps the pills slide down.

"Thanks." She slumps at the kitchen table. "Give me an hour to lie down and I'll be OK."

It's all she can manage.

"I don't know," Pete says, "you kick one football club where it hurts and you get waste shoved through your front door, tyres slashed, rape and death threats, actual attempted murder. Not exactly subtle, is it? Then you try and make the right decisions for your city – best of a lousy job, mind – and your reputation is trashed. Your comrades stitch you up and after, what, two months, there's a vote of no confidence? Nice that..."

They've reached a professional place in their relationship, united in their desire to get Nicole back, but his face is kinder.

As Pete looks directly into Anita's eyes, she forces herself to sit up straight. Fragments of herself spin in a mobile mix of memories, incidents of personal and political significance, screenshot images of small successes and disastrous campaigns, badges of belief, words and people merge and split. Her eyelids are dropping.

"They want me to give up," she says. "For myself; I could leave them to it, walk away, but Nicole... she has to get through this."

The girl, defined by her brother's death, needs to be able to live, to decide her own way. That is what's going to happen, she tells herself.

Nicole will live.

CHAPTER 53

The brass lion door knocker to Pinkie's house is a statement of strength on a social housing door.

"I'm not sure if you remember me, Mrs Patel? I'm Conor Walsh." He stops himself saying "from the council". Without the tag he feels insubstantial. His primary identifier has been stripped away.

"I wonder if I can have a quick word with Anita?" Conor is relieved to see Pinkie hold out a hand. An everyday handshake, the warm skin and common courtesy has Conor swallowing hard. He's worked out another piece of the Croft jigsaw.

"Please wait here a moment," Pinkie says. "I'll check."

The standard beige lamp in the hallway highlights the fine silver hairs at the old woman's temple. Twenty-five years ago, when he started at the council, Conor had processed Councillor Patel Senior's expenses forms. The Indian name had stood out back then.

The duty PC stationed outside the house already knows who he is. Conor is required to report his movements to DI Jones. He's desperate not to scratch his ankle. The electronic tag clipped to his calf is tighter than a swimming pool band, the irritating locker key reminding him he's on borrowed time, while the police decide whether to charge him or not.

"She can't see you now, mate." A man with a council lanyard comes to the door.

"I've got information. Please. Anita has to hear this."

"Tell me and I'll pass it on."

"It'll take some explaining, can't I just…"

"Not now."

While the PC looks the other way, Conor pushes past the member of staff. It's only a few metres down the hall and into the lounge. The house is similar to his grandad's old terraced property. In the unventilated room, a royal blue fabric throw covers a worn sofa.

Anita emerges from the kitchen. "Haven't you caused enough trouble? You're suspended, Conor, just go home."

Conor pauses. He can't go home. Jayne has chucked him out and he's been sleeping in a friend's spare room, temporarily he hopes.

"The police know I'm here, I've told DI Jones. Please, hear me out…"

"At least you've learned one lesson then. Look, Croft has got Nicole. We don't need you here."

Christ. Croft has Nicole. In his mind, the young Nicole he'd first seen picking up debris after the collapse of the stadium points a finger at him. He looks down at the smoky glass coffee table. On it is a forgotten jigsaw of Blenheim Palace, small piles of sandy colours sieved into categories, a reminder of the time when they had so little to worry about.

"Give me a chance… five minutes. I know why Croft wants Nicole now."

Being forced away from work has meant he's had the best part of the day to work it out.

"Five minutes. Come through."

The kitchen is lit by a strip of shop-like spot lights, the beams bounce off the heads of those seated at the table. It smells of coriander daal, of un-eaten lunch.

"This is Pete, the manager at Westmeade." Anita motions Conor to sit next to her. "And Wormy."

He watches as the young man nods slowly, keeping his hands firmly under the table. He recognises the former Welders player from a while back. He's filled out a bit, but it's definitely him. That season they thought they'd discovered a golden generation, their very own version of the Becks, Giggs, Scholes and Neville gang.

"Nic was at Croft's garages," Wormy says, "but when I got there, the place was clean." His shoulders slump in dismay. "I found a picture of Ash in a puddle." The image Conor has in his head of Ash is from the flier Nicole gave him all those years ago; a snapshot of a young player with his eyes on the future.

"The police checked it out, the trail's gone cold."

"Waiting for Croft to ring is killing me. I haven't been able to move…"

There is a mobile phone in the centre of the table.

"…The police are tapping it," Anita says.

The device has its own magnetic field, both holding their attention and repelling them from touching it.

"You know my Auntie Pinkie."

The older woman seems to see through his eyes into the gristle of his brain.

"So, Croft's motivation… I think I know what he needs. Or at least it's a theory." Conor notices the laptop charging on the washing machine. "Can I use this?"

A few clicks later, Conor finds the press release he's looking for, the tip from Selka. He turns the screen so that everyone can see. The page is headed with a Union Jack in the corner of a blue flag, next to it stands Saint Ursula and the lamps of her virgin followers.

"Caribbean, BVI?" Wormy asks.

"Correct." Conor continues. "Croft can't afford any scandal for the next 48hours until his fund is launched."

Anita rubs the back of her neck, wincing.

"This is Croft's scheme. It's an international private equity fund." Conor covers his mouth with a half cough.

"A hedge fund?" Pete asks.

"Similar."

Anita rolls her eyes, making the assumption that private equity is always bad, but she allows him to continue.

"In the small print, it claims the fund is publicly backed by the local authority, by our assets. It's a false claim we could call him on. It'll get media attention at least."

Anita makes a fist. "And this means Nicole is his bargaining chip to keep us quiet? Is that it?"

"And what are the consequences?" Pinkie asks, leaning in close to the screen.

Conor takes his time, "I'm pretty sure Croft wants Anita to sign the budget off, give up the legal action and stop any financial investigations. The investment deals are probably lined up now, but they won't know exactly how much is committed until the launch. We don't know the numbers, but my contact tells me Croft is putting in £100 million and could raise another £400 million on the back of it, maybe more."

"So he could afford to pay the council back with profit?"

"In theory…"

"It's an obscene amount of money," Anita says. "Are you sure they're not just asset strippers?"

"It's not always the case, a lot depends on the London fund managers, what their motivation is, what their expertise is." He takes a breath; they are all listening hard, trying to make sense of it.

"Essentially Croft is giving these professional gamblers all this money and saying join me, we can do better deals, we all make more. Whatever the number, this is huge."

"And if he succeeds?" Anita asks.

"Then he won't need the club. He could do anything, sell the stadium and disappear, and instead of owning a villa in the Caribbean he can buy the island. And as it mentions the stadium as an asset in the fund, if he did sell it, he won't be paying the council back, the shareholders in the fund will benefit."

"Do the police know this?" Pete looks sceptical.

"I am due to speak to the fraud squad this morning. The circumstances weren't ideal…" Conor squirms, recalling his release from the station, how he had to walk home.

Pinkie's quiet voice cuts through the collective indignation. "And the consequences for Nicole are?"

"After the launch is…" Wormy jumps up, banging the table with his leg, "is when he don't need Nicole no more… I know Croft, he disappears people, just like Ash. Why would he let her go?"

The realisation produces a physical reverberation. They all move. Anita grabs the phone. Pinkie shakes her head.

"We gotta do something man…" Wormy is ready to hit the ceiling.

"OK," Pete takes control, "let's you and me do a drive by Croft's manor and call round to see Dez, see if he'll tell you anything he won't tell the police, check the timeline."

Conor remembers that Dez is the fourth member of the Welders' promising stars: Odds, Wormy, Ash and Dez.

Anita protests, "The police have searched the stadium, Croft's house and his pubs, there's no sign."

Wormy's response is slow and determined.

"Yeah Miss, like I said. They ain't gonna know about all the rooms. Dez saw that crib, when they sold him off the last time. It's got a cinema, special *Crystal* cellar, well hidden."

"I'm serious, don't go near that house," Anita says. "The police have been there already. If Croft thinks he's being watched, it could jeopardise Nicole's safety."

"Course not. That's my sister, too."

Pete says, "There's working out why Nicole's been taken and there's getting her back. The lads know more than they think. They can help us unlock this."

There's a look of recognition between Anita and Pete, a trust that Conor makes him ache thinking of Jayne.

"Has anyone asked Mr Sizzle if he knows anything?" Conor remembers that Sizzle has helped them in the past.

"We'll do that." Pete thanks Conor.

When Pete and Wormy have gone, Anita takes off her neck support and lets her head fall onto the table. Conor notices a red slash on her neck, a burn from the seat belt maybe?

"I've been thinking the same as Wormy. Croft has all the cards; he's not going to let Nicole go, but I suspect it's for another reason. I believe Nicole was right about the link between the club and Ash's death. We've got a new timeline of events in 2008. I've tried to map in when the council decisions were made. There were clear financial incentives for Cornflower and Croft to cover up Ash's disappearance. I understand now why they might've done it, but not how. If Nicole's pieced that together, Croft will want her out of the way."

The timeline since the discovery of Ash's body is so packed with incident Conor finds it hard to track back. If the club did organise a cover-up on that night in 2008, why did they take Ash to the city farm? Why there? He searches for images of Les Underhill on his phone. There's a picture of Les and the pigs when he opened the place. There are no coincidences at this point. Conor decides to challenge Les on this later.

"The police will get Nicole back." Conor says this more from his own desire than from confidence. "Croft wants you to sign off the budget, but my advice is… don't. I might… have a way."

Anita looks at him as if he's about to go off on a drug-dealing spree.

"It's too late."

CHAPTER 54

Conor is clear he can't leave Auntie Pinkie's kitchen until he's said everything he came to say. The point is not to keep it in his head alone, not to pre-judge whether or not it will be heard or how it will be received.

"If you had the appetite for borrowing, there could be a solution. I want to help. I could talk off the record to Westwich. Anne-Marie Morton, the CEO, used to work here. She was involved in the previous fracas with Croft."

Les would've been too proud to ask the neighbouring council for help. Wouldn't ask a woman. Would he? Yes, but that's because for Conor going to another man would be harder. Both gendered responses, both unhelpful.

Anita sighs, "I will do what Croft says. Go along with anything he wants. If he wants me to sign off the budget, that's what I'll do."

"But…"

"We can't risk Nicole. That's also what the police say."

Conor empathises. "I totally understand. If it was my son, I mean, if it was someone I cared about, I would do exactly the same. But you might not actually have to say anything in public about the budget."

"Does anyone really have any money left?" she asks.

"Last time I asked Westwich they had reserves and I'm pretty sure they have cash."

"Shoved under the bed."

Conor has made a calculation based on the size of their own safe in the vaults of the building.

"Using fresh £50 notes, bank-packed, they might have say £5million?" Anita shakes her head slowly. "Actually in a safe?"

"Actually in cash."

Her jaw drops so low he can see her tongue. It's another thing he hasn't shared with her, has kept in his back pocket.

"You're kidding."

"With the prospect of negative interest rates, loaning it to us is better than paying someone else to look after it... we talked about it at a regional treasurers' meeting."

"Course you have." Anita's voice is toneless; she turns her shoulder away from the table and the phone that links her to Croft. "The world is truly mad. Their safe is full and ours is empty. Croft is talking about hundreds of millions; we're cutting grants to the food bank, shutting children's homes."

Conor had once thought that Anita was too beautiful to lead the council. Her face now looks like a pick and mix of disgust, dread and impending defeat.

"Let me talk to them off the record," he says.

"No, no more of that. I've nothing against neighbours helping each other, if the boot was on the other foot I'd be doing the same, we have to stick together, but it doesn't change anything."

Conor is on a roll now. He has her ear and isn't going to give up now. "It keeps the show on the road, services are delivered to people who need them, and wages are paid, all that matters. And it can buy you some time to think, re-group. Play the long game, change takes time." Conor lets Anita digest this. "Keep borrowing and carry on." He's quite pleased with that. "It's what the government are doing and families the same."

"And I was trying to do something different," Anita replies flatly. "We're managing a race to the bottom..."

"Anita, I'm trying to be pragmatic, not obstructive."

"I see that." Anita manages a wry smile.

Conor closes his eyes, processing. I've been a bloody idiot, he thinks, I've under-estimated this woman from the start.

"I'm going to publicly support Croft until Nicole is safe. I've got to look people in the eye and tell them I got it wrong about the club," she says.

He takes a deep breath. "But you didn't. I did, we did, me, Les, the others. It was our mistake. I'm sorry you picked up the poisoned chalice."

The admission sits between them as an offer he didn't know he was ready to make.

"Do you remember that first meeting after the stand collapsed?" Anita asks.

Conor settles his arms on the table. He's opened the way to talk about the hurt, to go deeper. Of course he can recall that meeting perfectly. It was bloody and humiliating for Anita and all she'd done was ask the right questions about whether it was the role of the council to re-build the stadium.

"It wasn't just you who wanted the council to step in and save the day." Conor hears a growl in her voice. "People... the general public wanted someone to do something and who else was there? No-one. It was a no-win situation. People don't trust us to do it properly, even though most of the time we do, and throughout this whole mess, no-one says, actually the greed-driven club is to blame."

It's a frustration Conor has felt and suppressed for the last few years.

Anita continues, "Our staff are sick of being shot at from all sides. No-one's in our corner. The government cripples us, sets us up to fail and happily shoves the blame in our direction for their decisions. And it sticks because there's no alternative story..."

Conor is caught by her words.

"I think people hate us, politicians or public servants, because we are like them. Fallible, gullible. Guilty of wanting to help when we know whatever we do, it will never be enough. If we didn't treat them like idiots, took the time and effort to show them how complex things are, were more transparent, we would be in a different place now. Les' simplify and exaggerate approach is an insult to the public."

Pinkie comes back into the room, restoring a sense of normality to the impromptu council of war...

"I'm making tea for the PC outside. Would you like a drink?"

Conor nods, realising he might be pushing his luck.

"For what it's worth," Anita says, "you were right to intervene, but you went about it the wrong way. Croft makes his own rules. You trusted him and Cornflower before him; they're the same. You gave him an inch and he took a hundred miles."

It's an absolution of sorts.

"That's the mistake people everywhere are making," she says. "I mean with this kind of turbo capitalism..."

"Hmmm," he nods. The deeply political nature of the words makes him uncomfortable. It's not that he doesn't accept it exists, it's all around him. Financial de-regulation, privatisation, the counterweights, the regulations that keep the economic system in equilibrium are being removed.

"...Or in our case the casino economy. It creates vampires like Croft. We can't win in that world."

That hits home. It's Stevenage Town v Real Madrid. Up until now Conor's believed the economy is a game and it's possible to play it better. You just need to excel at riding the waves, be smarter and cleverer. At the last public finance conference he'd sat and listened to an economist setting it all out in graphs. They'd clapped politely and moved on. Now it's happening in their back yard.

"We opened the door to that..." he says. It's a relief, a confession of sorts.

"The Welders aren't on their own stuck in no-man's land, not big enough to make it into the big time and too big to shoulder the costs, to be sustainable. We said we wanted the club to survive at all costs and that gave Croft a free hand. We got the worst of all worlds."

The phone on the table buzzes with a message. Pinkie drops the teaspoon in the metal sink. It's not Croft, it's Pete: *Where do the Debbies from the supporters' club live?*

Conor has no idea what they've got to do with anything. "I can find that out," he says.

The call brings their focus back to the moment.

Anita says, "Nicole's in danger – that's wrong enough. The club is all the horror I thought it would be, but what I didn't see were the opportunities. It has the fans, possibilities, people like Nicole. There are always options. In any case," she mumbles, "I'm accountable."

"Not responsible, though." He looks at Anita in admiration, seeing the tiredness in her eyes, knowing that, unlike Les, she will accept the consequences of her actions.

"We're in a post–truth world apparently; there's no difference anymore."

They both know it's not a good thing for her leadership to end like this. He doesn't want that. He sees her bravery as she gives him a defeated shrug. It's a gesture he's used himself. They are on the same side. He understands that now.

"So I'm going to tell Croft and the fans what they want to hear…"

CHAPTER 55

Anita bites at the fingernails on her right hand; her thumb bleeds at the corner of the cuticle. Ouch. She hasn't done that since she was a teenager. Pinkie washes the mugs in the sink, the gentle chink of the teaspoon against china the only sound.

"I guess my parents were right to send me away. I was always too much trouble."

Pinkie turns to look directly into Anita's face, making her turn away. Anita hates herself for taking the path of self-pity. The old lady she has come to love so much looks surprised.

"My dear, why would you think that?"

"It's true." Anita is hot behind the eyelids, "I deserved it."

Anita's anger at her parents had been like a permanent skin rash and on arriving in the UK she'd rejected Pinkie's affection. If Nicole is harmed, she thinks, I'll have to leave. I can't dishonour Pinkie. How could I face Pete? He's almost Nicole's father. How could I face the public... anyone?

"I didn't mean to let everyone down. I can't face starting somewhere new. I love you, I love this place, it's my home."

Pinkie sits at the table, gently massaging Anita's hand. "Your mother and father didn't send you here as punishment."

"They said I was... an embarrassment."

"Your behaviour was embarrassing at times... the dead mice at your cousin's wedding?" Pinkie smiles but Anita can't. "Your mother saw you were different. But she sent you here because she wanted you to be the person you needed to be."

Anita stares into Pinkie's eyes, scrutinising, wanting to believe it and desperate for evidence that it's true.

"Ammi realised it would be hard for you in India. Things change slowly there. And remember back home it wasn't unusual for families to send children off to live with relatives in better-off parts of the world. It was a practical solution and an opportunity for you," Pinkie says. "I didn't understand why you set yourself apart, but I see it now. You believed you weren't wanted. Unloved. It's a story you told yourself."

Anita's pulls her hand away from Pinkie, covering her mouth. There were signs over the years, signs of love that Anita had refused to acknowledge. When she'd had shingles her mother had shipped over her favourite chocolate-coated chempedak fruit. Her dad had posted her a photo of the papaya tree in their vegetable garden with her brother's face buried in the pulpy orange flesh.

"Sending you here was sad, pragmatic and opportunistic. They loved you. They wanted the best for you. The anger is all yours."

Anita's head feels lighter than it has since that first day in the council chamber. Tears fall. "Thank you," she whispers.

As she leans forward to hug her auntie, static electricity between Anita's wine-red shirt and Pinkie's patterned polyester jumper crackles.

"You can't give up." Pinkie looks up seriously. "People need you. Nicole needs you. You have opened things up, given people a different perspective, you need to keep going."

Giddy, Anita feels giddy. Pinkie is right again. It doesn't change the situation and yet it offers a possibility of feeling differently about it. It's a different fight. A battle to keep a grip on herself; to go against her instincts, to do the opposite of what she normally does, to act in the interests of one person. Because if one person doesn't matter, none of us do.

*

Croft's message comes as a jolt.

You and the accountant at the conference suite 6pm tomorrow. PR will send script for fund launch. Business dress. Just the two of you. No need for Jones.

It gives them a target, a time constraint, that's what they have to work with. If I'm going to fall in with Croft, she thinks, I want witnesses. I want ordinary people to see me standing beside him. Even if I can't explain everything that's happened, they've GOT to be able to see the difference between us.

The PR script arrives on her phone. She is required to say that she officially supports the launch of the fund. I will say that I support the scheme, she thinks. I can at least spare the rest of the councillors the reputational damage of implying this is a joint decision. Taking a deep breath she grieves for her career, for the future she might have had.

The script says that the arrangement will be an on-going collaboration. That the council's financial commitment to the club remains and that Anita looks forward to meeting targets and, she says aloud, "Making millions for you international, blood-sucking misery-makers."

Anita calls Conor. "I need you to help me get a small group of fans together tomorrow evening. Nothing that will jeopardise Nicole. And there's something else…"

Croft's event is at exactly the same time as Les' kangaroo court, the vote of no confidence. She smiles at the irony. They can vote her out if they like and the timing is good in one way.

"…Tell Les I can't come to his meeting, but if he wants to come along to Croft's fund launch that's fine. I've been meaning to ask him a few questions."

"I'm not sure about inviting fans… they can be, as you know… unpredictable. As can Les…"

"Unpredictable works for me right now."

"It could confuse things. I mean, it could get nasty."

"It could…" she says, thinking it already has.

Conor doesn't sound confident. The assured, downbeat delivery has been replaced by a hesitancy that gives her space. Uncertainty has its uses.

CHAPTER 56

They are in Conor's midnight-blue Volvo. Wind rages across the VIP car park, the lack of floodlights making it feel more like midnight than 7pm. Anita's mouth tastes metallic, her stomach leaden. This is not what she expected.

"We're early," Conor says. "Take a minute if you want."

It's already busier than she thought it would be. The concrete expanse makes a giant of the stadium, ready to pick up its feet and stamp, Godzilla-like, on the luxury cars. They are parked a couple of spaces away from a new black Jaguar XJS. A driver gets out, opening first one door then scooting around to the other, as two men in conspicuously expensive winter coats emerge. They have to be the fund managers.

Anita tries to concentrate on the speech she has to deliver. A small, brief press event with forced smiles to a camera, that's what she'd imagined. The fund would be launched and they'd be told where to find Nicole, but Jones had warned her that it might not be so straightforward.

In the background, the police are all over Croft, but still struggling for evidence. Nicole is a valuable asset to Croft. If he can extort benefits from an on-going situation, he will. As instructed, the police are not directly in attendance, but Jones is in a van around the corner. She suspects the young, black security men are on the lookout for undercover police officers to stop and search – a nice irony, if they see it.

Conor has a tiny wire inside his shirt, inside his black suit jacket. It's a back-up for the police. Everything will be recorded tonight on Croft's own CCTV. Anita grips her phone, constantly checking for news from Pete and Wormy. Their search continues.

Skulking behind the money men at the VIP entrance are a handful of men, fans wearing Welders scarves. This is also unexpected. Croft is packing the meeting with his loyal fans. They could be ultras or trolls, bound to hate her. Anita takes a breath, remembering Pinkie's advice: "When the world is going mad around you, the only thing you can do is choose to do the right thing." She'd tried that line on Les once. He'd looked at her as if she was insane.

"I took the liberty of inviting a couple of the fans myself." Conor points to a young couple. "They're friends of my son. I thought if you were going to make this compromise, at least some of our more reasonable fans should hear it from your own mouth. They'll support you for it."

She doubts that, but the idea isn't a bad one.

"And," he continues, "I invited Zoe from the LGBT network and Colin from the Disability Forum. Thought it might even up the odds. They are colleagues of yours, aren't they?"

Her anxiety level ratchets up another notch. "They might not be after this. They supported me for taking a stand against the club, but this will destroy my credibility with a lot of good people."

As they walk towards the VIP entrance, Conor touches her arm and nods back towards the car park. There's a procession of cars. Two men emerge, jackets flapping hard like seagulls' wings in the wind. It's Councillors Gent and Bardill. Les' gang are here.

By the entrance, Sizzle's van also crawls into view; he's never one to miss out on the possibility of brisk trade.

They climb the stairs to the conference facilities in silence. Past the purple-striped sofa in the reception area where Conor had told her what she'd thought was the worst of the financial mess. The sport seems so far away from this story that it's almost a surprise to enter the Cornflower suite, to see the banks of windows looking out onto the pitch. It's a dark field, a sodden battleground, the edges illuminated only by the reflected light of the stand.

In the centre of the room facing a small podium the seats are set out theatre-style. Next to the podium is a backdrop, a checkerboard pop-up screen plastered with the logos of the local Volvo dealer, an estate agent and a money lender. No friends of hers. A camera is set up and Croft in city mode looks to be making some kind of promo for the fund. Anita watches his understated performance, mimicking the money men in presenting a quiet confidence. Old Spice testosterone doesn't sell in their world anymore. The new testosterone is masked by algorithms, faux deference and male grooming.

Anita pictures Nicole, imagining what state she must be in, physically and mentally. In contrast, it's disturbing how convincing Croft looks. Except he struggles to take the lapel mike off and, dressed in full fan regalia, football shirts and scarves, the Debbies try to step into shot. They've clearly seen an opportunity to get Croft's attention. He's gritting his teeth, turning away from them, motioning for the one of the fund managers to say a few words.

The Debbies will test Croft's selective authenticity. How can he be all things to such a diverse audience? How will this play with his "man of the people" schtick? Is he going to start talking estuary English? The fund managers and investors want detail, they want professionals and they need big numbers to attract more of their ilk. They don't want a local lad done good. The only thing the Debbies and the men have in common is the hair dye.

Damn. Anita wishes she could lip-read. Maybe the Debbies have realised this is a terrible deal for the fans and want to have a word with Croft before this really gets going. More fans arrive and more community reps. Anita avoids eye contact, wishing time would speed up, that it would be over and they can get out of here alive. She concentrates on her phone. Still no word from Pete.

The PR woman tells Anita that they will film the men first. Of course they will. Les is heading to talk to Conor. Anita slides to the back of the room, she can't deal with Les now. Two skinheads burst into the room neck first, pumped up. Another stands arms folded, sneering at the fund managers' camera faces. Apart from Croft and the fund managers it's not clear who's on who's side, or what the sides might agree on.

The older Debbie tries again to talk to Croft, who has lost some of his earlier composure. He clearly doesn't like something Debbie has said. The younger one backs away sharply, shaking her head in disbelief or suspicion, Anita can't tell. But it looks like Mother and daughter are in a silent row. The young one stomps towards an emergency exit at the far end of the room. She stands under the green sign with the arrow pointing downwards, holding the door open until her mother reluctantly moves towards her.

When the door has closed Anita decides to follow them, only for a couple of minutes. She can't afford to be missed but this might be important. They can come and find me if they're so bothered about my public suicide, she thinks. Bizarrely, everyone is clucking and chuntering, the noise level is rising. While the PR is busy talking into a walkie-talkie, concerned about the numbers, Anita takes her chance.

The exit leads to a breeze block stairwell, the lights in cages on the ceilings buzz, it's cold, concrete; an instant shift from front of house to back. Anita closes the door behind her silently, wanting to overhear the conversation before she approaches the Debbies. With one step she realises that the heels of her ankle boots will make too much noise and slips them off.

The lights must be on a timer. Suddenly it's much darker, with a low, green glow guiding the way down.

"Christ, where's the switch?" the older Debbie coughs.

"Must be back up by the door." The younger one of the women

shines a torch light from a mobile. "I'll go."

Anita takes a shallow breath, not moving. She can reach the switch, but hesitates. It's a risk. One way or another they will know she's there.

"For god's sake, the phone'll do. Let's just get to the Crypt."

Cold sets in to Anita's stockinged feet. It can't literally be a place where bodies are buried. It has to be some kind of basement.

"She's faking." The smoky voice of the older woman sounds sinister. Are they talking about me, Anita wonders? I am faking it by standing with Croft, but how could they know that? Then she hears their argument re-start.

"The kid is sick. If Nicole dies, he'll blame it on us."

It's them. They've got Nicole. Anita freezes, shocked solid in the moment. Them? As she starts to breath normally she feels her blood begin to boil.

"She'll be OK as long as she doesn't keep pissing the Sweeper off. Mr Croft gave me his word."

"I don't know why you even agreed to this."

"I told you, whoever owns the club in future, we get to run the supporters' club. He'll see us right."

"He's keeping a kid in the bloody Crypt. Mum, please. However much trouble she is, that's way wrong," the younger Debbie begs.

The women are almost at the bottom of the stairs. Anita sticks to the wall, moving close enough to hear.

The old Debbie rasps, "You thought Christmas had come when Croft asked us to have a go at Patel. You enjoyed it, trashing her car. We're in this. We stay calm. The Sweeper is on his way down there, he'll know if she's putting it on. We're just the housekeepers, we do what we're told."

"But..."

"Do what you like. I'm going back upstairs." As the old woman turns, Anita begins to sprint up the stairs. She has to get a message to Jones.

"Someone's there. Oi."

Even if she does confront the women, wherever Nicole is, there's the Sweeper to deal with. Anita remembers now, when she visited Odds in prison he said to watch out for him. Breathing heavily, she opens the door, remembers to pick up her boots and walks quickly to the nearest chair, pulls on her boots, then ducks behind the podium. Before Les and Conor approach her, hands shaking, she sends a message to DI Jones.

Nicole in Crypt? Basement of stand?

*

Back in the room, Anita is reeling. Hold it together. Play for time. She pushes her hair behind her ear, wipes her forehead. Those women are sick. The police were only supposed to be around the corner. Where are they? Shit. There must be 30 people in the room now. They are oil, water, fans, financiers and politicians, a mix likely to combust. This can't be what Croft expected, too many people. A chant goes up.

"We're by far the greatest team…"

One of the fund managers raises an eyebrow; it's turning into a circus. Croft is talking to Les, backs to the growing crowd. Is that right? Croft wasn't patting Les on the shoulder, it was a squeeze. Another wave of shock hits Anita. Is Les in on the fund deal?

Bloody hell, come on.

As Croft moves quickly away from Les, a blink of anger crosses his face.

"We'd like you to join the stage now," the PR woman says. Anita's heart jumps. Croft appears to want to shake her hand on camera. She recoils; then, saving her, a fan comes up to take a selfie with Croft. They could be brothers. Croft tries to brush off his poorer, more shambolic self.

Les is on the front row surrounded by her fellow councillors, with Conor in the last seat of the row. Les takes the mike: "Order, order, calm it down, lads."

On the stage, a financial partner is in the chair next to a fund manager and there are only 30 centimetres between her and Croft.

"Let's get down to business." The money man's cut-glass vowels are heard above the melee. Anita sees puzzlement on the faces of the councillors and is relieved to see the young couple Conor invited have phones aloft, recording.

"Who are yer…?" Sizzle gets a laugh.

"Quite. Quite." The financial partner coughs. "It falls to me to introduce the launch of FACP68, our fully leveraged fund, offering substantial entry and governance rights. I want to start with a few words to our institutional investors…"

These are words designed to appeal to pension fund trustees and the like. Croft and his friends have other local authorities in their sights and Anita's legitimising this.

"What about the club?" someone shouts.

"What fund? Will it buy us a new striker?"

"Who owns the club?" Colin asks.

"Look, can we hold questions until…" appeals the financial partner.

Conor surprises her. "I want to check if the councillors here have any conflicts of interest to declare?" He's stalling, great.

"Sit down." Les wants to swat him away, but Conor is right.

Offence is taken at the back of the room and there's an altercation between the gobby fans and the security guards. Then it turns into a scuffle, a scrum of bodies surges towards the camera and TV backdrop, knocking the flimsy screen over. The PR manager panics, approaches Croft for instructions. Call it off? It's gone too far?

No, thinks Anita, we're here now, until it's over.

CHAPTER 57

A loud bang sends Anita's hands to her ears. First through the double doors to the conference room are three members of a firearms team, weapons ready.

"Clear," one of them shouts.

Councillors Berry and Ward drop to the floor. A few of the young fans run for the emergency exit. The rabble is shocked to a halt at the sight of the armour-clad bodies. Through the wall of police officers, darts Nicole. Alive. Electricity radiates from her, the crowd parts. She is at the head of a human triangle; Pete, Wormy and Jones are followed by a wider wave of uniforms.

Most people in the room don't know who this girl is or why she commands this army, but her significance smacks them into silence.

"Everyone sit down," DI Jones booms.

Anita launches herself forward to grab Nicole, holding her in a fierce press she wipes the hair from the girl's eyes. Anita gets a rush of pleasure; they are friends. It's the only word she has for their connection, but decides it will do. Friends can be everything. She gives Nicole a stupid grin, pats the torn rucksack that's stuck to the girls back.

"I heard them admit it," Nicole is babbling. "Croft and Cornflower. The Debbies are working for him, they, they…"

Police officers now block the main doors. The Debbies are nowhere to be seen. Relief chases out Anita's anxiety. Questions buzz. What happened? Are you hurt? The crowd is wired, the police comb the room, hands are placed on shoulders, the divisions temporarily contained. People return to their seats. The PR woman looks horrified. The fund managers huddle together, discussing their next move. Conor opens his jacket, no need to hide the wiretap now.

Holding out her hand to Pete, Anita lets him take Nicole to the safety of a nearby female officer. She scans the crowd. There's movement, the green light from the emergency exit door catches her eye.

"Croft!" Anita screams. "He's escaping!"

Police bundle across the room in pursuit of the chairman. Les' jaw has dropped open. This can't happen. Croft seems to be getting away.

"Sit down!" Jones bellows.

The temporary silence is awkward. The crowd expect her – as the leader – to say something sensible, to make sense of the chaos. She looks up at the ceiling, reflected lights dance from the phones held aloft like torches. Plenty of people are filming this. You wanted this, she tells herself. It's time to seize the uncertainty, to inject a new possibility.

Anita snatches the mike from the fund manager, grips it tight to stop her hands from shaking. Standing on the podium she's aware that under the stapled grey flooring is a flimsy structure, a soap box, the stadium beneath them unsettled by events.

"Croft has gone, the police are going to pick him up." Anita is not prepared to countenance any other outcome at this stage. "He's not coming back. To the club or the city, ever."

It's her message to Nicole, she is telling her she's safe, yet the audience teeters. Croft is a survivor, a man of clout.

"What d'you mean Croft's gone?"

"Where's he going?"

"Why would he run?"

"Croft and Cornflower, they killed my brother," Nicole shouts.

It's a similar assertion to the one Anita had heard the first day she'd met Nicole at Westmeade, but now it rings with the fire of truth and the fear of no-one.

"Lying little bitch," one of the skinheads shouts. The room erupts with conjecture. Pete steadies Nicole and the two huddle privately, away from the tumult.

It ought to be safe; there are as many police as there are fans in the room. DI Jones stands in front of the podium.

"Could you explain?" Anita offers the mike to Jones, but the detective doesn't need it. On the front row she sees Councillor Gent grab Les' arm, but Les is paralysed, hand fixed over his mouth. A picture of dread that Anita hasn't seen before. Guilt maybe?

DI Jones' gravelly voice fills the room. "Daniel Croft is wanted for questioning in relation to an on-going money laundering and fraud investigation..."

Anita looks across at a stunned Conor. The police must have found some proof.

"We'll be making a full statement as soon as we can."

Jones checks no-one is going anywhere.

Anita waits for the noise to subside. "I came here tonight to announce that the council was halting its legal action against the club. I was being pressurised by Croft to support this ridiculous scheme. It was a way to make more profit by leveraging the debt. It wouldn't have benefitted the club or the city. This isn't what I expected to say, but if we want the Welders to survive, it's down to us."

It's a strange kind of us. Anita recognises that she hasn't actually come to terms with it herself. And the fans still might not want an us that includes her – but they are listening.

"I remember my Uncle Jas, watching the old Boer war film, *Zulu*... In the face of the battle, a young private quakes. 'Why's it always us?' he asks his sergeant. 'Coz we're here sonny, and no-one else is.'"

Anita, with her breasts, her brown skin, sparkly Saturday night clothes, the badges and banners, could never be the same as the fans.

"I know for some people here, I'm your worst nightmare..." she says...

"...but I'm not your enemy and you don't need to be mine. We don't have to be the same to want the same, to share similar interests, to form an alliance..."

She takes a breath, shifts her gaze to Mr Sizzle, his bowl-shaped face is sceptical but attentive.

"I've learnt a lot about football in a short space of time... Nicole Brand has been my teacher. She helped me see the love of the sport, the commitment, the hope and pride that the game can bring."

Nicole's face glows. They are different women. It's the differences that have cemented their bond.

"Quite right, too," one of the councillors shouts.

"... And I've seen what a powerful left foot Nicole's got. We need the determination and spirit of players and supporters to benefit the whole city. And I understand the wider role of the club, of all sporting clubs now. I got that wrong. I'm sorry."

"So you should be," another voice calls.

But she sees Nicole nod, apology accepted.

"I saw the dirty business of the game and I wanted no part of it. And I couldn't understand why so many fans kept ignoring what was rotten at the club..."

She looks at Conor, Les and the other councillors, the fans in the room, clever men who could see that their loyalty, emotions and sense of identity were being exploited. Yet they switched off their critical faculties at the turnstile every Saturday. The club doesn't belong to them, the club wasn't their club, it was

Croft's. The fans' values were never part of the picture, yet they tell themselves it's just 90 minutes, put the reality to one side, suck it up and buy another season ticket.

Conor squirms in his seat, but he makes eye contact with Anita. His shrug says we're men, we can be a bit slow sometimes, but we'll get there...

Les' skin is whiter than usual. He's twitching, nervous and at the same time his face looks like he's deciding which fist he wants to throw first.

"There will always be fans who refuse to see the abuse of power, the intentions and implications. Or they see it and celebrate it, join in. The Cantona kick, the odd bung is all part of the game, as if it's a victory for the common man. As if Croft is a common man..."

She blows out a long breath, steeling herself.

"We are in the majority. We have power that people like Croft are scared of. It's in the interest of the likes of Croft for people to think the worst in human nature. It stops us acting collectively, in our own interest not his."

Take your time she tells herself, "...I didn't get that... Not when there's an alternative..."

The councillors in the audience look immediately alarmed.

"So I came here to announce business as usual when I really believed the club as it is needed to be shut down. I still do..."

This time Anita stops, pauses for effect. "I'm not going to save the club... you are."

This time it's a wave of incredulity that crashes at her feet. But as it subsides, the wash contains curiosity.

"If you want it, that is? I want to give you that opportunity..."

"Yeah, right," someone at the back shouts.

"Football is the same as many things in life, if you're passionate about it, if you really care..."

She keeps her face still, unsmiling. Her people are here, too. Good people are listening and others might, too.

"And if you want to carry on supporting the club, then you have to get involved. You can't stand on the touchline shouting the odds. Get on the pitch, get stuck in, try to do something together. We're good at that in this city..."

Anita looks at Conor. Or at least that's what they like to think. They like the image of themselves as people who work well together.

"I hear it all the time on the doorstep, in the street. Let's put it into practice. This will be a stiff test, a vertical learning curve, but we can do this."

"What exactly do you mean?" Sizzle asks.

Straightening her back; stretching the aching tendons in her neck, stomach listing, she says to the world: "I want the Welders to be the biggest, most significant, most successful fan-owned club in the country. That's the ambition. Out of this mess can come something new."

CHAPTER 58

On the podium, Anita has her back to the window. Without warning the full floodlights are switched on. She watches people shield their eyes, turn their heads slightly away, recalibrating. There's no way for her to judge their reaction to her proposition.

Nicole runs to look at the pitch. "Maaaaaann..." The security guard closest to the window gets his phone out. "Croft's running."

There's a stampede to the front, higher than the rest Anita watches the spectacle. Somehow Croft has broken through into the stand, careers down the stairs to the pitch. Heading for the tunnel maybe? One police officer is a few rows above him tracking his steps. Two more come from the Cemetery End.

"Go on my son..." one of the fans shouts in a bizarre, OJ Simpson moment.

Croft is lumbering, a rabbit in the floodlights, a gormless pitch invader zigzagging to evade the stewards. There's a small cheer as he's tackled at the half-way line, hands forced behind his back and cuffed, his expensive suit muddied by the turf. In the moment Anita enjoys Croft's public humiliation.

The atmosphere in the room is anxious, trying to take stock. Local lad done bad? They have seen the news happen in front of them, it's the golden shot on the fans' phones, yet they still can't believe it. The capture helpfully underlines that Croft won't be returning, but the crowd is undecided. Croft has resources, he can bounce back.

The group sitting around Les seems to lean in together, become more solid. The threat of a vote of no confidence returns for Anita.

"Show's over," Jones says, but there's no way people will remain orderly after that. "We'll let you know when we can clear the building."

Pete catches her hand.

"Keep going. It'll be alright. People aren't stupid."

Teeth clamped together, Anita tries to smile.

"The New Welders," Nicole says. "Cool."

"We've got to get Nicole to casualty," Pete says, "sort that hand out. She'll have to give a statement. Call me, as soon as."

"The Debbies, they…" Nicole's face is burning. Anita winces, noticing a bruise on the girl's forehead.

"Later, chick." As Pete and a policewoman lead Nicole away, Anita feels her heart race.

She holds the mike close, making herself fill the room. She starts again.

"We can't re-write history, but we can write the next chapter for the club. I want a club we can all be proud of."

"Fine words," Mr Sizzle chips in, "but where's the meat?"

Anita tries to remain calm. "OK," she says, thinking fast, "the deal could be something like this. *If* the council agrees, we transfer the stadium – not the debt – to the New Welders. And we give you a finance expert who is a lifelong fan…" She points at Conor.

"…on the basis that you re-invent the club for the benefit of everyone in the city. There would be conditions. It has to be a shared asset, the stadium open 24/7. It has to be affordable, pay what you can afford for your season ticket. Anyone doing business here has to be locally based. Turn the boxes into business incubator units. This becomes a community conference centre and part of the college. Women's football is played here, on the same pitch."

"It'll be a disaster," Councillor Gent interrupts.

"We design-in solidarity, with asylum seekers, with people with disabilities, our LGBT community and..."

"Burger eaters," shouts Sizzle.

"Hear, hear." It's a sign. The energy in the room creeps towards her.

"Our new club has to belong to everyone, not the same old boys' network. We all belong in different ways to different things. But this means active participation, not just pay your way in. You aren't just football fans, are you? You've got families, friends, experience, jobs, skills, we need all of that. Bring your whole selves and be open to others. I'm absolutely serious and you need to be, too. There is too much dividing us. We need a critical mass to make this work, we need to share the load and we need some real business experts."

Anita wracks her brains back to the night of research in the spare bedroom at Pinkie's place. "It's not going to be easy. Everything is hard these days. But AFC Wimbledon, FC United of Manchester..." she's relieved to have dragged that out, "other places have done it. Portsmouth..."

She turns to Conor for help.

"If others can do it, so can we and we'll do it on a bigger scale."

He sounds like his old downbeat self, the tone is guttural, but the content is positive.

"There's a different sort of approach at Chester..."

"That's not the same..."

"And Exeter are amazing..."

"And there's the German model, St Pauli..."

"Wurst-eating anarchists... all welcome here," Sizzle guffaws.

Anita steps back. It's starting. There are murmurs, positive in nature, but mainly talking. Talking is good. She lets it ride, wanting to hear their voices, but on tenterhooks in case Les makes his move. The anxiety is lifting. There is a sniff of optimism, it could work. She's said enough, but scared of a lull, an opening for Les to come in, she shouts above the hubbub.

"This is a leap of faith. Fans talk about having faith, have some in the people of this city. Have some in yourselves. I know some of you will be thinking we'll never win anything again. I see that's going to hurt, but none of us are winning now, are we? Not in the club or in the city. Let go of the idea of being promoted to the Premiership and concentrate on creating something real. See how far we could go. There are no short cuts... we've got to work out the details together... but it'll be on your terms, proper adult negotiations. Not just shouting like children from the sidelines because the new owner hasn't got deep enough pockets."

Anita loses her train of thought... pain shoots down her neck. Don't be too desperate, don't sound needy. She stops herself, shakes her head slowly.

What she'd been about to say, what she'd been thinking at the same time as speaking, was that the reason this is so important is because if we can't save the club, we can't save ourselves. And that goes for her too...

In that moment, she steps down and parks her backside on the edge of the podium, at eye level with people sitting in the front row, faces she knows and doesn't know, fund managers, fans, Croft's PR woman. Anita's smile is genuine. "Sod it," she says, "let's see if we can do something good together... Just don't expect me to turn up and watch the games..."

People clap. Sizzle is on his feet. Jones, even Jones, is nodding. They seem to be pleased; they actually want to have a go.

To the side of the podium she sees the younger Debbie nod. The Debbies are already guarded by police officers, awaiting arrest. The older one is slumped on a chair, still turned towards the pitch. Those women attacked my home, held Nicole captive. They clung onto some perverted idea that they had to serve this version of the club to the death. And, even sadder, that this was the only way to get the validation they needed. They were vulnerable to exploitation and hungry for power.

Anita can barely believe it. Quick, let's get out of here, she thinks. She begs Jones to let people go on a high, protecting the emerging energy, safeguarding the enthusiasm, and waves at a young man with a phone, relieved beyond belief. "You can post that right now," she shouts.

People begin standing, milling, searching for their phones. Anita makes her way towards Pete, to a place of safety. To the right-hand side of the room chairs are drawn into a corral.

CHAPTER 59

Conor watches people leave the conference room punch-drunk, boisterous, wanting more. DI Jones has given the group of about ten dazed councillors a few extra minutes before they need to clear the room. They are still in their corner, not ready for another round. Les has kept his power dry until now. The old man's nostrils flare, he's puffing and sweating, but he has the political experience to take it to penalties and then it could go either way.

"I propose we move ahead with the vote of no confidence."

Conor remembers the first time he'd seen Anita square up to Les in the New Mechanics, just after the stadium collapsed. She'd had a bright energy and a sparkly jumper, her questions had been effective, but they hadn't landed. Now Les is on his feet, static in the middle of a row of chairs, surrounded by his cabal. Tackling Anita is a different prospect, the energy has moved her way.

"Don't think any of that matters," Les threatens. "It meant nothing, completely irresponsible letting people walk away with false hope."

Les' taut face says that Anita's plan is far from certain to succeed. Yet Conor also sees doubt on the faces of the other group members. Has Les called this wrong?

"What the hell's going on?" Councillor Ward asks.

"Why is it false hope?" Anita cuts across the question. "Any kind of hope is better than lazy despair."

Les' strength is anchored by a deep resonance with his people.

"You're offering years of uncertainty when what people want is clarity. If this goes ahead, the club will be a mess. It'll cost us the next election."

True, Conor thinks, but anchors can be used to hold people down, to drown them. Anita hovers, pacing slowly along the side of the chairs; the eyes of the elected members follow her back and forth.

"Maybe. Maybe not," she says. "The New Welders could be a disaster or it could be an amazing success. Who knows?"

The group don't like ambivalence either.

Anita continues, "You're wrong about uncertainty Les. That's what gives me hope. How can things change if we're certain of everything, if the future is fixed?"

Les looks smug. "Our voters want the past not the future."

Conor knows Les is right, but Anita shrugs it off.

"The only certainty is change. It's a cliché, but it's true. We need to work with people to make the best change we can. Isn't that what we're here for?"

King Canute shakes his head.

"You always were naïve."

Anita rolls her shoulders back, takes a breath. Closest to Conor, Councillor Berry taps Gent's shoulder and whispers, "Did Les know about all this? The deal with Croft… I didn't understand…"

Anita ploughs on, "I'm not saying it will be easy. Hope gets you to the kick-off; hard work gets you the win."

Go on, Conor cheers silently.

"I don't want to fight you, Les." Anita surprises them all. "If this is going to happen, it needs you. The past is important, we need the memory of battles won and lost. We need your skill, your connections."

This isn't the Anita they recognise, that Conor recognises, barriers down, arms open.

"I can't deliver this alone. And you get to save your club!"

Whilst the eyes of the group turn to Les to hear his response, Conor's focus stays with Anita. She stops moving and holds onto the back of a chair, exhausted. It's another unexpected but costly move. Shrewd though and probably true. The New Welders will need all the support they can muster.

Conor has been standing a few metres away from the group. He could step forward, get Anita's back, but judges that she's doing alright and she might not want to lean on him.

Councillor Gent wants to buttress his friend. "Fans don't want to do things for themselves. I can't sell that on the doorstep."

I could, thinks Conor, relishing the prospect, a new sense of possibility arising from the mess of the last few days. Of late his gut feelings have been disastrous, but he puts a hand lightly on his stomach. This time he knows that a community club is the right solution, the only solution. He's been selling "good enough" ways forward to the staff for years now and this plan is actually good. It'll require something new, though. It means he will have to shift his focus, tell a new story with an open ending.

"Look," Anita says, her voice sounding full of gravel, "some won't buy it, but some will. We need to remind people that they are capable, that it's alright, that doing-it-yourself is better than alright, it's life-changing."

"What about the budget?" Hands by his side, arms heavy, Les takes a final punch. It's one that knocks them temporarily. Anita leans heavily on the empty chair. There is an uncomfortable silence.

"I'm not signing off a budget made in the shadow of Croft."

Evoking the chairman's name pulls everyone back to the reality of the situation. It unsettles Conor, but the effect on Les is worse. Still on his feet, Les starts to sway, stares in the direction of the pitch, his mouth moving but saying nothing.

Anita rubs at her sore neck. "We've been forced into making cuts that, frankly, I'm ashamed of. I won't do it anymore."

"Then you'll be sent to prison," Les says. They all know it's the law.

Conor reddens; he's used that line himself in the past.

"There's another reason I want to make the New Welders work," Anita says. "I'm talking about the council now, if we're going to survive and genuinely help sustain our people, we need to show that co-operative, creative solutions like this can work. People will be able to rely on what we do together, because they are part of it."

Conor grimaces, thinking about the "For sale" sign outside Westmeade. He agrees with Anita, but, in the end, the council might still have to sell it.

Councillor Gent asks, "Where's this going, Anita? If you aren't going to propose a legal budget, you have to step down."

"Please let me finish..." She is curt but polite. "Whoever the poor sod is that takes over Conor's role..."

Some of the group look confused. They don't know what happened with the drugs. The warm energy in Conor's chest sinks to his stomach. He's standing so close to Anita now that he could grab her arm. Christ. In the excitement he'd forgotten that there was no way he could go back to his old job. Conor feels the tag on his ankle itch, looks at his dirty shoes and recognises he's thinking that because he has loved that job, because it was important, it was worth doing.

"However much of a financial magician they are..." Anita looks at Conor like she did in the police cell that night, like she knows he's good, but he needs to get over himself and not act like he can control the world.

"...they can't make the numbers work."

"Wait," Conor says, stepping towards the group, "there is another way. I've started a conversation with Westwich Council, our neighbours have reserves. This isn't just about us. Others want to help, develop a co-operative approach."

This is to be Conor's parting gift: a sector-led financial solution. Les scoffs, but his reaction is over-egged; they all know he's been too proud to ask before.

Anita's voice is now hoarse; about to run out, "...We hold the potential for triumph and tragedy in our hands at the same time – all the time. We're good people, trying to do good in an impossible situation, but we're not on our own..."

Les is on the move, squeezing past the legs of Councillors Gent, Bardill and Berry to get to the end of the row. Where's he going?

"You don't need a vote of no confidence if you want me to go..." Anita says. "If I'm not the leader you need, then I'm not the leader... simple as that."

Les pushes through the confines out of the chairs, brushes past Anita and walks to the back of the room, towards the exit. He's not leaving now, is he? The old man is holding his arm, sweating, stumbling. For god's sake don't let him have a heart-attack. The group is swaying, bewildered, the plot has taken so many turns they are lost.

Anita looks spent, she staggers backwards a few paces and sits on the edge of the low podium, giving the group space to consider her words.

Conor is aware that this might be the last time he can speak as the voice of the bureaucracy. He summons what gravitas he can and steps forward, unwilling to let them come to a conclusion about Anita immediately.

"There are a lot of decisions to make, but it's too much for now," he says. "I'll make sure you get some independent help, a lawyer to work it through."

There's the relief of a process, of a next step. They have permission to slope off, to sit alongside the chances and choices ahead, to sleep in the dirt and the dreams.

Conor surveys the group. Anita is right, these are good people. In the main in their fifties and sixties, their kids and grandkids educated at the local comp. They don't see themselves as service users, but they probably are, probably always will be. Cradle to grave. They are not here for money, not motivated by private gain. They are local citizens, volunteers with one common purpose, to make democracy happen.

In the corner of his eye, Conor sees Nicole has returned, walking at speed towards Anita.

"Underhill? Who's Underhill?" the girl is shaking Anita's arm.

"Councillor Underhill, Les… you mean Les," Anita points towards the door. "What is it?"

"I forgot. Croft said 'I'll deal with Underhill.' He was talking to Cornflower about Ash's body being found."

CHAPTER 60

The air is sweaty and thick as the last group of people shuffle out of the conference room. Conor squints hard as if he's in a night club and the lights have suddenly been switched on.

"Les, wait!" He sprints to the doorway. Flanked by his ageing centurions Gent and Bardill, Les looks back briefly, but continues towards the main stairs. The police will interview the former emperor, but it's the last days of the empire and in the post-battle confusion Conor seizes the moment to get to the truth.

Barging between the men he places a hand firmly on Les' shoulder. A memory of the morning when the stadium collapsed has remained in his body. Back then, Conor had felt the downward pressure on his shoulder as an instruction from Les, an instruction to build, not bury.

"Traitor." Gent's white hair streak shines under the harsh lights.

Conor ignores the insult. If Les knew about Ash, maybe others did too.

"A quick word, that's all." Conor appears to be no threat. Bardill sneers and continues on his way home. Les wavers.

"We know," Conor says, not knowing exactly what Nicole meant.

Checking that no-one important is left, Les allows himself to be led to an empty part of the conference room. They stand by the windows looking out at the pitch.

"We built it," Les says, blinking hard.

In his years at the council, Conor was engaged by and committed to Les' world view. He had to be, in order to do the job. It's hard to look at the stadium and see it as a mistake, to see the distortion of the dream, to see it for what it has become.

"It's over, Les," he says simply. "You and Croft. You might as well tell me. Nicole heard Croft say you were involved in Ash's death."

She hadn't actually said that, but Conor wants to draw out the poison.

"How? No. I mean, no. It doesn't make sense. The girl's lying."

Les is sweating, biting his lip

"She was telling the truth all along. And Croft, he's in police custody. Is he going to say you had nothing to do with it?"

Suddenly the main flood lights are switched off. Conor finds the blackness in front of them soothing, the balm of a dark room to a migraine sufferer. Les leans forward, resting his head on the glass, spreading his arms out on the window ledge.

Slightly to his left he sees Anita moving towards them, unseen by Les. Conor puts a finger to his lips then points to his chest. The wiretap will still be recording.

Les moans like a statue, a voice boxed in.

"I wasn't involved, but I knew..."

Anita is right behind them now. Connor senses she's holding her breath. He is, too. Les shuts his eyes as if in silent prayer.

"That morning when the stand collapsed, Cornflower called me, said he was sending his car. I was surprised he wasn't in the Bentley, but when we got there, it was chaos... we had to do something..."

Conor swallows uncomfortably. He remembers the tangled mess of the stand, the debris blowing in the squally gusts. He'd mistaken Nicole for a young boy, turning over debris in the wreckage.

"I didn't know..." Les stammers, "about... about the boy. Not then. The stand collapsing, it was an accident..."

Anita's hand covers her mouth, the shock is all in her eyes, pupils wide, eyebrows raised. Conor looks around for DI Jones.

"A week after we'd agreed to re-build the stadium Croft rang me. That grating bloody voice... Said he'd be taking over Cornflower's interests in the Welders from that point on. Said it was a terrible tragedy that Ashley Brand had been crushed to death in the stadium collapse. I couldn't believe it. The lying bastard didn't give a shit about the boy..." Les draws a deep breath.

"...Croft said he could prove the council had been going light on health and safety. That Cornflower was deliberately running down the stand because I'd promised to rebuild the stadium. We shook on it."

As if there was some kind of honour involved?

"The poor kid was in the boot of the Bentley... and Croft said my prints were all over it..."

Cold races to the core of Conor's body. Anita had mentioned the Bentley. The police were looking for it. Christ. He'd thought of Les as a sentimental bully, a strong leader and a weak one, when it came to the fans. "It was blackmail. I told him I'd go to the police. I'd been in that car plenty of times. You've got nothing on me. Then he put the doubt in my mind... No smoke without fire, you'll be implicated. People'll believe anything, the truth doesn't matter anymore. I put the phone down on him, I did..."

And weak when it came to his own reputation. That Les would cover up the death of a young boy was unimaginable; that his moral compass was so firmly pointed at himself.

"...I suppose I bought into that lie..."

Post-truth? We all believe what suits us, Conor thinks; I believed Les was self-aggrandising, didn't want to think there was more to it.

"Days passed, the pressure was on. Cornflower disappeared. Croft told me that Cornflower would never set foot in this city again. The press demanded action. We were next in the firing line. The city and the club, it was a disaster. The economy was nose diving, the car plant gone, redundancies everywhere. The far right was making ground; carping on about the lack of leadership…It looked like we were going to lose the general election. We couldn't afford to lose the council as well. It would've been open season for the right to get in. A city this size has to have a functioning football club, we had to bring some hope, something to be proud of. I knew it was a risk not going straight to the police. For days I expected them to turn up to arrest me. It got to me…" Les knocks his head on the glass, "I… I phoned Croft."

Horrified, Conor questions himself. Even without political backing, it didn't occur to him to blow the whistle, to force Les' hand into holding Croft to account for the debt. It was always the same with Les. That was politics; Club, Council, Community, in that order.

"I never took a penny off Croft."

Conor's head jerks back as the reality smacks him hard.

"Don't try and justify this… For god's sake. Eight years and you said nothing?"

Underneath the political pushing and shoving, Conor had thought that Les was basically alright, that they were similar even. We all have our faults he'd thought. But he'd made assumptions. That because they'd worked together for twenty years, had supported the same team, that they knew each other.

From behind him, Anita finds her voice. "You lost the power you were clinging to the moment you made that call - Croft owned you. I know what it feels like to be threatened by him. In politics, we live or die by our decisions and in a hair's breath, we get them right or wrong. Before this, I was the one shouting from the sidelines. It's hard being the one who has to make those choices. I understand that now…"

Les shakes his head, he can't look at her. "Yes, but you stuck by your principles, you were right about the club all along…you risked the truth about the debt and tonight… you've put your faith in the fans, the people who were against you. That's leadership…"

Anita's body sways, Conor thinks she's about to fall.

"And I was lucky too…" she admits, more generous than Conor feels. "Look Les, when this is all over, we'll need to talk again… I'll come to see you…"

Les stares down at the red and black carpet tiles.

"You know where I'll be…"

Conor and Anita make eye contact, a look of recognition. Les will be in prison.

*

Before he'd left for the meeting tonight Conor had sat on the stairs at home with Jayne, hips squashed together as if it was matchday.

"Whatever happens, we'll be fine," she'd said. "Tonight isn't about you."

His wife had been right. Through all this, Conor had used his ego like a satnav, believing that his way was the right way, the only course between the rocks and the hard places.

"Use your heart and your head," Jayne had said. "At the same time. I know it can be tricky, for you men." She'd smiled and kissed him hard.

Right again. His rational self has driven his career, emotion suppressed for safety purposes. And when he realised he'd got it wrong, his grandad, the club, when he'd seen that he couldn't fix it all, he'd sped off, all heart, all hurt, out of balance. His new challenge is to be both.

DI Jones is clearing the room. Anita's cousin Vikesh and Aunty Pinkie have appeared to take her home. I need to get home, too, Conor thinks. He wants to be with Jayne, to begin his new story. He wants to be the man both Jayne and Anita think he is. And his son, he'll make Toby proud. More than anything, Conor wants to get on with it.

CHAPTER 61

May 2017

Regional Ladies' Cup Final

It's a perfect weekend. Last night's early evening canvassing had been followed by a Friday Biryani, fragrant coriander and chilli prawns with friends. They are the eight regulars in her ward, including a fit young couple, relatively new on the scene. They seem to relish delivering leaflets to flats where the lifts don't work. And there's a former resident of Westmeade, one of Nicole's friends, who lives in a shared house on the edge of the estate and is a fierce housing campaigner, some new youngsters attracted by the hopeful leadership. There are two weeks to go until the election, so every session counts.

When Aunty Pinkie had asked if Anita would stand again for the council, she'd taken her time to reply. Weeks in fact. The party's new regional organiser had re-cast Anita as a torch bearer for anti-corruption. The label felt awkward, as if that was all it had been. The new woman had offered to put Anita's name forward for the next available parliamentary seat, yet the suggestion rankled. It had come across as a perverse reward for the trauma she'd experienced. Equally, she suspected the party wanted to capitalise on the commendations she'd received for a successful handover of power to the fans.

Fan-owned or not, if the New Welders don't win, that might be short-lived. Success puts bums on seats, that's what everyone needs whether they are campaigners or football clubs

Anita is glad that people see her as a credible politician, although she'd prefer it if local people could see past that, to see her as a human being.

Pinkie had said, "You always wanted the moon on a stick."

"I'm not a career politician, I'm just into politics," she had replied.

"Yeah, all day every day," Nicole had laughed.

Councillor Berry had said, "Stay on as council leader, the fight isn't over. We've still got a government slashing services to pieces and you can help us to heal."

Anita felt heady hearing she was wanted; the appeal to her ego was persuasive, although that wasn't exactly what had swung her decision either. The process they had started with the New Welders had given her a broader sense of potential, a charge in her internal battery. People had come forward to help, stepped into a space, not just for the sake of the club but to be part of something. What was different was that they hadn't been defending their own corners at any expense; they'd focussed on what they had in common. It was a practical, progressive alliance spreading outside the bounds of their original project. At the heart of a radical centre is where I want to be, Anita thinks.

In the almond haze of a Saturday morning in bed with Pete, sex is the main agenda item. Anita would hate the opposition to win, but if she lost her seat... well, good news, bad news. There might even be time for a normal relationship, whatever that is.

The afternoon is taken up with the business of football. Yes. True, although they're actually calling it a festival of sport. Sunday will be a visit to see Pinkie and the cousins. Tea and tactics.

Walking across the tarmac to the People's Stand, Anita is partially caught by the almost nutty aroma of sizzling meat. With the briefest of nods to the big vendor, she heads inside. Nicole hadn't wanted it to be called the Ashley Brand Stand. It sounded naff and she wasn't keen to remind people that this was where her brother had died. There is a plaque, though; a photo and flowers in the reception entrance.

The VIP sign is gone and there's a hand-stitched banner stating as fact, "We are all refugees." The refugees get concessionary tickets and have proven as fiercely loyal as any of the Welders old guard.

Cornflower and Les have been sentenced; their legacy is gradually being over-written with every match report. Croft is awaiting trial; a clip of his demeaning end is a favourite on social media. Anita worries that the number of likes could have many meanings, but on balance chooses to see it as a positive response. In its old form, the stadium itself felt contingent, subject to the will of others, it smelled stagnant. Now, unburdened, it feels lighter, ready for the unknown, to be whatever its constituents need it to be.

And who knows, the Welders could even avoid relegation in a big six-pointer. The stock phrases are easy to learn. Her cherry red and black, sequin-edged scarf is a copy of an Alexander McQueen skull print, but she's showing willing.

Climbing the stairs Anita feels lightness in her legs; she must be in danger of getting fit.

"Here to watch your sister?" Anita asks. A boy of about six years old overtakes her – not that fit then. Anita nods to a short steward buried in a neon-orange vest.

"Unallocated seating," he says, "take your pick."

The stadium is almost half full. Thousands more than the Ladies have played in front of before. The crowd will be able to feel their nerves from here. Anita joins Zoe from the LGBT group. It's partly to share the excitement, but also to be near someone with a bigger mouth than hers.

On way. Pete's message makes her face smile and her stomach quiver. He will be here soon with his two sons. They weren't sure if it was the right place for them all to meet for the first time, but good as any, she judged. Not much time to talk.

It had been Conor's idea to hold the Ladies' Regional Cup Final match before the last game of the men's season. He predicted there would be plenty of men drifting in early to catch the second-half and the cheerleading competition. Anita had groaned. Apparently it's a sport these days. What could she say?

On the other side of the pitch near the tunnel, Wormy and Conor are picking up cones used in the warm-up. The first time she'd met Conor at the ground, Anita had almost walked past him in the corridor. Wearing a black, slim-fitting track suit, she'd assumed he was one of the coaches, a tall athletic man carrying a bag of balls.

"Wannabe coach, part-time driver and kit man for the ladies, full-time bean finder."

Bending easily, he throws the cones into a rough pile, then plays keepy-uppy with Wormy and one of the Ladies subs. The crowd cheer as they keep it going, for what might be a whole minute. Conor then packs the balls away and does a comedy forward roll to entertain the young mascots on the side of the pitch, before heading off down the tunnel.

The tannoy plays an old 1970s soul classic, "Ain't no stopping us now..." enough of it to make Anita's skin tingle.

"Ladies and gentlemen, boys and girls, time to give your support to our teams. And a rousing cheer for the New Welders Ladies..."

As she sees Nicole lead out the team, her heart lurches. Still shorter than many of the others, Nicole's square shoulders give her solidity. Anita notices the red gleam of her boots; the running is strong, effortless. They are all wearing black armbands as a mark of respect for Ash. Anita shoves two fingers in her mouth and whistles as hard as she can, not to get Nicole's attention, but in appreciation, in anticipation of a legendary victory.

ACKNOWLEDGEMENTS

I'd like to thank my amazing, supportive, creative friends and readers: Victoria, Sarah T, Diana, Thara, Judith, Claire, Fran, Moira, Joanna, Angela, Sue H, Sarah D, Mikenda, Swithun, Kate, Renee and Sylvester. The fantastic author Erin Kelly has been an inspiring and expert writing mentor.

For being open, generous, insightful and patient with my questions I'd like to thank: Bob Reeves, Sandy Ladies FC and Rachel Whitby; my friends at CIPFA, including Andy Burns, who has also been such a great reader, collaborator and guide, Chris Tambini, Mike Ellsmore, Jayne Stephenson (and dad) and Drew Cullen for the opportunity to work with so many talented and diligent public finance professionals as their writer in residence; Sonia Dean for the info on corruption in football; Adrian Besley, Paul Booth and John Latham for great football conversations; and John Read for the structural engineering advice.

This novel has also benefitted from important conversations about the creative process with Sarah Fenwick, Julie Hall and Geoff Bateman, and I've been inspired by, and learned from, many hard-working local councillors and campaigners, and the continued energy and commitment of people working throughout the public sector.

Thanks also to the fans at Arsenal FC, Watford FC, Stevenage Town FC, Dulwich Hamlet FC, FC United of Manchester, AFC

Wimbledon and Exeter – more power to UK's fan-owned clubs movement and good luck in the new season!

To Lisa, whose editing is a joy and who understands what I wanted to write and have written, to Ben for the beautiful painting that evokes the story so well, and to Kate for designing another beautiful book.

Finally, to Simon for being there and believing. And, as always, to my lovely family, Team Reeves.

ABOUT DAWN REEVES

Dawn lives in London and loves the Midlands. She makes change happen. She's motivated by social justice, and is fascinated by power and all the weird and wonderful things that happen under the surface.

As well as being a writer, Dawn is a facilitator and curator of three commissioned books of flash fiction and first-person narratives – *Change the Ending, Making our Mark* and *Walk Tall – Being a 21st Century Public Servant* – creative collaborations that bring stories that matter alive for organisations and individuals.

She has written for the *Guardian* and was the writer-in-residence at the Chartered Institute of Public Finance (CIPFA). *Hard Change*, her first novel, was published in 2013.

READ MORE

For videos, blogs and more info check out **www.dawnreeves.com**

If you enjoyed *We Know What We Are*, Dawn would really appreciate it if you could leave a review at **www.amazon.co.uk** and do please order it from your local library.

ALSO BY DAWN REEVES

Hard Change

When a girl's body is dumped in a bin, a city is forced to explore the boundaries of private interest and public good. *Hard Change* is a contemporary town hall thriller set in a midlands city with an alcohol problem. The girl's discarded body forces a council officer, a policewoman and an NHS trust manager to get out from behind their desks and make choices. Personal or political, public or private, professional or pragmatic, they must make those choices alone - but can they act collectively to do the right thing and prevent another murder?

Hard Change is available for order from all bookshops and online stores.

Lightning Source UK Ltd.
Milton Keynes UK
UKOW04f0838181017
311194UK00001B/251/P